THE CONTINENT OF
Arasin
ALIRIAN ISLANDS
FELIA
MALACHITE MOUNTAIN
TERECEAN SEA
KULAT
N
E
S
W

SALACEAN SEA
WASTELANDS
ALCHEA
KAI'MELEND
SILKAR DESERT
ALTAPECEAN SEA
CYNOSURE

BOOK 3 OF THREADLIGHT

Bonds of Chaos

BY ZACK ARGYLE

SYL

SYL PUBLISHING LLC

THE STORY UNTIL NOW

VOICE OF WAR

While expecting their first child, Chrys Valerian and his wife, Iriel, attended the Rite of Revelation for their friends, Luther and Emory. When the child is revealed to be an achromat (brown eyes), he is blinded and taken to be a priest of the Order of Alchaeus. Outside the Temple, Iriel almost loses their child but is saved by a stranger who also gives Chrys a thread-dead obsidian dagger.

Chrys goes on to investigate the Bloodthieves, where he rescues a young girl named Laurel, who runs away back to her home in the Fairenwild. When she returns to Zedalum, she loses her position as a Messenger, and also loses her best friend, a chromawolf named Asher, as he returns to his pack in the wild.

Eventually, Chrys discovers the truth of the Bloodthieves, that they are headed by an Amber threadweaver named Alabella, and fellow high general, Jurius, is working for her. Chrys' son, Aydin, is born and they take him in for his own Rite of Revelation, where they learn that, not only is he an Amber threadweaver, but Father Xalan is a Zeda spy. They run away to the Fairenwild where Chrys, Iriel, and Aydin narrowly escape Jurius with the help of a pack of hungry chromawolves and Laurel, while Father Xalan is captured.

Laurel brings Chrys and his family to Zedalum, where they meet the Elders and learn about Amber threadweavers and the coreseal. Shortly after, Chrys' mother, Willow, arrives and shares the truth: Chrys was born in Zedalum. They soon realize that Father Xalan is really Pandan, Willow's brother and Chrys' uncle. They devise a plan to rescue him. Laurel and Willow recruit Chrys' old crew (Luther, Laz, and Reina) to break out Pandan from Endin Keep's prison.

At the same time, far to the south in Cynosure, Alverax Blightwood wakes up in a pit of bones. He soon discovers that he is an Obsidian threadweaver and decides to use his new power to get revenge on Jelium (an Amber threadweaver) for killing his father. The plan backfires and he narrowly escapes. He decides to leave Cynosure and head north. The leader of the caravan betrays him and hands him over to Alabella, who takes him into the Bloodthieves.

While Laurel, Willow, and the crew try to break out Pandan, they come face to face with High General Henna. She chases them through the keep, and Willow leads the group to Jurius' room. When he emerges, a fight ensues, and Jurius kills Pandan. Then Laurel kills Jurius, and in his final moments, he turns the dagger around and stabs Laurel in the heart.

Alverax joins Alabella and a small army of Bloodthieves into the Fairenwild, where they set fire to the forest. The people of Zedalum abandon their treetop homes, dropping down onto the Wonderstone so they can flee. The Bloodthieves attack the unarmed Zeda people, and Alverax watches in horror.

When Chrys brings down Iriel and Aydin, the child's Amber powers lash out and bind Iriel and the baby to the Wonderstone, crushing them. Chrys, in an attempt to save them, finally gives into the Apogee and shows amazing powers as he slaughters dozens. He seeks out Alabella but is bound by Amber threads while she flees.

Alverax rushes forward when he sees a woman and child dying and uses all of his power to *break* the threads of the wonderstone. The earth shakes.

In the end, Laurel is still alive, but she has lost her ability to threadweave and is in the care of Alabella. Alverax is alive, heading west toward Felia with the Zeda people. And Chrys—still controlled by the Apogee—abandons his family and heads east.

The epilogue concludes with an odd woman exiting a holy cave in the Wastelands, looking for her brother.

STONES OF LIGHT

With the Apogee firmly in control, Chrys Valerian heads east over the mountains, picking up two soldiers—a man and woman—along the way. They arrive in Kai'Melend, the home of the wastelanders, and it is revealed that the Apogee is in fact an immortal wastelander god named Relek, and his sister, Lylax, is there waiting for him, having recently been released from her underground prison when the core-seal was destroyed. Relek and Lylax transfer their souls into the bodies of the Alchean soldiers, leaving Chrys for the wastelanders to do with as they please.

While imprisoned, Chrys meets Roshaw and three others. They make a plan to escape, using Chrys' Sapphire abilities and the aid of the chief of the ataçan, named Xuçan. Their plan is thwarted when they are forced to fight wastelanders in a pit near the Endless Well, a lake-sized hole in the ground with seemingly no bottom. After defeating several opponents, Chrys fights one of the corespawn, which he is unable to kill. He is saved by his mother, Willow, who wields Chrys' old thread-dead obsidian dagger.

Chrys, Willow, and Roshaw leap into the Endless Well where they discover the home of the third immortal, Relek and Lylax's brother, Alchaeus. He helps them hide, teaches them about theoliths (giving all three access to Sapphire, Emerald, and Obsidian), and takes them to the Convergence, a dome of warbling threadlight that bends space. Before they use it to travel to the Fairenwild on their way to Felia, they make a plan to create a new coreseal with the help of Alabella, the Amber-eyed queen of the Bloodthieves.

Back in Alchea, a thread-dead Laurel finds herself in the care of Alabella. Her withdrawals are tempered with the use of transfusers, but she still craves her threadweaver life, and Alabella has promised her a new theolith. Together, they travel to the Fairenwild in search of a cache of infused gemstones, where Laurel finds her home destroyed and her people gone. Instead of finding a cache of theoliths beneath the coreseal, they find a corespawn. They flee back to Alchea, and that night an army of corespawn wages war, devastating the nation.

Alabella offers her transfusers to Malachus, which will grant more soldiers the ability to see the invisible corespawn. However, when no second corespawn attack comes, Alabella and Laurel flee. While leaving Endin Keep, they run into Luther, who stole his son back from the priests and fled to Laz's cousin's farm. Laurel and Alabella travel to Felia and run into a pack of displaced chromawolves. Laurel finds her young chromawolf friend, Asher, and they form a bond. After arriving in Felia, she finds her brother just in time to watch their grandfather pass away.

After destroying the coreseal and fleeing with the Zeda, Alverax travels to Felia, where he meets the empress and her younger sister, Jisenna. They become friends, and he learns about the sacred nature of Obsidian threadweavers—as the right hand of the Heralds—in the Felian faith. When the empress is killed, Alverax is blamed and he narrowly escapes with the help of Iriel. The Zeda are imprisoned because of his actions, so he sneaks in through long pipes under the palace to convince Empress Jisenna, the Mistress of Mercy, to exchange his life for theirs. She agrees, and then, during his execution, allows him to live.

The truth is quickly learned when an army of corespawn attacks Felia with creatures as large as buildings. Watchlord Osinan, the head of the Felian faith, fights the corespawn alongside Alverax, wielding a thread-dead obsidian blade called the Midnight Watcher. He is mortally wounded and, before he dies, he names Alverax the next Watchlord.

When the corespawn return to Felia, Alverax is at the head of the army, Laurel and Asher have joined the fight, and Chrys, Willow, and Roshaw are on their way. When all seems lost, two figures fly in from the east and fend off the corespawn. They claim to be the Heralds, healing the wounded with golden water, then take to the palace where they kill Empress Jisenna. At the same time, Laurel finally takes revenge on Alabella so that the Heralds can't use her powers. Chrys rushes to the palace, saves Iriel and Aydin, then they all head to the docks. As they board the *Pale Urchin*, Alverax—still shocked from the death of Jisenna—discovers that his father, Roshaw, is still alive.

GENERAL THALLIN CLUTCHED the hilt of his blade, torn between faith and honor, between the very gods he worshiped and the moral weight of his own soul.

He looked at the five women kneeling before him—the elders of the Zeda—then out over the imprisoned crowd behind them. The sun was high, and a light breeze blew through the Felian courtyard from the west. Thallin hated what he had to do. But even more so, he hated himself for doubting the Heralds. So, he pushed aside the unrest, the fear and doubt, and breathed in his lifelong beliefs, letting them fill the cracks that ran through his soul.

The youngest of the elders, a woman in her early forties, looked up at him with tears streaming down her cheeks as he approached. "Please, I have a daughter."

Thallin clenched his jaw and ignored her words, refusing to let them shake him. Not now. Not in the midst of the first true trial of his faith.

"Please," she said again.

He drew his blade, and the familiar weight in his palm brought him comfort, reminding him of old doubts he'd fought through before. Doubts that he had overcome. Today, he would do the same.

This was his path.

The blade was his instrument, and he was ready to play its godly song.

In a blur, he lunged forward with perfect form and pierced the young elder through her heart. He retracted his blade, blood dripping from its edge, and watched as she toppled to the dirt.

"Gale take me," one of the other women cried under her breath. Somewhere farther back, amid the throng of Zeda, each of them bound and awaiting their fate, screams called out into the mid-afternoon sky.

He knew he should turn away, move on and forget. Instead, he stared at the elder's body until it stopped quivering. Her eyes were open, her brown tunic stained red. Helpless. He closed his eyes to pray for strength, and the irony of it broke his heart.

The next closest elder was a larger woman with a certain kindness in the wrinkles of her face. Though her lips quivered, she kept her head high. "You don't have to do this," she said.

Thallin took a step closer. "I will do whatever my gods ask of me."

He lunged again and felt a swelling of emotion in his chest as he watched the second woman fall to the grass.

Three older women still knelt before him. One with wrinkles deeper than the ocean floor. Another with fury brewing in her Emerald eyes. And the last looked to her fallen friends with a sadness that permeated every line of her posture and expression.

He approached the closest—the oldest of the five—and she opened her eyes at the sound of his footsteps. They were blue as the sea, and beneath their careful gaze, her lips curled into a smile. "I commend your faith," she said, taking a breath and offering a slight nod. "I am ready."

Thallin squeezed the hilt, letting all of his guilt seep into the polished steel. The old woman knelt reverently before him, a paragon of peace.

Faith is not meant to be easy, Thallin's mother had once said.

With a swift strike, he cut down the elderly woman.

Faith is meant to try you.

His stomach churned, and a dark cloud swirled in his mind.

He kept his eyes down, focused on his blade as he wiped blood on his pant leg.

"Violet," the next elder said with a growl.

Thallin did not look away from the sharp edge of his sword.

"Ivy and Ashwa," she continued. "Those women had names!"

He ignored her and set his feet.

"Violet, Ivy, and Ashwa!" she screamed.

"QUIET!" Thallin roared, finally bringing himself to look at her. The fire in his eyes clashed with hers. "You will die today, and you will be forgotten."

"And you will be damned," she spat.

He swung his blade and watched her corpse collapse face-first to the dirt.

Adrenaline flowed through his veins, burning him from the inside. He clenched his teeth with such ferocity that his jaw felt like splintered wood.

One more.

One more and his test was over.

The Heralds would see his faith.

The final elder was a kind looking woman with soft blue eyes. She looked at him with a profound sadness, like a mother who'd lost a child and blamed herself. The last death seemed to have hit her the hardest.

He took a few steps, and, as he set himself in front of her, she dropped her gaze to the ground. There was nothing about her that looked dangerous, no sign of evil or darkness. He didn't *want* to hurt her. An enemy in battle was one matter, but an old, grieving woman? It choked him from within. He'd always imagined exercising his faith would fill him with joy, but all he felt was a thick darkness deep in his core.

Tears dripped down the woman's cheeks, but she said nothing. She simply stared, shoulders slumped with age and grief.

The sword in his hand seemed to grow heavier with each moment. He feared that if he delayed, the weight would overwhelm him.

He lunged forward, fighting himself more than any enemy, and met her eyes as the steel cut flesh.

Wide-eyed, her lips moved.

I forgive you.

His heart swelled as the sword drove into her chest. She stared at him, choking, blood dripping from her chin. And, somehow, even through the pain and the sorrow, she looked peaceful. Content, despite the cold steel between her ribs. As she finally collapsed to the earth, her lips curled into a smile.

Thallin dropped to his knees. A flood of tears pressed against his skull like a dam ready to burst. He fought their release with every measure of strength he contained.

He hated himself for being so weak.

He hated himself for having such feeble faith.

He hated himself...

He would be better. He had to be.

"Stand up, Thallin Haichess," Relek said, draped in black robes. The second Herald, Lylax, stood beside him. A pale yellow crystal hung from a silver necklace that swung over her white robes.

Thallin lifted himself to his feet, with the tip of the blade dragging against the ground, and turned to the Heralds. "My gods, I have done as you asked."

"You have done well," Relek said, voice deep, prismatic eyes gleaming in the sunlight. He turned away from Thallin, toward the newly instated Watchlord, Rastalin Farrow, whose face brimmed with haughty pride as he stood in his black and gold garb. "Has he not done well, Watchlord?"

Rastalin lifted his chin. "He has done sufficiently well, my god."

"It is rare to find such devotion," the Herald added. "In the days ahead, we will need a man like Thallin by our side. A man whose actions speak louder than his clothing."

The Watchlord shifted in his boots.

"Thallin," Relek said, turning away from the Watchlord, "I am afraid this day may grow longer. I have two further requests."

"Of course," Thallin said, bowing his head with his blade ankle deep in the dirt. "Anything."

Relek's face grew still, his eyes void of emotion. "The Watchlord is meant to be the right hand of the Heralds, but this man," he said, gesturing toward Rastalin, "is unworthy. Take his life, and take his place."

Thallin turned to Watchlord Rastalin. The look of arrogance was gone. The fire in his eyes had gone cold. There was only fear. Rastalin reached for the sword at his side and pulled it from its sheath. Thallin took a step forward.

Something about the movement of the sword as it lifted in defense relieved Thallin. This man was not innocent. He was not valiant. This man was a coward. A nobleman who'd never had to sacrifice anything. Not for Felia. Not for the Heralds. Thallin hated this man. He hated how Rastalin spoke and how he walked. He hated that Rastalin wore the Watchlord clothes that once belonged to Alverax.

While each death of the Zeda elders had been a trial, this death would be the reward.

Thallin parried the Watchlord's blade with such force that the decorative replica of the Midnight Watcher shattered into a thousand shards of obsidian. Rastalin was left with nothing but a hilt and his broken pride.

One second later, steel was in his chest.

Ten seconds later, blood ran like the Tourmaline River.

Sixty seconds later, the former Watchlord lay still on the wet grass.

When Thallin turned back to the Heralds, he felt proud. All his life, he had fought for himself, for his own pride and accomplishment. Now, he would fight for his gods. He would be their most devoted disciple.

He would be their Watchlord.

And he would be their blade.

THE PALE URCHIN drifted over the Terecean Sea, rising and falling with each crest of the frigid waves. Chrys Valerian stood at the bow, holding his son and breathing in the salty air. His wife, Iriel, stood beside him, resting her head on his shoulder, and together they watched a flame-tailed halken soar high overhead, wings outstretched, twin tails flared in a wide arc. Against the backdrop of the setting sun, it almost let them forget about the rising darkness.

A woman's voice called out from behind them.

Chrys turned to see his mother, Willow, approaching from the middle of the ship, climbing up from below deck. Her clothes were a mess, though not as dirty as they'd been in the Wastelands. Every speck of dirt was a reminder of all she'd done for him. The sacrifices she'd made. He would never forget the look in her eyes as she'd dropped into the pit to stand between him and the corespawn.

"You look much too excited," Chrys said. "I'm a little scared."

"Come now," Willow said, brushing his comment aside as she looked up into the sky. "Oh, wow. Look at that. I would *love* to have a halken for a pet. They are so majestic."

Chrys raised a brow. "You hate pets."

"No one *hates* pets," she said with confidence. "I just haven't found the right one yet."

"If you haven't found it in fifty years," Chrys said, "I'm not sure there is one."

Iriel turned to Willow. "I never took you as a bird person. Always figured you'd be happier with a low-maintenance lizard or something."

Willow's eyes lit up. "Like Chitt! Oh my, I could definitely do that. But, ah! No more distractions. I came with something much more exciting. First, a question: how do the Heralds fly?"

Chrys looked back up into the sky. "I haven't really thought about it. I guess I assumed it was a power that came with having all four theoliths bonded together. Maybe related to lifelight?"

"A good guess, but no!" Willow shook a finger. "Think about what we *do* know. With Obsidian, you can cut your corethread and float."

"Sure, but that's not the same as flying."

Willow gave him a look. "Patience, little flower. Mommy's not done talking."

Iriel stifled a laugh.

"Without a corethread tethering you to the ground," Willow continued, "any movement would send you floating off. At first, I thought maybe we could create wings and use those to fly. But that wouldn't work, and the Heralds don't need them anyway. There had to be another way. So, again, what do we know? Do you remember the orange grove with the corespawn stampede?"

Chrys nodded. "I remember you made that force barrier by releasing a concentrated burst of Sapphire and Emerald."

"Exactly! Now watch what happens when you combine it all."

Multi-colored threadlight swirled through Willow's

veins, running down her arms, through her hands and neck, pulsing brightly in her eyes.

Chrys opened himself to threadlight, too.

In an instant, Willow's corethread was broken, and her feet drifted from the ground. Her lips curled into a smile just before she let out a surge of threadweaving. In front of her, she released a wave of Emerald. Behind her, a burst of Sapphire. Her body reacted, launching itself through the air like a hummingbird in flight. Quickly, she did it again in the other direction, counteracting the forces and bringing her floating form to a halt. She grabbed hold of the mast to keep herself from drifting off.

"Stones," Chrys cursed under his breath.

Iriel stared in awe but still managed to slap Chrys' shoulder. "Not in front of Aydin."

"He's a baby…" Chrys mumbled as Iriel took the child away from him, slipping the boy into the wrap on her chest.

At the far end of the ship, a group of sailors pointed, gawking and muttering to each other.

"It's a little dangerous to practice while on a ship," Willow said, steadying herself against the wooden beam. "But once we're on land, I'll be in the air every chance I get. Having an Amber theolith would make landing a lot simpler."

"And with three theoliths, we're the only ones besides the Heralds who can do it." Chrys paused. He pictured the frail image of his mother when they'd landed at the bottom of the Endless Well. The quiver in her hand. The tightness in her chest. Surging required a lot of threadlight. "Just be careful. It's a lot of threadweaving."

Roshaw came bounding out from below deck a changed man. His long shaggy hair from years in the Wastelands had been cut short, and his beard trimmed just enough to show the smirk on his face. "Sometimes I wonder which one of you is the parent." He winked at Willow. "She just showed you how to fly, Chrys. Give her the damn victory!"

"It's just—" Chrys began.

"Chrys," his mother interrupted, "our bodies are stronger than they've ever been. The elixir healed us, and our extra theoliths have given us even more strength. There's nothing to worry about."

Iriel chuckled to herself. "Asking Chrys not to worry is like asking the rain to stop being wet."

"I'm not that bad," Chrys said.

Iriel, Willow, and Roshaw all raised a brow.

"I'm not!"

They stared back silently.

"Whatever this is," Chrys said, gesturing to the three of them, "I don't like it. I'm going to check on the others."

He heard their faint laughter behind him as he walked around to the stern and descended a flight of stairs. At the end of a narrow hallway, he knocked twice and opened a door. Inside, he found Alverax lying on a long cot, with Laurel and her chromawolf companion, Asher, seated along the far wall beside several fixed crates of week-old Felian fruit.

Upon discovering his father was alive, Alverax had holed up in the cabin and refused to speak to anyone. After the first day, Laurel and Asher had joined him, silently sitting, not saying a word. Chrys had asked her once why she was doing it, and she'd simply replied, "It's not good to be alone."

She was right.

As Chrys sat down next to Laurel, he let out a long breath. "Captain says we're almost to Cynosure."

Laurel slumped further against the wall. "Too late. We've already died."

Asher mimicked her, collapsing across her lap.

Since the moment they'd first departed Felia on the *Pale Urchin*, the chromawolf had taken poorly to life at sea. From such a powerful creature, the delicate whimpers seemed to reach in and grab at the hearts of the crew. No matter how many times Chrys told Laurel that fresh air would help, they still stayed in the cabin with Alverax.

Chrys shook his head. "Everyone on this ship is so dramatic."

Laurel pushed herself back up and smiled, rubbing a hand down Asher's green-furred shoulder all the way to his paw. "Our kind is meant for land."

Our kind. The physical changes alone were enough to believe it—her hair had taken on more and more green throughout their journey—but, somehow, the curious bond between Laurel and Asher was changing them both.

"How's Alverax?" Chrys asked quietly.

Laurel looked over to the cot. "He's okay. Getting better, I think."

Chrys massaged his temples, then rubbed at his eyes. "I wish I knew what we could do to fix him."

Laurel lifted her chin and looked to Chrys with a certain intensity in her eyes. "You can't *fix* people." She paused, and Asher let out a low growl of agreement. "That's not how it works. People are like...trees."

"Trees?" Chrys repeated.

"Yeah," Laurel said thoughtfully. She turned her gaze toward the far wall, as if she were seeing another place in the distance. "You don't *fix* a tree. You can take care of it, sure, but it's the tree that has to heal itself."

Chrys thought for a moment, considering the wisdom in

her words. Alverax was broken and hurting, overwhelmed on top of it all. But if he refused to speak, there wasn't much anyone could do to help him. Maybe she was right, and all they could do was wait for him to heal himself. Alverax was a person, not some chipped blade that needed repair.

A month ago, Chrys wouldn't have labeled Laurel as *wise*, but she wasn't the same brash girl he'd met in the Bloodthief warehouse. She'd made mistakes—everyone does—but she was learning to move forward with a new focus.

He stood and offered Laurel a smile. "You know, you're smarter than you look."

She pursed her lips. "And you're nicer than you smell."

"Rude." Chrys smirked.

"I could smell you from across the hallway."

"Oh, come on," Chrys said.

"Asher's pack could probably track your scent all the way from the Fairenwild."

"It's not that bad, is it?"

Her only response was a flat stare before she laid her head back against the wall. The chromawolf nestled its head into her.

Chrys gestured toward Alverax. "Okay if I have a few words with him?"

Laurel gave a slight nod and closed her eyes.

As he stepped over to the cot, he found Alverax with his eyes closed, but Chrys wasn't convinced that the young man was asleep. A hint of black threadlight pulsed through Alverax's veins, even more pronounced due to the weight he'd lost while aboard the ship. The darkness surrounding his eyes extended across his face, shadows rolling over the gaunt edges.

"Hello again," Chrys said.

Iriel had visited Alverax every day of the journey, never speaking more than a few words, but often bringing him meals that she would lay on the side table. Chrys had visited a few times, but mostly to check on Laurel. Still, Chrys understood that he owed the young man so much, not the least of which was Iriel and Aydin's life. And if there was anyone who understood what it was like being trapped in your own mind, it was Chrys.

He took a seat on a crate and rested his head against the wall, feeling the sway of the ocean through the wood. "I know you don't want to talk. Which is great, because I really just need someone to listen. I guess I just need to say it out loud." Chrys took a deep breath and steadied himself, feeling the pulse in his chest begin to quicken. "I...am a failure. I'm trying—Lightfather knows it—but it just doesn't seem to matter. Nothing I do is ever enough. Or maybe it's just not *good* enough. It feels like I'm stuck in a rip tide, and no matter how hard I swim, the shore gets farther and farther away. And worse, everyone around me is drowning. The truth is...friends are *dead* because I wasn't enough."

An image flashed in his mind: Esme and Seven shuffling pieces over the makeshift Scion gameboard with Agatha laughing beside them. He'd brought them hope, promised them freedom. Then, he'd watched them die. Chrys closed his eyes and felt his heart seize in his chest. Tears welled, and he shut his eyes, as if closing them would dam the pain. But it was still there, beating away at him from the inside. So he opened them and looked to Alverax, whose chest seemed to be heaving as much as Chrys'.

"I don't know all that you've been through, Alverax, but I do know that empty hole in your chest that feels like it'll never fill again. More than anything, I just want you to know that you don't have to suffer alone. I made that mistake once." He turned and caught a glimpse of Laurel, eyes shut in the far corner. "A friend once told me that people are like trees. The way I see it, it doesn't matter how many broken branches you have, or how many leaves you've lost. If a tree is standing, it's no less whole than the trees beside it.

"I watched my friends die because I wasn't enough to save them, and I can still feel the pain where those branches split. But new branches grow where old ones break. No matter what it might feel like right now, how dark or empty you feel, it gets better."

A SURGE of emotion coursed through Alverax's body as Chrys stepped away from the room.

I watched my friends die, because I wasn't enough to save them.

Jisenna.

He could still see her face the moment she'd realized what the Herald was about to do. The seconds before the sword struck her down. The cold minutes after. Alverax opened his eyes and saw the Midnight Watcher staring at him from across the room, propped against the wall, shimmering in what little lamplight made its way to the corner.

Jisenna was dead, and it was his fault.

He'd told the Herald her title.

She'd saved his life, and now she was dead because of it.

And if that wasn't enough, the father whose death he'd finally come to terms with was still alive. Something about the revelation had broken him, as if the star he'd named had come spiraling through the night and crashed into his soul, shattering him into a thousand pieces, each reflecting a memory of his broken life.

Was he even alive anymore?

Perhaps this was the afterlife: an endless journey with nothing but painful memories for company.

AFTER AN ETERNITY OF QUIET, words echoed through the hallway from above.

"Cynosure, straight ahead!"

THE *PALE URCHIN* was nearly silent as a swarm of men stepped aboard, heavy boots knocking against the creaky wooden deck. Chrys watched them carefully, noting the cutlasses dangling at their sides and thick arms that knew how to use them. Their leader, a burly man who looked like he came from the farmlands outside of Alchea, stood nearly a head taller than the others, with a hooked nose and long hair. His hand rested on the hilt of his blade.

"Problem is," the man said, accentuating each syllable. "Ain't no ship ought to be dockin' tonight. Next ain't coming for three days. You folk didn't leave with the *Urchin*. Now you *with* the *Urchin*. So, question is...what the hell you doin' at my dock?"

Iriel stepped forward with Aydin tucked away in the wrap on her chest. "This is my family," she said. "I'm Iriel. There are...dark things happening in Felia. We just want to take our son somewhere far from there."

"Ship came in speakin' stories of gods and monsters," the man said, side-eyeing the others in the group. "Well...Iriel...what of the rest? Ain't no chance you all fami-ly." He turned and gestured to Alverax and Laurel. "You two lovers?"

Alverax stared at the man, but his face gave no hint that he'd even heard.

Laurel, on the other hand... Chrys held his breath, fearing how the erratic young woman might respond.

"Friends," she said with a strange sense of cool. "He's from here, spent some time working for Alabella, but she's dead now."

The man nearly choked. "What the hell you just say?"

"Alabella Rune, the Amber-eyed Queen of the Blood-thieves, is dead."

He clenched his jaw, nostrils flaring. "You sure?"

"Oh, I'm sure," Laurel said.

He pointed a finger at the others. "I don't care what the hell the rest of you do." He lunged forward, grabbing hold of Laurel's arm and pulling. "You're coming with me."

In a split second, Asher leapt out from behind a crate, dashed forward, and tackled the man, teeth bared mere inches from his face, slobber dripping down his snarling maw. The other guards reached for their blades, but Alverax —black veins ablaze—broke their corethreads without moving an inch. In a split second, the swarm of men were floating in the air, panic stricken across their moonlit faces.

Laurel said nothing when Asher looked at her, and Chrys swore the massive chromawolf nodded before releasing the man and taking a step back.

Chrys stepped forward, looking down at the man who suddenly seemed much less confident. As his eyes met Chrys', his brow furrowed and his jaw slackened. Chrys leaned lower and whispered. "We have no trouble with you or your friends. Tell us where we can find Jelium, and we'll be on our way."

The man, both confused and relieved, pushed himself to his knees, keeping an eye on the chromawolf. His gaze slid from person to person, finally seeming to realize their pecu-liarities. Alverax, blank-faced and black-veined. Laurel, green strands of hair matching the chromawolf at her side. Chrys, Willow, and Roshaw, eyes swirling with multi-colored threadlight. And Iriel, standing with the grace of a warrior, a child strapped to her chest.

"Who the hell are you?"

Chrys looked at his friends and back to the man. "Just a few friends looking to kill a few gods."

AFTER DISEMBARKING THE *PALE URCHIN*, they walked over to an enormous staircase carved into the face of the bluff. Thick rods jutted out from the face of the rock every few strides, attached at the ends to form a guardrail on the opposite end of the stairway. A complex pulley system ran from the peaks of the cliffside all the way down to the docks. Chrys, having lived his entire life with the safety of Sapphire threadlight, had never been afraid of heights, but he saw a hint of nerves in some of the others. He even caught Willow and Roshaw, who now knew they could fly, taking an occasional peek over the edge with a glimmer of doubt in their eyes.

As they climbed, the *Pale Urchin* became nothing more than a shine in the gravel. Chrys could still see the dock workers and sailors below, like tiny smudges on a midnight canvas.

When his head peeked over the top of the bluff, Chrys saw Cynosure for the first time. It was no Felia, yet, even still, the size of the separatist city was staggering. A giant sandstone protrusion loomed over half of the city, sheltering it from the elements and blocking even the light falling from the moon. Tents in various shades of brown, white, and black dotted the sandy world like weeds, with tall towers of stone built at seemingly random intervals throughout the city, burning red flames to light the night.

What surprised him more than anything was the amount of activity. In Alchea, when the sun dipped below the horizon, the city settled into a peaceful calm. Of course, there were areas, like the lower west side, that remained active, but even they kept their voices and activities hidden behind closed doors. Here, it seemed the entire world had yet to notice that the sun had set. People moved through the city like it was mid-morning, trading, joking, kissing, fighting.

Roshaw, having noticed Chrys' reaction, laughed and grabbed his shoulder. "You'll find that this city is late to rise and later to bed."

Chrys nodded. "I can see why you were so certain that Jelium would be available."

"I didn't just know he would be available," Roshaw said. "I told you exactly where he would be. The man is a creature of habit, and he has a habit of stealing from people and calling it a game."

Chrys licked his teeth beneath his upper lip. "The more I hear about Jelium, the more I'm afraid I might just try to kill him myself."

"Don't even joke about that," Willow said from his other side. "We need an Amber threadweaver to make the new coreseal, and he's the only option."

"Honestly," Roshaw added. "I wouldn't mind sticking a blade in him myself."

"It's not worth it," Laurel said from behind.

They all turned to the young Zeda girl.

"It doesn't make you feel better," she said.

Chrys raised his brows, looking hard at Laurel. The young woman looking back at him wasn't the same girl he'd met in the Bloodthief warehouse, not the girl from the Fairenwild. He felt an odd sense of pride watching her grow.

"She's right," Chrys said. "Besides, killing Jelium helps no one."

"I can think of at least twenty people it would help," Roshaw said with a shrug. "But you're right. We can't kill him. But we don't have to let *him* know that."

They traveled for a long while, down well-lit paths, past tents and stalls and flat-roofed homes built with clay and sandstone, finally passing through a large cave corridor into what Roshaw referred to as the Pit. Noise echoed from every inch of the enormous cavern. Alirian men puffed on long stems of sailweed as they wormed their way through circles of drunken Felians. Small wagers were taken as men squared off to fight, shirtless, exposing bodies of tattoo and brawn. Prowling whores leaned against the walls, heads high, lips puckered. Loud men shouted about their goods, gesturing to sprawling displays in open cases.

A woman bumped into Chrys, a giantess of a woman. Her thick arms tightened, and her heavy brows furrowed as she made eye contact with him, taking in the swirl of colors in his irises. Then she noticed the chromawolf standing beside Laurel and took a step back, vanishing with surprising speed.

"Let's keep moving," Chrys said, mostly to himself.

As they passed through the crowd, a shrill voice lifted above the chaos. Chrys looked and found a thin man with ghostly skin, smiling wide as he lifted a handful of shines into the air, shouting at the top of his lungs, calling for bets. As they moved, Chrys caught more and more of the crowd looking their way, some pointing, others scowling. A significant number of drunken men cursed and hobbled away at the sight of the chromawolf.

They continued their way forward, moving toward the stadium-like depression in the cavern leading to a sprawling racetrack. Even from the top of the Pit, Chrys could see the writhing necrolytes beating against their cages. When Roshaw had first told them about the races, no one had believed him; no one was doubting him now.

Without warning, the crowd began to settle.

A deep, booming voice broke through the quiet. "GATES READY!"

Chrys looked down and saw a tree-stump of a man standing with his arms raised at the front of the racetrack. Six men sat atop the caged necrolytes, hooked onto leather saddles that fit snugly between hand-wide spikes jutting from the creatures' backs.

Even before they were released, Chrys could imagine their movement. His mind drifted to the War of the Wastelands. He imagined men riding necrolytes into battle. Even if they couldn't fully control the creatures, fear and panic would roll through the enemy like a tidal wave. No sane man would stand up to such a creature. If they lived through this, Chrys was done with war.

"THREE!" the man yelled from far below.

"TWO!" Every Alchean, Felian, Kulaian, and Alirian, every man and woman in between, joined the chorus.

"ONE!"

The gates slammed open, and all six necrolytes burst forth.

Roshaw pulled on his arm. "Come on. Let's get down there while the crowd is distracted."

They descended a set of stairs with Roshaw in the lead, Chrys and the others trailing behind. While they walked, they watched the necrolytes race across the sandy track, crashing into each other with blunted tusks jutting out from their jaws like the wild boars of Kulai. Even before Roshaw pointed him out, Chrys found Jelium in the crowd, seated atop a makeshift throne near the front of the track, surrounded by women Chrys guessed must be part of his Hundred Brides.

Mixed throughout the retinue were guards in black, faces covered, eyes scanning the crowd. Rage boiled under Chrys' skin as a memory blossomed in his mind. The night he'd first failed as a father—the night Aydin was born—masked men had come through the trees. Iriel's birthing cries echoing from the house. The moon glaring down from overhead. The voice of the Apogee. He let a bit of thread-light into his veins to settle his mind.

"Alverax," Roshaw said with an air of warning.

Chrys turned and saw the young man with his black blade half pulled from its sheath, staring down at Jelium with fire in his eyes. It was more emotion than Chrys had seen from the young man since they'd stepped onto the ship. It was a look he'd seen before, from Luther. The look of a man who had lost something dear. The look of a man who wanted revenge.

Alverax's chest heaved up and down, but he slipped the blade back into its sheath.

They continued down and finally arrived at the edge of Jelium's roped off quarters. The race had finished and the excitement of the crowd had again been replaced by the buzz of activity. As they approached, a half dozen of the Masked Guard came to meet them.

Roshaw wasted no time. "We're here to speak with Jelium."

"You'll have to wait until after the races," one of the guards replied.

"Tell him Roshaw Blightwood is here."

"I don't care who you are," the guard said, his voice growing louder. "Walk away."

"Too late," Roshaw said. His eyes blazed to life with threadlight. In the shadow of a moment, he broke the corethread of all six guards and let a surge of Sapphire threadlight pulse from his body, like Willow had done when she was flying. The closest guard was rocketed through the sky, and the others stumbled back, tumbling through the air like autumn leaves.

"I guess we're doing this," Chrys mumbled as threadlight poured through his veins.

LAUREL'S EYES darted back and forth as men in black appeared from every direction, eyes alive with threadlight. Some held blades, others wore what Iriel had referred to as palmguards—the molded metal hand shield used by many Emeralds—but all crouched like wolves ready to defend their territory. In a way, Laurel felt bad for them. They had no idea what they were up against.

She pulled out the obsidian dagger and crouched.

The closest guard leapt forward, feet first, *pulling* himself toward her with unnatural speed. The world seemed to warp around her, warmth flowing through her limbs, and the masked guard's approach slowed. She stepped aside with ease and drove her elbow down into his stomach as he passed. She turned her head and took in the movements of the others. The entire world seemed to have slowed just the slightest.

Beside her, she saw Alverax parrying a blade with his own, backing up and tripping on the stairway. The guard attacking him made to drive his dagger down, but Laurel moved like the wings of a hummingbird, blurring through the air and closing the distance. Her boot crushed into the guard's shoulder, launching him back, tumbling down the stairs.

The warmth faded from her, and a frigid wind settled over the tunnels of her veins. She shivered and breathed, a similar feeling echoing in the back of her mind. Asher, only a few strides away, shivered beneath his dark green coat. The wolf nodded to her, and somehow she understood. He'd leant her his speed.

She reached down and helped Alverax to his feet. "I think you need a smaller sword."

"Not until the Heralds are dead."

Simple words, and yet they took her aback. They were the first words she'd heard him speak since they'd left Felia.

CHRYS LEAPT over the ropes surrounding Jelium's quarters. Masked guards appeared from the crowd, leaping down between him and their leader. Chrys, Roshaw, and Willow all released a wave of Obsidian threadlight, bursting apart the guards' corethreads. One of them attempted to throw a spear, which Willow flicked aside with an effortless *push*. Another threw a dagger. Both guards tumbled backward head over heel through the air. Chrys and the others strode forward with confidence as the remaining guards drifted into the sky.

"Well, I'll be damned," Jelium said, rising to his feet. His skin was bronzed, his hair dark and thick, and he smiled with the confidence of an emperor. Robes of black and gold flowed from a high neck down to his toes. Beneath the wrinkles and sagging skin, Chrys saw a spark of the man's true nature in the reflection of his eyes. "Roshaw Blightwood. I was ninety percent certain you were dead, and ninety-nine percent sure you would never again show your face in Cynosure."

Jelium brought his fingers to his lips and let out a shrieking whistle. The chaotic sounds of combat and fear cut off into an eerie silence. "There is no need for violence," he said with a booming voice. "Let us leave the Pit and have a civilized conversation in a more private setting." He paused, taking in the group, a flicker of a smile twinging his lips. "And you brought your son. You are full of surprises."

"More than you know," Roshaw said flatly.

Chrys surveyed the stadium, noting more Masked Guard arriving. Throughout the Pit, people stared, muttering amongst themselves, pointing, wondering what Jelium would do. Chrys could see their fear mixed with curiosity.

Jelium smiled. "Why don't we go to my home and have a conversation?" He turned an eye to Asher. "You'll understand, of course, that the dog will have to stay outside."

Chrys turned to Laurel, noting the snarl on her lips. "Laurel, why don't you and Alverax head out. We can handle the conversation. And if possible, keep an eye out for Felian ships. Last thing we need is unexpected visitors."

Laurel and Alverax gave each other a nod and walked off toward the stairs with Asher.

Chrys turned to Jelium. "Let's talk."

JELIUM'S COMPLEX was a maze of corridors, each seemingly identical to the last. Chrys was so convinced that they were being led in a circle that, at one point, he scuffed the sandstone wall with his boot and kept a look out for the mark. Shortly after, they were led to a wide room with a high, Felian-inspired domed ceiling. Jelium took a seat in a wide leather chair in front of a hexagon-shaped table with a game of Theo arranged atop it. As he had with many of his studies, Chrys had spent years mastering the complex dynamics of the game, even studying under the Alchean masters.

Chrys and the others remained standing, despite being encouraged to sit. The room was opulent, filled with the art of foreign peoples and wondrous places, both sculptures and paintings. Thick rugs lined the floor, and gold-threaded tapestries covered the walls. A trough of indented brass followed along the length of the walls with a stream of oil running through it, flames eating away at the source and feeding the room both light and warmth.

"Welcome to my home," Jelium said with a grin as the edge of the room filled with a retinue of Masked Guard. "Let us speak openly. Several of you have Obsidian in your veins. How? Alabella, perhaps? Doesn't matter. My power cancels yours, and yours mine. We are on even ground. And you,

Roshaw, old friend, you deserve an apology. I have long regretted our falling out."

"Our *falling out*?" Roshaw spat. "You tried to have me killed. And then you tried to have my son killed!"

"I never tried to kill your boy," Jelium said with a cool calm. "I gave him to Alabella—which was a success, I might add. After that, I simply wanted him on my side. I never had any plan to kill him."

Roshaw scowled. "They left him for dead in the desert."

Jelium smiled. "They did, true. But *I* did not."

"Enough!" Roshaw growled. The Masked Guard along the periphery of the room tensed. "What's done is done. There are more important matters." He gestured to the others. "This is High General Chrys Valerian of Alchea and his family, Willow, Iriel, and Aydin. The child is an Amber threadweaver."

Jelium leaned forward, intrigued.

"But we're here for something even more important." Roshaw pointed back out the door. "The Heralds have returned to Felia."

"Ah, so the reports are true," Jelium said, leaning his chin against his palm.

"Or some dark form of them," Roshaw corrected. "They're planning something. Revenge. War. We don't know. But a lot of people are going to die unless we stop them."

"You want to stop the gods, and you need...me." Jelium's lips curled into a sly smile. "I assume it's not because of my warmth and kindness. So you must need an Amber thread-weaver." He looked down at the baby. "One with more experience. And...hmm. It was only a matter of time before Alabella got herself killed. Was it the Heralds?"

Chrys ground his teeth as Roshaw's lip twitched. This was not how they wanted the conversation to go. Jelium already knew he had leverage. He knew they needed him for whatever they were planning. And now he knew that he was the only person in the world who could help.

Jelium reached down and grabbed a Sentry from the game of Theo in front of him, spinning the black circle in his fingers. "She was much more altruistic than I am. The greater good, at the expense of the few. Silly, if you ask me. That line of thinking has a tendency to get people killed."

Chrys took a step forward, glancing down at the gameboard. "We are not here to lie to you. Alabella is dead. And we do need you to help us stop the Heralds. This is not a problem you can ignore. Sooner or later, this war will come to Cynosure. And when the Heralds come, they will slaughter your people like hogs. And if you think you can fight them, I drove a sword through one's chest, and it did nothing more than annoy her. This is not about altruism, Jelium. It's about survival."

Jelium let out a roaring fit of laughter. His voice took on an air of mockery. "*This is not about altruism, Jelium. It's about survival. Ha!*" He settled back and wiped away a tear. "I don't know you, Chrys Valerian, but even I have heard of the Apogee, the so-called Butcher of the Valley. Why would I trust you? And why would I trust Roshaw who lied to me for so many years? From what we've heard, the Heralds saved Felia from an army of invisible monsters. That doesn't sound so malevolent to me. So, either you're all mad, or you're all fools who think they stand a chance against gods. Either way, I've no reason to help you."

Chrys started to move forward, but Iriel caught his arm. What he wanted to do was knock Jelium out, *break* his corethread, then carry him away like a bag of sand. But there were too many guards and too many good people who might get hurt in a skirmish. He needed to play to Jelium's weakness.

"You're a gambling man, no?" Chrys asked, hatching an idea.

Jelium tipped his head, raising a brow. "Perhaps."

"And, I assume, you play Theo?"

The large man leaned back in his chair and smiled. "I dabble."

"Let's make a little wager then," Chrys said. "We play a game. And if I win, you come with us to stop the Heralds."

Jelium stared at him, his eyes only half open as he weighed the proposal. "And what is it exactly you want me to do?"

Chrys lifted his hands. "We want you to use your Amber to create a sort of prison."

"Intriguing." Jelium's head nodded up and down as he thought through the proposal. "So, to paraphrase, you want me to leave the comfort of my home, risking my life and all I've built in order to fight a pair of supposedly immortal gods. In short, you win, I risk my life for your goals. Which begs the question: what happens if I win?"

"If you win," Chrys said, reaching to the sheath at his side, "I give you a one-of-a-kind, thread-dead obsidian dagger."

Chrys pulled out the knife and handed it to Jelium. The older man ran his hand over the blade, Amber threadlight shimmering in his eyes. He looked at the pommel, the grip, the cross-guard, then scratched a nail near the point.

"This is not obsidian," Jelium muttered to himself. "A true obsidian blade would shatter the first time it was struck. This is something different, though it does look quite similar. I would very much like to know where you found it. It would certainly be a worthy prize."

Chrys let out a breath, feeling a weight in his shoulders relax. "Then it's settled."

Jelium smirked. "I said it *would* be. Unfortunately, it is not enough."

"Jelium," Roshaw said with fire in his eyes. "Be reasonable."

"Be reasonable?" Jelium repeated. "You come to my home, spouting madness, demanding that I join you to imprison evil gods, then accuse *me* of being unreasonable? If I am gambling my own life for your plan, why should you not gamble a life for mine?"

A flurry of thoughts tumbled through Chrys' mind, one after the other, crashing, colliding, exploding into a million more ideas. He wanted to reach across the table and thrust the obsidian dagger into Jelium's chest. They could find another way to deal with the Heralds.

But he knew that wasn't true. They'd discussed it a hundred times on the ship from Felia. They couldn't kill the Heralds. They couldn't run from the Heralds. The only option was to trap them. And that left Jelium, and the game.

Fortunately, there were only a handful of people in all of Alchea who could beat Chrys in a game of Theo. Tucked away in a desert city of scum and lowlifes, how good could Jelium be?

"I'll do it," Chrys said confidently. "If I win, you come with us. If you win—"

"A life for a life," Jelium finished.

"Chrys," Iriel said sternly. "You can't...you... This is not your decision to make!"

He moved in close, grabbing her shoulders and lowering his voice. "Iriel, I know this isn't the first time I've asked, but you have to trust me."

"I do, but I don't trust him," she said, nodding toward Jelium.

"I'm going to win," Chrys said.

Her jaw clenched. "And what if you don't?"

Chrys hesitated longer than he wished. "I will."

Jelium, sitting quite pompously in his chair, reached out a hand. "Then we have a deal. If you win, a life is yours. If I win, a life is mine."

Chrys nodded and shook his hand.

Jelium placed his Sentry back on the board. "Well, Chrys. I do hope you're up-to-date on the latest theory, I'd hate to win without a good fight."

Chrys took his place at the other end of the table, straightening his nine Sentries and each pair of Emeralds, Sapphires, and...Heralds.

LAUREL AND ASHER rushed through the Pit with black-veined Alverax at their side, crowds scattering as men and women backed away from the oddly placed chromawolf. She felt a sense of relief wash over her once the crowds were behind them and they were back into the quieter part of Cynosure, though the streets still held varying degrees of activity. At least in the heart of the city there were no more watching eyes. No more feeling that someone would leap out and attack at any moment. Just the dimming hum of a city marching toward rest.

Neither Laurel nor Alverax spoke a word as he guided their path. They passed a woman packing up a cart of elletberries, the acrid smell wafting its way into Laurel's mouth. She looked to the south and Mercy's Bluff where, even at such a distance, all they could see was ocean all the way to the horizon. She didn't miss being aboard the *Pale Urchin*, with its constant rocking and cramped quarters, but she did miss the smell of the untouched air, and the solitude. She wasn't sure she would ever again want to live somewhere with so many people.

If they even survived the coming storm.

Eventually, they strode up to a small home with a shed out back and a wild pilliwick trying to nibble at a garden through a wooden lattice. She'd read about the creatures, with their unnaturally long tongues and penchant for kleptomania.

She watched as Alverax walked up to the front door and paused. For a moment, she thought of saying something—she knew he was still struggling—but instead, she waited, because that's what she would have wanted. Sometimes, people just need a moment, and, if that was the only thing she had to sacrifice to help him, she'd give up a thousand more.

Finally, Alverax pushed the door open, an inch at a time, the creak of it ringing out into the quiet neighborhood. It was dark inside. Quiet too. And as they stepped inside, Laurel felt an odd sense of nostalgia for her own home in the Fairenwild. But that home was gone. Alverax may have lost much, but at least he had a home.

He turned and looked at Laurel.

She nodded knowingly, then turned to leave.

CHRYS AND JELIUM sat across from each other, each staring down at the fifteen game pieces they controlled. Nine black Sentries. Two Sapphires. Two Emeralds. And two glass Heralds. Each piece had a black or white border; Chrys was playing black.

The most common opening was to advance one of the Sentries between the Sapphire and Emerald, opening the board and providing the more powerful pieces space to create threats. It was safe and led to a number of interesting variations, each with their own exploits and pitfalls.

Jelium, instead, slid forward a Herald's Sentry.

It weakened his position, unless you were going for...

Chrys advanced his left Sapphire, leaping over the Sentry in front of it.

"Good," Jelium said with a smirk. "You are familiar with the Agatos opening."

He pushed another Sentry forward.

"Made popular by Mennik Thorn," Chrys added, as he advanced one of his own. He had never been so grateful for the year he'd spent absorbed by the game. The Agatos opening had several nasty traps that worked well against many young players.

Jelium examined the board carefully. "And you wish to punish my opening with the Grievar Advance."

Chrys smiled. There was no immediate counter to his opening, which meant that they would enter the middle game with Chrys having more space and a stronger center.

Jelium clearly knew what he was doing...but so did Chrys.

As Laurel and Asher walked down dark, sandy pathways, she couldn't help but miss her own grandfather. Beginning with the death of her parents, it seemed that all life had to offer was loss, a slow biting tax for merely existing. Her parents, home, grandfather. Her threadlight. One by one, they had all been taken from her. And yet, despite it all, she was not alone.

Together, Asher whispered to her mind, feeling what she was feeling.

And they were.

Laurel and Asher raced through the outer edge of Cynosure. Despite the sand, it was hard to believe that on the other side of the massive sandstone wall lay a sprawling desert. There was an ethereal beauty to the scale of the cavern that housed the city, like the Father of All had scooped out a section of rock from a mountain and placed a city in its crevice. It felt so foreign, so strange. Hardly a tree in sight, and the ones that did grow were prickly or stunted.

As they ran, they passed a fenced enclosure with a dozen odd creatures. To Laurel, they seemed somewhere between a cow and a horse, but green and with spines covering their bodies. The creatures moved slowly, and, based on the abandoned carts beside the pen, she assumed they must be used as pack animals.

They continued, and Asher spotted a small, lizard-like creature. In moments, he'd pounced upon it, shattered the creature's shell, and bitten into its flesh. Watching Asher feast on his prey gave Laurel the odd desire to do the same. If only there were a duskdeer or a small rabbit. Her grandfather had the best herbs for cooking rabbit.

Finally, they reached Mercy's Bluff, where they collapsed on the sandy overlook. Asher crawled closer and rested his head on her lap. She brushed the green fur along his back, feeling each movement of his ragged breath beneath the thick coat.

They sat in silence for some time, looking out over the Altapecean Sea, an endless horizon of various shades of blue. A few weeks ago, the color would have given her pause, a reminder of her lost threadlight. But she was content now. Instead, the color faded away, and all she felt was the motion of the waves, like the rustle of leaves in the wind, and the explosive spray as those same waves crashed against the rocky shore.

"It's beautiful," Laurel said.

Asher's voice whispered in her mind. *It is.*

"I wish we could enjoy it."

Laurel leaned back with one arm posted behind her and watched the waves. Whether today or tomorrow or the day after, a ship would come hunting for them. Whatever measure of peace and confidence they felt now was just as likely to turn with the tide.

MOVE AFTER MOVE, Chrys and Jelium advanced their pieces, adding pressure, opening lines. The game was close, despite Chrys' strong opening. He'd played too defensively, worried about losing what little advantage he had. He needed to be more aggressive. This game was too important.

He had a clever idea and used his Emerald to *pull* one of the enemy Sentries forward.

Jelium laughed. "The Bessarion Gambit! Now, I haven't seen that one in years. Shawn Paul would be proud. It is, of course, a dangerous move were I to accept. The immediate advantage would require me to play nearly perfectly to account for the positional disadvantage. Which is tempting, to be clear. Tell me...Apogee, are you familiar with the Sarilla Countergambit?"

Chrys raised a brow as Jelium made his move. He could see the immediate threat, the potential fork after an Emerald *pull*, but it all seemed manageable. Chrys ignored the taunt, accepting the countergambit with his Sapphire.

"There is a funny line," Jelium said, swaying his head back and forth and reaching for a Sapphire. "Made popular by Nelson of Brun, though it first appeared in Eidyn, played by Khraen himself. A natural extension of our current positions. Are you familiar with the Volund?"

Chrys ignored Jelium to think, but the pressure was beginning to rise inside of him. He racked his brain trying to remember the line to which Jelium referred. He knew Khraen, of course. One of the most influential players in history. And Nelson of Brun had become a champion during his stay in the Alirian islands. But Chrys had no recollection of the game.

"It appears not," Jelium said, smiling as he moved one of his Heralds. "This should be interesting…"

With every move, Chrys felt the pressure intensify in his skull, a rhythmic beating that began with a simple tap, now ringing out like two mallets against a war drum. He didn't need books on Theo theory to tell him that his position was dangerous, but, even still, he held out hope. His Heralds were safe. And if he could keep the position defended long enough, he could find a way to get back on the attack.

"I must say," Jelium said, with his chalky voice, "that you have played impressively. You've warded off traps that would have fooled some of the most skilled players in Cynosure. However, as a man who has been in real war, you must see that the game is lost."

Chrys rubbed at his temples, staring intensely at the board. Jelium was taunting him. There were no immediate threats. "Your mind games won't work. My Heralds are safe. The game is far from over."

Jelium smiled, a single twitch of his upper lip. "Are you so certain?"

Adrenaline poured through Chrys like an old whiskey, burning him from the inside. He'd missed something. No. His Heralds were safe behind a wall of Sentries. There was no way for Jelium's pieces to get to them. Not unless…

Stones.

Together, Laurel and Asher stared out at the breaking waves in silence and solemn happiness, enjoying the calm before the storm, knowing that these days may be the last before the clouds of evil returned. Somewhere across the ocean, the Zeda people lay sleeping. Laurel wondered what was happening in Felia. She'd spent so much time away from the Zeda that she was beginning to feel a distance growing in her heart. In an odd way, Chrys and the others felt more like family than Bay now, and Zedalum felt less like home than the world at large.

She watched as, high above the ocean, a flame-tailed halken twisted in the air, diving toward the water, then pulling up and drifting as if floating. Two more halkens appeared, flying in a straight line from the northwest. Whereas the first seemed to be playfully tumbling through the air, these two seemed focused. They had a purpose, a destination. Laurel could appreciate that.

As she watched, the birds grew in size. They were massive flying creatures, lit only by a half-hidden moon. Suddenly, they paused in the air, as if all of their momentum had been taken away in an instant. It was then that Laurel realized: they were not birds.

"Gale take me," she cursed.

Danger, Asher added, his bright eyes fixed on the creatures in the sky.

They were both on their feet in an instant, eyes on the heavens, neither wanting to speak aloud the dark truth.

The Heralds had arrived.

No, no, no. There was always a move—that's what Malachus had taught him. Theo was like war; until the final move was played, there was always a way to turn the tide. And if anyone could find it, it was the Apogee.

Chrys scoured the game board, calculating exchanges, looking for the flaw in Jelium's position. More than once, he thought he'd found something, a way to at least even the match, but every line ended with his defeat.

Chrys moved a Sapphire, knowing full well that it would not stop the inevitable, unless Jelium made a mistake.

"Heralds have always been the heart of Theo," Jelium said, watching Chrys' eyes as they darted back and forth across the board. "Despite them being the most powerful piece on the board, most players prefer to keep them locked up behind a wall of Sentries. The fear of loss is greater than the eye for victory." His eyes dimmed, and he tilted his head to the side. "How fitting that a sacrifice will be what brings about your own."

Jelium moved one of his Heralds forward, capturing Chrys' Emerald with a sacrifice that would begin a forced sequence that would march Chrys toward defeat.

Willow brought a hand to her mouth. "Lightfather, no."

"What?" Iriel said quickly.

Roshaw took a step toward the board. "What is it?"

"The game is over," Willow said, her eyes wide with disbelief. "Chrys lost."

ALVERAX BREATHED as he entered his childhood home.

Silence.

Dark as it was, he felt a ghostly sway in his legs, as if he were back in the creaking cabin on the *Pale Urchin*. So many days lost in the memories that swirled in his vision like a noxious fog, infecting his mind, polluting his thoughts. He wanted to move on, to forget what happened to...her. But want and reality were at odds, and, no matter how hard he tried, he couldn't hide from the look in her eyes as she sank to the floor in the throne room.

There was a certain aroma that lingered in the air of his home. While living there, he'd never really noticed it, as though a hint of saffron had stained the walls from all of his grandfather's cooking. But now, returning after so many months, it filled him with warmth.

A few pebbles crunched beneath his foot as he took another step forward.

"Is someone there?" a voice called out in the darkness.

"Grandfather?" Alverax stepped toward the light.

A hunched man made his way out of a room on the far end of the house, a small candle illuminating his frailty. The old man rushed forward, slamming the candle's base down on the side table and wrapping Alverax in the warmest embrace he'd ever received. His grandfather's hands gripped tight against Alverax's back, squeezing, digging in with what little strength the old man had left. For a moment, Alverax forgot about the pain.

But only for a moment.

"My boy," his grandfather whispered, emotions adding an even greater quaver to his voice. "I knew you would come back."

"I..." Alverax didn't know what to say. He didn't want to talk about Jisenna, but he did. He needed to tell him about his father, but he couldn't. Instead, all of the pain and anguish, all of the fear and doubt and sadness, every bit of sorrow that had bottled itself in his broken soul came pouring out of him in a stream of tears.

Once, in a moment of stupidity, he'd told Elder Rowan that he wanted to bring hope to people. But now he understood that a shooting star was the sign of hope because it leaves as quickly as it comes.

His grandfather's calloused hands moved to the back of Alverax's head, and he pulled him in even tighter. "No matter what you've done, no matter how bad things are, I will always be here. You are a good man, Alverax...You are a good man."

He dug his head into his grandfather's shoulder and sobbed.

A few minutes later, Alverax collapsed into the soft fabric of a chair in front of the fireplace. His grandfather took a seat opposite him.

When Alverax finally felt ready, he spoke. "He's alive. Dad... Your son is alive."

His grandfather's eyes grew wide, the wrinkles along his forehead becoming deep chasms. "How?" His voice wavered. "How is it possible? Did you see him? Where is he now?"

"He's meeting with Jelium. We traveled here together—well, there was a group of us—but he and I still haven't spoken."

For a moment, his grandfather watched him, reading his story in the pain of his eyes and the weight of his shoulders. "You haven't forgiven him for leaving." His words were not a question but a statement of truth.

"How could I?" Alverax said, his voice growing with anger. "What kind of man abandons his family and never returns? And do you know where he was? In the Wastelands! What the hell kind of a father abandons his family for the Wastelands?"

"I'm sure he had his reasons."

Alverax shook his head. "You're defending him? He abandoned us. He abandoned you!"

Again, his grandfather gave a pause before responding. "When I was young, I carried deliveries all over the streets of Felia. Crates of fruit. Books. Flowers. It paid well enough. One of our clients needed a box of paper delivered to a small bookshop every other week, and I took the job. On the way there, I ran into a friend. When she found out where I was going, she asked if I could take a flower pot with me that belonged to the same bookshop owner. I agreed and set the flower pot on top of the crate of paper. But as soon as I lifted it, I knew it was a mistake. The pot was too heavy. But I was stubborn. So, I took it anyway. I was walking up the final hill when my arms finally gave out. The pot came crashing down. It shattered into so many pieces it was hardly recognizable. The crate, too, had broken.

"The point, Alverax, is that some burdens are handed to us, but others we pick up for ourselves. Our job is not to wallow in the gravity of it, nor to simply push forward and accept it. Our job is to ask ourselves which burdens are worth the weight and which are not. My boy, don't wait until you're falling over to lighten your load. This grudge you have for what your father did, you have to set it down."

Alverax took a breath. "I don't think I can do that. He doesn't deserve to be forgiven."

"Of course not—most people we forgive are undeserving —but the only person a grudge hurts is the one who carries it. If you want to live a life hunched over in pain, go ahead. But if you want to stand as tall as the world deserves to see you stand, then you need to shed your burden."

The words reminded him of *her*. She'd once told him that he would have to grow in uncomfortable ways, and he had! It felt like around every corner the world required him to change even more, and he wasn't sure he could handle it. Even if he didn't believe in himself, she did. But she was gone.

Alverax cried into his hands. "I can't."

"Not alone," his grandfather said quietly. "But you don't have to be. Alverax, I would take your burdens from your shoulders if I could. But I cannot. What I can do is share the weight, if you will let me."

So, he did.

While his grandfather stoked a small fire, Alverax told him everything. And when he spoke of Jisenna, his grandfather cried with him.

As THEY SAT in tired silence, an aggressive knock pounded on the door. Alverax stood quickly and pulled out the Midnight Watcher, gesturing for his grandfather to stand back. As he walked toward the door, it burst open, wood splintering where the lock had failed to keep it closed. On the other side, Laurel and Asher stood panting in the doorway.

"Laurel," Alverax said, startled. "What's going on? What's happening?"

"The Heralds are here!" she blurted out. "There's no time. We need to warn the others, and I need you to show me where they went!"

Alverax turned to his grandfather, jaw clenched, eyes filled with regret. "I'm sorry. I have to go."

"It's okay," the old man responded. "You have always been destined for more than this city. Seeing you again has brought me more joy than you will ever know. And to know that my son is alive...Tonight, Alverax, you have brought me hope."

Alverax gave his grandfather one final, ferocious embrace. "I love you, old man."

"The depths of the ocean could not see you as highly as I do." His grandfather pulled away and looked him in the eye. "Take care of yourself. And take care of your father for me. I would very much like to see him again."

Alverax smiled one last time. "I promise."

With that, they stepped away from the house and raced toward Jelium's complex.

CHRYS' vision warped as he stared at the gameboard, pieces slowly drifting away, breaking through the cracks of reality. He replayed each move in his mind, desperately searching for where he'd failed. But no matter how much he wanted to blame Jelium for cheating—Lightfather knows he would—Chrys couldn't hide from the truth.

Jelium leaned back, throwing his hands behind his head. "It was a good game, I will admit. One of the best I've played. You surprised me with the Bessarion. Despite the loss, you should be proud. You've clearly studied the game. But as it goes, the better man won."

"You knew," Chrys said with a snarl. "Spinning that piece around between your fingers. You wanted one of us to propose a game. You were probably going to suggest it yourself. You played us!"

"Be reasonable," Jelium said, failing to suppress a hint of amusement in his tone. "You came to me. I had no way of knowing that you even played the game. I am a man of my word, though. If I had lost, I would have willingly gone with you on your foolish adventure. But, alas, it seems that the game has played out differently. Perhaps, we can play again some other day."

"THIS IS NOT A GAME!" Chrys shouted, swiping his hands across the table, launching the Theo board toward the wall, sending pieces flying in every chaotic direction. The Masked Guard all drew their weapons. "People's lives are at stake!"

Jelium calmly rose to his feet, meeting Chrys' prismatic eyes with confidence. "People's lives are always at stake. How is that my problem?"

"Chrys," Willow said from behind him, shaking her head cautiously.

"Jelium," Roshaw cut in, raising his hands in an attempt to calm the rising conflict. "How long have we known each other?"

Jelium cocked his head to the side, scowling at Roshaw. "You. You're lucky I haven't gutted you. You think after a few years that you can return home and pretend like you didn't lie to me for more than ten? You will never be welcome in this city until you hand over whatever prized possession you brought back from the Wastelands. For the rest of you, the game is done. I won. You lost. The child is mine."

A shocked silence warped the room.

Chrys' head jerked to face Jelium. "What did you say?"

"I won," Jelium said with cold eyes. "And I want the Amber-eyed child."

"Over my dead body," Iriel said with a snarl.

"That was *not* the deal," Chrys growled.

Roshaw's eyes burned into Jelium. "You sick bastard. Don't you have enough children?"

Jelium's lip twitched. "For thirty years, I have tried to bear an Amber-eyed child. Not one of my wives could give me what I wanted. I have an entire army of children, and they're useless. Thread-dead, the whole lot of them. But your son...mmm. If he were with me, no one would even question it. He would be celebrated throughout Cynosure. He would be a king. Everything I have would be his."

Chrys gripped the hilt of his dagger. "It's not happening. The deal was my life for yours."

"That's simply not true." Jelium lifted a hand into the air, fingers extended wide. "If I win, a life is mine. That was the deal you shook on. A life for a life. And if you won't honor your promises, they will be honored for you."

Jelium closed his hand, the Masked Guards shifted, and the room went dark.

Fear crawled its spindly legs through Chrys' mind. Their biggest advantage was their threadlight. But if they couldn't see, the advantage was lost. And Jelium knew that. Chrys pulled his dagger out of its sheath, waiting for his eyes to adjust, but the door was closed, and the room had been cast into an inky void of blackness.

As he tried to orient himself, a body rammed into him, sending them both tumbling over and crashing into the wall. His eyes bulged as a knife bit into his thigh. Quickly, he threw his hips up and over the attacker, unable to see, but fully aware of his attacker's position. Once he was on top, he rammed his own dagger through the man's chest. Once. Twice. Three times. Squeezing his hips until the man went limp.

"The child is mine, Chrys," Jelium called out into the void. "Give him to me, and I will treat him as if he were my own flesh and blood."

"Go to hell," Chrys shouted back, before realizing that words would give away his position.

Jelium let out a roaring laugh. "Look around you. We're already there!"

Iriel's voice called out from the dark, a wordless scream of rage.

Before Chrys could move, a man's voice grunted out in pain from the same direction. A loud pop rang throughout the domed room, followed by the same voice calling out in agony.

"Who's next!" Iriel shouted. "I'll kill every last one of you!"

Chrys pulled himself toward her voice and whispered. "Iriel, you have Aydin?"

"I gave him to Willow," she said. "She's hiding in the corner."

"Chrys," Jelium's voice taunted. The room was quiet, save for the sound of feet shuffling. They were surrounded and without threadlight. There was no way out. "In a few minutes, there will be more than fifty of my Masked Guard surrounding this room. Give me the child, and I will let you leave the city alive."

"The Heralds will come for you!" Roshaw said. "And they will kill you first. They're hunting Amber thread-weavers, and you and the baby are the last. It's only a matter of time before they find you!"

Jelium let out a grunt. "Lies. You were a coward then, and you're a coward now. Now, GIVE ME THE CHILD!"

Just as he screamed the words, the door burst open, letting in a flood of flickering light from the hallway, illuminating three silhouettes. The first, a tall man with dark skin and a sword that dragged along the ground. The second, a woman with hair stained green and fire in her eyes. And the last, a beast nearly as tall as the woman, twin tails dancing in the firelight, crimson blood dripping from its maw.

Threads, like hungry eels, slithered out of the ground, latching onto the newcomers. But as soon as the threads were born, Alverax's veins pulsed with Obsidian threadlight, storm clouds swirling beneath his skin, and the Amber threads shattered.

"JELIUM!" Alverax shouted, stepping forward. Again,

threadlight surged through him as he broke the corethread of every barely-visible guard in the room. Those who moved lost their connection to the earth and began to float toward the domed ceiling. "This ends now!"

He ran forward, lifting the Midnight Watcher. Jelium's eyes glowed a brilliant gold as he tried to bind the blade, but it would not be touched. It could not be touched. This was its purpose. It was born to hunt Amber.

Chrys pushed himself to his feet, but he couldn't get there in time.

From the other side of the table, Jelium seemed frozen.

Alverax screamed out as he pulled the blade down over his head.

But he stopped, the shimmering thread-dead obsidian mere inches from Jelium's skull. He let it hover for a minute before speaking. "Let me be clear, Jelium. You are used to being the most powerful man in the room, but those days are over. If we want you dead, you are dead. If the Heralds want you dead, you are dead. You will help us, or we will find another way to stop them."

Jelium's lip quivered.

"Chrys!" Laurel shouted from the doorway. "There's no time. The Heralds are here!"

"Stones," Chrys swore. "In the city? Or on their way?"

"Here. Now."

Chrys turned to Jelium, a look of resolve in his eyes. "This is the first place they will look, and if they find you, you won't live through another sunset. Come with us if you want to live. Or stay and die."

The room grew quiet.

Jelium remained frozen beneath the Midnight Watcher, chest heaving up and down as he contemplated his position. His eyes darted back and forth between Chrys and Alverax and his Masked Guard, clearly unconvinced of the Heralds' arrival but keenly aware of his waning control of the situation. The man didn't have to say the words for Chrys to know his response.

"Alverax," Chrys said. "Lower the blade. Jelium is coming with us."

Everyone looked to Jelium, and he nodded.

Alverax sheathed the sword. "There are only three exits. The bluff. A tunnel to the northwest that spits you out into the desert. And another to the northeast that leads to the canyons."

"If we're heading to the Wastelands," Roshaw added, "we should take the northeast tunnel."

"Can we get there without being seen?" Iriel asked.

Laurel shook her head. "The city's too open. If the Heralds are in the air, they'll see us any path we take."

"Then we're going to need a distraction," Chrys said.

Alverax opened his mouth, then closed it with a wince. "I have an idea."

"What is it?" Chrys asked.

Alverax cocked his head to the side. "We're going to need a lot of rope."

AFTER THE MOON passed beyond the sandstone overhang, darkness spread over Cynosure. Chrys and the others peeked out of a window, catching short glimpses of the Heralds as they circled the city like bloodthirsty bats in a cave. Laurel was always first to spot them, marking their appearance with a growl.

It was time.

Chrys nodded to the others, then headed toward Jelium's underground passage with Willow and Alverax. It was a cramped, narrow passage, darker than night, lit only by the finely crafted bronze lamp Chrys carried. Below ground, he wasn't sure which was more unnerving, knowing where the Heralds were, or not.

When they finally exited the tunnel, they found themselves in a familiar setting from a new perspective. The underground stadium known as the Pit was lit by a single torch tower casting dwindling light from cooling embers. The track and stands crawled with unnerving shadows. In one corner, hidden away behind thick iron bars, nearly a dozen necrolytes slept coiled up in their cages.

Willow motioned to Chrys and they fell behind, whispering to him as they approached. "I really don't think this is a good idea."

"It's not," Chrys said, admitting the truth. "But we don't

need good ideas right now. We need a distraction. And if nothing else, this will be a spectacular distraction."

ON THE EASTERN edge of Jelium's complex, waiting for their signal, Laurel, Iriel, and Roshaw crouched in a small room with Asher and Aydin, staring out of a window. Behind them, a host of Masked Guard stood in the hallway with Jelium in their midst. Beyond her typical distrust, it took only a single moment in his presence for Laurel to decide that she hated the man. It wasn't his appearance, or even his demeanor, but a scent. A dank, putrid aroma. If darkness had a smell, it would be his.

High in the sky, the Heralds still roamed, gods surveying their kingdom while the people lay asleep in soft beds. Three times, Laurel had seen the two separate then come back together, hovering in the air like skyflies. For now, all their party could do was wait.

Laurel rubbed at her shoulder, then her chest and thigh. Her hands refused to settle. This moment—and her role— was too important. If Jelium decided to do something stupid, like try to take Aydin, Laurel and Asher had to stop him. Roshaw's Obsidian would counteract Jelium's Amber, and Laurel was certain that she and Asher could do the rest. Still, deep inside her, like a woodpecker tapping away at her ribs, the urge to act remained. But she was done listening to that voice. Laurel was willing to sacrifice for her pack, even if the sacrifice was time.

Suddenly, from the distant tunnel leading to the Pit, she saw the first of them.

Chrys stepped forward to the first necrolyte with a rope outstretched. He studied the spikes along the massive reptile's twisted torso, looking for two that were jutting out in opposite directions that could be used to lasso the beast. "There," he said, finding the perfect spikes. "Those should work."

"Careful," Willow said.

"Don't wake it up," Alverax added.

Without responding, Chrys used a y-shaped stick and lifted the end of the lasso toward the spikes. With the care of a surgeon, he looped the rope around the closer of the two spikes, letting the hemp fall toward the base without touching the necrolyte's scales. Then, taking the other end of the loop, he stretched it out as far as it could reach, but the lasso had tightened, and it wasn't wide enough. Carefully, he added pressure to the other end of the lasso, waiting for the loop to enlarge. The pressure pressed against the first spike, stirring the necrolyte from its rest.

He paused.

After shifting its position, the necrolyte returned to its sleep, the lasso still hooked around the first spike. Fortunately, its movement had loosened the loop, and Chrys was able to quickly wrap it around the second spike. He used the stick to tighten the lasso, then pulled it out of the cage.

Weight seemed to fall from his shoulders. He felt like he had when he'd pulled his first honeycrystal from the et'hovon hive.

"Easy," he whispered with a smile.

Willow shook her head. "This is such a stupid idea."

"It'll work," Alverax said.

"Oh, I know that," she replied. "Doesn't make it any less stupid."

One by one, they looped lassos around the caged

necrolytes, ensuring the rope ends would be free when the cages were opened. Then, once all of the ropes were set, Chrys, Willow, and Alverax tied the free end of the ropes together, creating a bouquet of thorned necrolytes.

Chrys and Willow stood at the gates.

Alverax wrapped the rope around his wrists.

Obsidian threadlight poured through their veins.

One by one, they *broke* the corethread of each necrolyte, a million tiny suns bursting through the air like billowing sand.

They opened the gates, and Alverax ran.

Chrys watched as Alverax pulled the weightless necrolytes along. Despite their broken corethreads, the massive creatures still had considerable mass, and it took a slow effort to get them moving. Chrys and Willow followed, being careful to keep their distance.

Alverax ran up the stairs and flailed for a moment as his feet lifted off the ground from the momentum of the necrolytes at the top of the stadium stairs. He recovered and took off down the entrance tunnel.

Necrolytes thrashed in the air behind him.

Crashing into each other.

Ropes groaning.

As they stepped out of the entrance and into the sprawling cavern housing the sleeping city, Alverax unknotted the ropes, spun, and hurled the necrolytes upward with every ounce of strength in his slender frame.

"Gale take me," Laurel cursed.

A writhing mass of necrolytes floated into the air, screeching, flailing...flying. Ropes fell from them like shedding skin. Slowly, they drifted apart, spreading out over the city like dragons in the night.

"Stones," Iriel cursed beside her.

The first scream broke through the dark sky as the people of Cynosure awoke to the sounds of the necrolytes.

Laurel turned to Jelium. "We leave at the next—"

Before she could finish her sentence, a choir of voices screamed out from the four corners of Cynosure. More and more people awoke. Fear flooded the night. Men, women, children. Lamps flickering through open doors, torch towers blazing to life. Shattered peace.

"We leave now," Laurel finished. "And leave your pack behind; they'll give us away."

"My pack?" Jelium raised a brow. "I'm not bringing—ah, no. They're coming with us."

"They stay!" Laurel shouted, her voice lined with a wolf's growl. "The Heralds will see a large group. If they come, we all die. You're in no danger from us. We need you alive."

"Damn it," Jelium grumbled and turned to the Masked Guard. "Stay here. Stay hidden. Don't let whatever those things are find you. I'll be back as soon as I deal with this."

Laurel pushed open the door and peeked around the corner into the night sky. There was no sign of the Heralds, though the necrolytes continued to spread out over the canopy like vultures. She waved for the others to follow, and they did.

Street by street, Roshaw led Laurel, Asher, Iriel, and Jelium toward the northeastern tunnel. As they moved, they passed frightened men and crying children, women wielding blades and others nocking arrows. Laurel felt the urge to comfort them, but the truth was that they had every right to be worried. Evil gods and monstrous beasts roamed the sky.

That was when the first necrolyte fell toward the earth.

CHRYS GRABBED Alverax and pulled him to a rocky corner where they hid, watching as the city sprang to life. Chrys wanted to shout at the people to stay in their homes, to bar their doors and windows. To stay safe. The chaos was only beginning, and when the necrolytes fell to the ground, some of them would survive, and people were going to get hurt. Chrys looked toward the northeastern tunnel passage. But they couldn't move until there was enough chaos in the city to keep the Heralds distracted.

As the pandemonium developed, Chrys leaned closer to Alverax and Willow. "I think we should go. The corethreads could reappear any minute."

"Ready when you are," Willow said in agreement.

"It's happening," Alverax said, looking toward the sky.

Chrys whipped his head around. "What?"

But then he saw it. One of the necrolytes was diving tusk-first through the air toward the ground, mouth wide open, teeth bared.

"Go, go, go!" Chrys shouted, taking off at a sprint along the eastern wall.

"I NEED TO STOP," Jelium groaned behind them, leaning against a sandstone wall, his chest heaving up and down.

Laurel growled. They didn't have time to stop. They needed to get to the tunnel as soon as possible. "Roshaw!" she shouted, an idea blossoming in her mind. "*Break* his corethread."

The older man looked at her, puzzled. "Jelium's?"

She nodded vigorously. "*Break* his corethread, and we can drag him along so he doesn't have to run."

Roshaw's eyes grew wide. "Brilliant." He let Obsidian threadlight pour through him and *broke* Jelium's corethread. In moments, the man was weightless and angry, but she also saw a flicker of understanding in his eyes.

"Asher," Laurel whispered, turning to her companion. "Don't make it gentle."

The chromawolf nodded, biting the sleeve of the big, Kulaian man's robes, and took off. Jelium bounced up and down against the sand, wincing while they continued their path.

Every few paces, Laurel would turn her eyes skyward to look for the Heralds and the necrolytes. The gods were nowhere to be seen, and most of the snakes were either writhing on the ground or falling through the air. One necrolyte was fumbling about against the edge of the eastern wall, throwing its tusks against large stone stalactites.

When they reached the tunnel entrance, Roshaw pulled Jelium down, and they hid behind a large boulder, waiting for the others.

CHRYS' heart throbbed in his chest as they ran, adrenaline and theadlight coalescing in an oily mixture that burned like lightning in his veins, surging through him and pushing him forward. He and Willow were *drifting*, lightening their weight and increasing their speed, leaving Alverax barreling after them, long legs striding over sand and rock.

Chrys' eyes fixed on their destination, where he could see the others crouched behind a boulder, waiting.

He smiled.

This was actually going to work.

Just then, a necrolyte fell from the sky, crashing into the ground not twenty feet away, between them and the cave entrance. The ground shook as it hit, and its body grew still.

Chrys and Willow slammed to a halt, staring, speechless.

Was it...?

The necrolyte stirred.

Stones.

If only he had Amber threadlight, he could bind the creature and run around it. Instead, the only way was through. "Alverax," he said without turning to the young man who had finally caught up. "How good are you with that sword?"

"I was trained by the best swordsman in all of Felia."

"Good," Chrys said.

"But only for, like, one week..."

Chrys turned to him. "Could have led with that."

Alverax shrugged. "I got pretty good in that week."

"Better than nothing." Chrys unsheathed his dagger. "We attack from both sides."

"Chrys Valerian," his mother said from behind them with a stern tone.

Both men turned around.

She shook her head. "Men are such idiots sometimes."

Chin held high, she strode toward the writhing necrolyte, massive spikes jutting out from its body, curled tusks cutting from its jaw, rows of teeth glittering in the moonlight. It saw her and coiled its body like a spring, preparing to pounce. The veins in her arms glowed with the ghostly mist of Obsidian threadlight, then she *broke* the necrolyte's corethread. It lashed out at her, but the absence of gravity caused it to flip over itself, bounce off the ground, and float back into the air.

She never broke stride, walking under it as it hissed from above.

"Damn," Alverax muttered.

Chrys shook his head and smiled. "That's my mother."

They took off after her, and in no time at all, they were reunited with the rest of their party. Chrys pulled in Iriel and Aydin for an embrace, kissing her forehead as he squeezed them close. He caught Laurel's eye, and she gave him a nod.

As he let go of his own family, he watched Alverax approach Roshaw. "I haven't forgiven you," the young man said. "But I'm ready to move in that direction."

"I'm sorry," Roshaw said, tears swelling in his eyes.

"I know," Alverax replied.

Laurel, unaware of their conversation, pointed to the sky. "Is that…?"

Chrys looked up.

The Heralds.

"RUN!" he screamed.

Everyone, including Jelium with a newly formed corethread, sprinted down the corridor.

A loud slam quaked through the ground from behind them.

"CHRYS VALERIAN!" Relek called out, his voice reverberating through the tunnel.

Everyone stopped and turned.

Relek and Lylax, the Heralds of Felia, the gods of the Wastelands, they-who-pervert-the-bond, stood in the mouth of the tunnel, looking down their noses.

"You cannot run from us," Lylax said, her gravelly voice biting through the air.

"Give us the child," Relek demanded.

Chrys took out his dagger and spun it in his hand. "Hey Lylax, how's your stomach?"

Iriel touched his arm.

Lylax took a step forward. "The mountain cares not for the fallen tree."

"Chrys," Iriel said.

He turned.

"I have an idea," she whispered, turning to the others and speaking quickly. "Four of us have Emerald threadlight. We're going to cave in the tunnel."

Roshaw nodded. "Hell yeah, we are."

"If we are," Chrys said, turning back toward Relek and Lylax. "We need to do it now."

"On three," Iriel said.

Relek took another step forward. "I must say that I was surprised to find that you had taken to the sea."

"One," Iriel whispered.

"I should have known," Relek continued with a sadistic grin. "You always run. At the Temple. In the Fairenwild. The Endless Well. Only now, there is nowhere to run."

"Two," Iriel continued.

They opened themselves to threadlight, and Emerald energy swam through their veins.

"It has been...fun," Relek said with a smile.

"Three!" Iriel shouted.

Their eyes blazed with viridian threadlight. The roof of the tunnel rumbled, shaking with the force of a hundred hammers beating against the stone. Rubble fell from overhead, then rocks the size of fists. Then, breaking apart from the surge of power that *pulled* it down, the tunnel shattered like a pane of glass, raining death from above.

Through the stone storm, Chrys saw Relek.

He wasn't angry.

He wasn't annoyed.

He was...amused.

And that scared Chrys even more.

RIXI STEPPED into Relek's Cave, followed by a group of three other wastelanders. After having guarded the entrance for so many years, there was something unnatural about finally stepping inside. But the stone felt like any other stone, and the damp air felt like any other cave. Still, he knew there was something inside. Something the false gods didn't want them to see.

He lifted a photospore overhead, the light glancing off the shiny skin of a half-healed gash on his forearm, and continued forward.

A small—but growing—division of the An'tara no longer believed in their gods. Not that they didn't believe they existed, but after Lylax had gone through body after An'tara body, discarding them like soiled clothing when they withered under her control, a faction began to wonder if the gods were worthy of their devotion. Some had already given themselves in defiance. It was not an easy path to walk —the An'tara were a hive, one mind united—but even the et'hovon must at times abandon their rose.

Together, the band of An'tara plunged deeper into the cave, through a winding tunnel system, farther and farther. It seemed empty, save for the occasional dripping of water from the ends of broken stalactites and the glimmering puff of photospore mist.

More than once, Rixi caught the others glancing back up the tunnel from where they came. Yearning, perhaps, to return to their home. Doubting, almost certainly, the path of disobedience they trod.

It would be worth it—he assured them.

There was something down here.

Something the gods wanted to keep for themselves.

They traveled deeper, down and down until, finally, a light gleamed ahead. They slowed their pace, careful to silence their steps. This was it; Rixi could feel it.

He turned the corner and entered a sprawling cavern, high and wide, lit by dozens of photospores and a strange light emanating from a pool of golden water at the far end. They stopped, mesmerized, afraid yet excited. There were signs of people living here, a table, chairs, bedding. Was this where Lylax had lived before she came out of the cave? Whatever the case, it seemed abandoned now.

No matter how hard he tried, Rixi could not stop his eyes from looking at the light emanating from the golden water. It called to him, singing. It was warmth, and his soul was freezing in the darkness.

He stepped toward it, and the others followed.

When he reached the edge, he kneeled, staring into the hypnotic light. He saw his face in the reflection, gray skin, tattoos down his nose. His brow was broader than it ought to be, the only physical change he'd experienced from his bond with the young ataçan, Koi'Ma. In a way, the pool reminded him of oka'thal, the water that kept their people alive, but its brilliance was ten-fold that of the life water. If oka'thal could sustain them, he wondered what this would do.

Rixi placed his hands in the water, cupping the glowing liquid in his palms, and brought it to his lips. It slid down his throat, cold but warm as it flowed through him.

Nothing happened.

As he stared down into the light, tears welled in his eyes, and his heart broke. This was it; he was certain. There was an answer here, somewhere. Some path forward for the An'tara without the gods. But maybe he was wrong. Maybe their only path was to submit themselves and move forward, content in knowing that they were nothing more than vessels.

Then, his heart burned. Small at first, like a hand held over a fire, but then the flames grew, a field of dry grass blazing. He gripped at his chest, crying out in pain, struggling to steady himself. His whole body burned. He was the dry grass, and his skin was the bonfire.

Suddenly, the pain was gone, replaced by a steady stream of warmth coursing through his limbs. He felt alive —more alive than he'd ever felt—like electricity danced in his blood.

When he stood, he caught a glance of his arm and smiled. Fresh gray skin had stitched itself together, leaving no sign of the painful gash. He had been healed.

And as he breathed in the stale, cavern air, he understood that, even more than the healing of his arm, something within him had changed.

One by one, the other An'tara drank from the golden waters, marveling at the transformation, wondering at the possibilities.

But a resounding voice broke their hope. "You should not be here."

Invisible threads latched onto the others, dragging their bodies to the floor before they could even scream. In seconds, the pressure collapsed their bones, and their bodies crumpled to the floor, blood pooling out from the mangled heap of sinew and organs.

And all Rixi could do was watch.

"I understand why you are here," Relek said, striding forward with his chin held high. "It is a hard thing we have asked of your people, but it is necessary. Tell me, Rixi." He emphasized the name. "Were you there when the Builders killed so many of your people?"

Rixi nodded. Only five years had passed since the Builders had come over the mountain, threatening to invade their land. And in so doing, they had killed thousands of the An'tara.

"With this," Relek said, gesturing to the glowing pool, "we can avenge those who fell. We can heal the An'tara and remove their dependence on oka'thal. We can lead them over the mountain. With the bond you hold with your ataçan, the An'tara look up to you. Together, we can unite the Hive. We can seek revenge on the Builders, if you will join me."

Rixi was no fool. He understood that, though there was a question presented, there was only one correct answer. But was it so bad? If he stood with the gods, perhaps he could protect his people. Perhaps, he could steer their path through safe roads. If there was no way to stop the gods, he would do everything in his power to limit their devastation.

Dropping to a knee, Rixi crossed his hands at the wrist, bending the fingers back to touch at the tips. "My god, we will unite the Hive."

A LIGHT BREEZE fluttered its wings through the canyons east of Silkar. A peck of pilliwicks darted across the hard ground, scuttling up and over the sandy walls. Chrys and the others were just as skittish as the wildlife, eyes constantly watching the sky, flinching at every shadow. Despite that, after a full day of wandering, the Heralds had yet to be seen.

Chrys had Aydin strapped to his chest, trailing behind Roshaw and Alverax, Iriel and Willow at his side. The canyons seemed to be an endless crevice wrapping back and forth, but Roshaw assured them that they were headed in the right direction. Still, Jelium complained with nearly every step. But if he ever stopped walking, Laurel and Asher were there, snarling to push him forward.

When the sun finally dipped below the western horizon on their first night out of Cynosure, they took shelter against a canyon wall with enough of an overhang to hide them from the open sky. The evening brought with it a desert chill, but rather than build a small fire and risk being seen by the Heralds, they pulled their clothes tight over their shoulders and dealt with it.

As they settled, Aydin began to stir, so Chrys passed the child over to his wife, who sat with her back against the sandy wall. She lifted her shirt and offered a breast to their son, who latched with ease. Chrys thought he saw the sliver of a smile on her lips as she watched him nurse.

As far as children go, they were lucky. Like most thread-weaver infants, the healing power in his veins made Aydin a healthy child who slept well and only cried when he was hungry. Still, Chrys felt guilty for the life he'd forced upon his son. Hopefully, if all went well, they'd be back in their cottage one day where Aydin could learn to crawl and walk and talk with a sense of safety and security.

Chrys sat back and laid his head against the wall beside Iriel's. His feet were tired, and his eyes begged him to rest. Instead, he watched the two people he loved most dearly in the world. "Remember how we talked about having another child?"

Iriel turned to him, brows raised.

Chrys held back a smile. "Seems like a pretty terrible idea right about now."

Iriel quivered as she held back her laughter, Aydin bouncing on her chest. "For a moment, I thought you were implying we should...here. I was about to make you sleep on the other side of the canyon."

"No, no," Chrys said, looking past the ledge into the star-filled night. "It's just that the entire world is growing darker, and if we can't stop the Heralds, who knows what will be left. I want to be able to think about the future, but part of me is scared that there may not be one."

"So don't," Iriel said flatly. "Why do we always have to think about the future? Look to the future. Plan for the future. Prepare for the future. Let's keep it simple. I have you. You have me. We have a beautiful, healthy boy. So forget about it. Forget about the Heralds. Forget about everything. Enjoy the peace we have right here, right now. Who knows when we'll have another chance."

She was right, of course.

"Iriel," he said softly, "I know I don't say it enough—I'm not sure I ever could—but I want you to know that if everything we've gone through, from the day we first saw Aydin's Amber eyes until now...if that was the cost of being here with you, I would pay it every day for the rest of my life."

She leaned into him and placed her delicate lips against his own. Warmth washed over him. Iriel was a warm blanket, and his soul had spent a season in the rain. Her kiss sent fire coursing through his veins, weaving its way through his blood like a flood of threadlight, warming him from the inside.

"I love you," he whispered as the last bit of their lips parted.

"I love *you*," she said with a smile, their noses still touching.

Chrys pulled himself closer and wrapped his arm around Iriel and the baby. "When I was in the Wastelands, I wasn't sure that I would ever get to say that again."

"I can't imagine what you went through."

"There were some really dark days, especially when Relek was in control. Part of me wanted to give up. It just...it felt like it was already over. Like I'd already lost. But I just couldn't stop thinking about you. I couldn't stop thinking that the last memory you had of me was," he faltered, his voice taking on the slightest tremble, "when I abandoned you."

She tilted her chin to look at him. "Chrys Valerian, don't you dare. There wasn't a single moment that I believed you had abandoned us. I know you: the man who would do anything to protect his family; the man who would miss his son's birth if it meant keeping us safe. When I saw your eyes from across the field before you walked away, I knew it wasn't you. *You* didn't abandon us."

"I don't deserve you," he whispered.

She smiled. "Probably not."

Chrys reached down and pulled out the pocket watch that Malachus had gifted to them. When he opened it, all three of the small hands continued their graceful rotations, each at their own pace. "When my mother found this in the mountains, she said it was a sign that I was alive. I think it's a sign, too, but for me it represents us. Our family. When she gave it back to me, it was like the Lightfather was telling me that we'd be together again. That we'd have a little more time." He squeezed the pocket watch shut and held it up to his ear. "As long as I hear that steady tick, I know that everything is going to be okay."

"Everything *is* going to be okay," Iriel said. "Now put that away and stop talking. I need you to be my blanket for the night."

Chrys smiled and gave her a gentle squeeze, laying his head atop hers. No matter what the coming days would bring, it would all be worth it if it kept his family safe.

ALVERAX SETTLED down on the edge of the camp, rubbing his hands together for warmth. He offered to take first watch, and the others took the opportunity to catch whatever sleep their minds would allow. He knew he wouldn't find much.

His father sat silently beside him while the others dozed off.

The stars overhead seemed brighter in the shadow of

the canyons. The Moon's Little Sister shone down at him, and instead of feeling overwhelmed with thoughts of Jisenna, he found an odd sense of peace. There was still pain—profound pain cannot fade so quickly—but the hurt seemed wrapped in a quilt of tranquility. Someday, he would join her in the stars.

"You can sleep if you want," Alverax said quietly to his father. "I'm not tired."

Roshaw's lips curled into a smile. "Couldn't sleep if I tried."

Alverax watched the man he'd admired for so many years. The man who had raised him, taught him, then abandoned him. When he was a child, his father was perfect in his eyes. Strong. Able. A provider. But as Alverax grew older, flaws seeped through the façade, and the shock of it made those flaws seem more than what they were. The promise of perfection had been broken, and all his angry eyes could see were the cracks. But now, Alverax could see more clearly, as if a fog had lifted from his younger lens. And it was enough to see that, despite the imperfections, his father was a good man.

"I have been debating with myself," Roshaw said. His eyes seemed pained.

Alverax took the opportunity to let out the words he'd been holding in, speaking before his father could finish. "We don't have to do this right now."

"I know, but," Roshaw said, rubbing at his temples, "it's just...there's so much I haven't... Sorry, I'm not very good at this."

"It's fine. We don't have to." Alverax felt an odd sense of dread. He was just starting to make peace with his life, and whatever it was that his father wanted to tell him, he wasn't certain he wanted to hear it. "Whatever it is, I'm sure it can wait."

Roshaw closed his eyes, relieved at the offer but still filled with the pain of withholding. For a moment, he said nothing. Alverax could feel the tension, the heavy decision his father was weighing. Some truths are painful to hold, and others are painful to share. Whatever truth Roshaw held, it hurt like hell. As Roshaw's chest rose up and down with each breath, Alverax was certain that this was the latter.

Finally, his father let out a breath. "Have you named a star for her yet?"

Alverax startled, looking to his father.

"I heard what happened," Roshaw continued. "Those bastards killed people I cared about, too. Three of them." He looked up into the dark sky. "The southern edge of the Broken Wheel. See those three stars? Those are theirs."

Alverax looked and saw the dim, little cluster beside the brighter circle. There was another cluster just to the east of the Wheel. One of those was his father's star. He pushed the thought aside, feeling an old grudge clawing away at his insides. "As soon as I looked in the sky, I knew what star would be Jisenna's."

"The Moon's Little Sister," Roshaw whispered as he stared up into the vast expanse.

Alverax nodded. "It was the only one bright enough."

"I think she'd like that." Roshaw's head bobbed up and down as he breathed in the night air. Quietly, almost as if to himself, Roshaw said, "It's the same star I chose for your mother."

A chill ran through Alverax. His father's life had not been easy. He'd suffered and lost, tried and failed. Alverax may not have forgiven him fully—not just yet—but he certainly felt like he understood the man more deeply than he ever had before.

And that was a start.

THE NEXT MORNING, before the sun was up, Laurel and Asher took off to hunt for water and a sandhog, both of which Roshaw claimed were in the area. Just one of the creatures would be enough to feed the whole group for several days. If it was large, maybe a week. Either way, it was refreshing for the two of them to get away from the pack for a while. If they could find food before everyone woke up, she might not have to listen to Jelium complain so much. Then again, a full belly wouldn't stop him from complaining about his smelly clothes, tired feet, or the dirt in his hair.

Together, they stalked through the desert. It was nothing like the Fairenwild. No shade. No grass. No trees. The only plants and shrubs seemed skeletal in comparison. Tall cacti. Brown clumps of balled up tumbleweed. Knee-high grass that was deader than a beetle in a treelurk web. There were hints of green, enough to give the illusion of life, but even the colors seemed muted and dulled by the heat.

Laurel wasn't convinced they'd find anything but the occasional leafling, and the small lizards were barely a snack. They wouldn't keep anyone sustained for the long journey ahead. Fortunately, after an hour of searching, they came across a herd of sandhogs grazing on what was certainly the brownest grass she'd ever seen. The patch sat at the base of a hill with a large rock formation beside it.

She felt Asher's excitement as they stalked forward in lock-step. Slowly, carefully, they inched forward, feet sinking into the sand with each step. They needed to get close enough so the sandhogs—with their wide feet that barely sunk in the sand—couldn't outrun them. When they were in position, they would decide on a single sandhog. Focused. A wolf that becomes too distracted by the bounty loses it all.

Without a word, they chose the closest sandhog, the fattest of the herd, with black freckles along its back and jowls that hung nearly to the floor. In perfect harmony, they pounced, feet dancing across the sand. They were one mind. Hunters in pursuit. Eyes fixed on their prey.

By the time the sandhogs noticed them, throaty squeals piercing the morning air, it was too late. The animals all scrambled in different directions, some running up the hill, others dashing toward the rock formation, and others, confused, running directly at Laurel and Asher, including the fattest of the herd. They leapt atop the sandhog, claws gouging its ribs, dagger tearing into its neck. The cleaner the kill the better, so they struck fast and hard, claws and dagger pulling in and out in quick succession. The creature took its last breath and flopped its wide head against the sand.

Overhead a flock of vultures grunted as they departed to the west.

Something about it gave Laurel pause. Wouldn't the vultures stay close so they could swoop in and steal the carcass?

Laurel turned her head to the south.

Two figures flew in the distance.

"Hide!" she shouted, scrambling on all fours toward the rock formation.

Laurel and Asher clawed their way to the stone and

leapt into the shadows of two overlapping boulders, nestling in as deeply as they could. Twenty feet away, the dead sandhog lay on the ground, bleeding out over the dead grass. Moments later, the two figures flew overhead, seemingly unaware of Laurel and Asher below. By the path of their flight, Laurel was fairly certain the Heralds had not flown over the canyon where the others hid. She stayed hidden beneath the rocks for several minutes before stepping away.

If the Heralds had seen them... This time, there was truly nowhere to run.

They needed to be more careful.

Laurel and Asher walked over to the dead sandhog, kicking away a red and black striped snake that had come to claim the prize. Asher bit down on the leg of the carcass and began dragging it in the direction of their camp.

The whole way back, Laurel watched the sky.

AFTER SEVERAL GRUELING days of travel surrounded by the constant threat of the Heralds flying overhead, Laurel and the others exited the desert canyons and entered sprawling plains. After another day of gentle flatland, they stepped into a thick, mossy forest. Asher was filled with excitement but lost his enthusiasm when the ground became soggy and wet. Soon enough, they were treading through Wasteland swamps with an inch of water ever present beneath their feet.

The paranoid joviality they'd shared over the previous days faded with the openness of the desert, replaced by the feeling of constant attention from their surroundings. Frogs calling from overgrown leaves. Birds chirping in the canopy. Snakes twisting around branches. And the odd, long-armed creatures that leapt from tree to tree, watching. Always watching.

Despite it all—despite the nagging feeling that told her she shouldn't—Laurel was beginning to feel hopeful. They were so close. A few more days and they'd be at the place the others had called Relek's Cave, preparing to trap the gods once more. But it wasn't over yet, and there were still a million things that could go wrong, so Laurel pushed aside her hope and clung to resolve.

The farther north they traveled, the more long-armed

creatures they spotted. At first, Laurel had thought that *they* were the wastelanders, but Roshaw and Chrys assured her that they were not. In fact, the wastelanders hunted and ate the creatures, which made Laurel wonder what the meat would taste like.

Perhaps the biggest surprise was Jelium's change in mood. He'd given up complaining—perhaps because Willow carried a stick she used to prod him with—and had instead taken on an air of curiosity. Every few steps, he had a question about a fern, or a mushroom, or some little bug crawling on his arm. After a while, Laurel wished he would stop talking and go back to the occasional complaint.

After four more days, Laurel and Asher had taken to hunting a variety of smaller creatures in the swamps. The sandhog meat they'd carried with them had not lasted as long as they'd hoped, but Laurel and Asher had become quite adept at hunting together. The most difficult part was finding places to sleep. The swamp was wet, everywhere. On rare occasions, they would find a patch of dry ground and take a rest, but the patches were small and rare. During their breaks, Willow had taken to weaving hammocks—they now had three—that they shared in rotation for those not on watch at night.

The next day, when the sun was high overhead and their feet moved thoughtlessly forward, Asher noticed something. A creature, with two arms and two legs, kneeling on the ground, motionless, partially obscured by the surrounding shrubbery. To be more precise, Asher smelled the creature—an oddly sweet smell laced with a familiar foulness. It wasn't human, and it wasn't one of the swinging creatures. This was something different.

They advanced carefully, poised to pounce in case the creature was hostile. As they grew closer, Laurel saw that there were two others beside the first, each kneeling in the same position, grouped up in a tight cluster. It soon became clear that the creatures were dead. They looked mostly human, though their skin was a charcoal gray. Their eyes were small and beady, and their earlobes were pointed, like downward facing triangles.

"Roshaw," Chrys said quietly. "Have you seen anything like this before?"

The older man nodded as he approached the closest. "Once, a long time ago. Maybe a month after I was first imprisoned."

Willow leaned closer, examining each of the three with curiosity. Finally, she touched one, and her brows lifted. "They're...hard. How is that possible?"

"*Pintalla mox*," Roshaw said. "At least, that's what I heard it called. Translates to *surrendered spirit*. The guards weren't exactly eager to explain the details, but I think it was some kind of wastelander disease. They separate themselves so the rest of the hive doesn't get sick."

"It sure smells like a disease," Laurel agreed.

"Certainly looks like one," Willow added. "But how would a disease kill all three at the same time in the same place?"

"Who said they all died at the same time?" Iriel kept her distance with Aydin in her arms.

Chrys gave a thoughtful nod. "If they were all sick, they probably came out as a group and let the plague run its course."

Jelium eyed the bodies warily. "The more important question that no one seems to be asking is: if the waste-landers are dying of a plague, why the hell aren't we turning around and getting as far away as we can?"

Laurel snarled at him. "Because not all of us are selfish

pricks who would rather let the world burn than catch a cold."

Jelium stared at her with more than a hint of anger. "I would watch my mouth if I were you. It would be a pity if I were suddenly unwilling to make your little coreseal."

Laurel ground her teeth together. As much as she hated Alabella, at least she understood the woman. She'd had a purpose, a goal. Jelium was nothing but a cancer, infecting the world around him with greed and pride. Didn't help that he smelled like sour sweat and piss.

"Three dead doesn't make a plague," Willow said, cutting the tension.

"Agreed," Roshaw added. "If it was a plague, it would have killed a lot more than the one wastelander I saw a few years ago."

Chrys stepped back from the three statue-like waste-landers. "Plague or not, our course is set. We're the only ones who can stop the Heralds. And the only way that's going to happen is if we can get them below ground and seal them in. If we get sick, we get sick. Either way, all roads lead to Kai'Melend."

"Great," Jelium said. "Not only are the Heralds waiting for us, but a plague is too."

Chrys smirked. "Let's not keep them waiting."

When Chrys awoke, the sun remained hidden below the eastern horizon. Iriel slept above him, hanging serenely in a large hammock with Aydin strapped to her chest, the pair wrapped in a warm blanket. Chrys and the others lay on a patch of raised grass above the murky water. Despite being several feet above the swamp itself, small beads of morning dew had still crept their way up the hill to settle on their sleeping bodies.

He stood and stretched, looking around the quiet swampland. The first thing he noticed was a grape-sized frog staring at him with big red eyes from atop a wide leaf. Chrys leaned forward and leveled his gaze, mesmerized by the beautiful array of green and yellow across its belly. He wondered if it was one of the poisonous varieties.

Soon, the others awoke, and they set out to the north.

Two days passed before they came to the outer edges of Kai'Melend. Keeping hidden, they watched the city, early afternoon sun filtering through the breaks in the trees. Where once there had been a small village, now there was a hive. Thousands upon thousands of wastelanders swarmed Kai'Melend, traveling the rope walkways, swimming the shallow waters.

Roshaw whispered to the others, "This is more wastelanders than I've ever seen. It looks like all of the nearby tribes have gathered to see the gods."

"No, this isn't just a gathering," Chrys said with confidence. "This is an army. Even the children have weapons. They're preparing for something."

Iriel looked to him. "Alchea?"

"Can't be," Chrys said. "They can't be away from the oka'thal waters for that long."

"Maybe the Heralds just don't care," Iriel said grimly.

Chrys scowled. "Either way, Alchaeus might know what's going on. Just another reason to get down there fast."

They left their perch and headed to the rocky overhang marking the entrance to Relek's Cave. By the time they reached the trees south of the cave, Chrys and the others were tired and wet, and what they found made matters even worse. The entrance to the cave was guarded by fifty wastelanders. With four Obsidian threadweavers, getting rid of that many guards wouldn't be a problem, but they needed to be discreet. They didn't want Relek and Lylax following them down until they were ready to create the coreseal. There had to be a way inside without being seen.

"We need a distraction," Chrys whispered to the others.

Everyone looked to Alverax.

"Don't look at me," the young man said. "I got enough grief for my last idea."

Laurel crouched beside Chrys, crawling forward on her hands and knees to get a better view. Her eyes were wide, her brows furrowed. Asher, beside her, bent low, as if ready to pounce.

"I could get their attention," Roshaw said. "Make them chase me, then once they're far enough away, I could launch myself into the sky. Circle back to the cave before they return."

Willow shook her head. "They wouldn't *all* chase you. Most would probably stay at the cave entrance."

Jelium, sitting with his back against a tree and his ass in the mud, shook his head. "You're all making this more difficult than it needs to be."

Chrys looked to the older man and scowled. "Please, enlighten us."

"Just kill the savages," Jelium said. "It would be so simple. I *yolk* them, and the chromawolf tears them apart. It'll look like some wild beast did it."

Alverax offered an unamused expression. "What kind of wild beast would attack fifty wastelanders...and win?"

"Ridiculous—" Roshaw began.

"Corespawn?" Willow said, thoughtfully. "We could make it look like the corespawn did it."

Jelium had a self-satisfied look in his eyes.

"That wouldn't work," Chrys said. "The Heralds control the corespawn. And it doesn't matter if it would work or not. If we kill them, we're no better than the Heralds. There has to be another way. During shift changes, or when they're eating maybe."

"We don't have time for that," Roshaw said. "If there were just one or two of us, maybe. But we're too many. If we spend another day out here, someone is going to see us, if they haven't already."

Jelium pushed himself to his feet, glaring at Chrys and the others. "I'll handle it myself."

"Stop!" Laurel hissed, jumping toward Jelium and shoving him back to the ground.

"Get off me, you little shit!" Jelium spat.

Asher darted in close, baring his fangs mere inches from Jelium's face. The Amber-eyed man snarled back but knew his place. Laurel glared at him with her hand on the hilt of her obsidian dagger. "You're not in Cynosure anymore. No more gambling with lives."

Jelium clenched his jaw and settled back against the tree. "I vote we kill them and be done with it."

"There has to be another way," Chrys repeated.

"Literally," Willow said, her eyes lighting up. "There *is* another way. The Endless Well. There's no way they can guard all of it, and it leads to the same place."

Chrys looked to his mother. "You're a genius."

"I am what I am," she said with a modest shrug.

Alverax leaned closed. "That's the big hole, right?"

Chrys nodded.

"And we're going...*down*...the big hole?" Alverax said. "Didn't that almost kill you last time?"

"It did," Willow said flatly. "But the second time is always easier."

Roshaw stifled a laugh. "Plus, we can fly now."

"I like it," Chrys said. "Unless someone has a better idea... Roshaw, do you know the way?"

Roshaw nodded and, with only the smallest measure of grumbling, they were back traveling through the swamps toward the place they'd almost died once before.

THE WALK through the swamps went as smoothly as it could have for a party of seven plus a baby and a chromawolf. Roshaw had done well keeping them distanced from the wastelander city, and Iriel had done well keeping Aydin quiet. The only eyes that watched their path belonged to the colorful birds perched in the trees. Though Chrys had grown accustomed to the putrid smells of the swamp, he was eager to take a big breath of the stale cavern air below ground.

Before they reached the clearing that led to the Endless Well, Chrys' mind drifted back to the day he'd last been there. The day that Agatha, Esme, and Seven had been killed. The day he'd failed to save them. But he couldn't think about that now. He may not have been able to save them all, but he *had* saved Roshaw and reunited him with his son. It was just as important to remember the good as it was to remember the bad.

As they approached their destination, Chrys pushed aside a veil of vines, blue skies bursting into view. But as the fields became visible, a wave of fear washed over him. Not because of the Endless Well, sitting like a lake of inky blackness in the center of the field. Not because of the jutting rock formations and wild waterfalls. It was the stench of two hundred dead wastelanders, blackened from the *pintalla mox*, kneeling motionless in the dirt like a field of statues.

There was no cursing, no jokes or mirth. The scene was too surreal. Too morbid. Macabre. A slight breeze rustled the leaves as Chrys and the others looked upon a field of the dead, a shrine of the surrendered.

The Endless Well stared from across the field like the Lightfather's all-seeing eye, beckoning them through a corpse-filled maze.

Finally, Jelium broke the silence. "What were you saying about it not being a plague?"

They all ignored him, and Chrys turned to the others, dropping the vines and concealing them once more. "Willow, Roshaw, and I should be able to fly everyone over."

"What if we're already infected?" Iriel asked, keeping the swaddle over little Aydin's face.

"Wouldn't change the plan," Chrys said flatly. "In fact, if we get infected, it would just be another reason for us to get below ground so we can drink the elixir. Roshaw, you take

Alverax. Willow, you can bring Laurel. I'll bring Iriel and Aydin."

"What the hell?" Jelium said. "You're just going to leave me here?"

Chrys nodded. "Unless you want to walk through a field of dead wastelanders, we'll come back for you and Asher."

"Take Asher first." Laurel set her hand atop the chroma-wolf's back. "There's something not right. A foul taste in the air."

"You're in a swamp," Jelium grumbled. "What is wrong with you all? Just go already. It feels like I'm the only damn person who wants to move forward."

Willow pursed her lips and winced. "While I don't agree with the tone, I'm with Jelium on this one. Looks clear to me, and I'm keen to move quickly."

Chrys looked to Laurel and Asher. "You two have the best eyes. Did you see anything?"

"Nothing," Laurel said, furrowing her brows. "But that's the problem. Where did all the frogs go? Snakes. Insects. They were everywhere, and now there's not so much as a bird call. I don't know what it is, but something doesn't feel right."

"IT'S A FIELD OF DEAD PEOPLE!" Jelium said. "Why the hell would frogs be hanging out in a grave? Look around. There's not a single savage in sight. You're acting like a bunch of frightened children. Here, you want proof?"

The large Kulaian man pushed his way out of the mass of ferns and onto the grassy field. This time, no one was fast enough to stop him.

Chrys panicked. His eyes darted back and forth across the tree line, up into the sky, and over toward the rocky cliffs. Jelium was the largest of their party. If anyone was going to be spotted, it was him. Chrys looked to the others and noted the same angry fear on each face.

A moment passed, and the wind glided quietly over Jelium, tossing his dark hair across his face. The bronze-skinned man smiled wide, lifting his hands, palms up. "You're welcome. Now, let's get on with it. I'm eager to meet the brother of the gods."

Just as the words left his lips, a thin, feathered shaft darted through the air and embedded itself in his shoulder. He looked down and pulled it out. Black ooze drooled off of the long needle-like tip. "What the hell?"

The trees just north of them rustled slightly, and a dozen more darts lanced through the air, whistling in the wind, piercing through clothing and sinking into Jelium's flesh.

"No!" Chrys shouted.

Alverax leapt forward to grab Jelium, but Laurel tackled the young man to the ground just as a series of darts flew over their heads. They rolled over, and she plucked one of the thin needles from where it had embedded in her shoulder, grimacing as it left her skin stained with the same black ooze.

"Laurel!" Willow shouted. "Are you okay?"

The young girl nodded as she and Alverax crawled back to the safety of the overgrowth.

It took all of Chrys' will power not to run forward to help. But if he ran out of their cover, they'd both be dead. Even now, Jelium was face-down in the dirt, spasming. Chrys grabbed Willow and Iriel beside him and forced them to the ground.

Chrys turned to the others. "We have to get Jelium to the Endless Well." They needed him. Their plan wouldn't work without an Amber.

"How?" Willow asked. "We can't fly with all those darts."

"We run," Chrys said. "You and Roshaw can create threadlight barriers to deflect the darts. Iriel, Laurel, and Asher will stay close and keep Aydin safe. If we can get to the dead wastelanders, we can use their bodies for cover. Alverax, help me carry Jelium; we can cut his corethread first, and I'll create a barrier for us. Our only hope is to get Jelium to the elixir."

Everyone nodded, including Asher.

"Good," Chrys said, looking back to Jelium and the Endless Well.

Jelium's chest heaved, his arms trembling along the grassy floor.

"No time," Chrys said quickly. "Go now!"

Chrys stood up and let threadlight flood his veins. As soon as they left the cover of the swamp, darts soared through the air. Willow and Roshaw's veins lit up with multi-colored threadlight, and a surge of energy pulsed around them. The darts struck the barrier, some stopping completely as they hit the wall, others passing partly through as if they'd been shot into a bubble of water.

Everyone moved in chaotic unison.

Alverax *broke* Jelium's corethread and lifted the big man over his shoulder like a bale of hay.

Chrys created a barrier for them.

The others took off toward the dead wastelanders faster than he'd ever seen them run.

The barrier Chrys held required too much threadlight to sustain, and he felt a sharp pain blossom in his chest. He let go just as they reached the statue-like dead, hoping the cover would protect them from the darts.

He glanced back, and his attention shifted to the sky as a flicker of movement fluttered above the trees. There, hovering in the skyline, he saw the last thing he ever hoped to see. Relek and Lylax stood in the air like the gods they were, smiling down at the chaos.

"FASTER!" Chrys screamed.

He watched as the others, staying low, dodged back and forth between the maze of dead wastelanders. Two steps forward. One step to the side. Twisting, leaping, sprinting, all while darts pelted through the open air. Plague or not, they needed to get to the Endless Well before the Heralds caught up. Chrys and Alverax trailed the others, Jelium's floating form knocking into dead bodies behind them.

The others slipped past the last of the dead wastelanders and reached the edge of the Endless Well, finally turning and seeing what Chrys had seen. Flying in their direction, the Heralds moved through the air like falcons on the hunt.

"Chrys!" Iriel shouted. She clutched Aydin with both hands, legs bent, ready to jump into the void. Even at a distance, Chrys could feel the fear in her eyes. It was the same look she'd had when she was bound by Amber threads on the wonderstone. Helpless terror.

He looked over his shoulder just as the Heralds swooped down from above. His veins sizzled with heat, and thread-light burned from his theoliths into his bloodstream. Despite the pain, he created another barrier, and the Heralds crashed into it, *pushed* back by the unseen shield. But the force knocked Chrys over, sending him tumbling into a pair of dead wastelanders, their hard skin cracking as they crumbled into the dirt.

Alverax continued to run with Jelium dragging behind him.

They were so close.

Chrys looked up and saw the others still standing at the edge of the well, waiting, feet set as they prepared to leap. He turned around just as the Heralds roared and shot forward. Chrys reached inside himself to create one last barrier, but his heart seized in his chest, refusing to provide any additional threadlight. His jaw clenched and fire burned beneath his ribs.

Without a barrier, Relek crashed into Chrys, slamming into him with so much force that Chrys felt his bones rattle. He rocketed through the air, sharp pain surging through his arm, and collided with a dead wastelander that shattered on impact. Chrys' vision blurred, but he pushed himself to his feet as the hazy shape of Relek approached at a steady pace.

Chrys threw a tight fist, but Relek caught it and smirked. Knocking the god's wrist away, he bent down and dove into him, but Emerald threadlight *pulled* Relek toward the earth, increasing his weight ten-fold. Chrys crashed into him like a brick wall. The Herald reached down and grabbed Chrys' neck, lifting him up like a sack of wheat. Relek looked deep into Chrys' eyes with the deformed smile of a mad god.

"Stop fighting," Relek commanded.

The words lashed out at Chrys' soul like a viper, squeezing its jaws against his will. Their intent seemed to echo in his skull, bouncing around, pounding away at the walls of his mind, a hammer on stone. But Chrys knew what would happen if he let Relek in. He threw his will against the command, refusing to succumb to the god's control.

"STOP FIGHTING!" Relek screamed, spittle raining down on Chrys' face.

But Relek was not the Apogee any more.

Chrys was.

"I...AM...IN...CONTROL!"

A blur of green leapt over him, barreling into the Herald. Chrys inhaled sharply, then turned to see Asher tackling Relek to the ground, ripping into his flesh.

Lylax took the opportunity to lunge at Chrys. She

moved with terrible speed, closing the distance nearly as fast as Chrys was able to lift his hands in defense. Her white robes blurred in the afternoon heat, and a pale yellow shard on a silver chain swung from her neck as she moved. He blocked her savage hands with practiced movements, barely able to keep on his feet as he stumbled on the foot of a dead wastelander. She pressed again, and he stepped under a wild hook. Using the mistake, Chrys landed a quick boot to her shoulder that sent her stumbling away.

Beside them, Relek roared in pain. Asher's teeth cut through skin and cartilage, disconnecting his left hand from his arm. The torn limb sprayed crimson over dead wastelanders, dripping over the Herald's black robes. Relek reached down with his other hand and gripped the chromawolf's neck, lifting it into the air and staring into its bright eyes, both snarling. Challenging. The mad god screamed out as he snapped Asher's neck, the crack reverberating through the field. He pulled his arm back and hurled the chromawolf through the air, over the open space, and down into the Endless Well.

Chrys watched in shock as the limp body of the massive chromawolf toppled over the ledge.

Laurel grabbed her throat as though Relek's hands were around her own neck. She stumbled back, choking, eyes wide with shock and fear. Her foot slipped on the edge, but she caught herself, still struggling to breathe. Her eyes rolled back, and she finally collapsed, falling from the edge and following Asher into the darkness.

Willow and Alverax dove in after her.

"Chrys," Relek said with a frown, watching as threadlight pooled along the edges of his stump hand. Slowly, as if watching a flower bloom outside of time, his hand reformed, tendon by tendon, until the stub became a hand once again. "You cannot stop us."

Lylax spat on one of the dead wastelanders. "You are a fool if you think you can fight gods."

Iriel's voice called out to Chrys from the edge of the Endless Well, but he kept his eyes on the Heralds. There was no fear in their eyes, no worry or doubt. To these immortal creatures, Chrys and the others were no more than mosquitos.

"If that were true," Chrys said, meeting their gaze, "then you wouldn't be here."

Snarling, Relek and Lylax stared back at him with dead eyes.

"No," Chrys continued. Keeping a hand behind his back, he signed a countdown to Iriel and Roshaw.

Five. Four.

"You're here because you're scared. Because we know your secrets. The elixir. Theoliths. Lifelight. It's only a matter of time. Whether it's us or another, there will always be people who see you for what you truly are."

"You always did believe you were smarter than your enemies," Relek said, lifting his chin. "Unfortunately for you, Chrysanthemum, men cannot outwit gods."

Three. Two.

Chrys lifted his chin in response, opening himself to threadlight, feeling the same sharp pain in his chest. "We'll see."

One.

Chrys turned and surged Sapphire, hurling himself toward the Endless Well. Threadlight burned in his chest as he *pushed* harder, blasting toward Iriel and Roshaw as they leapt into the well with Jelium in tow. Glancing over his shoulder, Chrys saw the Heralds flying forward.

He dove head first into the Endless Well, twisting in mid-air, keeping his eyes fixed on the ledge, waiting for the Heralds to appear.

Moments later, they did, flying into the center of the gaping hole but stopping as Relek held back his seething sister. For a few seconds, they simply watched, floating in the air side by side until threadlight began to blaze from their bodies with such otherworldly radiance that Chrys had to shield his eyes.

Threads. A hundred. A thousand. Ten thousand, pulsing and swirling in patterns of pure chaos. The mass continued to expand, larger and larger, until it surged and contracted, folding in on itself, compressing into a single point of limitless energy.

Relek and Lylax threw out their hands and the mass of energy hurled down the Endless Well. To Chrys, as he continued his descent into the darkness below, it was as though the sun were falling from the sky directly toward him. Toward his family. Toward his friends. He crossed his arms in front of his body, as if his feeble strength could stop such a power. But before the energy consumed him, it exploded.

Blinding light.

A burning in his veins.

But there was no wave. No burst of destructive force. Instead, the mass of threadlight spread its tendrils out like a sheet of pure power, rippling out from the epicenter, stretching across the Endless Well from edge to edge, extending its web through the stone and beyond.

As Chrys fell through the darkness, staring up at the pulsing threadlight above him, the truth struck him harder than if the sun had truly fallen.

Stones, no.

"LAUREL!" Willow cried out. "Laurel, wake up!"

The older woman crouched over the Zeda girl surrounded by dark waters at the bottom of the Endless Well. Alverax knelt beside her, photospore bulbs puffing their luminescence into the darkness, casting long shadows over the girl and her animal companion. Occasional drips of water sprayed over them from where the cascading waterfalls struck the underground lake.

A brilliant flash of threadlight erupted above her, filling the cavern. Willow shielded her eyes, waited a few moments, and then looked back up. Chrys floated down gracefully through the air beneath what looked like a net hewn of pure threadlight that covered the entirety of the well above them.

Iriel and Roshaw—now carrying Jelium—landed on their feet only a few paces away.

A moment later, Chrys struck the ground beside them.

"Chrys!" Willow called out. "Laurel and Asher are still breathing, but I don't think they're going to last long."

Roshaw leapt from stone to stone as he approached Willow. "We need to get them to the elixir."

"I'll take Laurel," Alverax said, already leaning down to lift her.

"I'll take Asher," Willow added.

"Let's be quick about it," Roshaw said. "The Heralds could be right behind us."

They all gathered themselves and made their way to the outer rim of the cavern, toward the tunnels leading to the elixir pool. Willow's veins turned black as she *broke* Asher's corethread; Roshaw did the same to Jelium. With Alverax carrying Laurel and Iriel holding Aydin, they all carried their burdens. All except for...

Willow turned and saw Chrys standing motionless in the center of the cavern, surrounded by jagged rocks and clear water, staring up at the threadlight-wrought enclosure high above.

"Chrys!" she shouted, her voice echoing in the wide-open space. "We need to go!"

He dropped his head for a moment, then silently followed.

The group arrived at the mouth of the tunnel together, taking one last glance up the Endless Well, ensuring that the Heralds had indeed not followed them down. As Asher's corethread reappeared, Willow let Obsidian threadlight pour through her, shifting the chromawolf once again into weightlessness.

Memories flooded through her as she recalled their first time walking through the tunnel. It seemed a lifetime ago. Back then, every shadow seemed to jump out at them, and every drop of water falling from the stalactites felt like a hand grabbing at her shoulder. She'd barely had a moment to enjoy being reunited with her son, and every step was filled with the fear of losing him again.

More than anything, what had changed was how long it took them to get from the Endless Well to Alchaeus' cavern. This time, there was no caution, no quiet steps. Instead, they trudged through the tunnel like a herd of corespawn, footfalls echoing through the wide corridor, announcing them in every direction.

When the familiar golden light of the elixir pool appeared ahead, they all seemed to find renewed energy, sprinting forward with even greater speed. The vaulted cavern was quiet—the pale, pink table still surrounded by the third god's oddities. From the far side of the space, Willow could see part of the collection of corespawn statues peeking out from behind the corner. The air was moist and warmer than she remembered. Beside the pool, she thought she saw the remnants of a bloody trail.

And was that...roses?

"Stones," Chrys cursed beside her.

Willow's veins blazed to life as she looked around for the source of the scent. There were no corespawn in the tunnel they'd come from and none in the far tunnel. She looked for Chitt, but even the small, lizard-like corespawn was nowhere to be found.

A scraping sound overhead was the only noise she heard before a corespawn with eight legs dropped from the ceiling. She tried to move, but Asher was still in her arms, and the chromawolf was too large to maneuver. She braced herself for impact—but before it crashed into her, the creature burst apart into a thousand beads of light, dissipating out into the open cavern air, then slowly drifting toward the pool of elixir.

When she turned, she saw Chrys with a scowl on his face and Obsidian threadlight in his veins. "I'll keep watch," he mumbled, walking toward the tunnel entrance.

Willow nodded, then approached the pool, sliding Asher into the golden waters. Alverax carefully set Laurel beside him. Roshaw placed Jelium on the ledge and pulled out the darts before lowering him into the water. They all watched as pockets of red misted out from each of the wounds. Jelium's body drifted away from the others, but Laurel and Asher seemed drawn together. Soon, as their corethreads reappeared, each of them sank deeper into the depths.

The room grew quiet.

Chrys' footsteps echoed as he stepped farther down the tunnel.

In the silence, they watched their companions, praying, hoping that the healing power of the elixir would be enough. Willow reached down and cupped a bit of elixir into her mouth. While it healed her physical wounds, her mind and spirit still ached.

Guilt swept through her as she realized that Laurel's death was her fault. She should have never let the young girl come with her to Alchea to rescue Pandan. Laurel should be with her brother and her people. If Willow had stopped her then, Laurel wouldn't be dying now. She was too young to die. Too young to pay the price of another's mistake. If anyone was going to die, Willow had lived a good life— longer than most threadweavers—and if it came to it, she would sacrifice herself for any of these people. Her son. Her daughter-in-law. A man she'd come to respect. His son. Laurel and Asher.

"How do we know if it's working?" Alverax asked with a look of worry in his eyes.

Roshaw leaned over the edge. "We should at least know soon whether or not they'll live."

"They will live," Willow said through clenched teeth.

Alverax stared into the pool. "I hope so."

"They will live!" Willow shouted, frustration and failure bubbling to the surface. The fire in her eyes faded as soon as it came, giving way to the same guilt that pervaded her mind. They couldn't be dead. She refused to accept that reality. "They will live," she repeated quietly.

Roshaw comforted her, wrapping an arm around her shoulder. "You're right. If the elixir can keep Alchaeus alive for hundreds of years, it can heal the girl. They're going to live."

Willow's chest heaved up and down as she fought back her fear. With her head nestled into Roshaw's shoulder, she watched the three bodies floating in the water. The golden energy of the elixir seemed to gather along the edges of their skin, flickering like a candle in a distant window. She looked at Laurel, floating beside her chromawolf companion. She remembered the crack of its neck, and Laurel collapsing into the well. Whatever bond they shared had caused Asher's pain to extend to Laurel. Now, Willow wasn't certain that either would survive.

No, she thought. *They* will *live.*

As if the young Zeda girl could hear her thoughts, Laurel's body heaved in the pool, spasming up and down. Asher's body followed suit, thrashing back and forth as the golden light glimmered across its green fur.

"They're choking on the water!" Alverax yelled.

"They can't drown," Willow said, taking a step toward the pool. "Not in the elixir."

Asher's eyes opened.

Roshaw and Alverax took it as a signal and jumped into the water, sinking to their chests before their feet hit the ground. They grabbed hold of Laurel and Asher, heaving them up and over the lip of the pool. The two bodies limped over the ledge and rolled onto the stone as Roshaw and Alverax pulled themselves up and over. Roshaw went to work checking Asher.

Alverax leaned down, fear and worry rippling across his

face, and moved his mouth toward Laurel's. But then her eyes opened.

He met her gaze, and she threw up a gushing river of elixir water all over his neck.

Alverax pulled back and looked down at his soaking shirt, wiping it off with his already wet hands.

Willow's chest was a torrent of emotions, laughter cut off by tears of joy, guilt crashing into hope. But when she looked over and saw Laurel and Asher embracing, all of it faded away, and all she felt was...gratitude. They were alive.

"Are you okay?" Willow asked, standing over the young girl's soaking body.

Laurel nodded. "We're okay."

"Good," Willow said with a curt voice. "Because if you ever die like that again, I swear I'll kill you a third time."

Asher lifted his head, and Laurel gave a strained smile.

"What about Jelium?" Alverax asked. "How much longer until he's healed?"

Roshaw leaned over the edge of the pool to get a closer look; Alverax and Willow followed. As she looked at the large, Kulaian man, she noticed that the dart wounds no longer leaked streams of red into the golden waters, but still he drifted aimlessly, his thick arms spread wide. As his body rotated, his bronze face reflected the golden light, and Willow felt a rush of sorrow. She knew that look—she'd seen it before.

Jelium's soul had fled from his mortal frame to travel the winds.

"Is he...?" Alverax asked, not daring to finish.

Roshaw stepped into the pool, waist deep in liquid magic, and moved Jelium toward the edge. Lifting his shoulders—and Alverax the legs—they pulled him out of the elixir and laid him on the wet stone. His cunning eyes were wide, staring at nothing, and his bronzed skin had taken on the color of pale sand. Roshaw placed a hand over Jelium's face and closed his eyes. Silence filled the air like a cloud waiting to storm—even Laurel and Asher had turned to watch. Roshaw opened his eyes and shook his head. "We were too late."

The words pricked the expanding bubble, and Willow felt every last ounce of hope fade away into the dark cavern. They'd come all this way, and for what? Without Jelium, there would be no way to create the coreseal. There would be no way to stop the gods.

They had failed.

"Dammit!" Roshaw cursed, kicking Jelium's dead body. "Wake up, you piece of shit!"

"Roshaw," Willow said, placing a hand on his shoulder.

He looked up at her with bloodshot eyes.

"It doesn't matter," Chrys said.

Willow hadn't noticed her son's return. He looked like how she felt. Instead of the passion he'd had while standing against two gods at the top of the Endless Well, Chrys seemed nothing more than a shell, as though his spirit had been ripped from his body.

"What do you mean?" Willow asked.

"We've already lost."

"Chrys," Iriel said, bouncing a squirming child in her arms. "What are you talking about?"

"No one's lost anything," Willow added. A rising bile in her throat proved that not even she believed her own words.

"Did no one else see it?" Chrys said, his voice rising. "They knew. The damn Heralds knew. And they were waiting for us. They wanted us at the Endless Well, and all it took was a small group of dangerous-looking wastelanders to shepherd us there. They knew what we were planning to do, and they beat us to it."

"What do you—" But Willow understood now. The events of the Endless Well replayed in her mind. The Heralds floating in the center of the shaft, threadlight shining like the sun, the explosion. The pattern forming. "Stones," she cursed. "The threadlight in the well. They created a coreseal…"

Alverax's eyes grew wide. "But we're—"

"—trapped," Roshaw finished.

"It doesn't matter," Chrys repeated one final time, an emptiness in his eyes. "They won. Jelium won't make a difference. Aydin won't make a difference. Even if we find Alchaeus, it won't make a difference. It's over. We lost."

"To hell with that!" Roshaw cursed, throwing his hands up in the air. "Alverax broke the coreseal once before. We can do it again. Hell, we have four Obsidians."

"With the power of the Convergence, maybe," Willow said, thoughtfully. "But if Alchaeus and Lylax couldn't break the coreseal when they were trapped down here, I have a feeling it won't be so easy for us either."

Roshaw rubbed a hand through his short hair. "So, what do we do?"

Willow looked to her son, feeling the defeat in his eyes. "First we rest," she said, eyes drifting toward the distant tunnel. "Then we find Alchaeus."

HIGH GENERAL HENNA stepped up to the study and pushed open the thick, mahogany door. When she entered, she found Great Lord Malachus seated alone at his desk, the curtains open wide to let in great beams of light that refracted from the tall windows behind him. He gave her a curt nod but continued to read from a thick, leatherbound tome. Henna walked up to the chair near the table but did not sit. She simply stood, the bag at her side weighing as heavily on her mind as it did her shoulder.

A minute later, Lady Eleandra entered, offering Henna a smile and a nod as she took her place beside Malachus. She whispered in his ear, and he pressed a piece of parchment into the center of his book, closed it, and set it aside, finally acknowledging Henna's presence. "Did you find her?"

Henna shook her head.

"Any news from Felia?" Eleandra asked.

Henna shook her head. "Still none."

After Alabella escaped, Henna had been tasked with finding her. The Queen of the Bloodthieves had moved quickly, making her way out of Alchea to the west. They had spies in Felia looking for her, but they'd had no news from Felia in weeks. The last they'd heard, the city had been saved by the Heralds—an utterly absurd claim—when the corespawn had attacked.

"What the hell is going on over there?" Malachus leaned back in his chair and ran both hands through his graying hair. He still had yet to name new high generals to replace Chrys and Jurius, so he'd taken their workload on himself. The few months of additional stress had aged him physically but had also given him a renewed sense of ambition. "And what of our preparations?"

"We have guard pits set throughout the north and west. Threadweaver lookouts rotate every two days with supplies to last three and flares to signal incoming corespawn. The only thing they've found was a herd of elk in the north. But I'm not here to give a report, sir."

He tilted his head.

Henna reached down and lifted the bag off her shoulder, dropping it on his desk with a jarring thud.

Malachus placed his forearms on the table and leaned forward. "You have my attention."

"Do you remember the thread-dead obsidian we found a few months ago? From the mine in the Everstones?"

Eleandra raised her brows. "Have you found another?"

"More than that," Henna said as she turned over the bag, unloading a pile of several dozen thread-dead obsidian shards.

"Stones!" Malachus cursed, a smile beaming across his face. "That's enough to make a full spear. Can you imagine? How much does it weigh? Is the material strong enough? Or would it break against iron? Hell, imagine a thread-dead shield! Or both. I can have my smith—"

"Malachus," Henna said, cutting him off. He scowled but stopped. "There's more."

Malachus failed to hide his disdain for being quieted. "More news or more thread-dead obsidian?"

"Both." Henna glanced back at the door, then leaned in

closer. "The recent quakes must have opened up sealed paths in the cave, because our people found crates—hundreds of years old by the look of it—filled with thread-dead obsidian. Malachus, we have a hundred times this amount."

"Lightfather be damned," he whispered. "We need to get it to the keep immediately. That cache is more valuable than all the shines in Alchea."

Henna nodded. "Already on it. I have a team of three loading it on carts and a team of thirty to bring the carts back. Only the loaders know what it is, and they're men I trust who have been sworn to secrecy. The transporters are all achromats, so even if they look, it won't mean anything to them. It will be safely within the keep's walls by the end of tomorrow."

Malachus reached forward and grabbed a shard, inspecting it with Emerald and Sapphire threadlight swirling in his veins. "This could be it..."

"Could be what?"

"My legacy," he said with a serious look in his eyes. "A man of my age often thinks of what he will leave behind. What he will be remembered for. The power you wield, the influence you amass, none of it matters unless it is attached to a creation of significance. Something the world can look at in awe. In one hundred years, no one will speak about my rise to power, nor this time of peace. Alchea was, and Alchea continued to be. Malachus the Dash."

Henna furrowed her brow. "I'm not sure I understand."

"There is a year attached to the creation of something and a year attached to its destruction. Those are the true moments of significance. Everything else is just a dash." He reached forward, grabbed a second obsidian shard, and held them both up. "But with these, this will be an unforgettable year. With these, we will create a legacy."

"What are you going to do with the obsidian?" she asked.

"Fight," Malachus said with a smile.

Eleandra looked to her husband. "War is the laziest way to build a legacy, and certainly the most brittle. If you want to be remembered for centuries, use that brilliant mind of yours and be creative. You have the chance to do something truly spectacular here. A new material with endless applications."

Malachus considered her words, then turned to Henna. "I want a spear and a handful of daggers. Have our smiths turn the rest into arrowheads. If we come up with a better idea, we can have them reshaped. Otherwise, we prepare for war. If the corespawn come, we will be ready. And if Felia has fallen, the Endin Empire has a nice ring to it."

"It will be done," Henna said with a nod.

As she left, she saw a glimmer of sorrow in Eleandra's eyes.

WILLOW STARED up at the coreseal with magic coursing through her veins. Like threadlight itself, she understood the *what*, but she still didn't understand the *how*. The Amber-wrought threads created a lasting mesh, a web of power that not only stretched across the width of the Endless Well, but through stone and dirt and roots. Given that the previous coreseal had stretched from beneath the wonderstone all the way to the Endless Well, she could safely assume that the opposite would be true. But did it stretch beyond? How far? Across the entire world? And how did it endure when other Amber threads faded? Was the Convergence feeding it power?

"It's pretty," a deep voice called out behind her. "In an eerie sort of way."

She turned to see Roshaw approaching. His eyes shifted between watching the coreseal and glancing at the ground as he navigated past rubble and puddles, finally coming to a stop a few feet away from her.

"Less pretty when you remember it's a prison," Willow said.

There was a profound sense of sadness in Roshaw's eyes. "We'll find a way out. And then it'll be them trapped down here staring up. Not us."

"I wish it were that easy." Willow sighed. "If I've learned

anything from this, it's that it's not so easy to outsmart people who have been alive for hundreds of years."

"I don't know," Roshaw mumbled. "I'm nearly fifty, and I don't feel like my age has made me any smarter."

Willow let out a clipped laugh. "Just wait a few years. When you hit fifty, the world will gift you an added measure of intellect."

"Can I request two measures?" Roshaw raised his brows.

"You can request it, but that doesn't mean you'll get it." Willow winked.

"Gah!" Roshaw said, throwing up his arms. "How are we so old? In my head, I'm still young and energetic, but damn if my body disagrees. I feel like a wheel that got left outside for too long. There's dirt in my axles. And you're over here, stomping through deserts and swamps and caves without complaining at all, while I've been secretly whining to Chrys every day since we left Cynosure."

"Once you've given birth," Willow said calmly, "you can handle anything."

Roshaw nodded. "Especially if you give birth to a baby with as thick a skull as Chrys has."

"Hey!" Willow said, slapping his arm. "He got that skull from me."

"I mean—" Roshaw grinned. "You said it, not me."

Willow let threadlight flood her veins and looked back up at the coreseal. There had to be a way to get past it. Some way to sever a few of the threads wide enough for them to squeeze through. Obsidian seemed the clear answer, but Lylax and Alchaeus had Obsidian all those years and never managed. She was beginning to doubt that the third god would know what to do either.

"How's *your* son doing?" Willow finally said.

"I don't know," Roshaw said. "Seems healthy."

Willow gave him a sardonic grin. "Seems...healthy?"

Roshaw shrugged, though a hint of sadness broke through the guise. "I'll put it this way: he is better than he has any right to be, especially after what I put him through."

"Have you talked to him about it?"

Roshaw paused for a moment, then shook his head. "I tried. But he's just finally talking to me at all—which is more than I deserve, honestly—and I don't want to ruin it. I just feel like, I don't want to rock the boat too soon after the storm, you know?"

Willow nodded along. "Seems reasonable."

"But at the same time," Roshaw continued, "he's a man now. And it's stupid because he's taller than me—probably stronger too, if I'm being honest—but I still just see him as a kid. Like he's still the wild toddler, running toward Mercy's Bluff until I scoop him up. Whenever I look at him, there's this burning desire to protect him, even from the truth. But I also know he deserves to know everything. So, I don't know what to do."

"Good parents protect their children," Willow said softly, "but not from themselves. You'll never have the relationship you want until you're honest."

"I know," he whispered. "I know, but I'm just not ready. Who knows, maybe we'll all die tomorrow, and I'll never have to tell him."

Willow glared at him. "If we're going to die tomorrow, all the more reason to tell him now."

Roshaw took a deep breath through his nose and exhaled through his mouth, rubbing a hand at his brow. "I'll tell him as soon as we get out of here."

The way he said it, she believed him. Whatever it was that he was holding back, it weighed on him. The truth was that Roshaw had been through as much hell as

Alverax. They both deserved to shed their burdens and move on.

All the more reason to find Alchaeus.

"In that case," Willow said, grabbing his arm, "let's go get the others. We have a man with at least six measures of intellect to find."

*D*RIP. *Drip.*

Hours passed. Chrys and the others watched their steps as they trudged through the dark caverns leading to the Convergence. Shadows danced from the subtle sway of photospores, feeding light to shimmering trails of water that fell from cracks in the ceiling and ran over the stone walls like tears.

They had no way of knowing if Alchaeus would be at the Convergence, but none of them were keen to sit and wait in the empty cavern, especially knowing that corespawn could arrive at any moment. If he wasn't there, they could always head back. After the first hour, they took Jelium's body and deposited it down an offshoot tunnel. None of them grieved.

Drip. Drip.

Another few hours and Chrys and the party grew quiet. The only sounds were the chaotic pounding of feet on stone and the rhythmic falling of droplets from gnarled stalactites. They were tired. They were hungry. But most of all, they were nervous. They no longer had a clear plan to work with. Now, all they had was the dim hope that Alchaeus might have answers. But that hope was a wet matchstick, and their souls craved a raging fire.

Chrys reached into his pack for his waterskin, knowing well that it was empty. Still, he brought it to his lips and tilted it up.

Drip. Drip.

A sliver of anger slipped its tendrils through his cold veins.

"There's some left in my pack," Willow said beside him. In her arms, she held Aydin, who was awake and staring up at the vaulted cave ceiling.

Iriel, who now carried Willow's pack, slipped it off and opened it. The waterskin was running low as well. She handed it to Chrys, who took a small drink, then she placed it back in her pack. As he looked at his wife, he felt guilt sweep over him. There was a deep fatigue in the curves below her eyes that he couldn't help but feel responsible for. No new mother should have to spend the months after birth hiking through swamps, chased by gods, all while continuing to breastfeed and care for her newborn. It was unfair, and he hoped that—if this ever ended—she wouldn't hold it against him. But she'd forgiven him for worse, and that gave him hope.

As he cinched up his pack, Willow stepped over to hand him Aydin. He tied the drawstring and threw it over his shoulder before taking his son. "Thanks for giving Iriel a break."

Willow shook out her arm, massaging it with her other hand. "He's already getting heavier. I should have borrowed her wrap."

As the party prepared to continue their journey, Roshaw let out a clipped laugh, shaking his head and stifling a slight smile. "Sorry. It's just...I know it's important to hold onto hope and all, but isn't all of this just a little bit absurd? I mean, you all are great, and if I had to choose a group of people to die with while trapped underground like a cockroach, I can't think of anyone better. But...I don't know. I feel like if I don't laugh about this, I'm going to remember how likely it is that we're all going to die down here." Roshaw glanced over to Alverax. "And I just don't think I'm ready for that."

Chrys felt a sharp pain in his chest as he saw the same uncertainty run through the others. Alverax, staring back at his father with doubt in both their eyes. Laurel, looking with sorrow at Asher. Willow, watching them all. When Chrys' eyes met Iriel's, they shared a moment of love and sorrow and pain.

"This isn't about us," Laurel said, breaking the silence. Her voice was filled with a certain sense of self-confidence. "It's about them." She pointed up. "We all have a reason we're here. Something we're fighting for. I'm doing this for my people. If there's any chance that this stupid plan works, I'm sure as hell going to try. For the Zeda."

Chrys nodded. "For Alchea."

Alverax stared at Laurel for a moment, then shook his head while his lips curled into a smile. "For my grandfather. And for the people of Felia."

A moment of silence passed before Willow placed a hand on Roshaw's shoulder. "Being the hero is never easy. But we don't have to do it alone. All of us here, we're in this together. Life or death. I don't know about you, but no matter the outcome, there's no one I'd rather try with."

Roshaw gave her the slightest smile. "I'm in if you're in."

"Then we try," she said.

"We try," Chrys repeated.

"Gale take that," Laurel cursed. "I'm not coming this far

just to try. And I'm not dying unless I can take the Heralds with me."

The entire group smiled, and Chrys felt a sense of pride. The Heralds may have won the fight, but they were damn well going to regret it.

CHRYS WASN'T sure if the feeling in his stomach was worry or excitement. As he rounded the final bend leading to the Convergence, Roshaw pressed a hand against his chest, keeping him from turning the corner. Without thinking, Chrys' stance widened, and his hand reached down to pull out his thread-dead dagger.

"You seeing this?" Roshaw whispered, eyes ablaze with multicolored threadlight.

Chrys followed suit and glanced around the corner. There, surrounding the massive dome of warbling energy, was an army of corespawn, still as Alchaeus' statues. From the massive monstrosities to the tiny scavengers, thousands of the creatures filled the sprawling cavern, some sitting, others standing. Only the smallest of the creatures made any movement at all, like skittering rats amid a field of scarecrows.

"What are they doing?" Chrys wondered aloud.

Roshaw shook his head. "I have no idea. Kind of looks like the *pintalla mox*, but how would a wastelander plague affect corespawn?"

"I don't think so," Chrys said. "At least some of them are alive. It looks more like they're waiting for something."

"Us," Laurel said, crouching low and peeking out from below them.

Chrys gestured for the others to pull back. "There's no way we're getting past that horde."

"I know a way," Alverax said, pulling the Midnight Watcher out of its sheath on his back. "Those things slaughtered the people of Felia. It's time to make them pay."

Roshaw shook his head. "There's too many."

"We've fought more with less," Laurel replied.

Chrys wasn't certain, but he thought he saw Asher's lips pull back into a toothy grin.

"Four Obsidian threadweavers," Iriel said, thoughtfully.

"Plus two obsidian daggers," Chrys added.

"And one obsidian longsword," Alverax finished.

"Against two thousand corespawn." Roshaw looked around the corner.

Laurel gave a wolfish grin. "Easy."

Chrys couldn't help but smile. He knew how they were feeling. The fear and worry were there, certainly, but all overshadowed by the incessant need to act. To do *something*. Anything that might get them closer to freedom. But they still needed to be smart about it.

"Let's take it easy," Chrys said. "Alchaeus isn't even here. There's no point in risking our lives for no reason. Besides, there's a good chance that Relek and Lylax specifically put that army there to stop us from getting to the Convergence. And if we die, we're not getting out of here."

"Ah," Roshaw said. "The Apogee's great wisdom."

Willow laughed. "He's right though. We shouldn't put ourselves in danger for no reason."

Suddenly, threadlight surged in the cavern like a pulsing star. Chrys ran around the corner and saw beads of threadlight floating through the air and into the Convergence. "Something's happening, but it's too far to see. Laurel?"

The young woman and her chromawolf leaned forward,

focusing their gaze on the chaos. After a moment, her eyes went wide. "One of the corespawn just burst. I think they're fighting each other. Over food? No, there's something else. I can barely see it through the corespawn. They're moving too much. I think...it's a person!"

Without another word, Laurel and Asher were sprinting forward at full speed toward the army of corespawn.

"Good enough reason for me," Alverax muttered as he took off after her. "For Felia!"

"For the whole damn world, honestly," Roshaw said to himself.

Roshaw and Willow took off after them.

Fire coursed through Chrys' blood, but just as he moved to follow the others, he turned and saw Iriel holding Aydin.

"I..." Iriel said, bouncing with Aydin asleep against her chest. Chrys saw a longing in her eyes as she looked toward the enemy army, but then her eyes rested on her son. "Never mind. Just be careful."

Chrys nodded as he let Obsidian threadlight course through his veins. "Your time will come. Keep an eye on the tunnels."

It took only a moment for the first corespawn to notice them, one of the smaller species, skittering along the floor on all fours as it screeched into the vaulted room. A ripple of enlightenment washed over the horde. They awoke from their pseudo-slumber, and their collective roar shook the cavern.

Veins raged to life with threadlight. Blades brandished. And the battle commenced.

Chrys watched as Obsidian threadlight lashed out at the oncoming horde. The fastest of the corespawn burst apart like bubbles to a pin, showering the room in otherworldly light. He reached out for the second wave, feeling the distance weakening his power. But he had three theoliths surging in his chest, and he could not be stopped.

One of the corespawn, a creature twice the size of a man with horn-shaped threadlight protruding from its light-wrought skull, roared as it trampled over smaller corespawn. Chrys reached out to it, feeling the pulse of thread-light running through its body, and *squeezed*. He felt the resistance, like a magnet refusing its counter, and pressed harder. The beast felt the pressure and roared in response, picking up speed. But, as it grew closer, Chrys' thread-weaving grew stronger. With one final clench of his mind, the beast exploded in a wave of threadlight.

As he looked for his next target, focusing on the larger creatures and leaving the smaller ones to the others, he saw Alverax swinging the Midnight Watcher in hectic twirls, cleaving apart several corespawn with each swipe, then reaching out and *breaking* others with his threadlight. Laurel and Asher were close beside him, pouncing on the smaller creatures with unnatural speed, Laurel slamming the obsidian dagger down to finish the creatures off. Willow and Roshaw stood side by side, speaking words that Chrys couldn't hear, but having far more fun than anyone ought to have in the middle of a battle.

Still, the fight had only begun.

A dozen of the same monstrosities that had toppled the walls of Felia came trudging through the cavern, sending quakes through the stone with each step and causing the smaller corespawn to dive out of the way. Chrys took a deep breath and readied himself.

His body rose into the air as he cut his corethread and sent a small surge of Emerald threadlight toward the ceiling. He rose, slowly, until he was thirty feet in the air, surrounded by thousands of beads of threadlight from the felled corespawn that glimmered in the air like fireflies. He sent a surge of Sapphire to steady himself. Floating, hovering above an army of corespawn, he could feel the power of his theoliths coursing through him.

Willow and Roshaw joined him in the sky, leaving Laurel and Alverax to the waves of smaller corespawn.

A few steps away from the Convergence, Chrys could see a man with a wide-brimmed hat amidst the chaos, Obsidian burning through his veins as he fought off nearby corespawn, struggling to deal with the sheer number. Looking at the monstrosities then back to Alchaeus, Chrys made a decision.

"Roshaw!" Chrys shouted to the closer of the two in flight beside him. "You two take the big ones. I'm going for Alchaeus!"

The older man nodded and turned to relay the information to Willow.

Chrys wasted no more time, surging Sapphire and Emerald in opposite directions, launching himself through the air toward Alchaeus far below. His feet slammed into the ground beside the third god with a burst of Sapphire to soften the landing.

Alchaeus looked to him, surprised. "You're back."

As several corespawn descended upon them, Chrys had an idea. Just like he did with Sapphire and Emerald during flight, he reached into his core and tapped into his Obsidian theolith. Then, in an unfocused surge, he unleashed a wave of threadlight that crashed into all of the surrounding corespawn in front of him, bursting them apart into thousands of beads of otherworldly luminescence.

There was a fire raging in Chrys' chest, and it felt good. "Are you okay?"

"I'm fine," Alchaeus said. "A bit confused."

Chrys noticed for the first time the items that Alchaeus held. In one hand, an oddly familiar leather bag, and in the other, an obsidian dagger. "Where did you get that?"

Alchaeus raised a brow. "Perhaps I should be asking if *you* are okay?"

A screeching corespawn the size of a man leapt forward, cutting him off, but Chrys' Obsidian was faster, and the creature burst apart just before it struck.

"We need to get out of here," Chrys said as more corespawn approached. "Can you fly?"

Alchaeus nodded with a look that said he'd forgotten he could, and they each *broke* their corethreads, *pushing* off into the air and leaving a group of hungry corespawn nipping at their heels.

Willow and Roshaw hovered in the air with two of the monstrosities charging toward them. A torrent of thread-weaving burst forward, latching onto the corespawns' threadlight core, surging, squeezing. Roshaw screamed out a guttural cry as he fed more Obsidian into the beasts. Willow grit her teeth. Both monstrosities exploded into billowing clouds of threadlight, specks floating in the vaulted cavern heights.

Chrys flew up to hover beside Roshaw. "Everything okay up here?"

Roshaw's eyes lit up. "You see that shit? Woo!"

Willow let out a laugh, though Chrys caught her pressing at the skin above her heart.

"Mother, you okay?"

She nodded.

"Who's next?" Roshaw shouted at the corespawn army.

A dozen more monstrosities were headed toward them, roaring at the destruction of their companions. Their rage overcame their care as they crushed the smaller corespawn beneath them. Each step killed five, then ten. In their wake, they left a flattened throng of corespawn, though the creatures all eventually rose again, their threadlight cores healing their bodies.

Chrys shouted over the frantic sounds of war. "Roshaw, you take the four on the left. Willow, the four on the right. Wait until they're closer, your threadweaving will be stronger the closer they come."

As Alchaeus flew up to join them, a massive tail whipped forward and crashed into his back. His leather bag opened, spilling a handful of golden slivers through the air that fell all the way to the cavern floor. The third god's eyes grew wide. "Save the shards!" he screamed.

ALVERAX FELT ALL of his pent-up rage release into each swing of the Midnight Watcher. It was safer to *break* the corespawn with threadweaving, but—going through the forms that Thallin had taught him, cleaving through the beasts like they were strands of wheat in a field—revenge felt good.

A larger corespawn came trampling toward him, waving a barbed tail high overhead. A single glance reminded him of the masquerade, of the moment Empress Chailani was killed. A black fire lit within him, anger for her death, for the pain it had caused Jisenna, for the pain it had unleashed on all of Felia, and for the sequence of events it had set in motion, all leading to the deceptive return of the Heralds.

Adrenaline pumped through his veins, swirling in a greasy mixture of Obsidian threadlight. He launched forward, swinging the Midnight Watcher overhead, but the creature's tail whipped out and knocked it from his hands.

Without hesitation, he reached his left hand forward, fingers spread wide, and squeezed. Threadlight flowed from him, latching onto the corespawn. Energy fought energy. Power defied power. Chailani flashed in his mind. Crying out. Falling to the marble floor. The creature's tail loomed over him, striking down. Alverax screamed and the corespawn shattered into a thousand pieces.

But it was different this time. Instead of dissipating, the shattered threadlight hovered in the air like fireflies, joining a sky already filled with threadlight essence.

A horde of smaller corespawn shrieked beside it, skittering along the stone floor toward him, but Laurel slid across the ground in front of them, dragging her black blade through their bodies. One by one, the creatures popped out of existence. She spun around and, in harmony with Asher, howled into the open air.

Alverax was glad she was on his side.

"Save the shards!"

Alverax looked up and saw an old man screaming as golden light refracted from something falling through the air. He ran over and picked up the closest one after it clattered to the ground. A pale, yellow light reflected from the transparent gemstone. It was thin, like a hiltless dagger, and something about it called to him.

LAUREL NODDED to Alverax then swiveled to face more of the corespawn. As she did, her vision split in two.

From her own eyes, Laurel saw the corespawn approaching like ripples of water, light-wrought limbs wavering, slapping against the stone, shrieks of chaos echoing from their void mouths.

From Asher's eyes, she saw red.

Together, they shared their strength, feeling each other's power.

The stench of roses filled the cavern, extending their rancid tendrils through her nostrils, infecting her mind. Her thoughts flickered to the caves beneath the coreseal. Then to the streets of Alchea. That smell, once so inviting, a reminder of the beauty of Zedalum and the floral guides of the Fairenwild. Now, a rotting stench that fueled her rage.

Side by side with her companion, her friend, her second soul, she met the onslaught of smaller corespawn with more energy than she'd ever had before. She was a flaming wall. She was the hand of death. She was the alpha.

Laurel dove forward and buried her thread-dead blade into the next corespawn just as a thin, golden shard struck the ground beside her, flickering in the light of the photo-spores. She placed the dagger in its sheath and picked up the shard.

Hiding behind the cavern wall, Iriel watched her husband and friends face down a thousand legendary creatures. It was absurd—she knew that—but she couldn't help but feel forgotten, as if they had purposefully excluded her. The truth was that, despite her years of martial training, she was nothing compared to them. Chrys, Willow, and Roshaw all had access to Sapphire, Emerald, and Obsidian. Alverax had Obsidian and the Midnight Watcher. And Laurel's bond with Asher made her faster and stronger than any woman her size ought to be.

Iriel's Emerald was nothing in comparison.

No, that wasn't true. She looked down at Aydin and felt a

tear roll down her cheek. She may not be as powerful as the others—she may not be able to fight the corespawn as effectively—but she had the most important role of all. She was a mother. And if all else failed, they still had Aydin, the last mortal Amber.

CHRYS SUCKED IN A BREATH, gasping as his chest sizzled like a volcano's core. Even with three theoliths, the threadweaving required to kill the monstrosities was too much, and there were still more coming.

He reached out to the next, extending his mind to the monstrosity's threadlight frame, and *squeezed* with all his might. Again, he felt the same resistance, power refusing to be broken, a bubble refusing to burst. His mind swirled. His vision blurred, but he blinked it away. He knew that he was on the verge of overextending his new powers. Shaking his head, he regained his vision, and the monstrosity's massive fist crashed into him from above.

Chrys tumbled through the air from the force of the strike. The wind instantly vanished from his lungs, and the world seemed to warp around him. He launched through the air and, just before he struck the hard stone, he surged Sapphire, counteracting the momentum provided by the attack.

Threadlight burned in his chest. Through hazy eyes, he watched as a massive fist flew through the air, smacking Roshaw out of the sky. The man tumbled through the air toward the entrance where Iriel remained hidden.

Chrys squeezed his eyes shut, fighting the clouds swirling in his mind. When he reopened them, a huge corespawn was there, swinging a wide fist through the air where he hovered.

"Stop!" a voice shouted from only a few paces away.

The monstrosity stopped in its tracks, a hundred Amber threads sprouting from the ground like hungry eels, latching to its body. Striding through the chaos with prismatic light swirling in his veins, a black dagger in hand, Alchaeus crossed his arms above his head and roared. The monstrosity reeled back, pain tearing through its light-wrought flesh. A moment later, the massive creature burst apart into ten thousand grains of light that filled the cavern like stars in the night.

Chrys looked to the third god, in awe at the brilliance shining from the man's veins. His eyes, lit like twin suns, seemed ready to burst. The colorful radiance coursing through Alchaeus changed, shifting from a prismatic swirl to an inky blackness. His shoulders pulled back as he screamed out. A wave of Obsidian burst from his body, like a flower blossoming petals of death and destruction.

Dozens of corespawn shattered into thousands of pieces, threadlight rising into the open air like a kettle's steam, joining with the incandescent light that already speckled the cavern's canopy. The entire room seemed to shudder as the Obsidian wave ripped outward.

The sounds of fighting stopped.

Silence permeated the cold air.

The remaining corespawn paused in their tracks, fear rippling through their numbers.

Gravity faded, and pebbles rose into the air from the cavern floor. Across the battlefield, Chrys watched as Alverax and Laurel drifted off the ground.

When gravity returned, everything came crashing back to the earth.

The fearful army of corespawn cried out with shrill echoing voices, turning and running into the Convergence, one by one disappearing into the warbling dome of threadlight.

Overhead, millions of beads of transcendent energy drifted through the air, slowly at first, almost imperceptibly, but then, as the moments led on, the energy moved faster and faster, sucked toward the dome like flecks of iron to a magnet, spilling into the Convergence, feeding it.

Chrys' skin tingled as a ticking noise called out from his pocket, each tick quicker than the last.

The Convergence grew, its dome expanding, spreading across the cavern like an avalanche. Chrys and the others tried to run, but threadlight surged through the room. A wave of power washed over Alverax first, then Laurel, then Willow, and Alchaeus.

Chrys felt a warmth wash over him and a brilliant, white light.

Tick.

LAUREL OPENED HER EYES, blinking and cringing at the thick smell of leather that surrounded her.

She was no longer in the cave.

And where was...Asher.

She looked around with frantic urgency, lifting her nose, searching for her companion. All around her, thick books lay stacked atop dark shelves. The air was frigid and stale, as though the pages had died and left nothing but ghostly memories floating in the dust. Laurel turned around and saw a heavy door looming over her, carved with intricate filigree and winding layers of brass inlay.

She reached out and felt the door, rubbing her hand along the patterns. It felt so...real.

It's just a dream.

On the far end of the room, a single source of light flickered from around the corner.

Voices.

A young man from the sound of it, and a young woman.

Laurel's hand clenched, and she realized she was still holding the thin golden shard. She ran a thumb down its side as she shifted to the balls of her feet, each step a silent advance along the stone floor. The voices grew louder, and the adrenaline in her veins pulsed to life.

"What the hell is that?" the young man's voice called out.

The young woman responded. "Looks like some kind of ritual, but the words don't make any sense. What is *ventricular*?"

"There's gotta be something down here besides books, something worth some shines."

Laurel stepped forward until she reached the corner. As she snuck a glance, she saw the backs of a boy and a girl— not much younger than herself—anxiously looking through each of the dusty shelves. The boy's gaunt jaw clenched as he flipped through a stack of pages. The thin, Felian girl placed a book back on the shelf and looked for another, tracing the edges of the dark wood with a finger, glancing at a few loose pages and leather spines. She lifted her finger and blew off the dust before reaching for another book.

"This one could be interesting."

The young woman turned around to show the boy, and Laurel saw her clearly for the first time, candlelight shining across flawless ebony skin. There was something about her that looked familiar.

The shape of her eyes. Full lips. The curves of her jaw.

The truth crashed into Laurel like a windstorm.

Gale take me.

ALVERAX LIFTED a hand and turned away from the blinding light.

He was no longer in the cave—that was obvious from the sand inching up the side of his boots—and for a moment he thought he was back in the desert outside Cynosure. But even before his eyes adjusted, he realized it was different. Ocean waves crashed over each other as they fought to gain ground. Salty air drifted on a warm breeze.

The sound of distant gulls. It almost felt like he was seated atop Mercy's Bluff, gazing across an endless horizon of blue.

For a moment, he reveled in the beauty. But the urgency of reality pulled it away.

Am I dead...again?

He took a step, expecting the sand to pull him under, as if the warmth of the beach was a veil with a nightmare crawling below the surface. Some dark tiding waiting to reach up its tendrils and consume him.

He spun around, taking in the rest of the landscape. Behind him, a copse of tall trees lined the edge of the beach, wide leaves spreading out from the top, circular brown fruit hanging from their stems. Along the ground, ferns grew in plenty, and lush veridian grass lined the floor like a rich rug.

Farther down the beach, a young kid—no older than twelve—walked toward him holding a fishing spear. Alverax wasn't sure if he should be excited or fearful. Whether it was a dream or something else, he wasn't keen on being surprised, especially by a boy with a spear. Watching, he let threadlight pour through his veins, but...

No threadlight came. No warmth. No euphoric energy.

He rubbed at his eyes, praying to see threads stretching across the world, but there were none.

His heartbeat quickened, and his hand reached for the Midnight Watcher, but even before he touched the empty scabbard, he remembered the skirmish at the Convergence and pictured the black blade lying along the floor of the cavern. His other hand—he remembered—held the pale yellow shard he'd picked up off the floor just before the Convergence consumed them.

The stranger continued his path forward, and as he approached, his free hand lifted in greeting.

Alverax lifted his own hand as well, praying for a peaceful encounter.

But as the boy came closer, bright sunlight reflecting from the ocean waves, illuminating the shadowed bronze skin of a handsome youth, Alverax's heart dropped.

No, no, no, no.

ALCHAEUS STOOD BESIDE A BEAUTIFUL CARRIAGE, the sun beating down from high overhead. He turned away, reaching a hand up to shield himself from the brilliance. To the east, a towering mountain range loomed over a sprawling city, larger than any he'd seen before. To the south, a slow-moving river wove its way through a lush valley.

As he stepped toward the edge of the carriage, Alchaeus looked down at his hands and frowned. Every drop of threadlight had vanished from his veins, Emerald, Sapphire, Obsidian and Amber. Where once chromatic energy had surged through his veins, deep wrinkles lined his hands and arms, sagging skin and sunspots. He reached up and felt the same profound grooves along his cheeks and forehead. He worried that—this time—it would be more than his body could handle.

"GEOFFREY!" a voice shouted from the other side of the carriage. "Get inside and find a doctor!"

There was something familiar about the voice.

The grizzly pitch.

The fiery passion.

Alchaeus took a single, slow step around the corner of the carriage.

A man and woman sat on wide steps leading up to an

enormous building with two floral-robed statues standing atop a domed roof. The man on the stairs was crouched beside the woman, staring at the ground and grinding his knuckles into the stone. The woman, partially obscured by the man, was in pain, sprawled on her back across a series of steps.

The man closed his eyes and shook his head with a clenched jaw.

Alchaeus saw him for who he was, and the slightest grin crept along his lips.

He was right.

Alchaeus placed the obsidian dagger into his bag and rummaged until he found what he hoped would be there. One left. The others lay scattered along the cavern floor. But he only needed one. Pulling down on his wide-brimmed hat, he stepped confidently around the corner.

He knew what he needed to do.

Chrys Valerian needed help.

Iriel needed a doctor.

And little Aydin needed an Amber theolith.

Laurel clenched the golden shard so tightly she thought it might break in two.

This is a dream.

But she knew it wasn't.

Somehow, impossibly, she stood on the other side of the continent, in the center of Felia, deep in the halls of the Hallowed Library, the restricted section, the Anathema.

And in front of her was a young Alabella.

ALVERAX'S EYES grew wide as he stared at the approaching young man. Shirtless, thin but strong, with tattoos running over a bronze chest. Shadows kissed the curves of his arms and the lines of his jaw. In so many ways, he looked like another man.

He was younger...much younger.

Alverax squeezed the shard, and it bit into the palm of his hand. He wanted to convince himself otherwise—maybe he was wrong. Maybe it wasn't him.

But when the young man smiled, there was no question that a young Jelium stood before him.

ALCHAEUS HURRIED FORWARD, trying to remember all that Chrys had told him during their time together. The names. The phrases. Everything. If he made the wrong move or said the wrong words, the Lightfather only knew what consequences would follow.

"Chrys Valerian?" he said as he approached. "I am a doctor and, if you want Iriel to live, you must trust me."

He stepped in close and began feeling for the child's head.

"What are you doing?" Chrys shouted. "Get away from her!"

Alchaeus turned to his friend, and a wave of deja vu passed over him. It was Chrys, but it was a different version of him. This man seemed years younger, his beard carefully manicured, his uniform well-pressed and orderly. Yet he still had the same fiery passion in his eyes. For a moment, a wave of sorrow poured over Alchaeus knowing what this Chrys would go through. But it had already happened.

Alchaeus caught Chrys' wrist as the desperate man tried

to push him away. "I am the only one who can perform such a surgery. Step aside and let me save her."

Chrys looked at him and furrowed his brow, drinking in thirsty gasps of air. Alchaeus could feel the struggle inside him, the pain of placing his beloved's fate in the hands of another. A stranger, no less. But after a moment, his shoulders relaxed, and Alchaeus saw Chrys' resignation.

"Good. Help me lift her into the carriage. Quickly now!"

Together, they lifted the pregnant woman up the steps and into the carriage, careful to give her space to lie down. Despite what he knew, Alchaeus still worried that he wouldn't be able to perform the surgery fast enough, that the Convergence would call him home before he finished his work. But if Chrys was right, then he'd already succeeded. There would be time, so long as he stayed focused.

Alchaeus inserted himself into the carriage doorway between Chrys and Iriel. "Give me space to work, and I promise you she will live. There's more at stake here than you know."

Lightfather, I've said too much.

Chrys, angry but resigned, stepped down from the carriage step.

Alchaeus closed the door behind him, opened his bag, and pulled out the two items he would need: a flask filled with elixir and a thin shard of Amber.

He was aging quickly now; he could feel it in the quiver of his hands.

The recoil would happen any minute.

There was no time to waste.

LAUREL STEPPED into the flickering lamplight of the Anathema, understanding her purpose. The Father of All had given her an opportunity to fix everything. A chance to make it all better. If she killed Alabella while she was young, none of it would happen. There would be no Bloodthieves. There would be no fires in the Fairenwild. Her people would be alive. The coreseal would never have shattered. The Heralds would never have returned.

And all she had to do was kill Alabella...again.

She stepped forward.

Alabella and the boy turned to see her.

Laurel looked down at the golden shard in her hand. It was thin, but it would do.

One jab, straight to the heart, and time would be rewritten.

She could save them all.

Laurel lunged.

RAGE SIMMERED in Alverax's thread-dead veins. In a way, it was a relief. His Obsidian threadlight was the reason for all their troubles. If he'd never become an Obsidian, Alabella would not have attacked the Zeda. The coreseal would not have shattered. The Heralds would never have returned. Jisenna would still be alive...

And it all began with Jelium. Every bad thing that had happened to Alverax—to the entire damned world—had started with Jelium. The world would have been better off if the man had never been born.

Realization dawned on him, a flash of light in a moonless night.

If this was real...

If this was not a dream...

Alverax set his jaw, squeezed with a fire in his veins, and thrust.

IN THE CARRIAGE, pressed for time, Alchaeus broke off the tip of the shard. Beside him, sprawled out on her back, Iriel cried out in agony, both for herself and for the child she knew was in danger. Alchaeus took the tiny theolith and held it between his trembling fingers, purpose overcoming his doubts. He took a deep breath, reached into the slit in Iriel's stomach, past blood and muscle and warm tissue, through the mother's sac protecting the unborn child—ignoring the agonizing screams—and placed the shard into the baby's heart.

LAUREL RAMMED the shard into Alabella's chest.

ALVERAX SHOVED the shard into Jelium.

ALCHAEUS LEANED BACK, tears forming in his thread-dead eyes, and placed the empty bottle of elixir back in his bag. It would heal her. He had done all he could. He'd played his part in the Lightfather's grand scheme. He only hoped it would be enough.

With a profound weariness, he pushed open the carriage

door and stepped to the ground. His body was so weak. The Convergence was leeching all of the magic that sustained his immortal life.

Young Chrys rose to his feet, his face a mess of emotion. Alchaeus wanted to tell him everything, but there was no knowing what dark consequences would follow. He did know, however, that he had already told Chrys something.

"They will be okay," Alchaeus said. This was his last chance to prepare his friend for what was coming. "The recoil will happen any moment. Chrys, you must listen to me. Your child is the key." He thought of Relek and Lylax. "They will come for it. You cannot let them have it. Whatever it takes, you must protect the child."

Chrys' brow furrowed. "What the hell are you talking about?"

"You will need this," Alchaeus said. He reached into the bag, pulled out the obsidian dagger, and tossed it to Chrys. "Use it to break the threads that bind you."

This was it.

He had set in motion everything that led to where they were now.

And even though it would be for the best, it was still the beginning of what would lead to his siblings' deaths. There was no hope for his sister—he could see that now. Perhaps, his brother...his younger brother. The brother who had once been his best friend before the elixir changed their lives. Before they had been separated for so long. For him, Alchaeus still held out hope.

"Relek, forgive me."

Silence.

A cold chill as shadows flickered in the darkness.

Chrys ran hands down his arms and looked at his surroundings. Patches of photospores grew like weeds between wet stone along the edges. Long stalactites hung from the vaulted ceiling. He was alone, standing in the center of a cavern as large as the courtyards of Endin Keep. Something about it made him feel so small.

His eyes followed the walls, past jagged edges and smooth granite, until they found a wide tunnel leading away from the cavern.

He knew that tunnel; he knew this cavern.

Chrys spun around in search of the Convergence. As he opened himself to threadlight, he found nothing but a hollow space inside of him. There was nothing there. No warmth. No power.

The cold chill shivered across his arms.

It was a nightmare.

That was the only explanation.

He remembered the wave of energy spilling out of the Convergence, washing over the cavern and consuming him. Consuming his friends.

Were they dead?

Was he dead?

Only a moment ago, the cavern had been filled with corespawn, filled with his family and friends, filled with drifting beads of light. Where were they? Where was any of it? And why did the silence feel so stifling?

Chrys walked toward where the Convergence had been. Only now, where once a warbling dome of multicolored threadlight had pulsed and shifted, there was nothing but stale air, wet rocks, and that damn chill biting at his skin.

Minutes passed as he stared into the empty cavern, waiting for the dream to fade, waiting for the silence to break. Nightmares were nothing new to Chrys. For years after the war, his dreams had been plagued by flashes of battle. Death, pain, tears, and suffering. But each memory had been filled with blaring trumpets, riotous battle cries, and the sounds of weapons clashing. Never had his nightmares been so very quiet. Never had they been so empty.

He couldn't remember the last time he was alone. Before the Wastelands. Before Cynosure and Felia. Before the Fairenwild. But even in Alchea, he had not truly been alone. Not since the war. Even in moments of quiet, the Apogee had been there, listening. Now, for the first time in five years, he was truly alone. And he did not like it.

Chrys wanted his family back.

He wanted to know they were safe. He wanted to hold them, protect them from the rising darkness. They needed to get out of this freezing cave. There was too much to do. Too much at stake. He didn't have time for this damn nightmare.

A man suddenly appeared in the middle of the cavern, standing where the Convergence had once been with a wide-brimmed hat and a hand over his eyes like he'd been looking into the sun. Chrys recognized him immediately.

"Alchaeus?"

The third god, who'd grown noticeably older since Chrys had last seen him, leaned forward as his eyes adjusted. "Chrys Valerian?"

"It's me," he said, glancing at a leather bag in Alchaeus' hand.

The old man shook his head. "I just had the strangest experience."

"Alchaeus," Chrys said, "you need to tell us how to break the coreseal."

"Coreseal?" Alchaeus raised a brow. "What are you talking about? The coreseal was destroyed." He gave Chrys a dubious look. "If you're here, where are the others? Why are you alone?"

Chrys turned and glanced back down the tunnel, a part of him still hoping he would see his wife hiding around the bend. He turned back to Alchaeus and a realization dawned on him. The hat. His skin, unblemished, yet sickly. Old, yet young. The leather bag. Alchaeus *was* the man who'd saved Iriel.

"It was you!" he said, unable to hold back his frustration. "You lied. You said it wasn't you, but it was!"

Alchaeus furrowed his brow. "I don't know what you—"

"You saved Iriel when she almost lost the baby," Chrys said, pointing a finger and stepping toward the old man. "Why did you lie to me?"

"I..." Alchaeus raised his hands. "I promise, if I—"

Chrys pulled out his thread-dead dagger and held it up. "After you saved Iriel and Aydin, you gave this to me. You said, 'Use it to break the threads that bind you.' Tell me how you got past the coreseal. And no more lies!"

"I didn't get past the coreseal," Alchaeus said. "And where is your threadlight?"

Chrys stepped up to Alchaeus and pressed a finger

against the old man's chest. "I don't care if this is a damn nightmare. You're going to tell me the truth. How did you get past the coreseal?"

"A nightmare?" Alchaeus' eyes grew serious. "Chrys, you need to calm down."

"Not until you tell me the truth," Chrys said, shoving the old man with his free hand.

Alchaeus unleashed an unfocused surge of Sapphire, punching into Chrys' chest and throwing him back. The thread-dead dagger dropped from his hand as he fell through the air, landing a few paces away on the hard stone. The old man reached down and picked up the dagger. "There is no time for foolishness. I made a discovery, here at the Convergence. Something that could change everything."

Just as he said the words, a skittering sound echoed over the stone floor. Then another a dozen feet away. Then more and more. Alchaeus' head swiveled back and forth, eyes wide as he took in their surroundings. Chrys saw nothing, but he did smell the sweet scent of a summer rose.

Alchaeus turned to Chrys. "Don't move."

Suddenly, a bright light appeared along the edges of his vision, expanding like a fire toward the center, filling his sight until there was nothing but light in his eyes. It was too bright, but he needed answers. He needed Alchaeus to tell him what to do.

He held up a hand to shield from the brilliance.

Then closed his eyes.

Chrys stood in the middle of the same cavern, warm and wondering what the hell had just happened. Was it a dream? Was the Convergence playing with his mind? It had all felt so real. Where was Alchaeus?

His eyes grew wide as bolts of energy suddenly crackled across the Convergence, branching out, warring with dozens of expanding bubbles along the dome, like a kettle boiling over. He turned and saw the others standing all around, dazed, backing away as the erratic energy grew.

Rocks danced along the ground from tremors pulsing through the cavern. Small at first, barely noticeable through his thick boots, but in moments they'd grown until quakes ran up through his legs, vibrating his bones. The cavern groaned, and stalactites rained down like stone daggers.

Then the Convergence exploded.

A cascading tidal wave of raw energy surged through the cavern. Chrys was thrown back, head over heels, tumbling through the air like a pebble in a windstorm, his mind swirling alongside his body. In a stroke of clarity, he embraced the threadlight pulsing through his veins, grateful that it had returned. Hot energy hissed beneath his skin. With a surge of Sapphire and Emerald, he stopped himself from spinning, then *pushed* against the jagged cavern wall just before he crashed. He dropped to his feet, shaking his head to clear the nausea.

Three loud thuds echoed throughout the vaulted cavern, then silence.

Chrys turned and saw Alverax lying still, crumpled along the rocky wall. Roshaw sprinted from the dark cavern entrance over to his son, thick boots stomping over fallen rubble, then knelt beside him, frantically checking wounds while shadows flickered over them from the light of the photospores.

Chrys was so disoriented that, despite his desire to do something, anything, he simply stood, staring at the aftermath of the explosion.

"Check on Alchaeus!" Willow shouted as she ran toward him, her face pale, veins alive with multi-colored thread-light. "I'll get Laurel."

Chrys was still furious with Alchaeus. They were friends. How could he look him in the eye and claim he wasn't the one who'd saved Iriel. There was something the old man wasn't telling them, and Chrys needed answers.

"Dammit, Chrys!" she screamed, spittle flying from her lips. "I didn't raise you to stand by. Not while the ones you love are hurt."

Chrys shook his head. She was right. Liar or not, they needed him. "On my way."

With renewed focus, Chrys spotted Alchaeus and ran to him. The third god lay against the jagged wall at an unnatural angle. His skin was wrinkled and gray, like he'd soaked in a warm bath for hours. Like he'd aged another twenty years since they'd spoken. Blood and water dripped down his face onto the wet stone floor, and his chest lay in such a way that Chrys was certain there were broken ribs. He knelt down and pressed a hand over Alchaeus' heart.

Nothing.

He leaned down and pressed an ear.

There. It was faint, but it was there.

"Alchaeus," Chrys whispered. "Alchaeus, wake up."

The old man's eyes fluttered open, like a newborn desperate to see a world that their mind couldn't comprehend. "C...Chrys?"

"It's me," he said. "I need to get you to the elixir."

"...did it," Alchaeus mumbled, coughing up a sizable chunk of red blood. He tried to lift his hand, but it fell back to the ground. "I was wrong."

"Come on," Chrys said, rising to a crouch and reaching his arm under Alchaeus' shoulder. "We need to get you up."

"It was me." Tears streaked his elderly cheeks. He rolled over and looked Chrys in the eyes. The old man's irises had faded, a layer of gray clouding the colors. "I didn't know..."

Chrys stared down at Alchaeus and felt his chest tighten.

Alchaeus' lip quivered as he reached for Chrys' hand. "Don't leave me."

"I'm not going to leave you," Chrys whispered.

"I don't want to be alone anymore."

Chrys felt tears in his eyes, swelling against his cheeks, pressure building as he watched an old man's desperate plea. If there was anything Chrys understood, it was the fear of being alone. "I won't leave you, Alchaeus."

The old man smiled and leaned his head back, his lips and cheeks twitching through a range of emotions. His hand grew heavy as his eyes moved to the empty cavern heights. A few quiet moments passed, a sense of peace in the pain, then Alchaeus' body grew still, his lips still parted with the slightest hint of a smile touching the corners.

Chrys closed his eyes and squeezed the old man's hand.

So much death.

And he couldn't stop any of it.

Not in the Wastelands. Not in Felia. Not now.

Would there be no end to their loss?

"Chrys?" Iriel's voice rose through the cavern like an angel's song.

He turned and saw her walking toward him, carrying their child through the silent aftermath of death and destruction. "Iriel."

"Is he?"

Chrys nodded.

"I'm sorry." She paused, Emerald threadlight running through her veins as she looked around the cavern. "What happened? I ran to check on Roshaw, and then the Convergence just...exploded. Is it gone for good?"

Chrys turned to where the warbling dome of threadlight had once been and found nothing but staggered puddles of fallen water and debris. Where once the energy had been, now there was nothing. No signs. No crater. Gone. Just like in his nightmare.

"I don't know," Chrys said. "But we should go."

Iriel nodded toward the body. "Are we going to leave him?"

"No," Chrys quickly replied. "I'll carry him. We should bury him at his home."

"I think that would be nice."

A minute later, Roshaw hobbled over with Alverax. The young man looked beat up but okay. Scratches along his cheek, blood seeping out from wounds in his shoulder, but he was alive, and he could walk. He would be okay.

When Laurel, Asher, and Willow joined them, the young woman seemed unfazed by the bone jutting out from her elbow. Chrys was going to ask, but could tell by Laurel's scowl that she didn't want to discuss it.

"Glad you're all okay," Chrys said as they gathered around Alchaeus. "I'd like to bring his body back to the elixir and bury him somewhere nearby."

"I'll help," Roshaw added.

Willow put a hand on Roshaw's shoulder. "We can all help."

Chrys gave them an appreciative nod. "I think we could all use a bit of that elixir as well."

After *breaking* Alchaeus' corethread, Chrys lifted the old man over his shoulders and began the melancholy trek through the winding tunnels to bury yet another fallen friend.

It was a long, grueling return through the caverns, following the white markings on the walls that Alchaeus used to signal the return route. At first, Chrys thought the party's silence had come because of the death of Alchaeus. But as they continued on, he realized that it was more than that. For months they had each been surrounded by death in its various forms, and their hands were just as dirty as any. This was not the silence of a death being mourned. This was the silence of secrets.

No one wanted to discuss what had happened in the Convergence. If any of the others had experienced a nightmare like he had, he understood why. Scared or scarred, they walked on in silence.

The cavern had shifted from the quakes caused by the destruction of the Convergence. In several places, massive stones had detached from the walls, blocking large portions of the way but never enough to fully impede their path.

By the time they reached the final tunnel, the light of the elixir shimmering beyond the bend, they were all tired and sore. Those who were able—Chrys among them—used Sapphire to decrease their weight for the journey, and still he felt a deep weariness. Laurel took the worst of it. Every step seemed to jostle her broken arm and, though she grimaced and growled, not once did she complain. And Iriel —Lightfather bless her—throughout it all, she endured with Aydin strapped to her chest, ever-thankful for the breaks that Willow provided.

Chrys took the final steps into the cave and breathed in the familiar sight. Golden light illuminated the vast cavern, though it too had changed. The rose-colored table had been split in two, rubble and debris scattered along the sides where a boulder had fallen from the ceiling, cracking the table down its center. Dozens of corespawn statues lay shattered along the far corner. And a massive crevice had opened along the wall above the elixir pool, deep and dark where the glowing light failed to reach.

"Damn," Roshaw said behind him.

Laurel and Asher stepped past Chrys, then moved to the elixir. In unison, they both bent down and lapped up a few sips of the golden water before Laurel reached over and placed her broken arm inside. In moments, her tense shoulders relaxed, and she flopped onto her belly along the edge of the pool, letting her arm drift in the water.

Chrys turned to the others. "Why don't you all take a little rest, and I'll start working on a burial mound for Alchaeus."

"I'll help," Roshaw said.

"No, it's okay." Chrys offered a solemn smile. "You go rest. If I use Obsidian, the work will go quickly."

The others understood his need to be alone, to work off

the pain of loss, and so they left him for the elixir. Chrys lifted Alchaeus' body one final time and carried him to the far end of the cavern, near a large pile of fallen rubble. One by one, Chrys lifted the stones, deciding not to use thread-light to ease the burden, embracing the physical labor of the work, and set them each down on top of his friend's body. Slowly, the mound grew, first along Alchaeus' feet and legs, rising to consume his chest and arms. Finally, Chrys built a wall of rocks around the man's head, setting aside a single flat stone which he would use to cover the face. The final puzzle piece to commemorate the life of a fallen god.

He stepped away from the burial mound, joining the quiet group still seated along the edge of the elixir pool. Already, they seemed healthier. The cuts on Alverax's cheeks had faded. Roshaw's bloody shoulder was clean. Laurel's arm, though still soaking in the elixir, was regaining its natural form. Iriel's pale face was now more full of life. And Willow...

"Mom," Chrys said, his brow furrowed tight.

"Yes, I did," she said with a laugh, not waiting for him to ask. "I rubbed some of it on my face, because it would be a pity to have this anti-aging juice available and not use just a little..."

Roshaw shrugged beside her. "I hadn't even realized there were wrinkles to begin with."

Chrys ignored them and turned to Laurel. "Are you able to take a quick break? I'm going to place the final stone."

The young woman nodded, pulling her arm from the elixir and bending it back and forth slowly. As she rose, they all followed Chrys over to the burial mound, gathering in a half-circle around Alchaeus' exposed face. They stood in silence for a few moments, staring down at their fallen friend. His skin had already gone nearly white. Thick wrinkles ran over the curves of his face, and the same delicate smile crept along the edge of his lips. Despite everything that had happened, he looked...content.

"What can we say about someone like Alchaeus?" Chrys started, unsure what he would say next. "You embraced us to your own danger, and you helped us when you did not have to. Never once, despite living in darkness for centuries, did you let it blacken your soul. I'm not sure any of us could have done the same. You were a good man, and a good friend. We owe you our lives."

The others remained quiet as Chrys reached down and lifted the flat stone. He paused, taking in the dead man's smile one last time, then placed the stone over his face. "The world may not remember you, but we will."

"May the winds guide you," Laurel whispered.

Willow nodded to the words.

"When we get out of here," Roshaw said, looking tired, "I'm going to find him a star in the east. He deserves at least that."

After a minute of solemn silence, the others stepped away, leaving the third god to rest beneath his stone shrine. Willow and Roshaw walked quietly over to the broken table. Alverax sat on the ledge of the elixir pool. And Laurel wandered over to the corespawn statues. Only Chrys remained, staring down at the man who'd risked his own immortality for them.

Just like that, hundreds of years of knowledge and memories were gone. Their best chance of destroying the coreseal. He didn't know how, but Chrys would finish Alchaeus' work. He would stop Relek and Lylax before they broke the world.

Chrys patted his side, looking for a memento to leave on the shrine. After touching his empty sheath, he realized that his thread-dead dagger was missing. He must have dropped it in the cavern. At some point, he would need to go retrieve it. But they had nothing but time.

He touched his pocket and felt the familiar, circular shape of the pocket watch he'd been gifted by Malachus. He pulled it out, thinking that it might make a worthy memento to leave behind. But when he opened it, a crack ran along the length of the glass, and the hands stood still. His own words to Iriel echoed in his mind.

As long as I hear that steady tick, I know that everything is going to be okay.

An ominous feeling crept along his spine.

Was everything going to be okay?

He looked at the pocket watch again and had a sudden realization.

The ticking sound.

Alchaeus' final words.

A string, held at each end, brought together.

If space was a string that could be folded by the Convergence, what about time?

Chrys needed to think.

ALVERAX STOOD at the edge of the elixir pool, staring down into the golden light. It called to him—not for healing, not the magic—the water itself. After his experience beneath the Felian palace, nearly drowning in a sea of darkness, he thought he'd never want to be in the water ever again. But he'd always felt some unseen bond with it. A reassurance. A connection that he only ever felt when he lay weightless and entombed.

His eyes drifted up to the massive fracture splitting the wall above the elixir. The earthquake caused by the destruction of the Convergence had done damage across the underground world, but this felt different. It, too, called to him, like a doorway opening to a new world.

Slowly, he stepped around the edge of the pool until he reached the wall. There was no ledge, so he stepped into the water, letting its golden glow crawl up his clothing. He felt a shiver of healing magic crawl across his spine, but his eyes never stopped staring at the fracture. The waters reached his chest as he made his way to the center of the pool's wall. He stared up at the gap, then jumped, grabbing hold of the edge and pulling himself up, lifting until his stomach lay flat along the base of the gap. He placed his hands down and pushed himself to his feet. The gap in the fracture was just wide enough for a man and ran deep enough that none of the golden light reached the end.

He looked back and saw the others. Laurel had moved to the tunnel entrance to keep watch. Roshaw and Willow sat at the broken table quietly talking. And Chrys stared down at Alchaeus' shrine, brow furrowed as he lost himself in his own thoughts. Iriel fed Aydin in the corner.

Alverax stepped farther into the fracture, into the beckoning darkness where jagged rocks flanked either side of him. He moved sideways through it until he reached the end and felt a pang of disappointment. His hand ran along the length of the wall, as if there would be some magical lever he could pull to open it. Unfortunately, there was nothing but stone.

But then he saw it, a speck of light flickering as he moved. A tiny hole at chest level, the size of a pebble. He crouched and looked through it. He had to squint at just the right angle, but he finally saw the other side. His eyes went wide as he took in a sprawling lake of elixir with hundreds of thick stalagmites piercing up through the water like stone swords. And there, in the center of the lake, an island. Even through the small hole, the island glowed like a threadlight sun.

Alverax stumbled back through the fracture, scraping his shoulders and shimmying his way through the jagged walls. Finally, he leapt down into the elixir and waded his way to the end of the pool. When he lifted himself up, his father was staring at him with a raised brow.

"Everything okay over there?"

Alverax stood and ran toward the alcove housing Alchaeus' corespawn statues, while pointing back toward the fracture. "There's something on the other side of that wall."

He stepped over one of the shattered statues—stone arms and legs broken from the torso though a short tail still stood firm—and found what he was looking for. He left the chisel and picked up the hammer, then grinned as he leapt over rubble back toward the elixir pool.

His father was now standing, joined by Chrys, Iriel, and Willow, all staring at him as he ran. Alverax ignored them, jumping down into the pool and making his way back to the fracture. He tossed the hammer up into the gap, then jumped and pulled himself up.

"Alverax!"

He turned to see his father standing at the edge of the pool, hands raised, palms up. Alverax raised a finger. "One second!"

After retrieving the hammer, he squeezed himself forward to the end of the fracture, then bent down to find the hole. He slammed the end of the hammer into the hole, blasting a chunk of stone off into the cavern on the other side. He bent down and took another look. The cavern was even larger than he'd seen the first time, the golden lake extending as far as the eye could see.

Again, he slammed the hammer at the edge of the hole. Then again, and again. With each strike, the hole grew slightly larger, revealing more and more of the sprawling cavern beyond. Once there was a hole the size of a man's head, Alverax stepped back, smiled, and made his way back to the other end of the fracture.

"You're all going to want to see this," he said with a grin.

Roshaw's veins lit with multi-colored threadlight just before he began to float into the air. With a surge of energy, he accelerated toward the fracture. Watching his father fly was still a surreal experience. He'd seen the three hybrids—Chrys, Willow, and Roshaw—practice flying during their journey through the southern Wastelands, but it never ceased to send a shiver of awe up Alverax's spine. He remembered falling from the sky in Cynosure like an awkward fish and felt a small measure of jealousy.

Before Roshaw made it all the way, Alverax leapt down into the elixir to clear the path. While he watched his father disappear into the crevice, he backed away, then pulled himself up over the ledge of the pool. He stood beside Iriel in silence while they waited for Roshaw to reappear.

After a few moments, Iriel turned to him. "What's in there?"

"I don't want to spoil it," Alverax said. "You're going to want to see this one for yourself."

As if to prove his point, Roshaw came bouncing out of the fracture with wide eyes and a wider smile. "Holy hell! You have to see this!"

Willow went in next, bringing Iriel up with her. They squeezed through the fracture one at a time while Alverax stood by his father, feeling quite proud of his accomplishment. By the time they came back down, Willow was in a fit of excitement. "It makes so much sense! The elixir pool is so small. It had to come from somewhere."

"Exactly!" Roshaw said. "I wonder if the lake feeds the oka'thal waters of Kai'Melend."

"Probably with some kind of diluted solution," Willow added.

"Did you look in threadlight?" Alverax asked.

Willow nodded. "Brighter than anything I've ever seen."

"Thought I'd gone blind for a minute," Roshaw joked.

Willow gasped. "It could be another Convergence! But if it is, where does it lead? It could be anywhere!"

Alverax glanced up at the opening. "Do you think it could be our way out?"

From the far end of the cave, Chrys came walking through the tunnel. He'd left without a word, looking quite thoughtful, but now there was a new sense of purpose in his stride.

"Chrys!" Iriel called out. "We might have found another Convergence!"

His eyes grew wide. "Really?"

"On the other side of the wall," she said. "Alverax found it."

"If that's true," Chrys said, eyes dancing between the members of their party. "Then we need to talk about what happened with the last one."

The buzz of excitement faded away as quickly as it had come. Alverax remembered the last image of his vision, a young Jelium falling to the sand with blood dripping down his bronze chest. If that was what Chrys was asking about, then Alverax didn't want to talk about it.

Chrys glanced back at Alchaeus' shrine. "If I'm right, then my mother, Laurel, and Alverax experienced something in there. It's probably why you were so quiet on the way back. I experienced something too, but I didn't understand it. I thought it was a magic-fueled hallucination, some kind of nightmare. But Alchaeus changed my mind. This changed my mind." He held up the pocket watch. "I might be crazy, but I think the Convergence took each of us back in time."

Alverax felt his pulse quicken. He'd considered it, hoped for it even. But it wasn't true. If he'd really gone back in time and killed Jelium, something would have changed. What happened in the Convergence was something else.

"It was just a vision," Alverax said. "If it was anything more, we wouldn't be here right now."

Willow's eyes darted about the floor as she pieced

together the puzzle. But as soon as Alverax spoke, her gaze shifted to him. "What do you mean we wouldn't be here?"

Everyone turned to him, and he immediately regretted having said anything at all. "What? No one wants to share their experience, but you all want to hear mine?"

Chrys took a step forward into the center of the circle, turning to meet eyes with everyone in the group as he spoke. "If there is another Convergence, no more secrets. There could be consequences. There could be information that helps us understand how it happened, maybe even recreate it. It could be what helps us break the coreseal and get out of here. Might even give us a clue about how to stop the Heralds. But if we don't talk about it, we'll never know."

"I'm with Alverax," Laurel said. "I think it was just some kind of a dream."

"What makes you say that?" Chrys asked. "Where did it take you?"

"The Hallowed Library in Felia."

Chrys raised a brow, taken aback. "And what happened?"

Laurel looked down at Asher, as if she were asking for permission, then looked back to Chrys. "I killed Alabella."

Alverax felt his mind beginning to spiral. Could her dream have been so similar to his own? Maybe the power of the Convergence just latched on to powerful feelings and placed you in a scene with those you hate. Did every vision end in death? That would explain why no one wanted to talk about their experience.

"You killed Alabella?" Chrys repeated.

Laurel's eye twitched. "This time, she was maybe fourteen years old?"

"So you did go back in time!" Willow said excitedly.

"But if she killed Alabella," Roshaw jumped in, "then we wouldn't be here, right?"

Alverax nodded. "Exactly."

Laurel placed a hand on top of Asher's back. "Like I said. It was just a dream."

"Mine was the same," Alverax added, remembering the beach and the hot sun. "I was in Kulai, and a young Jelium approached me. I figured if I killed him, then none of this would have happened. So I stabbed him with one of those yellow shards that Alchaeus dropped during the fight."

"That's what I used as well," Laurel added.

"Yellow shards?" Willow placed a fist on her forehead and closed her eyes. "Can you show me?"

Alverax shook his head. "It disappeared when the Convergence burst."

"Something's not adding up," Willow said thoughtfully. "I'm actually with Chrys on this. It would explain my experience perfectly. But if you two killed Alabella and Jelium, then why wouldn't...wait. Can you describe the shards you picked up?"

Alverax pictured it in his mind. "Handspan long, half a finger wide. Pale yellow. A bit like citrine."

"And you got it from Alchaeus?" Willow's eyes grew wide. "Stones, you didn't kill Alabella and Jelium. You stuck a shard of Amber in their hearts."

Alverax's heart dropped. He looked over and saw a fire in Laurel's eye and a dangerous twitch in her lip. He pictured the shard in his hand, dripping with Jelium's blood. The tip—such a subtle detail—had been chipped. Then when the Convergence exploded, the rest of the shard had been destroyed by the energy, crumbling to dust in his hand.

Willow continued. "Think about it. Alchaeus told us that no human has ever been born an Amber or Obsidian threadweaver. The only reason none of us have all four theoliths is because Lylax had hidden all of the Amber. Alchaeus must have finally found it. Then he went back and made Aydin an Amber threadweaver. Laurel placed a shard of Amber in Alabella's heart. And Alverax placed one in Jelium."

"Holy hell," Roshaw mumbled.

Iriel looked down at her son, asleep on a pile of wool blankets.

"No," Laurel said with a whimper. "I...I killed her! There's no way she survived that! I didn't. It can't be. I..." She stopped, tears welling up in her eyes as she looked to Alverax for help, but he had no solace to give. Every word, every pause, was a reflection of his own doubts and fears. He felt his chest tighten and tears creep out from his own tired eyes.

I created Jelium.

The truth of it was too much. All of the deaths caused by the Heralds—all of the pain they'd inflicted—was because of him. He'd had the choice. He'd made his decision. Somehow, deep down, he'd known that the shard was Amber. Of course it was. And he'd let his anger and bitterness win. What kind of a man tries to kill a kid? Without hesitation. Without regret. Every dark event that had eclipsed the good parts of his life was *his* fault.

"Laurel," Willow said, moving to place a hand on the girl's shoulder. "You were just trying to help."

"STOP IT!" Laurel screamed, swatting away Willow's hand and taking a step back while she wiped away tears. "I don't want to hear it. *Laurel, it's okay. Laurel, you couldn't have known. Laurel, you tried.* I'm sick of it! First Zedalum. Then Alabella. Now Alabella again. We're all going to die in these caves, and all I wanted was to do one good thing!"

With that, she stormed off with Asher at her side. The others all watched in silence as she disappeared into the tunnel leading toward the bottom of the Endless Well, but Alverax chased after her. She needed him, but he also needed her. They were the only two in the world who could understand what each other was going through. His grandfather had taught him the importance of sharing burdens. Now, he would share hers. And, hopefully, she would share his.

He ran toward the tunnel, wet boots squashing against the hard stone, dodging piles of loose rubble. It didn't take long to find her. Laurel was just around the corner, seated against the jagged wall with her head buried in Asher's fur. Her chest heaved up and down as she let out her tears. Asher rubbed his snout along her shoulder in comforting strokes.

Alverax approached slowly, remembering his weeks on the *Pale Urchin*, locked away in the cabin not wanting to speak with anyone. So, rather than trying to give an uplifting speech, rather than spinning some lie about how it would be okay, he sat down on the other side of Asher, his head resting next to Laurel's. Sometimes, the simple act of being there is enough.

They lay in silence for what felt an eternity. All the while, Alverax replayed the scene from the Convergence back in his mind. The handsome young Kulaian boy. The golden shard. And the moment he chose to kill. It felt like another man—Alverax was not a killer. But it was different with Jelium. Years of hate, years of anger and pain, had all combined to make the act so effortless. So deserved. Even after he'd done it and seen the fear in the young boy's eyes, Alverax had felt no regret. Maybe he was a killer after all.

"How do we make it better?" Laurel's voice cracked.

When Alverax sat up, Laurel's swollen eyes stared back at him, pleading, begging for him to offer a solution.

"Sometimes, there's nothing you can do," Alverax said, shaking his head.

"You don't believe that," Laurel replied.

Alverax looked at the ground. "Not every mistake can be fixed."

"That's not what I asked."

When he looked back up, he saw the intensity with which she looked at him. She was a woman of action—he could see it in her eyes—an arrow begging to be loosed.

"I know we can't fix it," Laurel added. "But I refuse to believe that there is nothing we can do to make it better."

Alverax furrowed his brow. "Make what better?"

"This?" Laurel said, gesturing to the cavern. "Our situation. The Heralds. The coreseal. I don't know, but we have to do something. This is just as much our fault as anyone's, and I'm going to do my part to make it better if it's the last thing I do."

His heart ached thinking of how much Jisenna would have liked Laurel. She was honest, brave, and willing to do what it took to protect the people she loved. Alverax liked to think that he was the same, but when it came down to it, he wasn't so sure.

"Come on." Laurel stood and offered him a hand. "I'm done feeling sorry for myself. People are like trees, remember? The least we can do is stand."

Alverax forced a smile, took her hand, and stood.

IT TOOK HOURS OF HAMMERING—EVEN with the aid of threadlight—to break open a hole large enough for a woman to fit through. After considerable effort, sweat, and cursing, Iriel finally managed it. The hard work felt good, like she was finally accomplishing something rather than waiting around for the others. She looked through the opening at the shimmering lake of elixir, ripples spreading across the surface like a siren's song, and breathed in her success.

There was something haunting in knowing that no one had set foot in this cavern, at least as far as Iriel knew. After what had happened at the Convergence, they were all a little wary of what this new phenomenon would hold. In some ways, it seemed so similar—brilliant rays of threadlight buzzing through the air—but in others, it was different. Like comparing the moon and the sun. She looked to the island, a beacon of power, the center of the threadlight.

It still seemed impossible that the others had traveled through time, everyone except her and Roshaw. It wasn't true—none of it was under their control—but it still felt like somehow they'd been excluded purposefully. Not this time. Whatever this new phenomenon held, she would be front and center to find out.

Squeezing her way through, Iriel entered the vast

cavern, overlooking the lake of elixir. Golden light emanated from the waters, illuminating the entirety of the cavern which stretched nearly as far as the eye could see. Even at a distance, she could feel the raw power buzzing through the lake, like static crawling over the hairs of her arm.

"Iriel?" her mother-in-law called out from behind. "You better not be exploring without me!" A moment later, Willow slipped through the crevice and stood beside her, staring down at the lake.

"Any chance I could have a lift to the island?" Iriel asked.

Willow smiled. "Just a warning, I still overcorrect sometimes. Might not be the smoothest ride."

Iriel glanced over the ledge. "Better than the alternative."

They wasted no time, flying forward roughly ten feet above the elixir, Iriel clutching Willow like a toddler clutching their mother. In the distance, ripples fluttered across the surface of the lake. The first were far away—nearly imperceptible as they flew—but then the ripples grew closer. Iriel kept an eye on them, but then the ripples stopped. Still, she watched, but no others came. Willow tried to convince her that they were just pockets of air trapped in the earth below the lake, stirring as the bubbles surfaced. Iriel wasn't so certain.

They continued their journey toward the island, which seemed to grow in size as they approached. Soon, their corethreads reappeared, and they touched down on the ground. Now that they were closer, standing atop the surface, Iriel could see that the island's surface had a shine to it, as if it had been polished or hewn out of a single, monstrous slab of onyx. And it was barren, nothing but wet stone and rubble with the occasional remains of fallen stalactites.

Iriel turned to Willow as they walked. "Think it's safe to look in threadlight?"

"Absolutely not," she said. "It was bright enough at a distance. I don't know if threadblindness is a thing, but I'd rather not risk it. What I'm really hoping for is some kind of an anchor in the physical world, a source. We never found one at the Convergence, but it doesn't mean there wasn't one. And I'm still not convinced this is a Convergence."

Iriel furrowed her brow. "I don't know. All I see is regular rocks, wet rocks, and broken rocks."

Willow stopped walking and looked at her with a blank face. "I think Chrys' sense of humor is rubbing off on you."

"Rude," Iriel said with a smirk.

They continued moving forward, and Willow pointed ahead to what appeared to be a stalagmite growing out of the ground. As they approached, Iriel saw it more clearly. Four transparent shafts jutting out of the ground, clear as diamond, twisting in a perfect helix and ending at twice the height of a man.

They walked closer, and the air seemed to hum. Sweat ran down Iriel's back, and her chest tightened. Their pace slowed—there was something about the diamond structure. With each step, Iriel's heart beat faster, a growing fire coming alive within her chest. Warmth flooded her veins. Comfort. Ecstasy. Power.

Her mind filled with the growing buzz emanating from the diamond. Transfixed, mesmerized by the helix, her mind drank in the energy with each step. Power crackled from the ends of her fingers.

It was so close.

She took a step.

It was beautiful. Distant elixir light refracted from the diamond, splitting into a rainbow of color.

A voice called out to her, but it was nothing more than a passing wind.

Another step.

Raw power expanded through her sizzling veins. Pressure building. Energy swelling. Power unending. With this, she could do anything. She could fight the Heralds themselves and win.

She reached out her hand to touch the helix. Tiny bolts of lightning crackled between the diamond structures and her fingers. A stabbing pain pulsed through her arm. But she didn't care. The pain was nothing compared to the deific power consuming her.

As soon as her skin touched the diamond structure, it cracked with a boom.

A wave of energy burst from the helix, launching Iriel away and snapping her back to reality. She tried to right herself as she tumbled through the air, but her veins were colorless, achromic, thread-dead. Panic consumed her. She was already weaker than the others. Anything but her threadlight.

The world around her shuddered. She closed her eyes and embraced the darkness, waiting for her body to crash into the marble stone. But she kept flying back, farther and farther, until she crashed down into the lake. The air forced itself out of her lungs as she fell below the surface. She struggled up, throwing her head above the water and gasping for air.

Iriel tried to remember what had happened, but the memory seemed to blur in her mind. She'd been approaching the helix. The power...she remembered the power. Had she reached it? The memory flickered in her mind, her fingers reaching out, bolts of electricity crackling between. The break.

Willow surfaced from beneath the water, gasping, and Iriel swam to her. Together, they made their way back toward the island, crawling up, then pushing themselves onto the slick surface.

A familiar glow flickered to life in her veins.

Iriel quickly opened herself to threadlight and felt the magic-filled warmth fight off the wet cold. Relief washed over her.

"What did you do?" Willow asked with an air of accusation. "I was screaming your name, and you just kept walking forward. What happened?"

"I don't know," Iriel said. "I couldn't control myself. That *thing* was filling me with more threadlight than I've ever felt. It was like a magnet, until the threadlight was ripped away from me."

"I lost mine as well." Willow looked down at her multicolored veins. "Thank the Father of All that it's back. Whatever you did somehow disrupted our theoliths. But the elixir was unaffected. How curious."

"How is that possible?"

Willow shrugged, turning to look at the diamond helix in the distance. "I don't know. I need to think more about it, unless..."

"What?" Iriel pressed.

"No," Willow said quickly. "Even if it were true, the outcome is the same."

"Willow," Iriel said with a glare. "What is it?"

The older woman clenched her jaw and glanced toward the helix. "Some believe threadlight comes from their god, the Lightfather or the Father of All. That the gods either create threadlight and offer it to the world, or that threadlight is their essence emanating out from their bodies. But there are others who believe that there is a different source. A Provenance."

Together, they stared in silence, contemplating the possibility.

"*The* Provenance?" Iriel repeated, knowingly. "You think that helix is the source of all threadlight? What if you're right?"

Willow backed away. "Then this is a very dangerous place to be."

CHRYS WATCHED as Iriel squeezed herself through the gap in the wall, side stepping through the fracture and *pulling* herself as she ran along the wall. Honestly, he was just glad she was alive. After the temporary loss of threadlight, he had feared the worst.

"What happened in there?" he asked. "We were resting when a gust of air came bursting from the fracture. Roshaw and I lost our threadlight for a moment."

"He's being way too nice about this," Roshaw said. "What he means to say is that we were both scared out of our damn minds. What the hell did you two do in there?"

Before Iriel could respond, Willow arrived, leaping from the fracture in the wall and landing beside them. Her clothes were as drenched as Iriel's, and her hair was a mess, but the serious look on her face was enough to quell any comments.

"We need to seal off that fracture," Willow said firmly. "Stuff it with rocks, cave it in, doesn't matter. We have to make sure no one else can get in."

"As much as I love to repeat myself," Roshaw said with a rasp to his voice. "What the hell did you two do in there?"

Iriel wiped away some water from her cheek. "We found something. And we're not certain, but we think it might be —Lightfather, but it sounds absurd when you say it aloud— we think we found the source of threadlight."

"The source..." Chrys repeated. Before he finished, his eyes lit up. "*The* source. You found the Provenance?"

Footsteps echoed from the tunnel leading to the Endless Well. Chrys and the others turned, hands instinctively reaching for their blades.

Moments later, Laurel and Asher came barreling through the photospore-lit cave. "The coreseal!" she shouted. "It's gone!"

"Slow down," Chrys said, holding up his hands. "What do you mean it's gone?"

Laurel glanced back at the tunnel just before Chrys heard another set of footsteps. "I don't know. We were in the Endless Well getting some water, and something happened. Alverax lost his threadlight, and I lost my Asher-vision. When it came back, the coreseal was gone."

"Damn," Roshaw said, running both hands over his face. "If that's true, let's get the hell out of here before it returns."

With that, Roshaw and Willow shared a look and raced off toward the tunnel. They passed Alverax halfway there, but the young man stopped and waved them on, bending down and taking in deep breaths.

Asher growled, and Laurel turned back to Chrys. "He's right. We don't know how long the coreseal will be gone. We should get out while we can. There's nothing we can do for the world while we're down here."

Chrys took one more glance back at the fracture above the elixir pool. If they had a chance to get out, they should take it. But what if they truly had found the Provenance. That kind of energy. Could they use the power? What if they could use it to travel back in time again? What if they could fix things?

Finally, Chrys nodded. "This might be our only chance to get free."

Laurel and Asher nodded in unison and took off.

He turned to Iriel. "You need to be more careful. You could have died in there."

"And you could have died fighting a horde of corespawn," she replied.

"That was different."

Iriel stepped over and picked up Aydin from a pile of blankets on the ground. "It was different because it was you. You're allowed to do dangerous things. All I'm allowed to do is carry the baby."

Chrys shook his head. "That's not true."

She didn't even look at him. "We need to go."

Chrys followed Iriel through the cave toward the Endless Well with a hollow sense of hope in his core. With all that they had been through, he'd begun to see that hope could not be trusted. Hope was a drifter, waving with one hand and stabbing with the other. This time, picturing the bright coreseal stretching across the expanse of the Well, Chrys tried not to let his hopes rise too high.

ALVERAX STOOD beside Laurel and stared up into the Endless Well. To his side, he could feel Asher's fur brushing up against his forearm. Maybe it was simply because they were close in age, but he'd grown fond of Laurel. She was strange, but in a good way. While on the *Pale Urchin*, she'd hardly said a word to him, but her companionship had meant everything to him. He would never forget those quiet days.

"They're taking a long time," Laurel said.

The subsequent silence grated on Alverax. His father and Willow had gone up to the surface to make sure there was no trap waiting for them. The only problem with their plan was if the Heralds were there waiting, Roshaw and Willow would be dead before they could share their findings. Every second that passed pecked at the raw fear in Alverax's heart. He'd lost his father once; he wasn't going to let it happen again. Not without a fight.

A moment later, Roshaw and Willow came flying down from the heights of the Endless Well—perfectly healthy and alive—and landed with a thud on the rocks beside the water.

Alverax took a step toward them. "Is it safe?"

"It's bright," Roshaw said, blinking and opening his eyes wide as he waited for them to adjust to the darkness.

Willow ignored Roshaw and gave a nod to Laurel. "Coreseal is gone, and there's no army up there waiting for us...yet. As soon as Chrys and Iriel get here, we should go."

"Chrys can get up by himself," Roshaw said. "We should go now."

Willow scowled. "If the coreseal reappears and they're stuck down here without us, they'll die. We stick together. All in or all out."

Asher gave a growl of agreement.

"I agree with Willow," Laurel said. "The pack stays together."

Alverax nodded. "What she said."

Roshaw shrugged, looking up toward the speck of light overhead. "Obviously I don't want them to die alone down here. I just wish they would walk a little faster."

The five companions stood in silence, staring up, praying for the coreseal not to reappear.

Alverax rubbed a hand over his shoulder, not quite able to scratch the itch on his spine where the large scar stretched below his neck. It had been bugging him since they got back from the Convergence. He remembered the first time Jisenna had come to his door, claiming that she'd come looking for a mysterious boy with a scar on his back. Later, she'd told him that he was scarred inside and out. Now, far away from Felia, deep beneath the ground where not even the Moon's Little Sister could see, the biggest scar of all was the one left by her death.

Footsteps broke the silence, and everyone turned to see Chrys and Iriel jogging down the tunnel, Aydin in arm. Willow waved them over, and Iriel offered Alverax a smile as they finished their approach.

"How's it look up there?" Chrys asked with threadlight swirling beneath his skin. "I don't see the coreseal."

Willow nodded. "It's still gone."

"Clear up top as well," Roshaw added. "At least when we checked."

Chrys clenched his jaw, looking up through the vast shaft of the Endless Well. "Then let's be quick, before that changes."

"All together," Willow said.

"I'll carry Iriel," Chrys said in agreement. "Roshaw, you bring Alverax. And mom, you have Laurel and Asher."

As they gathered close together, Alverax felt a rush of nerves flow through him. An hour ago, they thought they would never leave the caverns. Now, they were moments away from sunlight, fresh air, and freedom.

With a pinch of Obsidian, they were all soon floating in the air. Roshaw, Chrys, and Willow each surged a wave of Sapphire and Emerald, and soon the three clusters were blasting up through darkness, watching a single speck of light grow into open skies. Air rushed over Alverax's hopeful smile as they flew. As they approached the top, the blindingly bright skies glared down upon them. Alverax lifted a palm to cover his eyes, squinting as they left the darkness of the cave. The warmth of the sun kissed his skin. He hadn't realized how much he'd missed it.

And damn, the air smelled wonderful.

Willow landed first, dropping Laurel and Asher onto the patchy grass as their corethreads reappeared. Then Chrys and Iriel, landing softly beside them, both immediately surveying the surrounding jungle and cliffside. Alverax and Roshaw were the last to touch ground.

The first thing Alverax noticed was that the wastelanders who had died to the *pintalla mox* were still there, though he felt a hint of guilt at those whose bodies had shattered during the fight with the Heralds. Maybe it was just the angle, but it seemed like there were more of them now, each kneeling in clusters like stone statues.

"We should get out of the clearing," Chrys said, gesturing toward the jungle. "We can head west, avoid the dead. Laurel, do you see anything?"

She shook her head. "Nothing. Smells different, though."

"Not sure how to take that," Chrys said. "Either way, we should move. Conserve your threadlight. Laurel, you and Asher are by me. Keep your eyes open. Everyone else, stay close."

Alverax followed, feeling more stressed out than he'd ever felt in his life. Something about a quiet jungle sent a chill up his spine. The trees had always felt so alive, creatures scuttling over mossy limbs, insects darting back and forth across the swampy pools. Now, the only sound was boots stomping on ferns and splashing in puddles. The only movement was their own. Barely a breeze to tickle the leaves.

They tramped through the jungle, making their way west toward some goal that Alverax realized he wasn't quite sure of. But the mountains were west, and that meant Alchea. He hoped that was their destination.

Suddenly, Laurel stopped and Chrys raised a hand, gesturing for the others to lower themselves. Chrys whispered something to Laurel, and she snuck off with Asher while the others stayed hidden amongst the jungle foliage.

A minute later, Laurel returned, standing tall as she strode through the vines. "It's empty."

"No one?" Chrys asked.

"Not a single wastelander in the whole city. And their scent has already started to fade. They've been gone for maybe two days."

Roshaw stood up and looked through the trees toward Kai'Melend. "Where the hell did they go?"

"Tracks go west," Laurel said, gesturing with a nod of her head.

Willow stepped toward the wastelander city, a puzzled look on her face. "I thought they couldn't leave because of the mutation? What changed?"

"They can leave," Chrys said. "They just can't leave for long. I still don't like it. What if they found a way to sustain themselves? They could take an entire army over the mountain."

"Shit." All eyes turned to Roshaw. "The ataçan weren't at the waterfalls. They must be with the army."

"Gods and monsters," Willow said quietly. "Alchea wouldn't stand a chance."

"Unless someone warns them," Laurel added.

When they'd first escaped out of the Endless Well, the bright sun and fluttering breeze had instilled a sense of victory. A relief. It was so easy to relish in the small win that Alverax had forgotten about the greater danger. The Heralds didn't care about a few threadweavers. They wanted chaos. They wanted bloodshed. They wanted mankind to pay for their imprisonment. In a way, it was like Felia all over again. As soon as Alverax was free of his cell, a war was standing by waiting to be fought.

"Oh no," Alverax whispered, realizing a dark truth.

Roshaw turned to his son. "What is it?"

"The corespawn," Alverax said. "The army of corespawn fled through the Convergence. They're in the Fairenwild with no coreseal to keep them contained. Alchea could get hit from both sides."

"Dammit," Chrys said, gritting his teeth with a fire in his eyes. "There's no way we can beat the Heralds there. They can fly farther and faster than we can. But the wastelanders can't fly. And if this city is empty, then they have all of their young with them. They'll be slow. If we move quickly, we may be able to sneak past and warn Malachus before the full army arrives."

The group grew quiet, letting the plan sink in. Alverax watched them each digest the words. Roshaw, scowling but nodding his head. Willow, calculating their odds. Laurel, feet ready to take off at a run as soon as they said the word. Iriel, holding her child with a pained expression in her eyes.

She was the first to break the silence. "Then what?"

Chrys looked to his wife.

"After we warn them," Iriel clarified, "then what? We couldn't even beat the corespawn, let alone a wastelander army flanking from the other side. What's the point of going there if we can't win? Even if we destroy all of the corespawn, then kill the entire population of wastelanders, including the ataçan—which I'm sure is not so easily done —then what? The Heralds can't die. They'll kill us all eventually. The only Amber threadweaver we have is Aydin, and we have years before he can create any kind of coreseal by himself, if we even figure out how to do that. What's the goal?"

"We have to try," Laurel said angrily.

"No," Chrys said. "She has a point. We need a plan. There has to be another way to stop the Heralds."

Willow perked up. "I think Iriel already said it. The Heralds. Their immortality comes from their lifelight bonds to the wastelanders. If we killed all of the wastelanders, they'd be vulnerable."

"Hold on," Roshaw said. "We're not killing all of the wastelanders."

"Do you have a better idea?" Willow asked.

Roshaw threw up his hands. "We *just* started thinking of plans! Holy hell. The first plan is hardly ever the best, especially when it's genocide! We have time. If we head toward the Everstone Mountains, we can figure out a better plan along the way."

Alverax knew that his father had a soft spot for the wastelanders, despite his imprisonment. And it did seem unfair to sentence them to death because of a path they did not choose for themselves. But what was the alternative? Was the choice really who would die? The humans or the wastelanders? As long as the Heralds' immortality was tied to the lives of the wastelanders, could there be another way?

"I understand your hesitation," Chrys said. "This is no one's first choice. But it may be the only one we have."

"We're not—"

"Roshaw," Willow said, cutting him off with a hand on his shoulder. "We'll figure out the best option as we move. Like you said, we have time. And Chrys, just because we have one option doesn't mean that we stop searching for others. Too many lives are at stake. We cannot settle for anything less than the best path."

Chrys nodded, though Alverax could see a hint of annoyance in his lips. "Thank you, and I agree. Let's scavenge what we can from Kai'Melend. Food, water, weapons, anything you can carry. We leave in an hour."

The group advanced into the wastelander city, eyes darting back and forth as they searched for any sign of life, but the only movement came from the long-armed creatures swinging back and forth on vines in the canopy and the occasional bird in flight. Alverax meandered over to one of the lower huts while Roshaw and Willow flew up to homes built higher in the trees.

He pushed open a door—more like a curtain—made of two dozen braided vines that hung from the roof, then stepped into the small hut. There was only one room, with no furniture or decor. When he looked up, he saw a drawstring hanging from the center of a hammock that was tied up on the roof. He pulled it, and the hammock dropped down, secured on each end from one corner of the room to the other. While lowered, it filled up most of the hut. Alverax pushed open the dangling vines in the doorway, looked to see if anyone was watching, then set down the Midnight Watcher and jumped up onto the hammock. Despite the stature of the wastelanders, the hammock was plenty large for his height. Then he realized that there was only one hammock in the hut, which meant it was probably a shared bed for multiple wastelanders.

After a few minutes, guilt poked its head out from beneath the fatigue, and Alverax jumped down from the hammock. He grabbed his sword and moved on to the next hut, which was more of a rectangular shape with a solid—though thin—wooden door. Inside, he found a much larger space, with two hammocks tied off on the roof, several wooden boxes, and a bead curtain dividing the room at its center. He stepped in, pushed aside the beads, and moved to the largest of the boxes on the far side of the hut. Inside, he found a mortar and pestle and two crude daggers tucked beneath a pile of skimpy wastelander clothing. He placed the weapons into his pack and continued on. The other boxes in the room were empty.

Alverax walked out of the hut and back into the center of the wastelander city where a large statue of an ataçan stood on a raised pedestal. Not far away, Laurel and Asher were standing at the edge of the city, scanning the surrounding jungle with suspicion in their eyes. Chrys dropped down from a rope bridge a few strides away and joined them.

As Alverax approached, he saw that the head of the statue had been knocked off, crudely, with jagged edges jutting from the neck where the stone had shattered. A few paces away, the head lay in pieces, half-submerged in a murky puddle. Alverax stepped over and bent down, running a hand along the stone tusks. It was far from high quality craftsmanship but, in a place like Kai'Melend, he was surprised to see any kind of art at all. Maybe his father was right about the wastelanders.

Suddenly, Asher and Laurel growled behind him, and Alverax turned quickly, hand reaching over his shoulder. Before he touched the hilt of the Midnight Watcher, the earth shook, and an ataçan four times the size of a man with a broken tusk and four thick arms landed with an explosion of water. The earth shook a second time as the beast released a guttural roar, throwing all four fists high overhead and slamming down toward Laurel.

THREADLIGHT BURNED IN CHRYS' chest, streaming from his heart through his arms and legs as he threw up a threadlight barrier. Xuçan's massive hands struck the invisible shield, creating a ripple of force that shook the ground, sending shivers through Chrys' bones. He glanced over to check on Laurel, but, instead of finding a scared girl clutching the chromawolf, he saw she was already back on her feet, knife in hand, the tips of her boots digging into the dirt.

Asher attacked first, dashing forward and biting at Xuçan's thick leg. Laurel joined him, running and jumping, stabbing out at the ataçan's thigh. But then Xuçan's fist swung in a wide arc, backhanding Laurel and sending her tumbling through the air. Asher howled as Xuçan reached down and ripped the attacker off his leg, blood falling from the wound, and tossed the chromawolf aside.

Chrys stood alone in front of the massive ataçan and looked at the muscle rippling from every part of Xuçan's body. The extra pair of broad arms. The half-broken tusk. The spikes running down from his neck to his back. There was no wonder the wastelanders worshiped him as much as they did Relek and Lylax. Chrys reached for his dagger, until he remembered that it was gone. He'd found a blowgun in one of the huts and stashed it in his pack, but he didn't have any darts. Weapon or not, if they fought, Chrys was certain he would lose.

He remembered their previous meeting, bowing down and presenting the et'hovon honeycrystals. He remembered their words. Their shared disdain. The respect.

Chrys stood a little taller, raising his voice, and hoped that the chief of the ataçan would remember too. "Xuçan!"

Thick nostrils flared as the ataçan froze, looking down at him, a low growl reverberating from his throat. Xuçan's voice rumbled in Chrys' mind. *I know you, human.*

Chrys spoke slowly, carefully. "I am he-who-does-not-cower."

Xuçan leaned forward, bringing his face level, hot steam pouring over Chrys' cheeks with each of the ataçan's breaths. *No, you are not.*

The hairs on Chrys' arms stood at attention as if paying respect to the great chief of the ataçan.

You are he-who-sacrifices-all, Xuçan continued.

Chrys felt a wave of relief, knowing that he remembered their conversation, too.

Xuçan pulled back and looked to the side where Iriel, Willow, and Roshaw stood beside Alverax, watching in fear. On the other side, Laurel groaned as she pushed herself back to her feet, stumbling over to Asher who lay defeated in a puddle, chest heaving up and down. Xuçan pointed at them with a thick finger. *Those have perverted the bond. They are not welcome here.*

For the first time, Chrys made the connection. Whatever bond Laurel and Asher had formed was the same bond the wastelanders made with the ataçan. He remembered Xuçan's words the first time they met, when he referred to Relek as "he-who-perverts-the-bond." But Relek's bond was different; he used lifelight to bind his soul to others. Unless it *was* the same.

Chrys looked up at Xuçan and remembered that the chief had never bonded with a wastelander, despite having lived for hundreds of years. "They have not perverted the bond," Chrys said, an idea forming. "The bond that Laurel and Asher share is pure, mutually accepted. They are not like Relek."

DO NOT SPEAK HIS NAME! Xuçan's voice thundered in Chrys' mind as the chief beat at his chest with clenched fists. *They-who-pervert-the-bond have taken everything.*

Chrys recalled the empty rocks beside the waterfall at the Endless Well, where the ataçan had once been. "They took the others. They took your family."

Xuçan let out a single, pained whimper. *I could not save them. The collars. They-who-pervert-the-bond have grown too strong.*

"We are on our way to stop them," Chrys said, putting on an air of confidence.

They cannot be stopped.

Chrys tipped his head. "There is always a way." An idea blossomed in his mind. "Come with us, Xuçan. We can stop them together."

A series of raspy grunts came from deep in Xuçan's chest. *I will not bond a human.*

"That's not—"

For three hundred years, I have waited for the true King of the Hive. He-who-perverts-the-bond is not he. You are not he. No human can be.

"I am not asking to bond with you," Chrys said, though now that the idea had been spoken, a part of him wondered if there was something there. "They have taken everything from you. There is nothing left here. Come with us, and we will find your family. Together, we can stop they-who-pervert-the-bond."

Xuçan huffed and glanced over to the others.

Laurel and Asher had recovered, though both had taken a bit of a beating, and the others stood together in a cluster with Roshaw in front, holding them back. Chrys noted that Iriel had already managed to equip her palmguards.

"It's not too late," Chrys said as he turned back to Xuçan. "You can still save them."

As the words left his mouth, he wasn't sure whether they were for Xuçan or for himself. The people of Alchea—his people—were in danger. They needed every advantage they could get if they were going to stop the Heralds.

Xuçan slammed his fists on the ground, then leaned in close one more time. *He-who-sacrifices-all,* his voice boomed. *It is a good name. This is the hour of sacrifice.* He pointed a finger out toward the cluster of people. *I would speak to that one, alone.*

Chrys raised a brow, unsure which of the four he was referring to. He thought it might be Roshaw, since he was the only other that Xuçan had met before, but decided that it was better to verify. "Which one?"

The young male.

Alverax? A darkness grew in the pit of Chrys' stomach. Why would the chief of the ataçan want to speak with Alverax? He was an Obsidian threadweaver, but so were Chrys, Willow, and Roshaw. Maybe it was the Midnight Watcher. Could Xuçan have some need for the obsidian blade?

Chrys took a few steps toward the others, raising his voice. "Alverax, Xuçan wants to speak with you."

"With me?" Alverax said, pointing a finger at his chest.

Roshaw stepped forward. "No way in hell I'm letting that happen. He'll tear him apart."

"I don't think he means him harm," Chrys said, understanding Roshaw's protective thoughts. "It should be safe as long as Alverax doesn't do anything stupid."

"It's okay," Alverax said, stepping out from behind his father and approaching Chrys. "Did he say what he wants to talk to me about?"

Chrys shook his head as he stepped toward Alverax. As they crossed paths, he leaned in close and lowered his voice. "I invited him to fight the Heralds with us. Don't say their names. He calls them *they-who-pervert-the-bond*. They took his family. He hasn't answered whether he will join us yet. Try to convince him. Having Xuçan on our side could change the tide."

Alverax looked up at the massive ataçan. "No promises."

Chrys took a deep breath. "Good luck."

ALVERAX TOOK a few more steps toward Xuçan and felt his heart racing in his chest. The massive ataçan reminded him of the corespawn monstrosities, just a little more...solid.

He had no idea what to expect. Why did the ataçan want to speak to him? Laurel seemed the more obvious choice, since her animal bond seemed similar to what Roshaw had taught him about the ataçan bond. Why not his father, who had lived in the Wastelands and understood the culture and language?

What was special about Alverax?

You are not like them, a voice thundered in his skull, bouncing off the walls of his mind with a deep bass.

Alverax looked up and saw a pair of deep-set ataçan

eyes, shrouded by the cliff of his brow, staring down at him. Somehow, when Roshaw had explained that Xuçan could speak telepathically, the voice he had imagined had seemed more primitive. But the voice he heard was clear and confident.

Xuçan leaned forward, knuckles flanking either side of Alverax as he examined his body. *What are you?*

The question startled him, both the voice and the words. "I'm, um, Alverax. My name is Alverax Blightwood."

No, the voice rumbled, sending a chill up Alverax's spine. ***What** are you?*

Alverax swallowed and glanced back at Chrys, remembering his words. It wasn't the first time someone had told him not to do anything stupid. "I'm not sure I understand. I'm an Obsidian threadweaver?"

Xuçan let out a huff of air, then gestured toward Chrys and the others. *You are like them, but not. You are different. Tell me, he-who-does-not-understand, **what** are you?*

Still, Alverax had no idea what Xuçan was talking about. How was he any different than the others? If his father wasn't there, it might have been because he was Felian. If not for Chrys, Willow, and his father, it might have been his Obsidian threadlight. He was the tallest of the group, but surely that's not what the chief of the ataçan was referring to.

"I'm sorry," he said, bowing his head. How could he answer a question he didn't understand? "I am no different than the others."

LIES! Xuçan roared, standing up on his feet and beating his chest. As he came back down, all four fists slammed into the dirt, sending tremors through the ground and ripples through the swamp water. *You are not like them! They are human. You are not!*

Alverax startled back, hands trembling. "I don't... I *am* human." He pointed a finger over his shoulder. "My father is right there."

Hmmm, the voice boomed in his mind. *Perhaps. But you are not **all** human.*

His head whipped around to look at his father. His eyes wide. His mouth hung open. This wasn't happening. It wasn't possible. His mother had... She was from a small farm outside of Alchea. She wasn't...what? Inhuman? Was that even possible? No. Xuçan was an animal. Intelligent, powerful, but still just an animal. And he was trying to get into Alverax's head.

Roshaw took a few steps toward him. "Is everything okay?"

"I...I think he's trying to mess with my head." Alverax glanced over his shoulder, hoping Xuçan hadn't heard that. "I don't know what the hell is going on. He says I'm not human. Wants to know what I am."

And there it was, the compression in Roshaw's chest, the flicker of fear in his eyes, the pursing of his lips. Even before he said a word, Alverax knew something was wrong.

"I...I tried to tell you," Roshaw whispered, tears welling up in his eyes. "I wanted to, but I didn't know how."

Alverax took a step toward him, a hint of anger boiling beneath his skin. "Tried to tell me what?"

He remembered the night around the fire in the desert chasms north of Cynosure. His father had wanted to tell him something. But neither of them was ready. Neither of them was strong enough to open whatever chest the truth had been stuffed inside. Now, Alverax knew. In a wave of understanding, the truth was clear as day. And yet, he still needed to hear his father say it.

Roshaw glanced back toward the others with a look of

shame in his eyes, then sighed as he turned back to Alverax. "Your mother was a wastelander."

The swamp spun around Alverax, a twisting vortex of overwhelming reality. His knees quivered. His chest tightened. And his stomach filled with rotten truth. A truth that hovered in the air like a noxious cloud.

He was half wastelander.

"I should have told you ten years ago," Roshaw said, stepping toward him. "But you were such a happy kid. I didn't want to take that away from you."

Alverax took a step back, not caring that he was moving toward the massive chief of the ataçan. The world seemed to cloud over, a dark film blurring his vision so all he had were the words ringing in his ears.

Roshaw continued. "Before you were born—when I worked for Jelium—he would send me out scouting, exploring the world outside of Cynosure. The deserts, the mountains, the chasms. Looking for trade routes or treasures. I loved it, being in the wilderness, seeing places no one else had seen. But then I met your mother.

"On the outskirts of a small wastelander village. She found me as interesting as I found her. We spent the better part of a year together in secret, learning, teaching each other our languages. I never planned...didn't even think it was possible for her to get pregnant. I wish it hadn't been. I didn't lie when I told you she died giving birth. I just didn't tell you why." Roshaw rubbed his hands through his hair, his eyes a mix of desperation and sorrow. "Please, say something."

What *could* he say?

He was half wastelander.

He wasn't human.

The anger boiling inside him crescendoed, flaring in his chest. What the hell did it matter anyway? He'd already thought he was half Felian, half Alchean. Did it make any difference that he wasn't? Did it change who he was? He was still the idiot who broke the coreseal, fell in love with an empress, killed a thousand corespawn, and watched everyone around him die. Who a man is at his core has nothing to do with those who came before him. It may change where you are and who you know, but the true crux of a man is defined by him alone.

And yet...

He turned back to Xuçan and lifted his chin. "My father is human. My mother was a wastelander."

Xuçan's lips snarled into an eerie semblance of a smile. His voice thundered in Alverax's mind. *I have long waited for the true King of the Hive, one who would gather the tribes. He-who-perverts-the-bond claims to be this, but herding is not the same as gathering. Perhaps I have been wrong all along. Perhaps I was not meant to find the King of the Hive. Perhaps I am meant to make him.*

The chief of the ataçan knuckle-walked, stopping with his lower fists placed on either side of Alverax. Their eyes met, unblinking, then Xuçan placed one of his enormous hands atop Alverax's head, wrapping thick fingers around his skull. But rather than fear, Alverax felt a warmth spark in his chest.

It grew, and as it grew, the world grew darker. The jungle faded away, trees reduced to shadow, vines turning to strips of blackness. The ground vanished. He and Xuçan alone existed, hovering like two gods in the dark of the sky beyond. The strength of a dozen men flooded through his body. His veins expanded. His muscles tightened. Darkness slid through Xuçan's veins, and shadows enveloped them both until Alverax found himself alone.

Abandoned in a sea of black.

As the darkness filled his vision, he heard Xuçan's final words.

We are one.

WHEN ALVERAX AWOKE, the world was shrouded in night, and a sky filled with twinkling stars stared down at him. Before he could stop himself, his eyes drifted toward the Moon's Little Sister. It seemed smaller with the sprawling mountains on the horizon beneath it.

He shifted his weight and found that he was curled up in some kind of padded, furry blanket. But when he lifted himself, he realized it was actually Xuçan's thick arm.

The bond.

There, deep inside his core, Alverax could feel it. He reached out with his mind, touching the source of the bond.

Good, Xuçan's voice sounded in his head. *You are awake.*

Alverax sat up and looked around. They were camped in a valley at the base of the mountain near a small stream just outside of the Wasteland swamps. Tall grass whistled in the wind, lit by the light of a full moon. Small embers still burned from a long-dead fire, and a small fish with a flat face lay on a pile of nearby rocks. His father and the others were asleep.

As he pushed himself to his feet, he realized how hungry he was. "How long was I out?"

Three days, Xuçan said. *The humans left you food in case you awoke. The fish was cooked by the others.*

Alverax walked over to the embers and put his hands

close to feel the small amount of warmth that remained. On the grass beside the rocks, there was a small wastelander knife that Alverax picked up and used to cut into the fish, removing the head and bones. As he bit into the flesh, he was careful to remove any thin bones that remained, then devoured every last bite, despite it being cold and in dire need of a bit of his grandfather's seasoning.

Once he was finished, he stepped back over to Xuçan. "So, we're bonded now?"

We are.

"And what exactly does that mean?"

The massive ataçan shifted his weight, using his lower arms to support himself. *Our lives are tied together. Your strength is my strength. My strength is yours. If one of us dies, the other dies with them.*

Alverax pursed his lips. "That sounds like a bad deal for you."

Yes, Xuçan said flatly. *There is a reason I have never taken the bond.*

"So why did you?" Alverax asked. "I mean, I know it's too late, but Chrys really would have been a better choice."

He is human.

Alverax wanted to clarify, but there was something about the way Xuçan said it that seemed final, so he left it alone. "So the reason you chose me is because I'm half-wastelander?"

Xuçan let out a series of animalistic grunts. *The wastelanders believe they are a hive, like the et'hovon. When we find them and show them our bond, they will name you the King of the Hive. They will obey you, and they will release my family.*

It all made sense now. Just like in Felia, where the generals used Alverax as nothing more than a figurehead, Xuçan wanted the same. A tool to win a war. The only problem was that being a figurehead always demanded more responsibilities than just standing there.

"How did they take the other ataçan?" Alverax asked. "If your family is anything like you, I can't imagine they went without a fight."

Mmm, Xuçan grunted. *It is true that my family refused to go with them. Those-who-pervert-the-bond used threadlight to bind and collars to control.*

"Collars?" Alverax repeated, wondering what kind of collar could control an ataçan. "They put collars on your family? If we can get them off, would your family be free?"

Yes, Xuçan said with a single nod.

Alverax cocked his head to the side and raised his brows. "That seems doable. We just have to find them." He looked over and saw that his father was stirring.

I can feel them, Xuçan said. *But they are still too far. I cannot speak with them.*

"I'm sorry." Alverax knew what it was like to lose family. "We're going to find them, and then we're going to free them. I promise." The great ataçan nodded as he looked to the west. "Hey, Xuçan, if the wastelanders name me King of the Hive, what does that mean to them?"

You will be their new god. Xuçan said it with such casualness that Alverax nearly missed the enormity of the statement.

"What about Relek and Lylax? Aren't they currently their gods?"

Yes, Xuçan said. *The Hive will be yours, and they will expect their new god to destroy the old gods.*

"That's all?" Alverax said.

It will not be easy.

"I know," Alverax said with a laugh. "I was being sarcastic."

We do not have sarcastic *in the Wastelands. This must come from your human side.*

"I guess so."

Alverax looked over and saw his father pushing himself up. The old man looked over and saw Alverax awake, and his eyes lit up.

Based on the rising light, Alverax guessed it would be morning soon. The others would wake up, and they would be off. But truth be told, he didn't want to talk to his father. Roshaw had a hundred chances to tell Alverax the truth, even after that night in the canyons. The only reason he admitted it now was because the issue had been forced. Did he think Alverax was too immature to handle the truth? Or maybe Roshaw was embarrassed. He should be, after nearly two decades of lies.

Lies. The word hit Alverax like a slap in the face. After the canyon, Iriel had told him what happened at Jelium's complex. Supposedly, Jelium had mentioned some kind of *prized possession* that Roshaw had brought from the Wastelands when he used to work for him. Something he'd withheld for himself. What if that was...Alverax?

Roshaw came and sat beside him. "You're awake."

"I'm awake," Alverax said halfheartedly.

"Look," Roshaw said, his shoulders heavy with sorrow. "I should have told you about your mother a long time ago. There's no excuse. I had plenty of chances. I just didn't know how. Or I was scared. I don't know. For a long time, I told myself that you weren't old enough, not strong enough, not ready, or that maybe you never needed to know. But the truth is that I was the one who wasn't strong enough. I didn't know how you would react. And we didn't want you to feel like an outsider."

"Wait," Alverax said, grasping at his father's words. "We? Grandfather knew?"

Roshaw nodded. "I had to tell him. I didn't know what to do with your back."

Alverax paused. "What about my back? You mean the scar?"

"It wasn't a scar," Roshaw said. "You inherited it from your mother, Alverax. They're wastelander gills."

A lead weight dropped in his chest.

"Of course, we didn't tell anyone else," Roshaw continued. "Your grandfather helped me sew it shut, and then we told everyone that a surgeon had to fix a birth defect. They believed, because why wouldn't they. No one knew anything about the wastelanders anyway. Only your grandfather and I knew the truth. But you were safe, and that's all that mattered."

Alverax felt like such an idiot. How had he gone his whole life without understanding such an important part of himself, of his own body? Something he'd always carried with him.

It took only a moment to see the truth of it. He'd always been able to hold his breath longer than anyone. And in the waterways below Felia, he'd taken a breath. In the moment, he'd brushed it aside, grateful only that he'd survived, but it was true. He had breathed underwater. It was also how he'd survived in the river, unconscious, with his face submerged.

He also understood why his father had made the choice he did. If anyone had discovered the truth, they would have studied Alverax for the rest of his life. Alabella would have studied him, experimented on him. What if—it was all coming together—the reason he'd been the only one to survive the ventricular mineral graft was because he was a wastelander?

"Say something?"

"I'm..." Alverax began. "I should be mad. I deserve to be mad. You lied to me my whole life and were too much of a coward to finally tell me when you had the chance." He paused and his eyes softened. "But I'm not. You may not have been a perfect father, but you made a huge sacrifice to protect me. And it even worked. So, yeah, I wish you'd told me a week ago. But I also think it was the right decision not to tell me when I was younger. I was a stupid kid. I would have told everyone. And if I didn't, I would have told Truffles, and he would have."

Roshaw's eyes were swollen, but he choked out a laugh. "Truffles was actually a big part of why I didn't tell you. Never liked him much."

Alverax raised his brows. "You know he slept with Jayla?"

"No!" Roshaw gasped. "While you were together?"

"Well, that's where it gets a bit complicated." Alverax laughed. "I was technically dead at the time. But, it doesn't matter. We're done with Cynosure, and we're done with secrets."

Roshaw's lip quivered. "Thank you. I know I don't deserve to be forgiven."

"Most people we forgive don't deserve it," Alverax said, remembering his grandfather's words. "But some people do."

Roshaw threw his arms around his son and fought back tears. "Thank you."

Alverax felt a warmth flow through him. It felt good to let go. As symbolic as it was, he could feel the burden lifted from his shoulders. It might not matter—they could be dead in a week—but at least he'd walk those days with a lighter load.

"Just so you know," Alverax said, still wrapped in his father's thick arms. "If you ever leave again, I will find you, and I will kill you."

Roshaw let go of their embrace and looked him dead in the eyes. "I am where you are, from now until I die."

WHEN THE SUN rose and the party awoke, Laurel walked over to greet Alverax. Now that he shared a bond with Xuçan, she felt an even closer connection to him, even if Asher wasn't interested in a friendship with the ataçan.

Laurel and Asher led the way after they all packed up their bags. There was something intoxicating about the fresh mountain air, brisk with hints of lavender riding the breeze. After so long in the Wasteland swamps, Laurel's nose thanked her for the change of venue. It also helped that there were no longer puddles of unknown depth at every turn, no vines hooking at their legs, and no strange creatures laughing at them from the canopy. The mountains felt free, open, and alive. The best part was that she could take off her boots. There was nothing better than the feel of wild grass between your toes.

They followed a valley between two peaks, hoping to avoid the ups and downs as long as they could. Eventually, after stopping at a shimmering lake with fresh deer tracks, they made their way up the mountain. They were getting hungry, and Laurel wanted to hunt, but Chrys convinced them all to stay together and continue on their path. So, they collected berries and kept an eye out for wildlife.

The truth was that Laurel and Asher could have made the entire trip much faster. They were twice as fast as the others—maybe more—and possessed higher endurance. But she knew that it was safer to keep the pack together.

Asher growled, and Laurel turned.

Movement, his voice whispered in her mind.

She crouched low and stalked forward, senses honed in on where the creature had hidden. There was a tall patch of wheat grass beside a small alder tree. She listened, focused. Asher stilled beside her, and they set their feet. Without a word, they leapt forward together just as a small rabbit darted out from behind the wheat grass. Asher bit down, but Laurel's hand was faster. She snatched the rabbit by the back of its neck and lifted it up into the air, celebrating with a howl.

Chrys and the others gave her odd looks but smiled happily when they saw what she'd caught. It wasn't much, not for seven mouths, but it was better than nothing. They took a short break, struck up a fire, and feasted. As soon as the rabbit was cooked, Chrys threw dirt on the embers and watched to make sure it didn't cause too much smoke. They were getting close to where the wastelanders were likely to be. And while the wastelanders weren't likely to be watching their flank, even a passive eye might spot plumes of smoke.

As they continued their hike, they reached the start of the lowest pass. Chrys and Willow claimed to recognize the area, but, more importantly, they found tracks. Not the nearly imperceptible tracks that some game might leave as they sauntered by. These were the tracks of an army. Trampled muddy patches. Stamped dirt from thousands of small feet. And on the outskirts, the unmistakable prints of ataçan.

"They're only a day ahead by the looks of it," Laurel said as Chrys and the others approached.

Chrys nodded, crouching down by the prints. "They do

look fresh. Might have passed by as recently as this morning. Laurel, can you and Asher scout ahead?"

"On it."

"Just make sure you're not seen," Chrys added. "And be careful. Better to not find them than to have them find us."

Laurel gave him a nod and crouched down beside Asher. "What do you think? Stay on the trail? Or skirt around the outside?"

Outside, his voice echoed in her mind. *Safer.*

"I agree."

With that, they took off at full speed up a small hill on the left side of the pass about fifty paces from the main path the army had taken. It was mostly grass with wildflowers blooming at sporadic intervals.

Laurel knew that the bond had increased her speed, but as they ran and she kept pace with Asher—even at his fastest—she impressed herself. She couldn't imagine going back to a world without the bond. In a way, she'd become just as dependent on her connection with Asher as she had been with threadlight, replacing one addiction for another. She paused at the thought. No, that wasn't right. Her addiction to threadlight was based on fulfilling her own needs. It was selfish and destructive. Her relationship with Asher was based on fulfilling their needs collectively.

Either way, she loved him. At times, he felt like the only family she had left, even if she knew that her brother was out there somewhere. Probably still in Felia with his nose in a book. Maybe he'd found a pretty girl to settle down with. Maybe he was happy. Or maybe the Heralds had already killed him.

She pushed harder, keeping her focus ahead as she scouted for any sign of the wastelander army. She and Asher both paused beside a sprawling pine tree, taking in its scent.

But there was another taste on the wind, something foul that stained the woody aroma like oil dripped on a painting. Laurel shook her head, trying to get the scent out of her nose, but it lingered in the air.

The wind stopped, and the scent faded. Laurel looked to Asher, and they both nodded. They knew that scent.

Continuing their path, they traveled even farther away from the army's muddy tracks and slowed their pace. The wind swirled from the other direction, and they hoped the wastelanders wouldn't smell their approach. Crouching, they stalked through the grass, keeping low and moving from tree to tree.

Finally as they summited a small hill, they saw the source of the scent. A dozen wastelanders knelt in a cluster just off the main road, skin blackened and hard. The *pintalla mox* had claimed them. As they stepped closer, Laurel's heart dropped. Two children knelt in the mix, their hands held together. They were no older than three. So young. So innocent. Statues, undeserving of such an end.

The fact that the plague still continued to claim lives, even this far from Kai'Melend, worried her. But none of the others had shown any sign of sickness yet. Maybe humans were immune? What about Alverax?

Laurel and Asher left the statue-like dead and continued on until they reached a hill overlooking a sprawling valley. At the base, there were thousands upon thousands of wastelanders, short and thin, armed with spears, knives, and blow darts, dwarfed by two dozen ataçan with golden collars around their necks. Laurel and Asher crawled forward, careful not to be seen.

What surprised her the most was seeing the wastelanders living so carelessly. They cooked and laughed, played and slept. Rather than an army, it looked like they'd simply relocated the entirety of their people. Though, with only a few dozen tents erected, it was clear this was not meant to be a permanent home.

Laurel had seen enough. She needed to warn the others. But just as she moved, Asher growled, and she turned around to see the two Heralds flying in from the west. They passed the mountain peak and descended into the center of the camp, where a swarm of wastelanders crowded around them, some bowing, others crossing their arms over their heads. Laurel didn't understand it all, but when the Heralds waved their arms, the swarm of wastelanders parted, and the two gods disappeared into one of the tents.

She committed it to memory and left to gather the others.

WATCHLORD THALLIN HAICHESS sat in a carriage, surrounded by books. But they were not just any books. They were private writings, handed down from watchlord to watchlord, preserving the truths that ought not be spoken aloud. Some entries inspired, and others enlightened, words of holy men whose thoughts had shaped the lives of Felians for centuries.

He looked down at his notes where he'd written down a series of quotes that resonated with him.

> Faith is to swing the blade before the enemy
>   moves.
> — Watchlord Eleander

> It is easy to trust the captain when the sea is
>   still.
> — Watchlord Chedai II

> Faith is a new world that cannot be reached
>   by the ship of reason.
> — Watchlord Delathor

The truth that most resounded within him was that these men, whose names had been etched into the very fabric of Felia, were simply that...men. Their journals took Thallin behind the veil of poise to reveal lives filled with trials and victories, inspiration and doubt. On the one hand, it gave him strength knowing that they were able to perform their duties despite their struggles. On the other hand, he now knew that the very foundation of the Heraldic Ancestry was built on cracked stone.

In that moment, seated in a carriage on his way to war, Thallin's mind latched onto a short passage, ironically preached by a man he had known personally and respected above any other. A man who had passed away defending Felia from the corespawn.

The Heralds may never return, but this does not mean we cease to preach their coming. Men crave faith. They hunger for purpose and thirst for meaning. If we do not offer a path, they will search for one themselves. But those who wander are likely to find nothing, and there lies darkness. It is our duty to keep our people in the light. To offer a proven path of purpose. I find solace in knowing that we inspire goodness, whether or not our gods ever return. And if our words inspire goodness, are they not good in themselves?

—*Watchlord Osinan*

If only Osinan could have lived a few more days, he would have seen the Heralds for himself. Thallin wondered what the man would have thought. Would he have welcomed them with open arms and a ready blade? Or would he have followed Alverax in abandoning the gods? If he had lived, perhaps Thallin would not have had to kill so many in their name.

Perhaps the Heralds would have made him kill Osinan, too.

The carriage came to a slow and steady stop, the sound of footfall quieting beside them. When Thallin opened the door and exited, he saw the borders of Alchea, cottages and small homes, farmland and fields. Decades of peace cast in the firepit, ready to burn.

Two men strode up beside Thallin, hands clasped behind them as they, too, stared out over what would soon become a battlefield. Generals Nevik and Hish knew Thallin well. They had fought beside him against the corespawn, and they knew his interminable faith in the Heralds. So, despite their initial protests, they were resigned to leading the people of Felia to battle against the people of Alchea.

"The Alcheans are unprepared," General Hish said. "It would be wise to press an advance as soon as possible."

General Nevik nodded. "We could sweep through the city by tomorrow eve. Those who do not surrender would be forced to hide behind the walls of Endin Keep."

"No," Thallin said without offering them a look. "The Heralds have been clear in their command. We pitch our tents and wait for their return. I want a defensive perimeter established for the unlikely event of an Alchean offensive."

"You understand," General Hish said, "that if we establish camp now, we are giving Alchea a huge advantage. Our losses will multiply with every hour we delay. Many of our people will die if their army has a chance to properly assemble."

Finally, Thallin turned to the older man. "Do you not trust the Heralds? Do you think your wisdom greater than the gods? If they told us to bury our weapons, I would issue the command and drop my blade, knowing that the gods will provide a way to victory."

General Nevik bowed his head. "Of course, Watchlord. We will prepare for their return."

As the two generals departed, Thallin thought back to Osinan's words. In the coming days, the men and women of Felia would look upon the death and suffering of war, and they would question the gods. They would look to their Watchlord for answers, for purpose and meaning, and he would look to the Heralds. But Thallin knew he would find no answers there. The gods were opaque in their reasoning.

The only thing Thallin had left was his faith, and he hoped it would be enough.

CHRYS and the others followed Laurel to the hilltop overlooking the wastelander camp with a setting sun and cool mountain air to guide them. Clouds wandered through the sky like lost children, the light of the waning moon barely visible through the shadowed veil. Ten thousand wastelanders sat in huddled groups without fires while others patrolled the edges of the site. They were hidden away in a valley between two mountains, and Chrys was fairly certain that Alchea was just over the next ridge. Which made him wonder...what happened to the Alchean patrols?

Since the war, Malachus had always kept a watch on the mountains, despite the fact that the wastelanders had never taken the offensive. Still, the Great Lord had been prudent. Which meant that either Malachus had stopped watching the mountains for threats, or the patrols had been killed. Chrys hoped for the former.

"That's a lot of wastelanders," Roshaw said, lying on his stomach beside Chrys, gazing down over the sprawling army. "What do we do now?"

Chrys motioned for them all to retreat down the ridge a ways so that they could stand without being seen. "We're lucky," he said, addressing the entire group. "They haven't attacked yet, which means there's still time for us to make a difference. What ideas do we have?"

"Aren't you supposed to be the idea guy?" Alverax asked.

"I have some thoughts," Chrys said. "But I want to hear your ideas first."

Laurel turned to Alverax. "I don't think he has any ideas."

"Definitely not," Alverax said with a straight face.

"Not the time." Chrys gave them both a serious look. "People's lives are at stake. If you don't have any ideas, then listen. Let the rest of us figure out how the hell we're going to stop an army from slaughtering our people. We don't know how much time we have before they mobilize. We don't know if they have scouts patrolling out this way. We could be walking into another trap for all we know. If you'd ever been in a real war, you wouldn't be making jokes."

"Chrys," Iriel said softly. "Take it easy. They're kids."

"No, they're not." Chrys tried to breathe, but anger raged within him. "We're all the world has left. No one knows what we know. No one has the power or experience we do. The choices we make in the coming days will determine whether we live or die. Whether nations live or die. The time for growing up has passed."

Chrys looked to each of them individually, a general challenging his soldiers. Alverax and Laurel both stared at the ground. Roshaw and Willow gave each other a side-long glance. But Iriel met Chrys' gaze. A few seconds passed, then ten, then twenty. Even with Aydin in her arms, she was the only one of them who looked ready for war, which sent a shiver of pride through his chest, followed by a pang of guilt.

Maybe she was right, and he was being too harsh. None of them were soldiers. But if ever there was a time to understand the seriousness of the situation, the time was now. So as long as they looked to him as a leader, he would do what had to be done.

"Now," Chrys said. His anger had settled, but he kept the severity in his tone. "Does anyone have ideas on what we can do to stop that army?"

Willow spoke first. "I don't know how to stop the army, but we should also figure out a way to warn Malachus. One of us who can fly could go."

"Absolutely," Chrys said. "In the case that we can't stop the army, the next best thing is to have the Alcheans ready for an attack on their flank."

Roshaw gestured to the ridge. "No army is going to be ready to fight gods and ataçan."

Chrys nodded. "Which is why our first priority is to figure out how to stop the army in the first place."

"We can start by freeing the ataçan," Alverax said, lifting his chastised gaze from the grass. "Without them in the battle, Alchea could probably handle the wastelanders."

Laurel nodded. "Maybe Xuçan could convince the ataçan to fight for us."

Alverax shook his head. "The ataçan won't fight the wastelanders. This isn't their war. And Xuçan says that the wastelanders are just as much captives to Relek and Lylax as the ataçan. So, unless they're provoked, the ataçan will leave the wastelanders alone."

"Unless they're provoked?" Laurel said with her brows raised.

"We're not going to provoke them," Chrys said quickly. "Besides, Xuçan is right. The wastelanders are just as much captives as the ataçan."

"What about the collars?" Willow said. "If the Heralds are controlling the ataçan with some kind of collar, we're going to have to remove them if we want to free the ataçan. Maybe we can use the collars against the Heralds somehow. If they can control the ataçan, maybe they can control a god. Does Xuçan know anything about how they work?"

Alverax shook his head. "They lured him away, bound him with Amber, then collared his family. He watched it happen, and there was nothing he could do."

"That's terrible," Willow said. "We'll figure out how to rescue them. First, we need to get down there and examine the collars ourselves."

Chrys had the distinct feeling that his mother's interest was going to get her killed, and enough people he cared about had already died. As long as he was standing, he wasn't going to let it happen to another. "I'll go tonight while they're sleeping."

"No offense, Chrys," Laurel said. "But when you walk, I can hear it from the other side of the ridge. Asher and I are the scouts. We'll go check it out."

Roshaw took a step forward. "If either of you get caught, they'll kill you on the spot. I can speak their language. It makes sense for me to go in case something happens."

Iriel stepped forward and handed the baby to Chrys. "Can you take him for a minute? My stomach doesn't feel well." Chrys took his son as Iriel walked away from the group, holding her abdomen and waving away his concern.

Alverax raised a hand. "As much as I'd love to help, I don't think this sounds like the right job for Xuçan and me."

"It was my idea," Willow said, eyes bearing down into Chrys. "I'll go. And before you fight me on it, I'm not some old woman you need to protect, Chrys. I have three theoliths. If something happens, I can fly myself out of there."

Chrys clenched his teeth. "It has nothing to do with that.

I'm sure that any of you could handle yourselves if you got caught, but we can't get caught. The only advantage we have right now is that they don't know we're here. It's not that we can't get caught. It's that if they even see us, our advantage is lost."

"Then it's settled," Laurel said, raising her hands up. "Asher and I are the least likely to be seen. We'll go."

"I'm going," Chrys said with finality. "One person is less likely to be seen than two. And if it makes you feel better, I'll use a little Sapphire to *drift* as I walk so that I don't make as much noise. I want the rest of you thinking of ideas for how we can stop the army. And try to get some rest while you can."

The others, resigned to his decision, wandered away, back down toward the spot they'd chosen to rest. Chrys handed Aydin over to Willow before she followed the others. He looked in the direction that Iriel had walked. She was beyond his view, the night having grown darker as the clouds over the mountain thickened. Chrys walked back to the ridge, crouched low, and crawled the final stretch. He could hardly see the wastelander camp now. Even the tents had become nothing but blurry splotches on a black canvas.

It was going to be a long night. He would need to wait until well after midnight before making his approach. On the way down, he would need to use as little threadlight as possible. He didn't want his veins glowing, and he didn't want to waste any in case he needed to get out fast. At least until he was a stone's throw from the camp, he would walk. His eyes drifted toward the path he might take, and his heart stopped.

A figure moved stealthily off the beaten path. From his vantage point, he could see clearly. He knew that figure. He knew those shoulders. He knew that gait. There was no question in his mind. He'd been fooled.

Dammit, Iriel.

ADRENALINE COURSED through Iriel's veins as she crept her way through overgrown grass. She knew Chrys well enough to know that he would never let someone else go investigate, so as soon as they'd started to argue, she made her decision. Chrys was a good man, protective, a little too much at times, and he only felt useful when he was sacrificing his own safety for others. But Iriel had always been more suited to stealth work than he was, and she needed this.

While some of her feelings of inadequacy had faded, others had slipped their grimy claws into her skin. For weeks, she'd been the woman in the back, holding the child while the others made the plans. While the others did the *important* work. She was tired of being left behind. She was tired of not helping. And she was tired of hearing Willow talk about the gift of motherhood. It was as though she'd gained one title and lost all others. A mother, and nothing more.

Not tonight.

Tonight, she would prove that Iriel Valerian still had a fire in her chest and threadlight in her veins.

Chrys would be furious, but she didn't care. When she explained how she was feeling and why she did what she did, he would forgive her. He was nothing if not consistent —that's what she loved about him—but she also knew that if she explained beforehand, he still would not have let her go.

As she descended the hill, her foot slipped on a loose

rock, creating a small landslide. She reached out, embracing the Emerald in her veins, and *pulled* on each of the falling rocks. One by one, each of the falling pebbles shot through the air and into her hand. By the end, the landslide had stopped, and she had a dozen tiny stones in her palm. She bent down and placed the rocks in a flat place before continuing on.

After several minutes of watchful eyes and careful steps, she reached the bottom of the hill and hid behind a lone pine tree. The captive ataçan were now only a few hundred feet away. With a break in the clouds, she got a better view and counted at least two dozen of the large creatures resting in a pile of limbs. Even at a distance, she noted the difference in size between these and their chief. Xuçan was nearly twice their size.

Iriel looked back up the hill and saw a small head poking out from the vantage point. That meant that Chrys knew, and he hadn't followed her. That was good. He didn't have a reputation for subtlety. As mad as he likely was, he also knew that Iriel was better suited for the job.

A cluster of thick clouds drifted in front of the moon, casting a fog of darkness over the campsite. Iriel took the opportunity and moved. From tree to tree, she weaved her way closer, crouching low behind shrubs and grass until she made her way close to the ataçan.

She hid in a patch of long grass as a pair of wastelanders walked past. She kept silent and still, watching out of the corner of her eye. They came to a stop behind a thick pine tree, and the woman began removing a piece of clothing. Iriel turned away, blushing. At least she knew that they wouldn't be noticing her movements any time soon.

Finally, she reached the cluster of trees closest to the sleeping ataçan and crouched down low behind them.

Rather than approaching, she waited patiently. Only a few minutes passed before she saw the wastelander couple return from their late-night escapade.

She'd expected a longer wait...

Iriel looked out over the campsite and was taken aback by how human it all felt. For so long, she'd heard the wastelanders were cannibals, the savages of the east. She'd heard that all they did was eat raw flesh and fight all day. But these people were...people. They may have pointed ear lobes and gills on their backs, but they were still people. She felt guilty for judging Roshaw when the truth of Alverax's origin had come forward. She'd wondered how any man could sleep with a wastelander. Now she saw that, in reality, they were not so different.

As the last vestiges of commotion settled, Iriel moved to take her first step out of cover toward the sleeping ataçan, but just as she did, she saw movement at the entrance to one of the tents in the center of the camp. Out stepped three figures, short and stocky though they were shrouded in the dark of night. An ataçan seemed to appear out of nowhere from the other side of the tent, and one of the wastelanders approached it. Behind them, two taller figures pushed aside the flap and exited the tent. It took only a glance for Iriel to recognize the Heralds' silhouettes. Whatever they had been doing in the tent seemed to be over. Relek's jacket swept back and Lylax's dress trailed behind as the two siblings took to the sky, heading west over the final peak.

The three wastelanders returned to the tent, and the ataçan took a seat outside.

With the Heralds gone, Iriel decided that there would be no better opportunity to approach the collared ataçan. At least if something went wrong, she'd only have an army of wastelanders to deal with.

She stepped out from behind her cover toward the sleeping giants. From what Xuçan had told them, not all ataçan could speak telepathically with humans, but many could. As she approached, watching their massive chests rise and fall with each restful breath, Iriel hoped that—if one of them awoke—it would be one that could hear her.

The closest ataçan had its back to her. Gray hair covered blue-tinted skin, with bright yellow spikes jutting out along its spine. All of the ataçan slept in a pile atop each other, nestled in tightly, limbs entangled in a patchwork of muscle. As Iriel drew closer, she noticed that all of them were sleeping with their hands wrapped around their tusks. It was a small gesture—likely to protect the others—that Iriel found surprisingly compassionate. Xuçan was right; this was a family, and they were captives.

She took the last steps toward the closest ataçan and caught sight of a silver collar wrapped around its neck with gemstones embedded in the metal above the spine. She leaned in, squinting as she tried to get a better look.

Four.

Four gemstones, each a different color.

Iriel cursed as she noticed wet blood beneath the collar. She looked at the others. Every collar was the same. Four gemstones. Blood dripping beneath the silver. What the hell was going on? Xuçan claimed that the Heralds used the collars to control the ataçan because they were not weak-willed like the wastelanders. Aboard the *Pale Urchin*, as they sailed from Felia to Cynosure, Chrys had told her all about his experiences in the Wastelands. He'd told her about the humans that Relek had controlled in the mountains. He'd told her about the lifelight bond that Relek and Lylax had made with the wastelanders. He'd told her about theoliths and what happens when all four are combined.

Stones.

She looked back to the collar.

Green. Blue. Yellow. Black.

Those weren't gemstones; they were theoliths.

She tried to remember everything that Chrys had told her, but all she knew for certain was that, when all four were combined, something changed, which was why Chrys, Willow, and Roshaw still couldn't access lifelight. Which meant if the Heralds were somehow using the power of lifelight to control the ataçan, the collar needed all four theoliths to work. If she could remove one of them, the ataçan would be free.

Slowly, she reached for the collar, leaning over the sleeping ataçan's yellow spikes, extending a single finger toward the silver. A gap in the clouds sent a flicker of moonlight over the tangle of bodies. A nearby ataçan stirred, adjusting its shoulders amidst the mass of gray limbs. Iriel didn't move. She didn't breathe. Her hand hovered in the air like an Alirian statue. A few moments passed, and the clouds blanketed the moon once again.

She breathed and touched the silver, heart pumping as her skin met the binding metal. It was cold, but otherwise felt like any ring she'd ever worn. Still, she knew that the theoliths embedded along its surface were somehow working together to control the ataçan. With her hand still extended, she moved it farther up the collar, reaching for the first theolith, an Emerald like the threadlight running through her own veins. She imagined a similar shard embedded in her heart, feeding the blood that pumped throughout her body.

When her finger brushed against the theolith, she expected a jolt of energy, static, something to denote the power emanating from the stone. But nothing happened. It felt like any other gemstone. Part of her was beginning to wonder if they were theoliths at all, or if there was something else powering the magic of the collars. She stuck a fingernail under the Emerald and tried to lift it out, but it wouldn't budge. She tried again, this time using her thumb. Her arm quivered as she put her weight into it, but it refused to move.

Suddenly, the ataçan rolled over.

She leapt back, barely swooping beneath the giant's thick arm as it flopped down right where she'd been standing. She stood still, frozen, feet spread wide, ready to run. The ataçan's head rolled toward her, eyes closed as it once again wrapped its hands back over its tusks.

Iriel let out a breath and looked at the front of the collar. There was a circular lock embedded in the center. It looked oddly similar to threadlocks she'd seen used in Alchea. If she could get to it, there might be a chance she could open it.

But then the ataçan's eyes opened.

It stared at her, unblinking, dark shadows cast over its pupils from deep set brows.

Iriel didn't move.

It pushed itself up, nostrils flared as it leaned toward her, sniffing, then glancing over at the sleeping wastelanders.

All it would take was one grunt from the ataçan to wake the others. A single call to rouse the entire wastelander army. As she stood frozen, regretting every decision she'd made in the past hour, she lifted a finger to her mouth and whispered the only thing she thought might help. "Xuçan sent me."

The ataçan's thick brows scrunched at the center as it examined her, then a deep voice, female yet gravelly, echoed in her mind. *Xuçan. Alive?*

Iriel nodded enthusiastically, keeping her voice low. "Xuçan is with us beyond the hill. We are here to rescue you."

Cannot, the ataçan said. *Bound. Evil gods.*

"I know," Iriel replied. "I think I can get the collar off, if you'll let me try."

The ataçan eyed Iriel warily, then glanced back over its shoulder at the other sleeping ataçan. Its hand reached up and tugged at the collar, grimacing in pain. *How?*

The single word gave Iriel hope. "There is a piece on the front. Here." She gestured to her own neck, below the jaw. "If I can unlock it, the collar should come off."

Its voice resounded in her mind as it lifted its chin, exposing the silver collar. *Try.*

Iriel stepped forward, slowly, fear swirling through her like a poison. She was lucky that the ataçan had not attacked her, but that luck would not remain forever. If she somehow hurt the ataçan, or if she wasn't able to release the threadlock, the beast was strong enough to kill her in the blink of an eye. She needed to be careful.

As she approached the collar, she smiled. For once, she'd been right. The locking mechanism was a popular— but expensive—style used by many aristocrats with Emerald threadweavers in their employ. A threadlock had no key but was instead unlocked by *pulling* on a small steel disc at the back of the tumbler. Because the disc was the same width as the cylinder, there was no way to engage it without Emerald threadlight, making the lock inaccessible to the majority of the population. Wealthy Alcheans loved them, because all of the threadweavers worked for them. They were often paired with a more traditional lock for added protection.

But not here. The wastelanders had no threadweavers.

No one but Relek and Lylax had the ability to release the lock…until now.

She looked around, checking to make sure no waste-landers were awake and watching, then pulled her collar up and her cuffs down before opening herself to threadlight. Her veins came alive, swirling with veridian power. She leaned forward, trying to find a good angle to see into the lock, but it was too dark.

"Can you turn your neck toward the moon?" she asked. "I need more light."

The ataçan craned its neck to the side cautiously.

Iriel tried again, narrowing her eyes to find the hidden disc. As she stared, the clouds parted for just a fraction of a second, but it was enough to light the cylinder. Iriel *pulled* and felt the weight of the disc shift within the tumbler. The collar clicked, and the section beneath the threadlock split apart. She expected some kind of burst of energy, like when the Convergence had been destroyed, but there was no sign that releasing the lock had done anything.

The ataçan reached back and pulled the collar from around its neck, sneering as it came off. That was when Iriel saw the truth of the design. Four thin needles were built into the collar, embedded on the inside beneath each of the theoliths. Blood dripped from the ends of each as the ataçan brought the collar down and set it on the ground in front of them, staring at it in silence.

"Are you okay?" Iriel asked. "Do you feel different?"

When the ataçan looked up at her, its eyes were filled with tears. Iriel's chest tightened at the sight. She felt a swelling of pride knowing that she'd helped at least one of them, but she also knew that one was not enough. There were many more, and unless she freed them all and helped them get far away, who knew what the Heralds would do.

Please, the ataçan's voice begged. *Help others.*

"We have to be quiet," Iriel said, miming with a finger to her lips. "Can you wake them without making sound?"

A moment later, the entire troupe of ataçan stirred, gray limbs untangling from gray limbs, thick bodies rising from the mass of hair and hide. Iriel panicked as each of them shifted their dark eyes to her. They moved more gracefully than she would have expected, despite their size. After a short minute, every last one of the sleeping ataçan was awake and looking to Iriel expectantly, and none of the sleeping wastelanders had stirred.

The unbound ataçan nodded to her. *Family. Ready.*

Iriel took a breath and set to work.

One by one, she approached the ataçan, each of which gave her a dubious stare as she worked on the collar's threadlock. But each time, as she completed her work, their expressions shifted to awe and gratitude.

After a dozen had been freed, she heard a shout coming from the camp and whipped her head about to search out the source. A figure stood amidst a throng of sleeping bodies, pointing at Iriel and shouting. The other wastelanders awoke in waves, rising like skeletons in a graveyard, moaning and gesturing wildly one to another.

Stones, Iriel cursed to herself. *We're out of time.*

She moved onto the next ataçan, cursing the darkness for making it so difficult to see the disc in the cylinder. When a shadow fluttered overhead, she startled back, lifting a hand overhead to protect herself. Instead of an attacker, her husband landed beside her, veins glowing with multi-colored threadlight.

"What are you doing here?" she asked, adrenaline coursing through her veins.

"The wastelanders are awake," Chrys said quickly. "Come on. I'll fly us out!"

Iriel took a step back. "Not yet. We need to finish releasing the ataçan." She turned to the first of the freed. "This is my husband. He can help take off the collars. When everyone is free, head over that ridge, and we'll meet up with Xuçan."

The ataçan nodded and grouped up with the others who had been freed.

"Chrys, come on!"

He clenched his jaw but complied.

Together, they worked through the remainder of the threadlocks while the freed ataçan warded off the waking wastelanders. When the last collar fell, Chrys ran to Iriel. She gave one final nod to the first of the freed before Chrys took off into the air. Sapphire and Obsidian shot them into the sky, and Emerald guided their path. When she looked down, the troupe of ataçan were knuckle-running around the edge of the camp while a hoard of wastelanders chased after them.

Iriel's heart dropped when she realized that the entire army was following them toward the ridge...and toward her friends.

LAUREL DREAMED OF THE FAIRENWILD. Skyflies fluttering in the canopy. Roses sprouting between rocks alongside a gentle brook. The sound of the waters drifting through the darkness. Her feet wandered of their own accord, forward through familiar paths where shadows danced and bulbous photospores drifted in the staggered wind. She felt drawn to something, a beckoning light in the distance, a silent call.

After her first step, she realized that something was missing. She reached down and felt her pockets, trying to remember what it was. An emptiness. A loneliness. She should not be alone. Never alone. Where was…?

Asher.

She followed the beckoning light, hoping that her companion would be there. She'd made a promise that they would never part, and she would keep that promise no matter the consequence.

As she walked, she felt a tremor in the ground, and she crouched, swiveling on the balls of her feet in search of a source. But there was none; there was only darkness. Still the tremors grew in strength, the ground rattling like an old man's hands.

An odd haze fell over her vision.

She felt something on her shoulder. But when she

jerked around to look, there was nothing. The ground shook with greater fervor, and the world blurred even more.

Two invisible hands grabbed her shoulders and shook.

Laurel startled awake, fighting away the dreamland, the home she'd once loved, and breathed in the brisk air of reality. Asher and Willow, with Aydin in her arms, hovered over her, the fear in their eyes laced with a sense of relief. But it wasn't all a dream. Tremors still shook the ground.

She pushed herself to her feet, angry that she'd fallen asleep in the first place. "What's happening?"

Asher nodded to the ridge. *We must move. The army is coming.*

"Gale take me."

"Iriel must have failed," Willow said with a quiver in her lips. "Chrys will find her. We need to go, now."

Alverax and Roshaw stood beside Xuçan, walking toward the ridge. Could they not feel the tremors? Did they not know that an army was coming this way? Laurel had a thousand questions.

"Alverax!" Laurel shouted. "We need to get out of here!"

He looked over to her, a sense of resolution in his eyes. As he walked, something about him looked...taller. His shoulders were thrown back. His chin held high. Even standing beside Xuçan, it seemed like he'd grown in stature. Laurel wondered if it was real, like the green streaks in her hair. Was he changing? Either way, Alverax said nothing as he walked toward the top of the ridge.

"Willow!" Laurel shouted, looking toward the older woman who was already on the move with Aydin in her arms. Whatever Alverax was doing, she couldn't leave him behind. She couldn't leave her pack. "I'm going back!"

Without waiting for a response, she took off toward the others, Asher staying near her side. With her new speed, it only took a few moments for them both to bound across the mountainside and take their place at the top of the ridge beside Alverax, Roshaw, and Xuçan. When she looked out over the ridge and saw knuckle-running ataçan followed by a swarm of wastelanders, with Chrys and Iriel flying in the air above them, her loyalty and bravery withered beneath a mountain of doubt.

"Alverax," she said, hesitantly. "Please tell me there's a plan."

He took a quick glance at Xuçan before turning to her. "There is."

Laurel gave him a look. "A good plan?"

"Could be," he said, his gaze drifting toward the ground.

"And that is?"

Alverax lifted his chin and straightened his jacket. "Xuçan is going to tell them to stop."

Laurel looked over at the massive ataçan, each of its four fists pressing deep into the grassy ridge. The earth shook harder as the army grew closer. The shouts of wastelanders echoed through the canyon as they waved spears and hatchets in the air. Laurel did not like the plan, but they could still escape if something went wrong. Laurel and Asher were fast enough to run, and Roshaw could fly off with Alverax.

Staring at the oncoming army, Laurel decided that if she was going to die, she would do it fighting for those she loved.

XUÇAN'S WORDS echoed in Alverax's mind. It seemed that, once again, he found himself in a position where he had to convince strangers that he was worth following. But this time, where his role as Watchlord had been mostly symbolic, the wastelanders were just as likely to worship him as a god as they were to send him to an early grave. Fortunately, he had Xuçan, who had already communicated with his family. If nothing else, they would stand beside Alverax as they spoke to the wastelanders.

When the ataçan reached the top of the ridge, they took their place beside Xuçan, eyeing Alverax with curiosity. The chief lifted himself up high, reaching all four arms into the air, and let out a monstrous roar into the night. A spear hurled through the air toward him, and his lower arm snapped down, grabbing it out of the air and crushing it in his massive palm. Again, he leaned forward, lifting his arms high overhead, making himself appear even larger, and bellowed out a roar.

The army hesitated, wastelander men and women slamming to a halt, and the few bonded ataçan in their midst stopped alongside them. The closest of the army fell back, filled with fear. They had worshiped Xuçan for as long as any of them had lived. He was as much a god to them as Relek and Lylax, immortal, a protector. But where the Heralds had bonded the wastelanders, Xuçan had distanced himself. Another spear flung through the air, and Xuçan swatted it aside like a fruit fly. The rest of the army packed in close to their brothers and sisters, staring up at the chief, unsure what to do or how to proceed.

Xuçan brought his arms down, nodded to his family, then turned to Alverax and Roshaw. The next few minutes would decide their fate, and Alverax wasn't sure he was ready for it. His palms started to sweat, and his chest tightened. He was a fraud. The wastelanders would see through his façade as quickly as he presented it.

As all of his doubts surfaced, Laurel's hand slipped

under his own, followed by Asher's wet nose rubbing against the back of his arm. He looked to his friends, and they gave him a nod. It was a simple thing—a slight squeeze of his palm—but their support scattered the shadows from his mind.

This *was* going to work.

Xuçan had never shared a bond with anyone in over three-hundred years.

Alverax was the bridge between worlds.

He stepped forward and spoke. "My name is Alverax Blightwood."

Roshaw stood tall beside him, translating his words and speaking them out to the wastelander army in their native tongue. Knowing what he knew now about his mother, it made so much sense how and why his father knew their language so well.

"You do not know me, but I know you. You are the warriors of Kai'Melend. You are the faithful. You are the An'tara!" Alverax waited, letting his father emphasize the words. An agitated curiosity spread throughout the army. "You are also captives, enslaved by those-who-pervert-the-bond. By those who call themselves the Great Anchors. By one who named himself King of the Hive."

When Roshaw finished repeating the words, a buzz grew amidst the wastelanders as they relayed the words to the rest of the army. Alverax watched some of the warriors clutch their weapons tighter. Others spat on the ground, while some stood quietly, looking back and forth between the strangers on the ridge. An ataçan pushed its way through the crowd, a wastelander seated on its back.

"For hundreds of years, Xuçan has waited for the true King of the Hive, the An'tara who would finally bond the chief of the ataçan and lead the people to redemption. Relek tried to bond Xuçan, but the chief of the ataçan refused. I am here to tell you that Relek is not your King." Alverax looked out over the army and nodded. "Xuçan would like to speak to you now."

The chief took a step forward, causing a wave of movement amongst the army as they stepped back. What came next surprised even Alverax. Xuçan opened his mouth and spoke aloud in the wastelander tongue. Through his bond, Alverax could still understand the ataçan's words. "I am Xuçan, and I have found the true King of the Hive." He stopped and beat at his chest with all four arms, letting out a series of grunts before settling and gesturing with a single finger toward Alverax. "This is the true King of the Hive. He is human *and* he is An'tara. The bond is formed."

The freed ataçan broke out into a roar of approval, beating their chests and slamming fists into the ground. The wastelanders stared in disbelief.

As the ataçan settled, Alverax lifted his hands into the air. "I am the true King of the Hive, chosen by Xuçan himself. The son of two worlds."

He stood tall in front of the wastelander army as he unbuttoned his shirt. Slowly, he turned around and dropped the shirt to the ground, exposing the elixir-healed gills along his spine.

Gasps and murmurs spread throughout the army. With his back turned, he couldn't see them, but he trusted Roshaw and Xuçan to keep him safe if a wastelander decided to hurl another spear. When he finally turned back around, the freed ataçan were bowing and wastelanders were beginning to follow suit, arms held high, crossed, with the tips of their fingers touching. More and more followed the others, bowing down before the true King of the Hive.

Suddenly, his corethread *broke*, and he began to hover in

the air, on display for all to see. When he turned to look, his father looked just as surprised to see that Xuçan had Obsidian running through his veins.

As he looked out of the prostrated wastelanders, he felt a swelling of relief.

They had accepted him.

It had worked.

He was the true King of the Hive.

And now the Heralds were going to pay.

CHRYS AND IRIEL flew past the others, who stood defiantly at the top of the ridge. By the time they set foot on the ground, Chrys' chest was burning hot, each surge of threadlight flowing in like a drop of magma through his veins. He let go of Iriel and stabilized himself with his hands on his knees while he took in deep breaths.

The Heralds could fly across the entire continent, but Chrys could barely fly up a mountain without feeling on the verge of death. Alchaeus had told them that the power of each additional theolith was exponential, but he'd also said that the Heralds grew stronger with each wastelander they bonded. The implications of such power were frightening.

When he finally caught his breath, he looked to his wife, who was standing with her back to him, staring back at the ridge where the others awaited the oncoming army. Xuçan let out a monstrous roar, arms high overhead.

All of the anger that had been building up inside of Chrys as he'd watched Iriel descend the ridge came pouring out, like a tea kettle reaching its boiling point. "What the hell were you thinking?"

She spun around without an ounce of regret in her eyes. "The plan was to rescue the ataçan. So I rescued the ataçan."

"You sneaking down there *alone* was not the plan."

"No," she agreed. "*You* sneaking down there alone was

the plan. I bet you told the others that you should be the one to go down and investigate."

Chrys clenched his jaw.

She continued. "And they probably didn't agree with you—Laurel and Asher are the clear choice—but you made the decision anyway. Because you can't stand putting someone else in danger, even if they are more capable than you for the job."

His heartbeat quickened. His breaths shortened. Where was all of this animosity coming from? She was mad at him for trying to keep everyone safe? How was that fair?

"Chrys," she said, looking him straight in the eyes. "You don't get to save the world on your own. All of us are in this together, and we're all going to play a part. Ever since Aydin was born, you coddle me as much as you do him. I'm not just a carriage to cart our kid around."

The words landed like a punch to his gut.

He wanted to be mad—the anger seething in his chest demanded it—but she was right, and it nearly broke him. Before she'd become pregnant, Iriel had been one of the most capable Emerald threadweavers in Alchea. Had he forgotten that? In a way, he *had* expected her to cart their child all across the continent, all while he did what he felt had to be done to protect everyone. If the roles had been reversed, how would he have felt? Backgrounded. Standing by as everyone else used their new threadlight abilities and bonds.

Worthless. That's how he would have felt.

That's how his wife had been feeling, and he'd been too stupid to notice.

"Iriel," he said softly. "You're right. I haven't been treating you as a partner, and you deserve better than that. I'm sorry."

Iriel stared at him for a moment before letting out a breath and shaking her head. "You know what the worst part is? I knew you'd forgive me. I knew you'd be mad, and I knew that after I explained myself you'd apologize. After everything you've been through, how are you still such a good man?"

Chrys let out an exasperated sigh. "Being good is all we have left."

"Some people might say that being good is what got us here."

"Some people would be wrong," Chrys replied. "Us trying to be good is the only reason the Heralds haven't won yet."

Iriel's smile faded, and she looked back toward Xuçan and the others. "Speaking of, wasn't there an army coming over that ridge?"

Chrys furrowed his brow and watched as Alverax took his shirt off at the top of the ridge. "What the hell?"

"This night just keeps getting weirder."

A moment later, Roshaw turned, saw Chrys and Iriel, and waved for them to join the others. Chrys spun around, taking another look for his mother in the wild surroundings, but saw only an empty mountainside and the cluster of statue-like wastelanders in the distance. Wherever Willow was hiding, he was certain she would be safe. If nothing else, his mother knew how to protect a child.

Chrys and Iriel walked side-by-side until they reached the top of the ridge where the others stood. Alverax was now hovering in the air with a broken corethread. Whatever they'd done had worked. On the other side of the ridge, the entire wastelander army was bowing to Alverax, making the same odd sign they'd made when Relek had first appeared in Chrys' body and claimed to be the King of the Hive.

A thick wastelander with an unnaturally deep-set brow spoke with Roshaw as an ataçan loomed over them.

The moment was so surreal that it felt like a dream. Chrys was so used to their plans failing that this one victory seemed impossible. With the wastelanders on their side, they might actually be able to beat the Heralds.

But then reality struck. The ataçan had been controlled by the collars, but the wastelanders were still bound to Relek and Lylax. Even if they pledged themselves to Alverax, when the Heralds returned, they could control the waste- landers like Relek had controlled the Alchean soldiers in the mountains. He wondered at the extent of their power. Could they control all of the wastelanders at once? If the ease with which they flew was any indicator, Chrys felt certain that they could. The war was just beginning. And when the Heralds returned, they would bring with them the wrath of centuries.

Unless they didn't know.

Chrys and Iriel stepped up beside Roshaw as the waste- lander and his ataçan returned to the army. "Who was that?"

Roshaw ran a hand across his brow. "Rixi. He leads the wastelanders while the Heralds are away. He's bound to that ataçan. Says the wastelanders are willing to defy the false gods but only if there is a plan."

"Tell them to return to the valley and go back to sleep," Chrys said. "They are still bound to the Heralds, which means they can be controlled against their will. If Relek and Lylax return and see this, we'll be dead before a ten count."

Roshaw raised a brow. "Even if they go back down the valley and pretend like nothing happened, won't the Heralds know?"

"I don't think so," Chrys said. "They're not omniscient. When Relek was in my head, he only knew my active thoughts. They could command the wastelanders to tell them what happened. But if they have no reason to ask, they won't be any wiser."

"Even with the wastelanders on our side," Iriel added, "we still don't have a way to kill the Heralds."

"We still have the one option," Laurel said indifferently.

"No," Roshaw said quickly. "Look out there. We are not slaughtering those people."

Laurel shook her head. "We don't have to kill them. Alverax is the King of the Hive. You're the one who told us so enthusiastically about the et'hovon and how the wastelanders see themselves the same. That they are willing to sacrifice themselves for the good of the many."

"Is that a joke?" Roshaw's eyes were bulging. "You can't seriously think that is the same."

"You have a better option?" Laurel asked.

"Enough," Chrys said. "Even if we find a way to get rid of the bonds, the Heralds still have their threadlight. They are still stronger than us. They still have the corespawn. Hell, they could still create new bonds."

"Unless they couldn't," Iriel said. All eyes turned to her. She opened her mouth to continue, then paused, shifting her eyes from Chrys to the others and back to Chrys. "I know we're getting short on ideas, but hear me out. What if we destroy the Provenance? Cut off the source of their power."

Chrys felt his mind reel at the thought. What if? What if they did destroy the Provenance? Could they even destroy it? Would every threadweaver in the world lose their threadlight?

"No way," Roshaw blurted out. "Our threadlight is our best weapon against the Heralds."

"It would hurt them more than us," Iriel said.

Roshaw pursed his lips. "That still hurts us."

"It's worth considering," Chrys said, giving his wife a nod.

"Would it destroy their bond with the wastelanders?" Roshaw asked.

"It should," Iriel said. "We can't know for certain, but I don't see why not."

Roshaw waved his hands in the air. "You realize it wouldn't just be the Heralds, and it wouldn't just be us. Destroying the Provenance would destroy threadlight for every single person in the world. There would be no such thing as a threadweaver anymore. Are we really okay with that?"

Chrys tilted his head. "If the options are death to all mankind or death to threadlight, I think we would go with the latter."

"It's crazy," Iriel said. "But I agree."

Laurel let out a small laugh and mumbled something inaudible to herself.

They all turned to her.

"Alabella always said that the great unfairness of the world was that some people were born with threadlight while others weren't. She wanted to give everyone the chance to be a threadweaver. She wanted 'equality.' Looks like she might get what she wanted, just not in the way she planned."

There was a moment of silence as the idea sank in. Were they really considering the end of threadweaving? It seemed the kind of decision the Lightfather should make, not a group of runaways with everything to lose.

Chrys looked over the sprawling army below the ridge. Their leader, Rixi, spoke to them with his ataçan standing beside him. One by one, then in waves, the wastelanders rose to their feet, a cacophony of emotions rippling through their numbers. Awe. Fear. Curiosity. Doubt. Faith. They were trapped between evil gods and their long-awaited King of the Hive. Chrys couldn't imagine how confusing it must all be for them.

When Alverax finally drifted back to the ground, he turned around to see the group, still without a shirt and the smoky glow of Obsidian threadlight in his veins. He looked to his father first. "Looks like we have ourselves an army!" he said excitedly. When he noticed the thoughtful looks on everyone's faces, he raised a brow. "Did I miss something?"

"We'll explain later," Chrys said. "First things first, we need to figure out what to do with the army. The Heralds could return at any moment, and unless they see a bunch of wastelanders asleep, we'll all be dead before the morning comes."

Roshaw grit his teeth. "I just don't think it will work. Why don't we take them away? Hide them back in the Wastelands or something?"

"As nice as that would be," Iriel said, "where are we going to hide ten thousand wastelanders where the Heralds won't find them? They can fly, and it's not like a marching army won't leave a trail."

"Maybe we can find a cave," Roshaw said, throwing up his hands. "I don't know. There has to be a way we can get these people to safety."

Chrys felt sorry for Roshaw. He knew how much these people mattered to him. How much he cared for them, the last remnant of Alverax's mother. "Roshaw, the truth is that as long as they are bonded to the Heralds, there is nothing we can do."

"He's right," Iriel added. "We should send them all back down and tell them to do everything Relek and Lylax ask. Be perfect subjects. Fight the Alcheans if they have to. When the time is right, we'll have Alverax give them a sign and they can turn on the Heralds."

"I don't like it," Roshaw said. "And I don't think Rixi will like it. But I don't have a better idea."

"Great," Chrys said. "Because you're the only one who can tell them."

Roshaw let out a breathy laugh. "Right."

"And Alverax," Chrys added. "Put a shirt on. You look ridiculous."

Alverax looked down and laughed. "Right."

As soon as he said the word, he and Roshaw looked at each other, but it was Iriel who spoke first. "Like father, like son."

Laurel looked around the group. "What about us? Where are we all going to hide? Xuçan isn't exactly subtle."

Chrys nodded. "No, you're right. Roshaw's comment earlier reminded me. There is a cave not far from here. We can head there and use it for cover."

"Sounds like we have ourselves a plan," Iriel said triumphantly.

Laurel placed a hand on Asher's head and nodded. "The start of one at least."

"Almost," Chrys said, turning around and looking back over the wild mountainside, eyes drifting over the statue-like dead, marked by the *pintalla mox*. "We still need to find my mother."

WILLOW KEPT RUNNING until she could no longer feel the quaking of the army's approach. Images of the others standing atop the ridge, defiant, flashed like bolts of lightning through her mind. Laurel and Asher. Alverax. Roshaw. Even with Xuçan at their side, there was no way they would survive the assault of an entire army. But what worried her most was Chrys and Iriel. They had both been down there, amidst the sleeping wastelanders and collared ataçan. They could be dead already.

She threw herself under a rocky ledge, ripping at nearby branches and shrubs to build a makeshift wall, a poor attempt at obscuring their location. The child in her arms had not stopped crying since she'd fled the ridge. All of the jostling and stumbling had woken him to a world of darkness and hunger, without a mother to succor him. Willow pulled Aydin in close and tucked his swaddle back around to tighten the wrapping and hold down his hands.

With a soft voice and her grandson bouncing in her arms, she sang an old Zeda lullaby that she'd once sung to her own son so many years before.

When the lights fade out, and the faithful doubt,
You should know there's calm in the shadow.
In the darkest days, when the faithless prays,

Close your eyes, find calm in the shadow.

Willow closed her eyes, sending up a plea to the Father of All. She prayed that Aydin would stop crying. She prayed that her son would be okay, that her daughter-in-law would live to care for her child. She prayed that Roshaw would survive to live out his days with *his* son. He was a good man —so was his son. After all he had been through, Roshaw deserved to retire in peace. She prayed that Laurel and Asher would be safe. And then she prayed for herself, a heart-wrenching plea to a god that felt too distant in a world of living legends. She prayed for courage. For comfort. But above all, she prayed for the strength to accept whatever outcome fell upon her family. Even if that outcome left her alone in the world.

No, she thought. *There is still a chance.*

She wiped away tears and looked down at Aydin, who had fallen back asleep sometime during her prayer. It seemed such a small victory compared to the events around them, but even small victories lend a credence of hope.

As she sat in the dark of night, hiding from the waste-lander army, she realized that this was not the first time she had run away with a child. The thought took her not to the Fairenwild or Zedalum, or even to her quiet arrival in Alchea. Instead, it took her to the Convergence. It took her into the warbling mass of threadlight that had expanded to fill the space of the vast cavern. And that, in turn, had taken her to the past.

Willow opened her eyes, standing in a familiar room, in a familiar house on the northeast edge of Zedalum. She saw a new mother sleeping beside the rickety old bassinet her father had made. A newborn child, two days old, who slept as peacefully as Aydin did now, wrapped in the pale blue blanket Rosemary had gifted. The new mother was Willow.

She had been so young, so beautiful, even though she'd hardly slept since the child had been born. Willow remembered feeling like little Chrys would never wake up if she weren't there watching over him, but she also remembered being too tired to keep her eyes open any longer. And the peach-colored gown that her husband had loved so much looked otherworldly beneath the light of the autumn moon.

She remembered being that woman, asleep in that chair, then waking to see an older version of herself standing above her, a specter sent from the Father of All. Only now she knew the truth: she was no specter at all. She was flesh and blood, sent to the past by a Convergence that had folded the thread of time. She pictured Alchaeus' string, one end brought to the other.

The young Willow awoke, and the elder Willow told her that she needed to take Chrys away from Zedalum. A storm was coming, and the Fairenwild would not be safe.

The memory faded, and Willow returned to her hovel in the Everstone Mountains. She feared that the son she had sacrificed so much to protect might be gone, that the mother of the child she held in her arms might be dead, that the man she...

Breath fled from her lungs, and her heart swelled. Could she? No. Thirty years of pushing away every man who'd come to her, fearing the consequences should they discover the Zeda tattoo on her back. But that was over, and she couldn't deny the feelings any longer. The truth of her past was out in the world. She was free to love however and whomever she wanted.

Despite a dozen reasons why she shouldn't, her heart had chosen that bear of a man who'd traveled across the world with her. His thick arms and coarse hair. His foul mouth and the way he looked at his son, so protective, an echo of herself. A weight seemed to lift from her chest as she admitted to herself, once and for all, that Willow Valerian was falling for Roshaw Blightwood.

The slightest smile touched her lips.

But it might not matter. The last she saw him, he was standing atop a ridge with a wastelander army rushing toward him. And even if he did survive that and if she did find them again, what then? The world was still on the verge of collapse.

One step at a time.

Settling in against the rocks, she tucked in a handful of wheatgrass where the stones were sharpest and watched as the clouds drifted through the night sky. There was still no sign of the wastelander army, and she wondered if she had waited long enough to leave her shelter. She needed to know what had happened to Chrys and the others. But if she was the only one left, then she had to stay alive. She needed to get to Alchea to warn Malachus and Eleandra.

She pushed herself up with one arm, careful to keep her movements smooth so as not to wake the child, and peeked up and over the rocky ledge.

Nothing.

No wastelander warriors, dead or alive.

No Heralds lurking in the sky.

No family.

Willow continued to watch, refusing to accept that her son would not walk around the bend at any moment. There was still a chance.

Time passed, and no one came. A slight breeze fluttered

through the grass and brushed through the leaves of the trees, an earthy scent lingering in the air. Still, she watched, threadlight trickling through her veins to offset the chill in the air. She couldn't wait forever; Aydin would need food soon.

She sat back on the dirt and rock, the remnants of her once strong hope streaming away. This couldn't be the end. Not after all they'd been through. She should have stayed with them. If they were going to die, they should die together. But she knew that wasn't true. Aydin needed to grow up. He needed to live a full life. If Willow's sacrifice was being the one who lived so that Aydin might too, then, Lightfather-be-damned, she would not die on that mountain that day.

She stood, lifted her chin, and stepped out from her rocky hiding place.

CHRYS STOPPED at the mouth of the cave as the others stepped inside. Ghosts flashed in his mind, figures standing in a line, terrified as they watched their comrade slit his own throat. Chaos. Sorrow.

The memory faded, but the feelings remained. What had at the time seemed such inconsequential violence from the Apogee, Chrys now understood as the beginning. The introduction to the Heralds' grim rule and disregard for human life.

And yet, worse than the memories was finding specks of dried blood crusted to the cave wall.

He breathed, uncertain whether the smell of death was real or his mind clinging to the past, then stepped in after the others. A few paces into the cave, they found a collection of abandoned equipment, pickaxes, dead torches, a small cart with a broken wheel, and hemp sacks. Chrys was certain that none of that had been there before. He wondered if the equipment belonged to Alchea—likely under the continued direction of Henna—or if it belonged to the Heralds.

The others stood around the remains of an old fire pit while Roshaw worked it to life, chipping away at a piece of flint. They were all there except for Xuçan, who was too large to fit in the cave. His bond with Alverax allowed them to communicate, even at a short distance, and he'd already sent word that he'd found a gully not far away where he could hide.

When a shadow flickered over the mouth of the cave, Chrys expected to see Xuçan's looming silhouette. Instead, Laurel and Asher had returned.

With Willow and Aydin.

Iriel sprinted forward, grabbing Aydin from Willow's arms, pulling him in tight and kissing his head. Chrys joined her as they looked down at their son. He thought he'd convinced himself that Aydin was safe. But seeing them now, he realized that the doubt had never quite left.

He turned to his mother and wrapped her in a tight embrace. "I'm so glad you're safe."

"I thought I'd lost you," Willow replied.

Beside them, Iriel unwrapped Aydin and checked every inch of his body before finally taking a breath. She then excused herself and stepped away to give the child an overdue feeding.

Beside the fire, Roshaw and Alverax stood watching, hands stretched toward the flames, smiling at their friends' reunion. And there it was. At first, Chrys hadn't seen the resemblance. But looking at them now, smiles as wide as a river...they were two gems cut from the same stone.

"Come," Roshaw said to Willow, gesturing toward the fire. "I saved a space for you."

Chrys turned and saw Willow fighting back a smile.

They migrated toward the warmth, Laurel and Asher arriving first. The big chromawolf stretched out on the rocks a few feet from the fire. Alverax took a seat on the hard stone next to Laurel and ran a hand down Asher's thick, green fur, laughing over some quiet joke shared between them. On the other side of the fire, Roshaw unpacked a blanket and wrapped it around Willow's shoulders, rubbing his hands in front of the flickering flames.

Silently, Chrys watched them with a sense of wonder stirring in his chest. These people weren't just traveling companions anymore—they weren't soldiers or smiths or butchers with a job to perform that Chrys would soon forget. These people were family.

When Iriel finally returned with a sleeping Aydin bundled in her arms, she stopped beside Chrys. "What did I miss?"

They all turned to her with a blank look.

"You've been discussing the plan, right?" Iriel added.

Nothing.

"We're hiding in a cave," she said flatly. "There's an army outside. Gods who want to kill us. Impending war. And we're not discussing a plan?"

Roshaw shifted in his boots. "I wanted to hear about what happened to Willow. She wanted to hear about the army."

Alverax pointed to Laurel. "She was telling me more about her bond with Asher."

Iriel turned to Chrys. "And you were just watching?"

"Actually, yes."

Iriel let out a clipped laugh and shook her head. "The world deserves better heroes than us."

"Who said we were heroes?" Roshaw said. "I see us more as the world's toilet stick, and the Heralds are just diamond crusted shit stains."

Alverax burst out in laughter. His lively response ushered in an outpouring of giggles from the others. Even Iriel joined in, unable to fight the wit and charm of the older man.

"You are quite the oddity," Willow said, shaking her head at Roshaw.

"I am what I am," he replied with a grin.

Chrys cleared his throat, and everyone turned to him. "Shit stains or not, Iriel is right. We need to figure out a plan. I had an idea, but it might not work."

"What is it?" Willow said excitedly.

"The caves." Chrys gestured down the dark corridor. "It's possible these caves connect with the others. If they do and we have a path to Alchaeus' cave, then we should seriously consider destroying the Provenance."

"Wait," Willow said, shaking her head. "Did I miss something?"

"Ah," Roshaw groaned. "We all discussed it earlier."

Alverax pointed to Iriel. "It was her idea."

Willow slowly looked around the room, settling on Chrys, but it was clear that her mind was mostly within itself. "Destroy the Provenance. Destroy threadlight. Cut off their power. They can't fly. They can't fight. The bonds would be broken. They would be mortal..."

"That's the hope," Iriel said proudly.

Willow's eyes grew wider. "It's brilliant. And terrifying. But if it works, brilliant."

Laurel jumped to her feet. "Asher and I can go check the cave. We're faster and see better in the dark. I'll find some photospores, and we'll be back in no time."

"I can go with you," Alverax said. "My bond with Xuçan is already making me faster. I'm keen to try it out."

"Hold on," Chrys said. He was surprised by the speed with which everyone agreed, despite the glaring reality that such an action would create. A world without threadlight. Were they so willing to offer such a sacrifice? Was *he* willing to offer such a sacrifice? A threadweaver was what Chrys had always been. Since he was a child, he'd always had the power and respect that came with his Sapphire eyes. And now, he had the strength of three theoliths, power beyond even Great Lord Malachus. "Are we certain?"

Their faces grew a little more somber as they remembered the truth. Iriel looked to Aydin. Alverax and Roshaw looked at their own veins. Laurel looked to Asher.

Willow gave a slow nod. "I lived without threadweaving for thirty years. It was difficult at first—I won't lie to you. But as time went by, the sky was still as blue. The sun was still as warm. And the flowers still smelled as lovely as ever. As long as the people of Arasin have each other, alive, healthy, and free of the bonds the Heralds have placed on the world, it will be enough. Take people away from magic, and the power is lost. Take magic away from people, and their power remains. The world will move on."

"The world will move on," Roshaw repeated.

"*We* will move on," Iriel added.

Alverax looked down at the black veins visible on the top of his hands. "In my experience, threadlight brings nothing but pain. We'll all be better off without it."

Laurel nodded but remained quiet.

"Okay," Chrys said. "Then let's hope this cave leads to the tunnels."

A raucous noise rolled up the hill and into the mouth of the cave, thousands of voices cheering in unison. Chrys and the others turned, looking out where the morning sunlight had begun to illuminate the Everstone Mountains.

"Laurel and Alverax," Chrys said. "Check the tunnel. We're running out of time."

The Zeda girl and Asher took off without question, Alverax following closely behind as they darted into the depths of the cave. Chrys ran toward the entrance, his breath ragged with worry for the people of Alchea. As he exited the cave, he could see the valley in the distance, filled with wastelanders standing, staring up at two figures that hovered in the air.

His heart pounded in his chest. This was the moment of truth. If the wastelanders turned on them, letting their fear of Relek and Lylax outweigh their belief in the King of the Hive—their trust in Xuçan—then this could be their last day. If they hid in the caves, the Heralds might create another coreseal. But it was more likely that the Heralds would put a definitive end to the mosquitos that had been nipping at their skin for too long.

As Iriel and the others joined Chrys, the Heralds spun in the air, turning toward the cave. Iriel was the first to hit the ground, but Chrys and the others followed suit with urgency. Together, they lay on the dew-glazed grass, the sun rising behind them, blood pumping through their veins as they waited to see what the Heralds would do. Iriel's hand slid over Chrys' and squeezed.

Another rowdy cheer exploded from the wastelander army. The earth shook as they stomped on the ground, slamming their spears into the dirt. The ataçan—with collars back in place— stood beside them like mythic sentries.

Eventually, the noise died, and the Heralds flew back toward the west. The army immediately began taking down the tents and packing up their belongings. It seemed the wastelanders had held to their promise. Whatever the King of the Hive was to them, it held more weight than their fear.

"Damn," Roshaw said, rolling over onto his back and running his hands over his face. "It actually worked."

"Alverax must have made quite the speech," Willow added.

"You should have seen it," Roshaw said. "Xuçan *broke* Al's corethread, and he hovered in front of them like a god."

"Xuçan broke his corethread?" Willow asked.

"The bond goes both ways." Roshaw said, as if it were obvious. "And you should have seen when Xuçan named him King of the Hive. The entire army bowed down."

Willow smiled. "You have quite the kid."

Chrys pushed himself to his feet and looked back down the cave. Wherever Laurel and Alverax were, they needed to work fast.

With the wastelanders on the move, they were running out of time.

ALVERAX RAN through the dark tunnel, holding a cluster of photospores in one hand. With each step, he could feel Xuçan's strength flowing through his body, muscles expanding against his skin, Obsidian veins oozing with power. Even still, Laurel and Asher were faster. Every so often, they would glance over their shoulder to make sure he was keeping up. He knew he shouldn't be annoyed by it, but he was.

They passed a narrow section of the tunnel with rocks piled up to the ceiling where the tunnel must have been blocked at one time. From the look of it, the recent quakes from the coreseal and the destruction of the Convergence must have opened it. Carefully, they climbed up the pile, rubble falling down the mountain of rocks as they slipped through a narrow opening at the top.

As they moved farther into the cave, he thought about the Provenance, and what life would be like without threadlight. No Masked Guard with their glowing eyes. No Jelium fixing necrolyte races. No acrobats performing wondrous feats at the docks of Felia. The inequalities brought about by threadweaver birthright would be gone. But Alverax wasn't a fool either. He knew people well enough to know that if one reason for lording over others disappeared, another would wriggle its way in. Still, he believed that—maybe, eventually—if enough of those reasons were removed, the world would become just a little better each time.

Suddenly, Laurel and Asher stopped at an intersection.

"Gale take me," Laurel muttered.

"What?" Alverax said, running up behind them. He looked down each corridor, seeing nothing but darkness and the flickering light of distant photospores. "What is it? Which way do we go?"

Laurel silently stepped over to the wall. "Look." She gestured toward a white stain along the stone. "One of Alchaeus' markings."

"That means if we follow the marked tunnel"—Alverax felt a buzz of excitement flow through him—"it will lead all the way back to the Provenance!"

"That's what we came for," Laurel said. "We should go tell Chrys."

Without another word, they backtracked down the tunnel the way they'd come. Alverax felt alive, running even faster on the return than he had on the way down. It surprised him how even his endurance had improved so quickly. Laurel and Asher trailed close behind him, letting him take the lead. He knew it was stupid, but being in front gave him a sense of purpose that he hadn't felt when following. It was silly—he knew that—but still he appreciated that they'd allowed him that small win.

When they reached the narrow opening in the tunnel, Alverax scrambled up and over the pile of fallen rock, squeezing his way through the crevice. He slid down on both feet, smiling as he leapt off the bottom. He took a few steps forward, preparing to continue the run, but paused when he realized he couldn't hear the others.

He turned and saw Laurel standing in the narrow opening, looking down from a mountain of rocks with a boulder in her arms that seemed too large for her frame, Asher's bond fueling her strength.

"What are you doing?" Alverax called out to her.

Her teeth were clenched, and there was a strange look in her eyes. A dark feeling grew in the pit of Alverax's stomach.

"Why are you holding that?"

Her lip quivered. "I have to do this."

"What?" Alverax furrowed his brow and shook his head. "What are you talking about?"

"I'm doing this for the pack," she said flatly.

Before he could speak, Laurel slammed the boulder against the wall so hard that the tunnel shook. Rocks and dust rained down from the ceiling, filling parts of the narrow gap in the tunnel. A thin crack split along the ceiling just above the opening.

"Laurel!" Alverax screamed.

As her name left his mouth, understanding settled over him. When Iriel had touched the Provenance, she'd been blown back by some unseen force. If their plan was to destroy it, whoever volunteered was going to die in the process. Laurel was offering herself.

But if anyone deserved to die, it should be him. Alverax wasn't even supposed to be alive. Time and time again, he'd evaded death's sting. But for what? So he could destroy the coreseal, unleashing the corespawn? So he could release the Heralds from their prison? So he could watch the woman he loved die? If justice demanded recompense from anyone, it was Alverax.

"Laurel!" he shouted again. "This is not your choice to make!"

She stopped after slamming the boulder against the wall once more, the narrow opening already half-filled with rubble so that he could only see her torso. The cracked veins in the ceiling grew larger. "It has to be me."

"You have family!" he said. "A brother in Felia, right? He's ill, isn't he? Laurel, don't do this!"

The words gave her pause, but still she slammed the boulder into the wall once more. "You have your father and your grandfather. Chrys has his family. All I have is Asher, and we made a promise to each other. When the Provenance is destroyed, it will destroy our bond. We would rather die together, so that you all can live your lives with the people you love."

"We can find another way!" Alverax said.

"Just...do me one favor," she added. "When the light goes out, make sure the Heralds pay for what they've done."

"Laurel, stop! There has to be another—"

With one final thud, Laurel heaved the boulder up, throwing it with Asher-enhanced strength toward the ceiling. It struck with such force that the entire cave vibrated. Cracks along the ceiling splintered, rippling down the tunnel. Rubble rained down like hail, and the ceiling above the narrow opening collapsed, causing a landslide of dust and stone to fill the gap.

Alverax threw himself back, narrowly avoiding a massive chunk of stone that fell from the ceiling where he'd been standing.

When the dust settled, she was gone.

Alverax stood, alone, tears in his eyes, angry, heartbroken at the thought of losing Laurel, the one who had sat by his side for weeks while he coped with the death of Jisenna and the return of his father. And yet, the longer he stared, the more he understood. Her words echoed in his mind.

I'm going to do my part to make it better if it's the last thing I do.

He walked over to the mountain of stone and slammed his boot into it, Xuçan's bond sending a wave of force through the rocks. "I'm your family, too!" he screamed, tears flooding down his cheeks, unsure if she could even hear through the wall of rubble. Again, he kicked, as if some kid from Cynosure was strong enough to fight the earth itself. "I'm your family, too!"

She was selfish and impulsive. And if she failed, the whole world would burn. With the tunnel closed, they wouldn't get another chance. On top of that, she didn't even give the others a chance to say goodbye. Willow had treated her like a daughter. Chrys like a little sister. Roshaw and Iriel. They deserved a chance to say goodbye. But, now...she was gone.

Alverax turned around and let himself fall, his back sliding against the cold stone as he closed his eyes. He was just so tired. Of running. Of fighting. Most of all, he was tired of losing everyone he cared about.

"We were all your family," he whispered to himself.

Chrys glanced back down the cave. They needed to leave...now.

Since the Heralds had left, the entire wastelander army had packed up and begun its ascent over the final peak. Soon, they would drop into the southeastern countryside of Alchea. Chrys was beginning to worry that the only plan they'd come up with wasn't going to work. If the tunnels didn't connect, the cave outside of Kai'Melend was too far, even for Laurel and Asher. And even if the caves did connect, it still might be too far.

From deep in the tunnel, footsteps echoed, growing louder and louder as a lone figure came into view. Alverax, clothes covered in a new layer of dust, slowed to a walk as soon as he saw the others. He held his head high, but the droop in his shoulders was enough for Chrys to recognize that something was wrong.

"Alverax," Chrys said, running over to the younger man. "What happened? Where's Laurel?"

"They stayed behind," Alverax said quietly.

By then, the others had joined. Willow looked over his shoulder. "What do you mean? Stayed behind? Where?"

"She's gone!" Alverax shouted, the façade cracking. His lips quivered, and his breathing grew more frantic.

"Father of All," Willow whispered as she turned away. "The tunnels connect."

Iriel's eyes grew wide. "She's going to destroy the Provenance."

"She'll die," Roshaw added.

Alverax closed his eyes. "She and Asher didn't want to live without their bond. She said to make sure the Heralds pay when the light goes out."

Emotions swirled in Chrys, a stinging in his chest, a pain in his heart that belonged to that young girl he'd met in the Bloodthief warehouse. The girl who'd saved his family from the chromawolves and from Jurius' soldiers. No matter what he may claim, a man's heart never truly grows accustomed to loss. He may believe it has, but it's not the loss that has grown dull. It is the depth of his love, driven by fear, which has grown shallow. Chrys loved Laurel. He loved who she'd become, her strength and gallant resolve. Her loss would weigh on his heart forever.

But...she had given them a gift. The world was in danger, and her sacrifice would lend them their best chance at stopping the Heralds. He would not let her loss be for naught. They needed to be ready when the Provenance was destroyed.

They needed to leave...now.

"The army is on the move," Chrys said softly. "If we want to make sure the world never forgets the sacrifice that Laurel made today, we need to get to Endin Keep before the wastelanders get over the mountain."

Iriel looked toward the cave. "Shouldn't we—I don't know—*try* to stop her?"

"Her course is set," Willow said, nodding her head thoughtfully. "Besides, Laurel and Asher are faster than any of us. If they're on their way to the Provenance, there's nothing we can do to stop them."

"She's right," Chrys said. "We need to be ready when the Provenance is destroyed and threadlight disappears."

"*If* it disappears," Willow added.

"If?" Roshaw repeated. "I thought we were certain here."

Willow's eyes seemed tired. "As certain as we can be. Unfortunately, when you do something that has never been done, there can be no certainty. For all we know, that wasn't the Provenance, and destroying it will do nothing. There is a real chance that our plan will fail, and we'll be left with no way to stop the Heralds. Still, even if all we have is uncertainty, we have to try. If there is any chance that we can make a difference, that's all we can do."

Chrys smiled as he looked to his mother. She'd given him a similar speech a dozen times when he was younger. Whenever a task was too difficult, or a project too overwhelming in scope, Willow would look him in the eyes and tell him that "Valerians never give up." When the world needed them most, that same spirit burned within her. Now, Chrys could see the same flames burning in the eyes of each of the others. No matter the outcome, they were all in this together.

"Damn," Roshaw said softly, looking at Willow with admiration. "You sure you don't have some of that Heraldic mind control stuff? Because I'm pretty sure I'd jump off this mountain right now if you asked me to."

"Not the time," Willow said.

Chrys' eyes lit up. "That actually gives me an idea..."

An hour later, after meeting up with Xuçan and trudging through the wild growth of the mountains, they arrived at a peak overlooking the city of Alchea. To the south, they could see the wastelanders preparing to descend the mountain pass like a swarm of ants scuttling down a cobblestone path. It wasn't until Chrys looked west that an icy cold surged through his chest.

At such a height, Chrys could see an army sprawled out on the western border of Alchea. And there was only one nation large enough to march an army of that size. If the city was already under siege from the west, the wastelanders would obliterate them from the east, like an arrow loosed at their back.

That was exactly what the Heralds wanted.

They wanted to stand back, smiling, while Felia, Alchea, and the wastelanders tore each other apart. And if he had to guess, the corespawn would arrive just in time to finish the job. If this war wasn't stopped, there would be no one left alive.

Iriel stepped up beside him. "Chrys, is that—"

"It is," he said.

"How did they get here so quickly?" she asked.

Chrys' nostrils flared as he looked over the countryside. "It's been a long time since we left Felia. The Heralds must have sent them after we departed."

Iriel's chest rose up and down, Aydin cooing against her breast. "Are we too late?"

"No," Chrys said quickly. "But we're running out of time."

Multi-colored threadlight came to life, swirling in the veins of his neck and hands. Willow and Roshaw walked up beside him, their own eyes glowing with otherworldly light.

"Wait," Alverax said.

They all turned to the young man, who gazed over the countryside toward the surrounding army.

"I'll be no use to you in Alchea," Alverax continued. "But if I can get to the Felian army, maybe I can talk them out of the war."

Willow raised a brow. "That doesn't seem like—"

"They'll gut you like a sandhog!" Roshaw blurted out. "You're a traitor there. If you walk into that camp, you'll be dead the second they recognize you."

"I still have a few friends inside," Alverax said.

"Had," Roshaw said. "They've been waiting hundreds of years for the Heralds to return. It would take a hell of a friendship to win over that kind of zealotry."

Though he tried to hide it, Chrys caught a flicker of sorrow in Alverax's eyes, which surprised him. He'd expected to see anger or annoyance toward Roshaw. But instead, the young man held an air of sadness.

"Alverax," Chrys said, placing a hand on the younger man's shoulder. "Each of us will walk a critical path in the coming days or hours, and all of these paths will lead to sacrifice of some kind. But not all will lead to self-sacrifice. Laurel's path is not yours."

"Stop!" Alverax shouted, throwing Chrys' hand away with surprising force. "I know what I'm saying. Stop treating me like a child. If we do nothing, the Felians will kill who knows how many Alcheans, and speaking to the Alcheans isn't going to stop that. We need to consider every angle. For you, that's speaking to your friends in Alchea. For me, it's speaking to mine. One of the highest generals in Felia is a friend, and he's a good man. If I can talk to him, maybe I can delay the army until Laurel can destroy the Provenance."

Roshaw puckered his lips. "It's not worth the risk. They'll—"

"He's right," Chrys said, feeling a measure of guilt as he cut off Roshaw. "If Alverax can delay the army—even for a few hours—it would make all the difference. It could save thousands of lives on both sides of the war."

"But...it's...my..." Roshaw's voice fell to a whisper as his lips quivered and his chest convulsed. He turned away to hide the tears in his eyes.

Chrys felt tears form in his own eyes as he watched the big bear of a man break down. They all knew what Roshaw was thinking, and they could imagine what he was feeling. But imagining pain and feeling it for yourself are not the same. No matter how hard a man may try, he never truly understands hurt beyond what he has experienced himself. Roshaw, a man who had already lost his child once, was faced with the real possibility of losing him again. Chrys looked over to Aydin and felt a swelling of pain in his own heart.

"I know you're scared," Alverax said. "You don't think I am? But like Chrys said, we all have our path to walk, something that only we can do to help. I'm not a hybrid thread-weaver like you. Until the Provenance is destroyed, I can't lead the wastelanders. There's too much at stake for me to sit around waiting for that to happen, especially if there's a chance I can help."

Roshaw's breathing steadied, and he looked to his son with bloodshot eyes. "How the hell did you turn out to be such a good man?"

Alverax let out a small laugh. "Sometimes the bad examples help more than the good."

"I'm coming with you," Roshaw said with a sense of resolve. "I can fly you close and watch your back since Xuçan won't be able to come to the camp."

Alverax nodded. "Let's do this."

. . .

CLOUDS HAD GATHERED over the mountain range, blanketing the city in a dreary darkness that brought with it an icy chill. The few rays that made their way through the gray felt muted as they reached toward the high stone walls.

Chrys and Iriel took off toward Endin Keep, flying faster than they ever had before with Willow and Aydin beside them. If Laurel managed to destroy the Provenance in that very moment, they would tumble through the sky to their deaths. If they were going to fly at all, they needed to get it over with quickly.

As they drifted toward the keep, memories flooded through him. Toward the base, he saw the room where he and his mother had once lived thanks to Eleandra's kindness. Beside it, he saw the window he'd once shattered while playing as a young boy. Higher up, he saw Jurius' study, where he'd spent countless hours in conversation before the Bloodthieves had compromised the high general. And higher still, he saw the window that his mother had used with Laz and Laurel to break into the keep in order to save Chrys' uncle, Pandan. It seemed an eternity ago. So much had changed since then. The world. The dangers. The people most of all.

Chrys shook his head, trying not to be distracted by the past. Alchea was at war, and while they were not likely expecting an aerial attack from the mountains, soldiers would be out in force. He was a hybrid threadweaver, filled with otherworldly power and fast-acting healing, but a single, well-placed arrow could still take him—or his family—out of the sky as quickly as a crow.

They began their descent, shooting down as the cold wind bit at their skin. While there was no entrance on the top of the keep's highest towers, it was still the best place to touch down and regroup. Chrys glanced back to check on

Willow and Aydin, then let out another surge of Emerald to speed up the descent. Surprisingly, two guards stood atop each of the towers, looking out toward the Felian army to the west. He'd never heard of guards posted there before, but it took only a moment of thought to realize that Malachus was smarter than he was. If the Heralds had been as cavalier about flight as they had been in Felia, Cynosure, or even the Everstone Mountains, then the Great Lord knew that he needed to watch the skies. What better way than to station a few Emeralds on the highest point of the city.

Unfortunately, Malachus' wisdom made Chrys' job just a little bit more difficult.

Chrys *pushed* off the stone as he landed, hitting the ground with a louder thud than he'd anticipated. The two guards—one male, one female—spun around in unison, veins flared with Emerald threadlight.

"Soldiers," Chrys said with a nod.

The woman, her thin frame accentuated by the baggy uniform, opened her mouth to speak, but nothing came out.

Chrys offered a sly smile. "Last I heard, your uncle was feeling much better. Is he back in the smithy yet?"

A small grin formed in the corner of her mouth. "He is, sir."

"Good." Chrys looked to the other guard. "I know I did not leave on the best of terms, and you likely have orders to capture me—"

"Sir," the woman interjected. "You—"

"Please," Chrys cut her off. "We are here to speak with Great Lord Malachus, to share information that will aid Alchea in the war. There is no need for us to fight, and it would only go poorly for you, I promise. I would much rather this visit be peaceful."

"High General," the woman said with force. "You were

pardoned by the Great Lord months ago. You're free to come and go as you please. No one in Alchea will stand in your way."

Chrys was taken aback. Malachus had pardoned him? Why? Surely defiling the Temple of Alchaeus, colluding with a spy, and directly leading to the death of a dozen soldiers on the edge of the Fairenwild couldn't be so lightly forgiven. But then he remembered what his mother and Laurel had told him about their failed attempt to rescue Pandan. They'd also told him about High General Henna's role in exposing Jurius. The nation needed someone to blame and, where once Chrys Valerian—the butcher of the valley—stood, Jurius had taken his rightful place as traitor.

The revelation gave Chrys a measure of hope, but he knew the truth. There is nothing more dangerous than a measure of hope when the meal is war.

"Good," Chrys said, feeling a weight lighten from his broad shoulders. "I would have hated to kill you." He smirked as the second soldier, a man with bags under his eyes, clutched his sword a little more tightly.

"Chrys," Iriel said beside him. "We need to go."

He nodded, then looked to the soldiers once more. "When this is all over, I'll see to it personally that the both of you are rewarded for your diligence. Keep your eyes in the sky, and watch the mountains. A wastelander army is coming."

With that, Chrys, Iriel, and Willow stepped over the edge of the tallest tower, flaring Emerald threadlight as they walked down the wall, defying gravity. A single skyfly drifted in the air below them, translucent wings fluttering at an impossible speed. It dropped lower as they walked down, taunting them to approach. For a moment, Chrys' heart dropped as he remembered his son. He turned to look and saw the child safely wrapped up and held securely against his grandmother's chest.

Finally, they reached the window to Malachus' study. It looked the same as it always had. For some reason, Chrys had expected a change, as if the darkness that had come over the world would have rusted the hinges or clouded the glass. He paused, remembering his conversations with Malachus as they sat opposite each other. With a glance below to ensure no one would be hurt, he used the pommel of his dagger to shatter the glass, then launched himself inside with an unfocused surge of Sapphire.

The room was empty.

Chrys walked in, smelling the familiar scent of leather books and mahogany shelves. Broken shards of glass dotted the rug near the window, and Chrys felt a hint of guilt knowing how difficult it would be to pick up every piece. Iriel entered next, leaping down off the sill and steadying herself with a hand on the desk. Willow came in last, floating down gracefully with a combination of Emerald, Sapphire, and Obsidian.

Iriel straightened her hair and checked her side for her dangling palmguards. "So far so good."

"Should we wait for him here?" Willow asked.

Chrys shook his head. "No time."

Iriel was already moving toward the door. "He'll have sent Henna up to the front lines to manage the defenses. Too dangerous for him to be there with the Heralds around."

Willow raised a brow. "You think he's hiding?"

"Definitely not," Chrys said quickly. "He's too proud for that. I bet he's in the keep though. Somewhere visible but safe. Like the briefing room." They both turned to him. "It was built for wartime safety of the Great Lord and his family. Reinforced walls. Metal-framed windows with multiple panes. And a collection of bolts and latches for the only door that leads in. The perfect place for him to communicate with his generals safely without fear of the Heralds or the Felian army."

"Sounds like hiding," Willow mumbled.

Chrys gave his mother an unamused look.

"What?" she said. "How is that *not* hiding?"

"He's not hiding," Chrys repeated.

Iriel cocked her head to the side. "It does sound like hiding."

"It doesn't matter," Chrys said, annoyed at both women. "We know where he is, which means we know where we need to go."

"Ready when you are," Willow said.

Iriel gestured toward the entrance of the study. "Lead the way."

Chrys grit his teeth.

"But to be clear," Iriel said with no small hint of levity in her voice, "it's definitely hiding."

Until that moment, Chrys had never questioned his marriage.

He opened the door.

NEARLY EVERY PERSON they passed in the halls of Endin Keep recognized them, though Chrys only recognized half in return. Still, it did not stop their flight as they raced down marble stairs, ignoring whispers and quizzical looks, turning around familiar corners until they reached the hall leading to the briefing room where they hoped Malachus would be. Five sentries stood at attention guarding the thick mahogany door.

A promising sign.

Chrys took a step forward, raising a hand to greet the guards when footsteps sounded behind them. Before he could make a move, Iriel had already turned around, lifting a hand and shouting as threadlight flowed through her body. A small, steel dagger flipped through the air from the other end of the hall, flying directly toward Chrys' back. As it flew, its trajectory shifted, drawn toward Iriel and her Emerald threadlight. The dagger finished its arc, landing point-first in the center of her palmguard. Everyone stood still as the sound of metal on metal rang through the air.

The guard who'd thrown it stood slack-jawed as he took in the intruders. "Stones! High General, I'm so sorry. I didn't recognize you! I never would have thrown it if I'd known it was you."

Chrys didn't know the young man, but he did recognize

his sincerity. "You are in the middle of a war, and I have been away. I won't hold that against you. But you *are* lucky that my wife was here. If I had a knife in my back, I would not be so forgiving." He turned to the guards at the door. "I need to speak with the Great Lord."

One of the guards looked familiar, a Sapphire with a birthmark on his left cheek and hair to his shoulders. "Of course, High General." He turned and knocked in a specific pattern, and, when he finished, the door swung open from the inside.

The guards stepped aside, and Chrys entered with Iriel, Willow, and the baby.

The inside of the room was dim and windowless, lit by a collection of small lanterns that heated the space to an uncomfortable level. In the center, men and women sat around a circular table with a map sprawled out, filling the entire surface. Small figures and tokens lay strewn across the parchment. Chrys recognized each of the guests, though a few stood out. A surprisingly solemn Tyberius Di'Fier. Stone-faced General Rynan. And the white-haired High General Henna. On the far end, with wavy dark hair that framed his bichromic gaze, Great Lord Malachus Endin rose to his feet.

"Chrys?" Malachus said with a hint of surprise. "You're alive? And with Willow. Come in, old friends. Where have you been?"

A dozen images flashed through Chrys' mind. From the Fairenwild to the Wastelands, the caves below the Endless Well, the Convergence, the Provenance, Felia, Cynosure, and back. "It's a long story."

Malachus gave a sly grin. "With a beard like that, I can only imagine. Now the real question is why have you returned, and why now? I cannot imagine it a coincidence that the Apogee has returned when we are on the precipice of war. Have you come to turn the tide once again?"

"That," Chrys said raising his brows, "is also a long story. But there is no time for that. We are here because Alchea is surrounded." He let the words sink in, puzzled looks passing from person to person around the table. "Your focus is to the west, toward the army on your doorstep and the so-called Heralds. But that is not your only threat. Do you not find it odd that they have traveled all this way and have yet to attack? Almost as if they were waiting for something?"

The Emerald-eyed General Rynan huffed. "They haven't attacked, because they've seen our new weapons."

"New weapons?" Iriel asked, taking a step up to stand beside Chrys.

High General Henna smiled. "We found more thread-dead obsidian. A lot more. Enough to make ten thousand arrowheads."

"Enough to take those damn Heralds out of the sky if they fly too close," Rynan added.

Chrys' mind flooded with thoughts. With an arsenal of thread-dead obsidian arrows, they could wipe out thousands of unexpecting Felians. It would win any ordinary war. Unfortunately, this war was anything but ordinary, and there was more than just Felia to deal with. "It's not enough."

Malachus leaned onto the table, knuckles down, staring into Chrys' eyes. "They *are* different," he said. "I thought it was a trick of the light, but your irises have changed hue. Where have you really been, Chrys?"

Quietly, Chrys pulled out a blowgun from Kai'Melend and set it on the table. "We've been in the Wastelands. The Heralds are in reality wastelander gods, and their army is traveling over the pass as we speak. Soon, you will be attacked from both sides." Chrys slid the blowgun across the table, knocking over tokens and figurines until it stopped at Malachus' hand.

The Great Lord lifted it and turned it over in his hands. "We would know if there was an army coming over the mountains."

Chrys paused, cocking his head to the side. "Would you?"

An uncomfortable silence settled over the Alchean leaders. Chrys could see it in the slump of their shoulders, the heavy breath in their chests. They knew it was true. The mountains at their back were safe. The wastelanders had never led an offensive attack, always content with keeping the outsiders away. They had always stayed on their side of the divide.

Rynan broke the silence, his gruff voice littered with frustration. "Why would the wastelanders attack now? To take advantage of the war? How would they even know there was a war? I don't buy it. Not until I see the wastelanders for myself."

"By then it would be too late," Henna said, turning to Chrys. "If we're going to redirect forces, we need to do it before the wastelanders enter the valley."

Malachus continued to stare into Chrys' multi-colored eyes. "Still doesn't answer how you know all of this."

Chrys turned to Iriel and Willow, who each gave him a nod. "I'll try to make this brief, and it may sound unbelievable, but I promise you that it is all true, with my wife and mother as witnesses."

With that, Chrys told them about the Apogee. He told them about the Wastelands and Alchaeus, the coreseal, Felia and the corespawn. Then he finished with their failed plan to create a new coreseal to capture the Heralds, ending with their escape and the wastelander army. By the end, each of the leaders looked at him as if he were completely mad. Even Malachus, who had known Chrys since he was a young boy, closed his eyes with flared nostrils as he considered the words.

"If you want proof, look at my eyes," Chrys said. "When I left Alchea, I was a Sapphire. Now, I am a Sapphire, an Emerald, and an Obsidian. My mother as well. A gift from Alchaeus himself." With that, Chrys *broke* the corethread of every leader sitting around the table and watched their eyes gape open as they began to float, gripping their chairs to stay down. "Give it a moment, and your corethreads will reappear. Until then, listen carefully. If you do not delay the wastelander army from joining the war, Alchea will be destroyed within the week."

As if on cue, the leaders all fell back into their seats. Rynan took the opportunity to stand and draw a serrated dagger from his belt, holding it out toward Chrys.

Tension built like a boiling kettle, until Tyberius lifted the lid with a fit of boisterous laughter. The large man stood to his feet and pressed on Rynan's arm, forcing it down. "Invisible creatures, flying gods, now blessings from Alchaeus... What a time to be alive!" He turned and addressed the rest of the room. "We all know Chrys, many of us since he was a boy. He has never been one to lie or even stretch the truth. With all that we've seen in the past months, I'm keen to believe his story. I vote that we redirect some troops immediately to the east, even if just to disable the bridge over the Jupyter River."

Rynan crossed his arms, the dagger still in his hand. "And what if he's working for Felia? Trying to thin the troops on the front lines?"

"We still have the thread-dead arrowheads," Henna said.

"Even if we redirect troops, the Felians would take a heavy loss if they attacked."

"I would not use those arrows quite yet," Willow said, raising a hand. "You're going to want to save them."

Malachus rubbed at his forehead. "Willow, speak straight. Why should we split our troops and not use our greatest weapon?"

She raised a finger. "First off, Chrys and I are now your greatest weapons. Secondly, the Heralds control the corespawn, and we suspect they will be returning to Alchea as well."

"Dammit!" Malachus shouted, slamming a fist down on the table, tokens and figures tumbling around from the quake. "The wastelanders are coming. The corespawn are coming. The Heralds are coming. How the hell are we supposed to deal with all of this?"

"We have a plan." Chrys turned again to his wife for strength. Iriel gave him a nod, standing tall and strong beside him. "We found the Provenance of threadlight. And we're going to destroy it."

"Destroy—" Henna's eyes grew wide.

"The Provenance?" Tyberius blurted out. "Ha! This just keeps getting better!"

"Quiet!" Malachus scowled. "The Provenance is real?"

Chrys nodded.

"And you want to destroy it?"

"That's correct, sir."

Malachus' eyes looked up and to the left, toward a blank section of the wall. "I don't see how destroying all threadlight would help us. It would do exactly the opposite. It would completely cripple our army and even the playing field for Felia."

"It's not about the army," Chrys continued. "The best

war is no war, and that starts with the Heralds. The problem is that they're immortal due to their unique connection with threadlight. We believe that if we can remove that connection, then they can be killed. If the Heralds are dead, we can try for peace with Felia. And we're confident that we can convince the wastelanders to leave as well."

"No," Malachus said flatly.

Chrys' brow twitched. "Malachus..."

The Great Lord leaned forward. "You will not destroy the Provenance."

"Malachus," Chrys said. "If we don't do this, thousands of people are going to die."

"Tens of thousands," Iriel added.

Malachus loomed over the table. "Threadlight is power. And not only that, it is our way of life, woven into the fabric of each and every day. We will find another way, without destroying threadlight, even if that means war with Felia."

Chrys clenched his jaw. "I understand your hesitation. We all had our doubts. But there is no other way to fight the Heralds. Trust me; we've tried. Besides, the plan is already in motion. We have someone traveling to destroy the Provenance as we speak. The only remaining question is if Alchea will be ready for it."

"Dammit, Chrys!" Malachus spat. "That was not your decision to make!"

"I know," Chrys said calmly, hoping to cool the rising heat. "But there was no time and no other way."

Willow put a hand on Chrys' shoulder. "If there was another path, Malachus, we would have taken it. The Provenance could be destroyed at any moment. Today. Tomorrow. We don't know. But we need your help to buy time. We can take it from there."

"You make it sound so simple," Malachus said, his chest

still rising and falling with fury. "Stop two armies—three if you count the corespawn—and two immortal beings, for an indeterminate length of time. Are you sure there's nothing else?"

The sarcastic tone gave Chrys an odd sense of reassurance. "There is one other thing."

Malachus frowned. "Dear god, what is it?"

"Your watch broke." Chrys pulled out the pocket watch and held it up. "But that...is an even longer story."

THE WASTELANDERS WERE such tiny people.

Laz watched them cross the valley and thought they looked an awful lot like ants. Holding up his thumb and index finger, fitting the army between, he pretended to squish them. Sometimes just one, sometimes a dozen or more. The game made the waiting go faster.

"What are you doing?" Reina looked at him with the same goofy look she often gave, as if she were too dumb to understand what he was doing. Laz still liked her, even if she was simpleminded. She also looked quite silly on that big, white-haired horse. It looked like it could be her cousin.

"Is too hard to explain," he said.

Laz still couldn't believe that Chrys had returned. Now *that* was a man who was not so simpleminded. He always had a plan. Laz missed that. Ever since Chrys had left, Laz had had nothing much to do but boring patrol routes. It did give him an excuse to visit Luther once. That was nice.

On the other side of the river, the wastelander army grew closer, and Laz noticed the other soldiers glancing back toward Endin Keep more and more frequently. But their orders were clear: destroy the bridge. They were also supposed to wait. Don't destroy it until the army was close. That way the army would waste more time finding a new path. There wasn't another bridge across the wide, rushing river for miles.

Just in case, there was a battalion of soldiers with Laz. And not just any battalion...*his* battalion. It was the first time Laz had ever been in charge, but Chrys said he needed someone he trusted, who he knew wouldn't be afraid of the wastelander army. They were so small, Laz wasn't sure why anyone would be afraid. He lifted his fingers up and squished the army one more time for good measure.

"We should do it now," one of the soldiers said. A pretty man, thin frame, nice long hair. Laz did not think he should be a soldier.

"Is not time," Laz said.

The soldier gestured toward the army. "But they'll be on top of us in less than five minutes!"

Laz gave the man his hardest look. "Then we wait four."

The soldier cowered back quietly.

Reina still sat on her horse beside Laz, but she waited for the soldier to step away before speaking. "We really should probably do it soon."

"Soon," Laz said, offering her a toothy grin, "is last chance. If you want to swing the axe, I will let you."

"No, no, no. I think you're definitely the right person for the job."

Laz rubbed his hands together. "Good. This thing will be very fun!"

With Reina trailing behind, Laz walked toward the bridge with a satchel at his side and a skip in his step.

"HOLD!"

High General Henna crouched and held a thick shield

over her head alongside thousands of Alcheans. If she closed her eyes, it sounded like a wild hailstorm beating against the small cottage she'd grown up in. Only those storms weren't broken by the screams of unlucky soldiers being struck by arrows that her Emeralds were unable to redirect.

"Rise!" she screamed.

As her words were repeated down the line, soldiers rose to their feet, keeping their shields overhead and a careful eye on the outlying army. The Felians had continued their sporadic barrage of arrows for several days, but they had yet to launch a full offensive. Unfortunately, something had changed that day. Whether they were running low on arrows or supplies, the Felians had begun a slow advance. And with the troops recalled to prepare the eastern walls for the wastelander army, there were more Felian soldiers than Alchean on the western front.

One of her captains rushed up beside her, an older man named Kith who'd seen war before and had taken it personally that the Felians had forced him into it once more. "High General," he said respectfully. "The Great Lord needs to reconsider. They're too reliant on their Emerald shields. A single barrage of thread-dead arrows would devastate their ranks and stop their advance. They wouldn't know what hit them."

Henna glared at him. "For the last time, keep the arrows ready, but do not fire them until I give the order."

"We're just going to let the dark-skinned bastards walk right up and slaughter us when we have a way to stop them?"

Henna stepped forward and struck Kith in his face, quite sure she felt something crack in the process. Whether it was her own knuckle or his cheek, she didn't care. "We have men and women of Felian blood fighting in our army. Speak like that again and you'll find out just how sharp those arrows are."

The older man stepped away, rubbing his cheek and grumbling. If Kith had not been hand-selected as a battalion leader by Malachus himself, Henna would have sent him to the front lines. But she would need men like him, who held the respect of the other soldiers. When fighting begins, strength and respect are the only currencies.

One by one, messengers approached, detailing the advancement of the Felian lines. The other generals saw the slow approach as a sign of weakness, as if the Felians were afraid of a full-scale clash. Some even thought a spy had tipped them off about the thread-dead arrows, but Henna wasn't convinced. She knew the Felian generals personally, and she knew they were not fools. If they were moving slowly, then they were waiting for something.

Another messenger—a scrawny man with thick scruff and shaggy brown hair—came sprinting down the line, shoving a younger soldier out of the way and waving his hand in the air. When he finally arrived, out of breath, panting, fear in his eyes, Henna finally discovered what the Felians had been waiting for.

Chrys was right.

"Corespawn!" the messenger shouted. "Coming from the Fairenwild!"

Henna looked to Kith, the older general she'd sent away. "And that's why we saved the arrows."

THE WASTELANDERS still looked like children the closer they came to the bridge, but the swamp gorillas were another story. Laz wagered they were twice his size, which lined up with Chrys' warning, but even still, something about their movements gave Laz the strange desire to wrestle them. But they also had spikes on their backs, which would make wrestling slightly less fun.

Maybe another time.

Laz stood at the end of a twenty-foot-wide bridge that spanned the nearly one-hundred-foot-wide river. They'd sabotaged the whole thing, rigging it to collapse with a few swings of his lucky axe. Reina had tried to convince him not to let any of the wastelanders onto the bridge before he collapsed it, just in case they were able to somehow make it across, but Chrys wanted the army as close as possible. Their goal was to slow down the army, and the longer they spent approaching the bridge, the longer it would take them to find another route.

So Laz waited, and Reina stood beside him with a thick shield and Emerald threadlight in her veins. When the first arrow landed on the other end of the bridge, they decided it was time. Laz stepped up to the first thick rope holding the partially-deconstructed bridge together. He lifted the heavy axe and slammed it down. The sharp edge cut through the hemp with ease, snapping the taut rope and sending a tremble through the structure.

Laz turned to Reina and smiled his toothy grin. "See? Is easy!"

He moved to the next rope and lifted his axe. In a way, it brought with it a sense of nostalgia. Growing up in the farmlands outside of Alchea, he'd spent many summers cutting wood with that very same axe. The grip felt as though his calloused hands had rubbed their way into the wood, leaving perfect indentations for each of his fingers.

With a burst of strength, Laz let the axe fall. Again, the

rope snapped, shooting forward at the bridge in a wild arc. The entire structure teetered, tipping onto one side as the second of the four anchors released its hold.

Laz and Reina quickly made their way to the third rope, eyeing the oncoming army which, despite the developments of the bridge, still hurled forward at surprising speed. When they reached the rope, Laz lifted his axe.

Thud.

He looked up and saw an arrow sticking out of Reina's shield and Emerald threadlight glowing through her veins. The look she gave him was enough for him to swing hard and fast. The third rope blasted away as it split in two. The bridge shuddered, the final rope groaning under the weight of the tipping bridge. Laz was surprised that the thick rope held and smiled as he thought of cutting it loose.

Thud. Thud. Thud. Thud.

Laz ignored the incoming flurry of arrows, grateful that he had someone beside him that he trusted, even if she was simpleminded. With adrenaline coursing through his veins, Laz lifted his lucky axe one final time, swinging it down with as much force as he could muster. As soon as the blade hit the rope, the axehead snapped off of the handle, leaving him holding nothing more than a jagged piece of wood.

He looked to Reina.

She looked to him.

They both looked at the wastelander army as the first warrior reached the other end of the bridge. Another flurry of arrows and darts loosed from their front line, drawn to Reina's shield as she *pulled* on a dozen fast-moving threads.

Keeping her eyes on the next wave, Reina screamed, "Do something!"

Laz looked down at the broken axe shaft.

Stones.

"HOLD!"

High General Henna stood behind a legion of archers, all equipped with thread-dead obsidian arrows. She felt an overwhelming gratitude for Chrys Valerian, the man she'd once believed to be a traitor, but who had proven himself to be the most important ally that Alchea had. If he hadn't warned them about the wastelanders, they would have been blindsided. And if he hadn't warned them about the corespawn horde, teaching them that thread-dead obsidian is the only weapon against the creatures, then they would have wasted their arrows on the Felians. They would have been left with no way to fight them. They would have been torn apart.

Instead, it was their turn to do the devastation.

"Loose!" she screamed, her voice carrying through the legion, her message relayed until every man and woman holding a bow heard.

The sky darkened as a storm of obsidian rose into the air, falling like a hailstorm of shadows. Thousands of arrows fell, crashing into the unseen horde. General Kith stood beside her, Emerald veins glowing beneath his uniform, eyes fixed on the fields to the north. Henna had no way to know if their arrows would truly work on the corespawn, only Chrys' word that they would.

Her heart skipped a beat as the first arrows touched the ground. When Kith's Emerald eyes doubled in size, a dark cloud swirled in the pit of her stomach. If the thread-dead arrows didn't work, today would be the day Alchea fell. For a moment, she wished that they still had transfusers left over from the Bloodthieves, or anything that would let her see the corespawn and know if their plan was working. Instead, she was left standing still with a rampaging heart as she awaited verdict from the threadweavers around her.

A choir of guttural roars flooded the battlefield mixed with shrill squeals that harmonized like children's screams in a thunderstorm. The ground shook. Henna looked to Kith beside her, whose mouth was left agape at whatever demonic sight he'd seen in the realm of threadlight.

"What the hell is happening?" Henna shouted.

Kith turned, but his eyes seemed fixed to the battlefield. "It's...beautiful."

"Tell me."

Kith shook his head. "The corespawn hit with the arrows burst apart, like popping a bubble. The sky filled with beads of threadlight that quickly faded."

"So it's working?" Henna clarified.

Finally, he turned to Henna with a smile. "Hell yes, it is."

A few cheers rang out from amongst the infantrymen, but only long enough for them to remember that one volley does not win a war. They scrambled to prepare their next thread-dead arrows and aimed with guidance from thread-weavers evenly spread throughout the legion.

With the corespawn under control, Henna turned to keep an eye on the approaching Felian army, Emerald-led shields spread through the ranks like life-saving magnets. Regular arrows would do nothing to stop their advance, and Henna worried what would happen when the larger force clashed with her own.

From the back of the Felian army, two figures streaked through the sky, passing their soldiers and slamming onto the ground between the opposing forces, snarling as they looked at the dying corespawn. The Felian lines halted their advance, and a cold stillness rippled through the Alcheans.

The male Herald, thick-armed with hair like fire in the blinding sunlight, wore a long, black robe with gold trim that shuddered in the wind. The woman was dark-haired and shorter than the man and wore a white robe also trimmed with gold. Side by side, there was no doubting who they were. They looked oddly familiar to Henna, but she couldn't place from where.

When the male Herald finally spoke, his words rang out in the open air.

"CHRYS VALERIAN!"

LAZ SCRAMBLED FORWARD and grabbed the broken axehead off of the grassy ledge, nicking the side of his smallest finger as he lifted himself back up to his feet. With great urgency, he slammed down the axehead on the final rope. It bit into the hemp, but not nearly enough to break the overwhelming tension. He slammed it down again and the axehead slipped, twisting and cutting his wrist with the jagged bottom.

He made the mistake of looking up and seeing a swarm of wastelanders throwing themselves across the tilted bridge. They were still tiny, but now he could see why people might be afraid of them. He lifted the axehead once more, ignoring the pain in his wrist, and swung down with every ounce of anger boiling inside him. For the wastelanders and the friends that had died at their hands during the war. For the pain in his wrist. And for his lucky axe. The metal head cut down into the rope, strands snapping off and flying toward the river.

Almost.

"Now would be a good time to finish!" Reina screamed

while another volley of arrows and darts rained down toward them.

Laz lifted the axehead a dozen more times, slamming it down on the rope, blood dripping from his hands and wrist, rage flooding his mind and body. He felt like a butcher hacking a boar. Again, he swung. And again, the tension refused to break. The front-line wastelanders were halfway across the bridge now, and more were joining, their eyes fixed to the creaking wood and taut ropes.

Finally, the rope snapped, flinging up and over the bridge, landing in the middle of the confused wastelanders, but the bridge did not collapse.

Laz stared, wide-eyed, counting the cut ropes. One. Two. Three. Four. That was the plan. That was supposed to cause the sabotaged bridge to collapse. Instead, some unseen force kept the bridge from falling.

"Reina." Laz swallowed hard.

Reina strapped the shield on her back, turned from the bridge, and set her feet as she screamed, "Get to the horses!"

Laz slipped the lucky axehead in his pocket and ran, but he only made it two steps before the ground trembled and the bridge behind groaned like an angry whale. When he turned, he saw the end scene of the bridge collapsing under the weight of the wastelander army. Thick beams snapped in half, tumbling into the rushing river that pulled them downstream to the west. A dozen wastelanders fell into the water, rope and wood collapsing atop them as they disappeared into the depths.

In a matter of seconds, the bridge was in shambles, ripped apart by the fast-moving current, boards floating down the river by the dozens. The rest of the wastelanders stood on the far edge of the river, staring with their beady eyes across the water that rippled with refracting beams of mid-day sun.

Laz's lips curled up into a grin. "Ha!" He lifted his hands high overhead.

Beside him, Reina glanced back and forth between the wastelander army and their small battalion, particularly their horses.

"Relax," Laz said. "We won!"

As soon as the words left his mouth, a resounding thud sounded on the shoreline. Laz swiveled around and cursed as he saw one of the swamp gorillas soaring through the air over the rushing river to land beside another. Each of them had a wastelander straddling the back of their necks, like a child on their father's shoulders. By the time the first curse left his mouth, another ataçan had knuckle-run with incredible speed, then launched itself over the river, joining the others. At the same time, the wastelander army huddled in close, linking arms, and walked calmly into the river until the water covered them completely. Line by line, the army disappeared below the water, moving in unison through the rushing river as if it were nothing but a babbling brook.

Laz looked to Reina. "I do not think we won."

ALVERAX COULD FEEL Xuçan's rage along the edges of his soul. On the one hand, he'd wanted to bring the ataçan for protection, but traveling with a creature four times the size of a man wasn't much in the spirit of stealth. So instead, he'd left a very upset—to put it lightly—Xuçan in a valley at the base of the Everstone Mountains.

He gripped his father's wrist with both hands as they flew just a few feet over the ground. The cold wind found its way through every opening in his clothing, reaching its tendrils up his arms and down his chest.

As Roshaw's chest grew hot, they landed and continued their trek on foot. They could already see the Felian camp, and they hoped that—because of their Felian heritage— they wouldn't be attacked preemptively. Still, they knew there would be guards, and it would not be so easy to get in.

When they finished their approach, a host of guards converged on them, and Alverax's mind flashed back to his time in Felia. Guards lining the path to the rose throne when he'd first met Empress Chailani with the elders. Guards floating in the air in the same room while Alverax bartered his life for the Zeda people. And he would never forget the two guards, like opaque shadows, trailing Jisenna wherever she went. In fact...

"Innix?" he said.

One of the guards stepped forward, bringing a hand up over his brow to block out the ambient sunlight. It was one of Jisenna's guards, a man who'd shadowed their walks on many occasions. And though the man had given Alverax many dubious looks over that time, Innix had always been respectful to him as an outsider. "Watchlord?"

The others shifted in their boots, palms placed over the hilts of the swords dangling at their side. A few even unsheathed their weapons. As they looked back and forth at each other, Alverax could tell they were unsure how to react to his return. Which meant that there was likely a bounty of some kind on his head. More than likely, the Heralds had called for his death. Fortunately, he'd built up a bit of a reputation for himself, particularly with the whole becoming a watchlord and using his Obsidian powers to fight off the corespawn from destroying the city ordeal. They knew what he was capable of, and they saw the Midnight Watcher at his side.

Alverax stood tall and walked forward, letting Obsidian threadlight radiate in his eyes. He looked at the guards, one by one, meeting their gazes with his own until he'd reached the end of the line. Seventeen. But from the corner of his vision, he could see more were coming.

Finally, he spoke. "It is good to see you again, Innix." He gestured to Roshaw. "This is my father. As you can see, he is also an Obsidian threadweaver, though his power is beyond my own. We are not here to fight you. We are here to speak with General Thallin regarding an urgent matter."

"*Watchlord* Thallin," Innix said, emphasizing the new title. "Shortly after you left, the Heralds... Well, he became their right hand. I do not think it would be wise for you to speak with him."

Alverax nodded, taking in the information. If Thallin

was Watchlord, that was good news. His word alone could stop the war. "Thank you, Innix. The Mistress of Mercy looks down on you kindly from the stars."

At the reference to Jisenna, Innix's composure faltered, and Alverax saw a subtle twitch in one eye and a shiver across his lower lip. It was clear that the man had cared for his charge. The two of them shared a nod of mutual understanding.

"Are we good here?" Roshaw asked with a deep, resounding voice. He looked to the guards with his head held high, multi-colored eyes shining with threadlight.

The guards parted, opening a gap for Alverax and Roshaw to enter the makeshift Felian war camp.

If there was a single word to describe the camp, it would be "muddy." Ten thousand soldiers walking through half-dead grass after a morning of dew—the entire camp had transformed into a cesspool of congealed dirt, made all the more clear thanks to Felia's penchant for white fabric. Tents were stained. Clothes were mottled. And strips of fabric—old clothes and bandages—lay half-buried in the tar-like substance that coated the field. Every step felt like Alverax was back in the Wastelands, trudging through the swamps surrounding Kai'Melend.

Fortunately, the rest of the camp was not as diligent as the outer guards. Alverax and Roshaw, in their own muddied clothes, blended into the bustle as if they'd been there since the beginning. Alverax tried to keep his head down, especially after spotting several familiar faces in the crowd, including General Hish, the older man who'd pissed and moaned when Alverax had first become Watchlord—although Alverax couldn't fault the man for the sentiment.

After another ten minutes of wandering around and

keeping their heads down, they finally found the black and gold tent of the Watchlord. Alverax felt his chest tighten and his pulse quicken as he glanced at the guards standing sentry in front. It was now or never. And if he failed, thousands of lives would be wasted, including his own.

Roshaw leaned over and whispered, "Last chance to go back."

For a moment, Alverax considered it. Even though Thallin was the greatest swordsman in all of Felia, Alverax was an Obsidian, and his father was even more. If all else failed, they could *break* Thallin's corethread and walk away. The danger wouldn't be Thallin, it would be getting out of the camp. But then again, they could fly...

"No," Alverax said with a healthy air of resolve in his voice. "If we can save lives, we have to try." He turned to his father. "You don't have to come."

Roshaw looked to Alverax with surprising intensity. "Yes, I do."

Alverax turned away, understanding that his father was still trying to make up for years of absence. But if Alverax was being honest with himself, he did want his father there. Even if it put them both in danger, he wanted him by his side.

Without a word, they approached the Watchlord's tent. The sentries stepped forward to meet them, swords drawn, eyes gleaming with Emerald threadlight. Alverax noted that they each wore a palmguard on their offhand, which he'd never noticed before seeing Iriel's. He almost *broke* their corethreads but didn't want to cause a scene.

"Gentleman," Alverax said, keeping both his pitch and volume low and steady. "If you have not already recognized me, I am former Watchlord Alverax Blightwood. This is my father, a threadweaver with access to Obsidian, Sapphire, *and* Emerald. We have come to speak with Watchlord Thallin. We mean him no harm. When I am finished speaking, you will step aside, and my father and I will enter. If you try to impede our progress in any way, you will regret it."

The confident shoulders and stoic eyes of the guards seemed to vanish while he spoke. By the end, they were nervously looking to each other for guidance. From the corner of his eye, Alverax caught the slightest smirk curl over Roshaw's lip.

"Gentlemen," Alverax repeated as he stepped forward with his head held high. He opened himself to threadlight, allowing the ghostly glow of Obsidian to radiate from the pit of his eyes. Hesitantly, the guards stepped aside.

Roshaw pushed back the flap and allowed Alverax to enter first, keeping an eye on the guards until they were both inside.

As soon as Alverax entered, he saw Thallin, but the man had changed. He seemed thinner, frail despite the bulging veins in his neck that peeked through the black watchlord garb. Golden tassels hung from his shoulders, and a sword hung at his side. When their eyes met, his face was a torrent of emotion, swirling through tides of fury, joy, and sorrow. In the end, a strangely cool calm settled over him.

Thallin unstrapped his sheath and placed it on a thin wooden table. "I am surprised to see you," he said, walking over to a side table and bending down to retrieve a bottle of whiskey.

Alverax felt relief wash over him. "Thallin, it is so good to see you. To be honest, I wasn't sure how you would react."

The Watchlord turned his back, pouring a bit of whiskey into three cups. "I'm not sure how I should react either. The people of Felia are quite torn about you." He turned around and carried two of the cups over to Alverax and Roshaw. "Your heroism against the corespawn hasn't been forgotten, but abandoning the Heralds? There are those who believe you should be killed for such a thing."

Alverax took the cup. "And where do you stand?"

"Please, drink, relax." Thallin stepped over to the table and lifted his own cup to his mouth, drinking a hearty amount. "I stand ready to listen, if you are willing to share."

Something about the way Thallin looked at him both calmed him and sent a chill through his spine, but he couldn't have asked for a better opportunity. If Thallin was willing to hear them out, then Alverax was going to do what he came to do. He lifted his cup and took a drink, cringing at the potency that burned as it slid down his throat.

"First things first," Alverax said, glancing over to Roshaw, "I guess I should introduce you. Remember when I told you that Blightwoods don't die easy? Turns out, I was right. Thallin, meet my father, Roshaw Blightwood."

Thallin stared for an uncomfortable length of time at Roshaw. Straight-backed, his hand rested on the table beside him. His eyes seemed almost lifeless, as if he were seeing something beyond the world.

Finally, Thallin set his hand on the grip of his sword and pulled it from its sheath. "Did you really think you could just walk back into our world as if you had not abandoned our gods?" Each word was spoken with crisp enunciation, blades in and of themselves.

"Brother," Alverax said, lifting his hands. His heart quickened, and his mind raced with the sudden shift.

"I am not your brother." Thallin's eyes burned fire.

"Thallin, please, let me explain."

"No!" Thallin screamed, switching the point of his sword back and forth between the two intruders. "You are a heretic! A black-hearted traitor to your gods! I should cut you down where you stand!"

Alverax's chest compressed. His heart was a clay pot, and each of Thallin's words sent a tremor along its surface. Hope leaked from a dozen cracks. Pain echoed in the emptiness.

"You know me," Alverax said with no more than a whisper. "Look me in the eyes and tell me what kind of man I am."

"It doesn't matter what I think," Thallin said, blade shaking in his outstretched hand. "My perception of truth is nothing compared to the wisdom of the gods."

"Bull shit," Alverax spat.

Roshaw gave him a nervous glance. "Careful, Al."

"No," Alverax continued. He took two steps forward until the point of Thallin's blade pressed against his chest. Head held high, he looked into Thallin's eyes. "Did they tell you what happened to Jisenna? Because I was there. When the Heralds arrived, they called the two of us into the throne room. They said they were going to test our loyalty. But then they—" Alverax choked on the final words, tears swelling up in his eyes. His chest heaved with the blade still pressed against it. "Relek took the Midnight Watcher. He lifted it up. And he drove it into her neck. And do you want to know why? Because I told him she was a merciful ruler. You want to talk about the *wisdom of the gods*? Tell me, Thallin. What kind of a god fears mercy?"

His heart raced. Tears streaked his cheeks. But he saw it. A flicker of apprehension. Thallin didn't want to kill him. And somewhere, deep beneath the walls he'd built, doubts scraped against their coffins. But faith isn't a weed that can be plucked out. Its roots run deep through the soil, latching onto every part of a man's life, *affecting* every part of a man's life. Expanding until there is little room for anything else.

They become so entangled that it becomes difficult to see where a man's faith starts and his own mind begins.

Thallin's hand remained outstretched, a slight tremble in the blade. "I could tell something was different when you walked in. Is that it? Are you so filled with pride that you think yourself equal to the Heralds? I remember you pissing yourself at the top of the tower, and now what? You're wiser than the gods?"

Alverax breathed, letting the words pass over him like a cool breeze. "No, Thallin. I don't think I'm wiser than the gods. I just don't believe that the two you call Heralds are gods at all."

With a scream, Thallin slashed his sword across Alverax's chest. The blade cut through fabric and skin, leaving a streak of blood from shoulder to hip. Pain rippled through his body. All the way from the valley, he could feel Xuçan's rage-filled response.

Roshaw charged forward, launching a thick boot directly into Thallin's chest, knocking the Watchlord back. Alverax grabbed his father, throwing all of his weight into restraining the bear of a man.

"LET ME GO!" Roshaw roared.

Alverax, with the strength of an ataçan flowing through him, shoved Roshaw back toward the entrance. "This is not your fight!"

Roshaw growled. "When a man draws my son's blood, it becomes my fight."

"Not this time." Alverax turned around and looked at Thallin. The Watchlord stood with his back against the black tent, sword hanging like a natural extension of his arm. "Thallin, I understand what you must be going through. But you have to see that faith for the sake of faith is worth nothing. It doesn't matter *that* you believe. It matters *what* you believe. And a god that chooses to slaughter innocent women does not deserve your devotion."

The final words seemed to crash into Thallin like a tidal wave, as if they'd been hurled with the weight of a thousand regrets. The Watchlord stumbled back against the wall, eyes closed, clutching his sword so tightly that his knuckles whitened. Alverax finally felt a trickle of hope return.

Thallin shook his head violently, then sent a chair flying across the room with a swift boot. He brought his sword up with both hands, screaming as he slammed it down onto the thin table. The wood split and collapsed with a crash. He shoved the halves apart and sent them crashing to the ground.

The enraged Watchlord lifted his sword once more toward Alverax, heaving with each breath. "No more lies."

"Shit," Roshaw cursed, panic laced in his tone.

Alverax turned to him. "What is it?"

"My threadlight is gone."

Alverax opened himself to the otherworldly energy, sending a horrible burning sensation through his veins. He groaned and cut it off.

Roshaw grit his teeth. "Laurel has the worst timing."

"This isn't Laurel," Alverax said, glancing at his black veins. When he looked back up, Thallin tilted his chin up just the slightest. "The whiskey."

"The Heralds said it would take quickly," Thallin said. "A wastelander herb, I'm told. Now, raise your blade, Alverax Blightwood. No tricks will save you this time."

Alverax grabbed the hilt of the Midnight Watcher. Thallin was the greatest swordsman in all of Felia, and Alverax had sparred with him dozens of times. He knew first-hand that his own ability was no match, at least not before. Now, because of Xuçan's bond, he was faster and stronger.

"Thallin, we don't have to do this," Alverax said, clutching the hilt of the blade in its sheath.

"Yes, we do." Thallin lifted his own sword into a dueling stance. "And this time, I will not hold back."

ALONE IN THE darkness of the cavern tunnels, everything looked the same. Wet rock, a patch of malformed photospores, stalactites dangling from the ceiling like nature's knives, and more wet rock. If not for Alchaeus' markings, Laurel would have been lost. At each intersection, he'd marked the way home. Between each, they ran faster than they'd ever run before.

A chromawolf's eyes are accustomed to the dark of the Fairenwild, and Laurel found her own eyes adjusting in quite the same way. After a while, she'd dropped the bunch of photospores she held—which had done nothing but slow her down—and ran, fueled by her unique bond with Asher.

What she hadn't considered was how much time she would have to reconsider her decision. For endless hours on end, they did nothing but run. Even when they stopped to rest, she couldn't rid herself of her own thoughts. She found herself missing the annoyingly idle chatter of the others. Without it, she had nothing but her own thoughts to haunt her. And she couldn't stop picturing her younger brother. How had she forgotten Bay so easily? She tried to repeat the lie to herself that Asher was the only family she had left, but the words did nothing but curdle in her stomach.

But it didn't matter. She'd set her course. She'd even caved in the tunnel, which was as close to burning a bridge as she could get. There was no turning back. The others were counting on her. Unless the Provenance was destroyed, there would be no way to stop the Heralds. Maybe—she hoped—by sacrificing herself for the greater good, she could pay back the myriad mistakes she'd left scattered along the road.

As they continued forward, a bright light shone in the distant tunnel. Laurel and Asher raced on, increasing their pace for what they hoped would be the final stretch. When they rounded the bend, she felt a weight lift.

Alchaeus' cave.

She saw the rose-colored table, broken in two. The storage room filled with corespawn statues. And more importantly, just above the far side of the shimmering, golden elixir pool, was the fracture in the wall, the earthquake-wrought crevice leading to the Provenance.

Laurel stepped forward, eyeing the fracture as if it were an enemy. It was, in a way. A sentry standing guard at the entrance to the Heralds' home. Once she passed the fracture, there was nothing left to stop her but the Provenance itself.

Something touched her foot, and she leapt back with a growl. When she looked, there was nothing but cold cavern air. But when she took another step, she felt movement skittering up her leg. She swatted at it, still unable to see whatever it was that molested her. Tapping into her bond with Asher, like she'd done many times before, she reintroduced the world of threadlight to her achromic eyes. A small, lizard-like shape clutched the side of her thigh, its head moving back and forth as it looked up at her.

Laurel raised a brow, no longer afraid of any real danger. "Are you...Chitt?"

Its head cocked to the side, looking at her with curiosity.

She reached down, and it scuttled into her hand, crawling up her arm and resting on her shoulder. It shifted its feet again and again until it found just the right position. Laurel smiled before she could stop herself. As she craned her neck to stare at the little corespawn, a question she'd not considered surfaced in her mind. A question with consequences far greater than for Chitt alone.

"What's going to happen to you?"

If it truly was the source of all threadlight, and the corespawn creatures were made of threadlight, what would happen to them when the Provenance was destroyed? Would they react as they did to the obsidian dagger? Or would they be more like a person's corethread, which seemed to have been unaffected by the previous disturbance? Looking down at the friendly little creature, Laurel wasn't sure which answer she hoped would be right.

"Come on," she said. Whether to Asher, Chitt, or herself, she wasn't sure. Either way, whatever happened at the Provenance would affect more than just the three of them.

Laurel stepped over to the edge of the elixir pool and gazed up at the fracture in the wall. It looked too narrow to fit through, but if Roshaw had done it with his broad shoulders, then Laurel and Asher ought to be able to fit as well. Slowly, she stepped into the elixir, letting the healing waters rise up to her chest by the time she reached the opening. One step at a time, she scaled the wall, slipping her hands into breaks in the stone and locking her feet atop jutting rocks. With lithe muscles reinforced by her bond with Asher, she quickly reached the fracture, placed two hands atop the ledge, and lifted herself the rest of the way.

She pushed herself to her feet and looked down at Asher, who still stood on the edge of the elixir pool. His voice echoed in her mind. *I will need you to catch me.*

The large chromawolf took off at a sprint along the border of the elixir pool. Just before he reached the end, he leapt up onto the stone, using his speed to run horizontally along the wall toward the fracture. Laurel's eyes widened, and she steadied her feet. A moment later, Asher vaulted across the fracture, paws outstretched. Laurel lunged forward, grabbing his torso and yanking him into the opening, throwing them both into the wall of rock.

Laurel rubbed at her arm where a jagged rock had bit into her skin. "A little more warning next time," she said.

I am sorry.

"No, you're not."

Tiny feet skittered along Laurel's back as Chitt found his way back onto her shoulder. She reached up and touched the little corespawn's head, which was much more solid than she'd expected. Being made of threadlight, she'd assumed its body would be more like a thick mist.

Laurel slid her way through the rest of the fracture until she reached the end, where Iriel had hammered away a section of the wall. Ahead of her, a lake of golden elixir shimmered in a cavern so vast it could have fit the entirety of Zedalum. Stalactites the size of men hung from the ceiling in sporadic intervals, glimmering from the golden light that filled the expanse. And there, in the center of the cavern, far away from where she stood, was the island Iriel and Willow had described.

Asher nuzzled up behind her, peeking his green-furred head from under her armpit to look out into the cavern. *It is time.*

Laurel grit her teeth. "I don't know how to swim."

It is easy.

"Not for a human."

Asher said nothing.

Laurel looked down at the water. "Just make sure I don't drown."

You will not die in the water.

Whether intended or not, the grim humor lingered in the air like a noxious fog. They were one cold swim away from death. A few shivering strokes from destroying threadlight for the entire world.

Laurel couldn't think about that. Not now.

One step at a time.

This was one decision she couldn't allow herself to walk back on. If she did, Chrys and the others didn't stand a chance against the Heralds. This was the path she had to walk, no matter how wet the road.

She scratched Asher's head. "Let's go."

With that, they leapt together from the fracture, sending waves tumbling through the lake of elixir. Cold heat tingled across her body as she sank below the surface. For a moment, she did nothing but float. Specks of light shimmered all around her like sparks of lightning that flashed in and out of existence. On the lakebed, broken stalactites lay scattered like fallen soldiers with clusters of transparent fern-like plants that grew on the crystals, wavering to and fro. Laurel kicked her feet until her head poked back out above the surface and drank in the cavern air.

She turned and reached toward the center of the lake, Asher following beside her. As she awkwardly kicked her way along, she thought of Alverax. Even after seeing the gills along his spine, the idea of a man being able to breath underwater seemed impossible. But her own hair was tinted with green now, and she'd seen an ataçan-bonded wastelander with a spike growing from the base of his skull.

As they swam in eerie silence, she realized that swimming wasn't so difficult after all, at least with Asher-enhanced strength and endurance to aid her. As they came closer to the island's shore, a dark feeling pricked at her skin. She turned and saw a ripple in the water not far away, moving quickly toward her. Adrenaline pumped through her veins. Any enjoyment she'd felt turned to an overwhelming sense of vulnerability. If there was something in the water, what could she do? Wolves are not meant to fight in water.

Opening herself to the bond, threadlight flooded her vision. She saw little Chitt, skittering across the top of the elixir water like a pilliwick on hot sand. Fear washed away as she remembered the friendly corespawn, happy to have him joining them for their final journey.

Suddenly, an explosion of water blossomed from the surface of the lake as a massive creature, hewn of pure threadlight and with a jaw that could swallow a man whole, enveloped the little corespawn as if it were no more than a grain of feyrice. The creature let out a deep, whistling groan that filled the vaulted expanse.

"SWIM!"

Laurel and Asher took off toward the island, moving with as much speed as their paddling arms and flailing legs could give them. Whatever that creature was—some kind of aquatic corespawn monstrosity—Laurel wasn't going to sit around and let it eat them before they had a chance to destroy the Provenance.

The island grew closer, and Laurel swam harder, Asher keeping pace beside her. Just before they reached the sheer edge of the shore, Asher's body disappeared below the surface, Laurel's heart sinking along with the chromawolf.

She dove down, reaching for the dagger strapped to her thigh, its black blade glistening in the golden light of the elixir. When she opened her eyes, she saw Asher thrashing back and forth. One leg was trapped in the massive maw of the corespawn while the others swiped their deadly claws to no effect. Laurel stuck the dagger in her mouth and swam as hard as she could toward the light-wrought beast. It saw her and turned, opening its jaw and releasing Asher, while its tail fins sent it torpedoing directly toward Laurel.

It was too big. Too fast.

Her eyes grew wide as she watched the monstrous corespawn swim toward her. Fear threatened to take hold, but if she was going to die, she was going to die fighting.

Laurel grabbed the obsidian dagger from between her teeth and kicked her feet until she was aimed directly for its open mouth. Just before it reached her, the creature twisted back and forth, a deep groan emanating from its throat. It thrashed its tail, and Asher went flying through the water with a chunk of corespawn flesh glowing in his jaws. Laurel didn't hesitate; there was no time. She kicked forward, reaching her hand back with the dagger high overhead, and slammed it down into the creature's body. The dagger shook in her grasp, fighting the considerable amount of raw threadlight powering the corespawn. She squeezed the hilt with every ounce of strength she had, now grabbing hold with both hands and screaming under the elixir water as bubbles shot up toward the surface. Finally, the massive beast exploded into thousands of beads of threadlight that glittered in the lake like stars in a glowing sky.

Suddenly aware of her need to breathe, Laurel kicked up to the surface and drank in the cold cavern air. With the dagger secured back on her thigh, she spun around, looking for Asher and feeling a sense of dread. Only a moment passed—though it felt much longer—before his green-furred snout broke the surface of the lake. She swam to him and wrapped her friend in an embrace, which submerged them both.

They quickly swam the rest of the way to the island, and when they reached the edge, she pulled herself up and flopped down on the jagged stone, dripping from head to toe and laughing. The longer she lay, the more she laughed, until her voice filled the cavern.

Asher shook out his fur and looked at her. *I do not understand.*

Laurel stared up at the man-sized stalactites hanging high overhead. "Sometimes it feels like the world wants me dead, but it doesn't want me to choose the time and place." She pushed herself up to her feet and looked out over the vastness of the cavern. "GALE TAKE YOU, WORLD! I CHOOSE WHEN I DIE!"

The chromawolf understood well enough and howled beside her. She laughed again—only this time a hint of sorrow found its way into her tone—and rubbed a hand along Asher's wet back. One of his legs was bleeding, but the glowing water congealed around the wound already worked its healing magic.

"We're so close," she whispered.

Can you feel it? Asher asked.

Laurel closed her eyes. In the cavern, there was no breeze. No scent beyond the freshness of the cold air. No sound but their own. And yet, as she reached out through her bond to the world around her, she could feel a buzz, like the rustle of a morning wind through autumn leaves. A song, quiet but alive, calling to her from the center of the island. An instrument begging to be played.

"Is that the Provenance?" she asked.

I think yes.

"Asher," she said, suddenly feeling the weight of reality.

"I…I've never been good with words. But I just need you to know. When Elder Rosemary showed up to tell Bay and me that our parents were dead, I felt like my entire world had been ripped away from me. I cried for days, and it felt like this thick cloud of darkness surrounded me. One day my eyes just went dry. I remember staring at a wall for hours and feeling like only a moment had passed. I started to think that maybe *I* should just pass. Ride the winds with my parents. At least then we'd be together again. I just…I missed them so much. But then my grandfather brought me down to Cara's nursery, and I met you. You climbed up onto my lap and fell asleep. I remember feeling so warm. So loved. It was a little thing, but that was all it took. Suddenly, where there had only been a dark emptiness, there was this spark of warmth.

"I will never forget what you did for me, and I just want you to know how grateful I am. You were my spark of warmth, Asher. You saved me."

The big chromawolf, still drenched in cold elixir, approached Laurel and nuzzled his head under her arm. His deep voice filled her mind. *It has been worth every moment.*

They held each other for some time in silence, knowing full well the fate that awaited them, then stepped toward the Provenance.

IN THE HIGH towers of Endin Keep, Willow felt like a child staring out the window in the middle of a thunderstorm. From the west, the Felian army advanced. From the north, the corespawn. To the south, the wastelanders finished their trek through the river and made their way to the edge of the Alchean border. The world was growing smaller, compressing, a bubble waiting to burst as pressure squeezed from every side.

Willow stood quietly beside a child swaddled in a sky-blue blanket, who slept as though he could not hear the storm. And all she could do was wait.

The skirmish between the two human armies seemed to have ceased. Whether that was good or bad, Willow did not know. She only hoped that Laurel would act quickly.

"You know," she said aloud, mostly to herself, though her eyes looked down at the sleeping child. "When this all began, we thought that you were going to save the world."

A knock came at the door, and Willow saw a familiar face enter. A beautiful woman with golden skin to match her golden hair and wrinkles along her eyes that told the story of a life filled with joy and comfort. Lady Eleandra Orion-Endin, the Gem of Alchea and wife to the Great Lord, looked older than Willow remembered.

"May I come in?"

Willow offered a weak smile. "Not much to see here. Just the end of the world."

Eleandra rushed inside and threw her arms around Willow, squeezing with the strength of thirty years of friendship. Willow wanted to say something pithy, but Eleandra had always had a way of disarming her. So, instead, she found herself weeping while her old friend held her tight.

Her mind returned to the day she'd first stepped foot in Endin Keep. She remembered being introduced to Eleandra. She remembered lying to her about where they'd come from. And she remembered the unreserved generosity. Willow had cried in her friend's arms that day, just as she did now.

Eleandra pulled away and looked into Willow's eyes. "I have missed you." She stopped, mouth agape. "Malachus told me, but your eyes. They're astounding."

"Oh," Willow said with a hint of color flushing her cheeks. "I suppose they are."

"And your skin!" Eleandra's brows shot up. "Is that part of the magic? You look ten years younger than last I saw you. Is there any way you could share a bit? I wouldn't mind..." She paused and let out a simple laugh. "I'm sorry. You were never one for such conversations. Regardless, you needn't worry. Everything is going to work out just fine. You'll see."

Willow wiped away a tear from her cheek and smiled. "It's so good to see you, even if I don't quite share your optimism."

"It's not optimism," Eleandra said, shaking her head. "It's that I know who fights on our side. I've never met a man as cunning as Malachus and no one as tenacious as your son. Together, there is nothing in this world that can stop them."

Willow looked at the regal woman, surprised to see such sincerity, such deep faith that they would emerge victorious.

But Eleandra had never been through true defeat. She'd never had people she loved ripped away from her. She'd never seen the real darkness of the world. Hell, as an achromat, she'd never even seen the corespawn, let alone the immortal Heralds. The more Willow thought about it, the more hollow Eleandra's words became.

"I'm not so sure."

Eleandra walked over to the window and looked over the chaos enfolding. "I know you think I am weak."

Willow felt her stomach drop.

"Everyone does," Eleandra said quietly. "And they've every right to believe that. But not you. I don't want you to see a pampered woman who has never suffered. I don't want you to see a wealthy woman with no foot in reality. Not you. Not now." She paused and turned to Willow. "The truth is that I was never in love with him."

Willow furrowed her brow. "What do you mean?"

"Malachus," she said flatly. "If there is one truth that I hold above all others, it is that the world cannot be made better without sacrifice. But I'm not a warrior. I'm not even a threadweaver. If I wanted to make the world a better place, I had to sacrifice my life in a different way. I remember the day I first met Malachus. He was handsome, brilliant, and dangerous. I saw a cold darkness inside of him, leaking through. With those bichromic eyes, I knew that he would become Great Lord someday. I knew what I had to do. I finally knew what my sacrifice would be. What I could do to make the world a better place. So, I married him.

"I've never told anyone that before. I suppose some truths are too sacred to share. But I just—in case you're right —I wanted someone to see me."

"Eleandra," Willow whispered, staring at the woman she'd known for so long and misunderstood so thoroughly.

A veil lifted. And behind it, Willow saw a woman who had given her whole life to shelter the world from one man's darkness. She saw a woman who had seen a grim future and offered her own happiness to prevent it. A woman bearing the weight of a nation with no one to witness. Willow didn't know what to say—what could she? Instead, she pulled her friend into an embrace and whispered, "I see you."

Eleandra's chest constricted as she fought back tears. "That's all I've ever wanted."

As they pulled back, Eleandra rested her head on Willow's shoulder. Together, with a warm sun bathing the chaos, they watched the greatest war the world had ever seen.

CHRYS STEPPED through the legion of Alchean soldiers, hands instinctively touching the waterskin of elixir at his side. Iriel walked beside him.

Across the way, Relek and Lylax stood in their resplendent robes, sunlight flickering over their wavering forms, paragons of godhood. With each step, Chrys prayed for the destruction of the Provenance. There were no more tricks, no traps, and nowhere to hide. This time, one of them was going to die.

They entered the trampled grass between armies, weaving between broken arrow shafts and littered cloth until they arrived a short distance from the Heralds.

"Chrysanthemum," Relek said with a sadistic smile.

"Relek," Chrys said. "And here I thought you were supposed to be all-powerful gods. What kind of a god needs an army to fight their wars for them. Let alone three."

Lylax lifted her chin and snarled, speaking with a cold, calculating voice. "When this is over, I am going to carve out the eyes from your corpse and feed them to your orphaned child."

Iriel squeezed her fists until her knuckles went white. As she leaned forward, ready to fight, Chrys put a hand on her arm. The last thing they needed was to expedite the fight.

The only real chance they had was to delay and pray that Laurel could make the Heralds mortal again.

"What I don't understand," Chrys said loudly, "is why? If you succeed and everyone dies, then what? You'll have no more souls to bind. No one to play god to. You had hundreds of years to plan your triumphant return, and this is the best you came up with?"

Lylax took a step forward, but Relek held her back. For a moment, Chrys saw a grim reflection of him and Iriel. He wondered if Relek and Lylax had always been so cruel, or if time had simply stripped them bare. Before the elixir, before lifelight, had they been more like Alchaeus?

"You assume too much." Relek's eyes grew cold, as if he'd grown tired of the game. "Step forward, old friend, and let the world watch. I have been looking forward to this for quite some time."

They couldn't wait any longer.

Chrys pulled out two newly minted thread-dead daggers, gifted to him by Henna. Beside him, Iriel slipped off her palmguards, letting them drop to the ground as she unsheathed her own black blades.

The Heralds were waiting.

Come on, Laurel.

ALVERAX STUMBLED out of the tent, swinging the Midnight Watcher in wild arcs as he parried a host of lunges and thrusts. Were it not for the speed and strength Xuçan's bond provided, Alverax knew he would not have lasted five seconds against Thallin. Even so, he nearly took a blade to the shoulder from a clever feint at the start.

Thallin followed him out of the tent, dragging his sword

along the dirt. "The Midnight Watcher does not belong to you," he said. His eyes seemed darker, shrouded by shadows cast from the midday sun. He strode forward with such confidence and pride that Alverax considered trying to lunge forward to catch him off guard, but he didn't want to fight. He still held out hope that Thallin would see reason.

Alverax tried his plea once more. "I don't want to fight you."

"Neither do I," Thallin said without thinking. His hand squeezed the hilt of his blade. "But it doesn't matter what I want. My faith compels me."

"Quit using your faith as an excuse!" Alverax shouted. "If you don't want to fight, then don't. Faith isn't a living creature with the strength to compel you. Only you have that power."

"Enough!" Thallin shouted, throwing himself forward. His blade came high overhead, but Alverax parried with ease. At the same time, Thallin threw a kick at Alverax's knee, but he wasn't fast enough. Every move was fueled by so much rage that the Watchlord was nearly foaming at the mouth.

For a moment, Alverax felt a surge of confidence. He swatted away the next lunge and leapt forward, throwing a hard boot into Thallin's chest, hurling the Watchlord back. A crowd began to grow, weapons drawn, shouting. A guard ran forward, but Thallin screamed for him to step back.

"I'm not asking you to give up your faith," Alverax said, lifting his hands. "It's one of the things I admire most about you. All I want is for you to find something more worthy of your devotion." He pointed toward the east where the war was raging between the two armies. "Relek and Lylax. They do not deserve the faith of a man as good as you." He gestured to the growing crowd. "The Heralds do not deserve the faith of any of you!"

"You don't understand," Thallin said, shaking his head with flared nostrils, lower lip quivering. "You don't know what I've done."

"Thallin," Alverax whispered. He looked to his friend and watched the veil fade away, revealing the skeleton of a man, a corpse barely standing as the last remnant of his soul drifted into his blade. A man whose faith had consumed him. Every piece of Alverax's soul wanted to help him, wanted to *save* him. The Heralds had already taken Jisenna. They could not have another.

Tears fell from Thallin's eyes. "My faith is all I have left."

"Brother," Alverax said, feeling the weight of his friend's burden. A weight filled with loneliness and doubt. A weight that Alverax longed to help Thallin bear. "You have me."

THE PROVENANCE WAS different than Laurel had expected, nothing like the warbling mass of threadlight that formed the Convergence. Instead, it was a physical structure, a helix of three twisted, diamond stalagmites twice her height in the center of a deserted island. Something deep inside her yearned to touch it, to embrace the power she could feel emanating from its surface.

Asher whimpered beside her. *I do not like this.*

"I know," she said.

Back in the Fairenwild, when the coreseal was still just the wonderstone, the chromawolves had avoided that place like a poisoned well. Now, Asher was willingly approaching something infinitely more powerful and dangerous. Laurel felt a surge of gratitude for her friend. If this was to be her last day before she rode the wind, she was glad she would spend it with Asher.

Laurel gripped the obsidian dagger. She remembered her first experience with it, sitting beside a feytree and trying to cut her own corethread. She'd felt so embarrassed for thinking that such a thing could be possible. But now, after meeting Alverax and spending time with Chrys, Willow, and Roshaw, she understood how close she'd been to the truth. What worried her now was that the same dagger that was unable to *break* a corethread would be unable to destroy the Provenance.

They strode forward, step for step, as energy poured into them. Laurel felt more alive than she'd ever felt, like the bones beneath her skin were buzzing with power.

The Provenance was so close.

Raw energy sizzled like static across her arms.

It was so beautiful. Hypnotizing. Powerful.

It was power.

She was power.

Infinite.

Free.

Laurel was no longer in a cave.

She was in the clouds.

A bird.

A skyfly.

No, she was the wind itself.

Freedom incarnate.

The world belonged to her and she to it.

As she drifted through the sky, she wondered where she should go. She thought, perhaps, that there was something she was supposed to do.

But she could not remember what.

CHRYS RAN FORWARD and crashed into Relek, both thread-dead daggers ripping into the wastelander god's body like a butcher. Again and again, he thrust into Relek's chest, blades sinking hilt-deep into thick flesh. Every ounce of bottled-up enmity came flooding out of him like a broken dam. Relek was the Apogee. The Apogee was the darkness within. If he could kill Relek, Chrys would be free.

Beside him, he caught glimpses of Iriel, her own dagger biting through snow white robes and staining them with the red blood of Lylax's stolen body. Iriel was a whirlwind, a torrent of lethal grace.

When Chrys finally pulled back, Iriel did the same.

Relek and Lylax stood tall, red blood leaking from dozens of gashes, dripping onto the dry grass. Despite their outward appearance, the wastelander gods smiled. A ghostly light glowed from their myriad wounds, weaving in and out like a surgeon's thread, knitting their injuries back together with borrowed lifelight.

Somewhere in the valley south of Endin Keep, Chrys imagined a wastelander falling to the earth, their life forfeit for Relek's immortality.

Relek breathed in the stolen life, then brushed his hands down his shredded robe. "You cannot win."

"Who said I wanted to win?" Chrys said, spinning a dagger in his hand. "I just want to see you suffer."

Relek snarled. "Perhaps you would like to see your wife suffer."

Iriel gasped.

Before Chrys could react, Lylax reached a hand out as if gripping Chrys' neck from a distance. A ghostly tendril stretched forward, reaching into Chrys' chest, reaching into his very soul, his lifelight. Chrys fought the energy, throwing up a wall, a mental barrier to protect against Lylax's control. Still, it battered against the barricade, slithering around in search of a single crack to worm its viral energy inside.

Let me in, her voice shivered in his mind.

Chrys screamed, and the tendril shattered.

"Give in!" Lylax shouted as she walked forward with fury in her eyes. She lifted her hands, and dozens of rocks rose into the air. She hurled her arms forward, and the rocks launched toward Chrys. He crossed his arms and surged Emerald and Sapphire, bringing the stones together then blocking them with a threadlight barrier.

Lylax rushed him, sullied robes flowing behind her. She launched a flurry of reckless strikes that Chrys narrowly dodged. He lunged in beneath her arm and drove a dagger up toward her neck. She deflected it at the last moment, but the edge caught on a thin chain necklace beneath her robes. The force of it ripped the necklace free and launched it to the ground.

She snarled and reached for the necklace just as a black spear struck her in the chest, sending her stumbling back, barely able to keep her footing.

Chrys turned to see Great Lord Malachus Endin striding forward with a second black spear in his hand. "You shouldn't be here," Chrys said.

"You're right," Malachus said, taking his place beside Chrys. "But neither should they. This is *my* empire. My people. My home. Not theirs. And you were right before. Threadlight is not my legacy. My legacy is what happens right here, this day. Life or death. If we have to destroy threadlight to make it happen, so be it."

A thrill of energy danced within Chrys' heart as he remembered Malachus' old words. "Let's burn the world."

ALVERAX'S HEART pounded so powerfully in his chest that he swore he could feel each beat down to his boots. The crowd had grown quiet, all eyes turned to Thallin, who stood opposite Alverax with a gleaming blade still in his hand. But Thallin had grown quieter still. His head was down, fixed to the dirt near his feet. Alverax held his tongue, though he nearly spoke a dozen times as he waited. But he'd learned from Laurel that sometimes silence is more powerful than words.

Finally, Thallin lifted his head. His eyes were bloodshot, wet and weary. Alverax wasn't sure if it was acceptance of the truth—that the Heralds were no heroes to be worshiped —or if they were tears of submission to the faith that had so fully engulfed him. When Thallin took his first step toward Alverax, he reckoned he would soon find out.

Thallin said nothing until he stood only an arm's length away. "Alverax Blightwood," he said, his head held high, "the Heralds have sentenced you to death."

A shiver ran through Alverax, and he glanced at the sword in Thallin's hand. He wanted to make a plea one final time—his friend *would* see reason. Surely, the truth would prevail.

"For blasphemy and treason, you are condemned by Felian law." Thallin lifted the sword slowly with both hands. "As is our custom, you have had your opportunity to address the people."

From the corner of his eye, Alverax could see Roshaw's chest heaving up and down from the edge of the crowd as his gaze darted back and forth between the soldiers, Thallin, and Alverax.

There, again, Alverax felt a tremble in the ground, a

rhythmic beating. It wasn't his heart. It was something different. Something big.

Thallin's eyes grew cold. "As Watchlord—as the right hand of the Heralds themselves—I find you guilty."

Alverax closed his eyes, embracing his failure. If nothing else, he had tried. Perhaps the distraction, small as it was, would be enough. If Laurel could destroy the Provenance soon, maybe Chrys and the others could still stop the Heralds.

"As a man," Thallin continued, standing motionless. "No, as a friend to one who has brought me hope in the darkness, I offer my life for yours."

Thallin tossed his sword to the ground and fell to his knees, smiling with tears in his eyes. The image was a ray of light to Alverax's soul. A heavy rain on the parched earth where his hope was planted. His grandfather's words about chosen burdens echoed in his mind. Thallin had finally accepted that his faith in the Heralds was not worth the weight on his soul.

And now, with his support, they just might be able to stop the war.

The thought gave him pause.

Alverax turned and looked at the soldiers encircled about them. Some looked confused. Others looked angry, unsure how to respond to their Watchlord's betrayal. Roshaw looked stressed out of his mind.

Suddenly, with the sound of an awl punching through leather, an arrow soared through the air. Alverax ducked, but the arrow was not meant for him. It struck Thallin in the neck, just below his chin, knocking him off his knees onto his back.

"No!" Alverax screamed. He dove forward, grabbing

hold of the spear, ready to pull it out until Thallin grabbed his hand.

"Stop..." Thallin coughed up a thick gob of blood as he tried to speak.

Alverax again felt the rhythmic beating of the earth beneath him, but all he saw was Thallin. "We can fix this. You're strong. You can pull through it!"

"B..." Thallin wheezed, blood oozing down his chin. "Brother." He looked up into Alverax's eyes, and his lips curled into a smile. His lips moved, but no words came out. And yet, somehow, Alverax understood. *It is better to die free of guilt than to live shrouded in its shadow.*

Thallin's head tilted back, the trembling in his chest growing still as his body relaxed into the grass.

For a moment, Alverax felt like the sky was falling, as if every star in the night was tumbling toward him and all he had were his hands to stop them. He let go of the arrow, staring at the bright blood on his hands. *Lightfather, please. Not again.*

"Al!" a voice shouted.

His father.

Alverax turned and saw Roshaw standing with his hands raised, using an upturned table as a barricade. Dozens of arrows thudded into the wood, some breaking through, some nearly striking his father as they found their way through the openings.

"We need to go!" his father yelled.

Alverax looked around, but they were surrounded. A host of Felian soldiers contained them, weapons in hand, though many seemed nearly as confused as he was.

An arrow slammed through the table and cut across Roshaw's cheek. "Al!"

Thud. Thud.

Again, the rhythmic beating shook the ground, stronger now, like the earth's heart was thudding through the dirt.

The arrows stopped, and the soldiers ran forward.

Roshaw threw the table down and grabbed Alverax as if he was going to fly up into the sky, but their powers had not yet returned. There was no threadlight to save them. No words to convince the soldiers to stop. No tricks to escape.

But there was...

Boom.

The earth groaned as Xuçan landed beside Alverax.

Black veins glowed throughout the ataçan's body, his eyes oozing mists of darkness. Obsidian threadlight surged off of him, spreading over the field like a black wave and *breaking* the corethread of every soldier within fifty paces.

Xuçan opened his mouth and roared.

SHRIEKS SWIRLED TOGETHER in a storm of chaos as the armies finally clashed on the battlefield. Faithful Felians threw themselves at the Alcheans. The largest of the corespawn monstrosities trampled through the frontlines with Obsidian arrows stuck in their bodies like tiny thorns.

Chrys reached down and grabbed the necklace. It looked familiar, and he remembered seeing it when they fought in the Wastelands. But it wasn't until he saw it up close that he understood what it was. On the end of the chain, wrapped in wire mesh, was a small shard of Amber.

Before he could think, Lylax ripped the spear from her chest, lifelight filling the hole, and lunged back in, swiping for the necklace as she attacked. Malachus stepped in, jabbing with his thread-dead spear, forcing the Herald back. She was faster than either one of them, but it took more than speed to deal with two hybrid threadweavers at the same time.

That's when Chrys saw her.

Iriel stood beside Relek with tears dripping from her chin, but her eyes had gone cold, emotionless, submissive.

Relek turned to look at Chrys. "Kill your husband."

No, Chrys thought.

He knew what she was feeling, how difficult it was to fight, like a battering ram against a city wall, except the ram knew the weakest points in your defenses. But Iriel was strong, and her will was iron. If anyone could rebuke Relek's touch, it was her.

She had to.

She wouldn't...

Iriel reached down and picked up her thread-dead daggers, then turned to Chrys. With cold eyes, she stepped toward him.

Chrys had to do something. He couldn't fight Iriel. He *wouldn't* fight the woman he loved. He needed to break Relek's bond. But how? Dammit, where was Laurel? Was she even still alive? What if they were waiting for a miracle that would never come? No, he couldn't wait for her. He needed to do something now.

An idea blossomed in his mind.

"Malachus," Chrys said.

The Great Lord glanced at him while keeping an eye on Lylax, Relek, and Iriel.

"Keep them occupied," Chrys added.

Before he could convince himself otherwise, Chrys slammed his dagger into the shard of Amber, breaking it into a dozen pieces, then grabbed the smallest sliver of the shattered theolith. In one swift motion, he turned the dagger on himself, ramming it into his chest, deep into his heart, gasping as the pain rippled through his veins. He pulled it out, choking on his breath, and shoved in the sliver of Amber as deep as his bloody fingers could manage, moaning as he dropped to his knees from the pain. He fell to his back, struggling to breathe, frantically clutching at the grass beneath him, a thousand daggers cutting him from the inside. He slapped at his side, grasping his waterskin and undoing the drawstring. With a frantic jerk, he dumped half of the elixir into his open wound.

His chest sizzled from the inside.

Lylax's raging form appeared over him, driving a sword toward his chest. But Malachus *pushed* her steel blade away and countered with his own flurry of strikes. He was taller, with long arms and a longer spear. He stood above Chrys like an angel of death, swinging his thread-dead weapon in wide arcs, forcing Lylax and Iriel back while Chrys lay on the ground in blurry agony.

If any moment would leave a legacy for Malachus, it was this glorious clash of titans. Lylax raged, and he swatted her hands away with the tip of his spear. Iriel reached, and the butt of his weapon whipped out at her.

But the truth was...the Great Lord was no match for a god.

Malachus lunged wide, and Lylax stepped in with inhuman speed. Her hand reached up for his neck, continuing until she grasped the Great Lord's jaw and ripped. A loud crack popped as his head jerked to the left. Lylax spun on her heels, swinging the steel blade around until it cut through Malachus' neck. A clean slice through tendon and bone, muscle and sinew.

The world seemed to slow as Lylax turned to Chrys.

Malachus' head toppled to the ground.

In that moment, the world seemed to shift. A flickering spark of red energy glowed inside of Iriel. Two sparks danced in Lylax. And a dim, fading light flickered within Malachus.

Iriel stepped forward, standing over Chrys with thread-dead daggers in her hand. But even as she lifted the blade to strike, her arm trembled, and her jaw clenched tight. The blade inched forward, reaching, but she fought it with everything she had. Chrys could see the struggle in her eyes.

And that was when he saw it. There, surrounding the

flickering spark in her chest, a clear thread, like a rope lassoed around it. Chrys remembered Alchaeus' words, his description of lifelight, and realized what he was seeing. Without thought, he let Obsidian flood his veins, reached out to the transparent thread with the last remnants of lucidity in his mind, and *broke* it.

Iriel gasped, and Relek roared.

Chrys caught Iriel as she collapsed.

Amber threadlight swirled in his veins like liquid gold. He could feel the full strength of a fused theolith in his heart, pounding, surging, expanding within him. His chest burned, a raging fire of power.

When he turned to Relek, for the first time he saw fear in the god's eyes.

Laurel was the wind.

A god.

Drifting in a sea of endless power.

She *was* the sea.

Wavering. Rising. Static creeping along her arms, sizzling like water on a fire. A fire that burned within her, around her, consuming. Eating. Taking. Inviting.

A single tone rang in her skull. Buzzing. Beckoning.

She closed her eyes and listened.

The tone vibrated through her, echoing in her bones, reverberating through her veins.

It grabbed hold of her, and she was the stream feeding the ocean.

Music flowed from her, adding to the chorus.

Art.

Beauty.

Euphoria.

She was alive.

She was power.

She was...

LAUREL!

Asher's voice broke through the dissonance, shattering the false reality that clouded her mind. Suddenly, she was back in the cavern, golden light shimmering up from the ends of the island, blinding threadlight beaming from the helix. She fell to her knees, dazed and scared, feeling like every muscle inside of her had been ripped from her body.

So weak.

So tired.

Perhaps, she would simply lie down and sleep. Is that not what she had come to do? What *had* she come to do? Her mind was so fuzzy, her thoughts so fleeting. It had something to do with the helix. Or was it the elixir? The world was too bright.

She closed her eyes to shut it all out.

Laurel!

Her eyes snapped open, and her memory returned.

The Provenance.

She had to destroy the Provenance.

Laurel felt a nudge from behind and turned to see Asher pressing his nose against her back, pushing her forward as he whimpered from his own pain. She looked to the helix and took a step. Her limbs felt so heavy, her bones on the edge of shattering. But she was so close.

Just. One. More. Step.

She lifted the obsidian dagger.

Her arm shook from shoulder to fingertip.

Asher, she thought.

His voice came through, shaky and pained. *I am here.*

Laurel turned to him, the blade quivering in her hand. *May the winds guide you.*

Asher rubbed his cheek against her side. A single tear fell from the chromawolf's eye as his voice filled her mind. *And carry you gently home.*

Laurel slammed the dagger into the helix.

The earth shook.

Bright light enveloped the cavern.

Endless pain scorched through Laurel's body.

Burning.

Devouring.

Together, Laurel and Asher howled one final time as the light consumed them.

ENDIN KEEP SHOOK as if the world had unleashed its wrath. Walls trembled. Buildings groaned. Books fell from shelves and art leapt from walls. Oil splashed against glass as lamps rattled in their metal cages. Outside the room, screams echoed through the halls as a quake unlike the world had ever felt rippled through the earth.

Willow acted fast, swooping down and lifting Aydin from the bassinet. He cried as if he knew just how dangerous it was to be in the tower. She cradled the child close to her chest as she hid beneath a desk. Across from her, Eleandra sat with her back against the wall, knees clutched to her chest.

For a full minute, Willow sat huddled there, eyes shut tight, holding her grandson in her arms and praying that the walls would hold.

But then, realization struck her, and she opened herself to threadlight.

She stood, carefully, and moved to the window, eyes wide as she strained to look out over the battlefield. In the distance, she could see the horde of corespawn. Massive monstrosities dwarfed their companions as they trampled through the warring armies.

Suddenly, a wave of force rippled through the air like a tidal wave washing over the land. Pain erupted in Willow's chest as she clutched the bedpost, gasping as her eyes took in their last glimpse of the battlefield. The force enveloped the corespawn, and they exploded, blossoming like a mushroom that reached up to the clouds.

Eleandra dove out from the wall and caught Aydin from Willow's shaky grasp. The child's piercing cries filled the tower.

"Willow," she said, eyes filled with worry. "Are you okay? What is happening?"

The room grew quiet as the quaking ceased and the pain faded.

Eleandra gasped, and her eyes grew wide. "Your eyes."

After a moment of confusion, Willow understood. She opened herself to threadlight, but none came. No warmth. No power. No pain. Where once there had been a fire burning inside of her, there was only cold nothingness.

She looked down at Aydin, searching his eyes.

Eyes that had sparked the return of the Heralds.

Eyes they once believed would save the world.

And now, their Amber sheen was gone.

THREADWEAVERS CRIED out in pain as the earthquake wreaked havoc across the battlefield.

Corespawn screeched and roared as their bodies burst.

Agony.

Like a tidal wave, it crashed into them, then faded away.

Sprawled on his back, Chrys drank in heavy gulps of air, feeling empty, lifeless, hollow. He rubbed at his chest, terrified that the pain would return. When he looked at his wife, he saw tears in her eyes as she stared up into the sky.

Then he remembered the Heralds.

Chrys pushed himself to his feet, finally ready to unleash the full force of his retribution. Relek would pay for all the pain he'd caused. The death. The sorrow. And he would pay for reaching his grimy hands into Iriel's lifelight.

Taking in a deep breath, Chrys opened himself to threadlight.

But none came.

His heart shivered as he waited for threads to appear, for the world to grow chaotic with a myriad of otherworldly connections. But nothing happened. Threadlight never came.

Not now.

He knew what it meant—Laurel had succeeded—but why did it have to be now? He could still feel the raw power like a phantom swimming through his veins. He wanted it back. He needed it to fight the Heralds! He had become a god himself! He could still imagine the flickering sparks of lifelight.

But it also meant...

"Iriel!" Chrys said, crouching by his wife. "Threadlight is gone. The Heralds are mortal."

Iriel clenched her teeth, pain written in her eyes. "I can't," she said, pointing toward the Heralds. "It has to be you."

Chrys rose from the dirt, turning to face the Heralds. For a brief moment, the fighting had stopped as both sides recovered from the quakes. An eerie silence settled over the battlefield. Pain and confusion as men and women realized that their greatest strength, their blessing from the Lightfather himself, had been stripped away.

Relek stood, chest heaving up and down as he looked to Chrys. "What have you done?"

Chrys kept his focus. Every advantage the Heralds held was gone. Chrys may have failed at many things, but if there was one thing he knew, one thing he understood above all else, it was how to kill a man.

He ripped a spear from a dead soldier's hands and hurled it with every ounce of strength in his body, years of martial training flowing through his form, extending back and lunging forward, stretched to full extension as the spear soared toward its target. Time seemed to slow as Relek reached out his hand to *push* the spear away. His eyes went wide as the bladed tip continued forward, blasting into his chest, launching him backward, sliding across the grass and dirt.

Lylax snarled, then screamed a smattering of unintelligible syllables as she dashed toward Chrys. He pulled out a dagger and focused on the fight. Her white robes moved like the wind as she countered his every movement. She pressed harder, redirecting his hands, driving a fist into his ribs and another into his kidney. Chrys' shoulder throbbed. No matter how fast he moved, she moved faster. He pushed forward, trying to stay close so his dagger would keep its advantage, but with every step forward, she slipped back. Finally, she slid beneath his arm and threw a punch into his stomach that sent him doubling over.

Her hand reached out and gripped his neck.

She was strong.

Impossibly strong.

Though she was not tall, Lylax lifted Chrys off the ground, squeezing against his throat, choking his breath. He tried to move, but his body was too tired. And all his mind could think about was how impossibly strong she was. She shouldn't be that strong. She was mortal.

Chrys reached out with his dagger, choking as his mind and vision blurred. With his last clear thought, he rammed the dagger into the side of Lylax's neck.

She stumbled back, dropping Chrys to the ground, pressing a hand against the open wound. Blood gushed down her white robes, dripping through her hand.

Chrys gasped for air, coughing, wheezing, and watching the Herald bleed.

"Try to survive that without threadlight," he spat.

A smoky essence swirled along the curves of her neck and into the wound, glowing, stitching the gash shut piece by piece, skin growing until it stretched across the gaping hole. Lylax turned her gaze to Chrys as a vile fit of laughter rose up behind her. Relek pushed himself to his feet, the spear still lodged in his chest, blood dripping down his black robes. With both hands on the shaft, he pulled it out, coughing and laughing in equal measure as both armies watched in horror. Swirling mist gathered in the fatal wound, filling it with healing energy.

Finally, Relek lifted the bloody spear and pointed to Chrys with a horrid smile. "Threadlight is not lifelight."

Chrys felt his world come crashing down.

Destroying the Provenance had only destroyed their threadlight, but the Heralds' bond with the wastelanders remained.

They were still immortal.

And Chrys was powerless.

ALVERAX AND ROSHAW leapt atop Xuçan's back, preparing to flee as fifty soldiers floated in the air around them. Then the quakes hit. Xuçan steadied himself against the ground with all six of his limbs, but Alverax could still feel the trembling ground shaking the great ataçan. A sudden gust of force washed over them, nearly knocking Alverax and Roshaw off of Xuçan's back.

Pain tore through Alverax's body, hot fire filling his veins. He clutched one of Xuçan's spikes, squeezing as if doing so would ease the pain. His father beside him did the same, groaning in agony. Around them, Felian soldiers collapsed to their knees, their screams and cries filling the air.

But as soon as the pain came, it was gone, and all of the floating soldiers came tumbling back toward the ground.

"Go!" Alverax shouted.

Xuçan grunted, then threw himself forward, knuckle-running out of the circle of soldiers as small men leapt out of the way of the massive ataçan. Alverax clutched with all his strength, feeling much like how he expected the necrolyte racers would feel.

That's when he realized his veins were no longer black.

"Laurel," he said aloud.

Roshaw turned to him, still rubbing a hand over his heart. "What?"

"She destroyed the Provenance!" Alverax said. "Xuçan, we need to get to the wastelanders, now!"

In what seemed the blink of an eye, Xuçan bounded out of the Felian war camp and into the southern plains where they could see the amassed wastelander army. They advanced on Alchea like a swarm of shadows. Spears. Daggers. Bows and darts. All mixed in with the wild clothing of the wastelander people and their bonded ataçan. A few lone arrows rained down from the Alchean walls, but not nearly enough to slow the advancing army.

The chief of the ataçan picked up speed, and Alverax held on for dear life, wishing—if only for the briefest moment—that he could use Jelium's trick and bind himself to Xuçan with Amber threads.

As soon as the wastelanders spotted their approach, whispers rippled through their ranks, and they stopped their advance. Xuçan came to a halt in front of the army, and Alverax leapt off of his back, stepping up to the waste-landers.

"The bond is broken!" he shouted.

They stared.

Roshaw strode up beside him and repeated the words in the wastelander tongue. Cheers rose up, filling the air with excitement and joy. Some lifted their hands high overhead. Others fell to their knees, weeping, or embraced those near to them.

But not all were cheerful. Their leader, Rixi, who had spoken with Roshaw in the mountain valley, walked forward with his ataçan beside him. The other warriors stepped aside to make room as he continued until he stood just two paces away from Alverax. He spattered off a collection of unintelligible words in Roshaw's direction.

"What's he saying?" Alverax asked.

Roshaw furrowed his brow. "He says that the bond is *not* broken."

Alverax looked at the wastelander. Rixi was short and stout, his arms as thick as any man Alverax had ever seen and his brows set so unnaturally deep his eyes were shrouded in shadow. The hunch of his shoulders gave him the look of one who had spent more time with ataçan than his own people. It was then that Alverax realized that his bond with Xuçan had not been broken. And if his had not been broken, and Rixi's had not, then it was likely that no bonds had been broken at all.

"It didn't work..." he whispered.

Roshaw turned fully to Alverax, giving a quick glance up at Xuçan. "What are you talking about? Our threadlight is gone, and not just from Thallin's poison. I can feel the emptiness in my chest. She definitely did it. It worked."

"She did," Alverax repeated, realizing the implication.

Laurel was dead.

His friend...

He blinked away the tears before they surfaced and shook the thought aside. "It must have only destroyed the threadlight but not the bonds."

Roshaw stepped in closer. "So, the Heralds are still immortal?"

"Most likely."

"Most likely?" Roshaw repeated, raising his voice. "What the hell are we supposed to do now? As long as the bond is in place, there's nothing we can do!"

"There has to be another way," Alverax said.

"There's not!" Roshaw exploded. "I *knew* this was a

stupid plan! We don't have threadlight anymore, which was our greatest weapon. We're all split up. Gods know where Willow is. Chrys and the others, too. And Laurel..."

"Stop!" Alverax shouted, closing his eyes and breathing. "There *is* another way. Just let me think."

It only took a brief moment for Alverax to realize the truth: if there was another way, they would have thought of it already. He wasn't as smart as Chrys or Willow. If they couldn't come up with an alternative, then there wasn't one. Destroying the Provenance was all they had. No threadlight, no bonds. No other way. Not unless they were going to...

Xuçan understood his thought before he finished it. The ataçan's booming voice echoed in Alverax's mind, *I will not.*

"I didn't ask you to," Alverax said, turning to Xuçan.

You did not have to.

Roshaw looked confused. "What are you talking about?"

"It's..." Alverax didn't want to say it aloud, but if there truly was no other way...

"Al, what is it?"

Alverax glanced at the wastelander army, each of the warriors watching with interest. "There is another way."

Roshaw looked at him skeptically. "What is it?"

Alverax kept his father's gaze.

For a moment, Roshaw was silent, but then it hit, and every grain of joy in his eyes turned to red-hot anger. "No. Absolutely not."

"Do you have any other ideas?" Alverax asked.

Roshaw exploded. "We are not killing off an entire race of people!"

"I didn't ask *you* to either," Alverax said defensively. Roshaw and Xuçan shared a glance, as if his father finally understood the previous exchange. "The problem is the bond. Think of it like a moldy loaf of bread. You can either cut off the mold or throw out the bread."

"These are people!" Roshaw said with a look of disappointment. "They're not something you can just discard. Especially when there's still a chance we can cut out the mold."

"That's the thing." Alverax looked to the wastelanders, to their young and old, their men and women. "It's no longer a matter of if; it's a matter of when. If the bond doesn't kill them today, the war will kill them tomorrow."

"Doesn't matter. It's not our decision to make." Roshaw pointed to the army. "If this is really the only path forward, they might have something to say about it. Rixi might have something to say."

"You're right," Alverax agreed, annoyed that his father was insinuating that he didn't care about the wastelander's opinion on the matter. "They should know the truth. Can you translate for me?"

Roshaw reluctantly nodded, and Xuçan's voice entered Alverax's mind. *Be careful, King of the Hive. Your words carry weight now, and it is you who must live with their consequence.*

Alverax opened his mouth to respond, then realized the wisdom in Xuçan's words. If he asked the wastelanders to lay down their lives, and they did, would he be strong enough to live the rest of his life knowing what he'd done? He wanted to bring people hope, not death. Light, not infinite darkness.

The real question was: did he have any other choice?

Alverax remembered his father's words on the path to Kai'Melend, teaching him about the wastelanders and their reverence for the Wasteland bees, the et'hovon. How, like the bees, the wastelanders believed they were a hive, each individual adding to the greater whole. One heart and one mind. Each willing to sacrifice for the benefit of the hive.

If this was the only way, he would give the wastelanders the choice.

Xuçan roared, beating at his chest, then settled and let Alverax begin.

"Our plan failed," Alverax said, loud enough for them all to hear though they could not understand. "You have watched your brothers and sisters die to give life to the false gods and, because we failed, your lives are still bound. There is no breaking the bond. There is no fighting the gods. In the coming days, each of us will die, whether by the blade or by the bond. There is no stopping it. It is inevitable. As long as you live, Relek and Lylax will win."

He paused, letting the wastelanders absorb his words as his father translated. In their eyes, Alverax could see that they already knew. Many hung their heads, others gave a nod of understanding, and others stood tall, trying to be strong in the face of defeat. Rixi watched with intense focus.

"Though our plan failed, it did not fail completely," Alverax continued. "Relek and Lylax are no longer threadweavers. The bond is their last advantage. There is only one way now to stop the false gods, but it is a dark path. And it is a path that only the An'tara can walk."

Rixi stepped forward and spoke.

Alverax turned to his father.

"He said they are not afraid." Roshaw stepped closer to Alverax. "This doesn't feel right. We can't do this. There is no way in hell the Alcheans would do the same. There has to be another way."

"You know there's not," Alverax said. "But you're right that we can't do this. It needs to come from one of them." He looked to Rixi, and his father translated for him. "The false gods cannot create new bonds, but their bond with the An'tara still gives them power. There is no way to stop them so long as the An'tara live."

Rixi looked to Alverax, the tattoos along his nose shifting as he furrowed his brow and replied.

"What of the children who are unbound?" Roshaw translated.

"They would be cared for," Alverax promised. "The choice is yours. The Hive will follow you."

Rixi nodded, taking a minute to consider the request. Finally he turned to the army of wastelanders, his head held high. "An'tara!" he called out. "Look around. See our brothers and sisters, friends and children. We are the et'hovon, and this is our Hive!" When Roshaw finished relaying the words to Alverax, they watched as wastelanders nodded, gripping arms with their neighbors, quiet but empowered. Rixi continued. "There is only one way to stop the false gods, and only the An'tara have the power. But only if we are undivided."

Alverax looked at Roshaw as he translated with tears swelling in his eyes. He loved these people, despite all he had been through, and the truth sent a flood of emotion through Alverax's chest. The wastelanders reminded Roshaw of the woman he loved, the woman he'd lost. Alverax looked up and imagined how he would feel if the Moon's Little Sister suddenly vanished from the sky, and his heart broke for his father.

"If we surrender our spirits," Rixi continued, "the false gods will lose their power. The choice is ours. Let the false gods live. Be their anchor and die tomorrow. Or give our lives today, and take the false gods with us."

The entire wastelander army stood stunned. Not a word was spoken, only the cool breeze fluttering through the grass and the distant sounds of the rushing river. Their eyes all seemed to focus on the ground, as if looking at each other would bring them shame.

Finally, Rixi turned and looked at the rest of the army. He lifted his spear into the air. "If we are to die, I say we die of our own choosing, and for our own purpose! We are the sacrifice. We are the Hive. We are the An'tara!"

The wastelanders stood a little taller, nodding as the Hive made their decision.

Tears fell from Alverax's brown eyes, both for the wastelanders and for his father. And because he knew what was to come.

CHRYS FELL to his knees and felt every last vestige of hope trickle from his pores. Even still, he was not empty. Familiar words expanded within him, lies that choked his bones like a weed. They laughed at him, echoing, mocking him for ever having believed their vitriolic message.

I am in control.

The truth was that Relek had always been in control. Even when he was no more than the Apogee, whispering in Chrys' mind, he'd set the stage for his release. And now, kneeling in a grassy field in the midst of two armies, staring at the gods he'd failed to stop, Chrys finally accepted the truth. He had failed, and the world would suffer because of it.

"Get up."

He turned and saw Iriel walking forward, strapping a palmguard onto her left hand, holding a dagger in her right. Dried blood congealed beneath her nostrils, and mud covered her clothes. Her hair was a ratty mess. And she was ready to fight.

"Get up," she repeated, though her eyes remained fixed on the Heralds. "It's not over until we're dead."

"It didn't work," Chrys said.

Iriel looked to her husband, somehow offering disappointment and rage with the same look. "Then we will make them suffer."

"That's enough for me," he said, pushing himself up.

"Besides," she added. "There are only so many waste-landers. The bonds will run out eventually."

"There are thousands," Chrys said.

Iriel hit the hilt of her dagger on her palmguard, a metallic thud echoing out from the strike. "Then we have a lot of stabbing to do."

Chrys felt a surge of strength flow through him. Iriel was right. If they were going to die, they would go down fighting. Relek was going to regret not killing Chrys in the Wastelands.

He clutched tightly to his daggers as he looked to Iriel. "If this is the end, I want you to know—"

"It's not," she said quickly.

He had a whole speech that he wanted to give about how she was the strongest woman he'd ever known and a better mother to their child than he could have ever asked for. A better wife than he deserved. That she made him a better man. But she already knew, and that truth filled his soul. Even if he'd failed everywhere else, at least he had not failed the woman he loved.

Together, they stepped toward the Heralds.

Chrys made eye contact with Relek, whose prismatic eyes had faded to a deep brown, so dark they nearly matched his torn black robes. Beside him, Lylax's white robes were stained with a hundred streaks of red. For the briefest moment, as Lylax watched their advance, Chrys saw a glimpse of Autelle again. Perhaps, it was the brown in her eyes, but Chrys wondered if she was still inside, crying to be released, or silently watching with no hope of return.

Between the earthquakes, the corespawn, and the loss of

threadlight, none of the soldiers knew what to do. So, both armies stood still as the Heralds, Chrys, and Iriel, all circled each other in the center of the field. They watched with reverence, scared to come between gods and legends, wondering what other dark tidings the day would bring.

Chrys and Iriel stood across from Relek and Lylax, each holding a thread-dead blade, though it no longer made a difference. Wind rustled through the grass. Silence swirled through the open air. Fate drifted down on warm rays.

"I should thank you." Relek looked at Chrys with dead eyes. "All of this is because of you. When there is no more left in this world but death and decay, it will be because you were unfit to protect your family. Because you needed me. Because *you* let me out. Tell me, old friend. Was it worth it?"

Chrys' blood boiled beneath his skin, rage sizzling through vein and sinew. His hands shook and his nostrils flared as he fought back his urge to attack. It was what Relek wanted. It was what Chrys came to do. But he would fight when he was damn well ready. Instead, Chrys decided to try another avenue.

"Your brother loved you," Chrys said, waiting for a reaction. Relek gave nothing away, but Lylax, on the other hand, trembled at the mention of the third sibling. "He never wanted to live forever. He did it because he loved you both. He wanted to help you hold onto your humanity. I want you to know that he died helping us. Because in the end, Alchaeus saw what you had become, and it broke his heart."

"Say his name again, and I will cut out your tongue," Relek growled.

Chrys gripped his blade. "If I die today, I will die fighting for the same cause your brother died for. If anyone has a right to speak his name, it's me. When *Alchaeus* died, he was no longer your brother. He was mine."

Relek and Lylax lunged like ravenous wolves.

"Lightfather be damned," Roshaw said, stepping away from Rixi.

"What is it?" Alverax asked. "What did he say?"

Roshaw ran both hands over his face. "*Pintalla mox...* We were so wrong."

"The plague?"

"It's not a plague." Roshaw shook his head. "It's protection from a plague. The translation is literal. The wastelanders can surrender their spirit to protect the Hive. The dead wastelanders we saw didn't die of a disease. They knew that the gods were using them. They saw their brothers and sisters dying to the bond. But they couldn't convince the rest of the Hive to fight back. So they surrendered their lives in protest. First at the Endless Well, and again in the mountains. They sacrificed their own lives. The wastelanders have been preparing for this moment since the gods returned."

Alverax's mind swirled. Confusion. Awe. Disbelief. Even beyond the shock of the revelation, the implications gripped Alverax from the inside. He pictured the wastelanders who had given their lives through the *pintalla mox*, kneeling, skin blackened, statues gathered together in protest against the false gods. The solemn image took on a whole new meaning as tears formed in his eyes. He pictured Thallin, also kneeling as he too gave up his life to protest the Heralds.

He closed his eyes. In the darkness, free of the surrounding world, free of reality, free of the truth, he could almost forget the path he'd set for the wastelanders. He could almost revel in the beauty of it without letting the crushing weight take hold. Just because the wastelanders would, did not mean they should.

He turned to Xuçan, craning his neck to look up into the ataçan's shadowed eyes. "Are we doing the right thing?"

Xuçan let out a huff. *You wish me to justify your path.*

"No," Alverax said, knowing it was a lie. "It's our only choice—which I guess makes it the right choice—but that won't make it any easier to live with."

You are truly he-who-doubts-his-path. The chief of the ataçan bent down low, nostrils flaring with each breath. *If you cannot trust the path you tread, you are already lost.* With that, Xuçan rose up and stepped back, settling on a bed of grass and dirt beside a group of the other ataçan.

Alverax repeated the words in his mind as he looked out over the wastelander army, their Hive. He thought about what they were going to do, and he felt a strange sense of pride. These were his people as much as the people of Felia. But the selflessness they displayed in such abundance was something no human civilization could ever accomplish. They may have a different lifestyle, but they had grown beyond the men of the west in a way that mattered so much more. Thinking of his time in Felia, sacrificing himself for the Zeda people, he wondered if the wastelanders would be proud of him, too.

Trust the path, he thought once more.

Alverax stepped over to Rixi, and, without a word, he wrapped the short man in an embrace. Rixi hesitated, then returned the gesture. Warmth and kinship flowed through them until Alverax let go, grabbing Rixi by the shoulders. "May the true gods embrace the Hive."

As Alverax let him go, Roshaw translated the words. Rixi gave Alverax a final nod and stepped over to the waste-lander army, who awaited his command. Quietly, calmly,

Rixi and his ataçan companion fell in line with the others, as if they were just any other warrior and ataçan pair. He got down on his knees and the entire army followed, a wave of reverence rippling through their ranks. He set down his spear and lifted his hands overhead, crossing them at the wrist and curling his fingers back so the tips were touching. Every last warrior of the Wastelands followed his lead. Finally, he dropped his hands and bowed to the earth.

The wastelanders—these beautiful, selfless people—did not deserve such an end. But sometimes life does not give the most to the deserving. Sometimes, life takes, and it takes until the once-filled well runs dry. Sometimes, it is cruelest to the kindest and coldest to those already bitten by the frost. It is brutal, callous, and most of all, unfair. And so, it becomes the work of men to bring balance. To fill the empty wells. To warm the shivering shoulders. To sacrifice for the greater good. The wastelanders understood that, and Alverax would never forget.

Without a sound—so calmly that Alverax would have missed it had he not been watching carefully—Rixi's gray skin turned black, an onyx statue in a veridian field. His bonded ataçan collapsed beside him.

Alverax choked back tears. His lips trembled, and his chest convulsed. Roshaw turned away, tears streaming down his face, no longer able to watch. Alverax stepped over to his father and wrapped him in a fierce embrace. But he did not turn away—he had to watch. This was his path, his responsibility to bear.

One by one, each of the wastelanders grew still, their skin fading to black.

Alverax watched them all, still clutching tightly to his weeping father, but now, he no longer fought back the tears. Instead, Alverax embraced the sorrow and welcomed the pain. Men and women, families, side-by-side, holding hands as they surrendered their spirits. What started with Rixi spread through the wastelanders, until the field of grass had transformed into a steppe of statues.

When all that was left was the sound of small children crying, Alverax closed his eyes and dropped his head onto his father's shoulder.

So much death.

No matter how many times Chrys' dagger connected with Relek's body, the Herald continued his attack. Blow after blow, strike after strike, an endless barrage of power and strength. After several minutes of fighting, Chrys could barely move either arm, and Iriel wasn't faring much better. She had a dozen cuts across her arms and a slash across her cheek that had nearly taken her ear. When she fell back to the ground near Chrys, he knew it was over.

He could feel it in his bones.

He could smell death in the air.

Relek stepped over him, sword in hand, eyes alight with claimed victory. "Good bye, old friend."

He lifted the blade high into the air, holding tight with both hands.

Then his eyes went wide.

Relek's body convulsed. His mouth opened, and he gasped as his limbs trembled. The sword fell from his shaking hands. Lylax groaned beside him, gulping in ragged breaths. In the shadow of a moment, they both collapsed to the ground, clutching at their chests.

Chrys watched in awe.

Something was happening.

Had Laurel found another way?

Whatever it was, he had to act. If there was any chance that their bond with the wastelanders had been severed, he had to take it.

Chrys stepped forward, straining with every movement, fighting limbs that had already given in to defeat. The world seemed to tilt around him. He shut his eyes for a moment, the Heralds still groaning only a few paces away, and took in a steady breath. When he opened his eyes, he saw Iriel on her knees, crying as blood trickled from a dozen wounds. He stepped over and grabbed her hand.

"One more fight."

"I..." Iriel wrestled with her tears. "I think this might be it for me."

"One more fight," he repeated, shoving a dagger into one of her hands and pulling her to her feet.

They were a mess, dirt and blood splattered across their bodies, open wounds peeking through torn clothing. But as terrible as they looked, the Heralds looked worse. Their black and white robes, speckled with red, lay draped across the grass as both Relek and Lylax stared up into the sky, mumbling to themselves.

Chrys and Iriel stumbled over, daggers in hand, and stood over them. All of the power and primacy that had once emanated from these so-called gods had faded, leaving nothing but cracked vessels. These two beings had caused so much pain, so much death and destruction. For centuries, they had cast their poisoned shadows over the earth.

But they failed.

And now, standing over their broken bodies, Chrys was finally in control.

The Heralds' lips quivered, each breath a choking battle.

For a moment, as tears swelled in Relek's eyes, Chrys saw vestiges of humanity in the dying man. Perhaps, now that his powers were gone, he could be redeemed. Perhaps, he would atone. Use his centuries of accumulated knowledge for the betterment of mankind. Alchaeus had once believed his brother had goodness left in him.

But Alchaeus was dead, and so were countless others.

Chrys leaned down close to Relek's ear, dagger in hand. "Who's in control now?"

Together, Chrys and Iriel Valerian slammed their daggers into the hearts of the Heralds.

ALVERAX GRIPPED his father as he watched mourning children wander through a field of statues. Though the wind blew, all he could hear were the cries of those too young to understand. Too young to join the sacrifice. The unbound few. Alverax looked to Xuçan, hoping to glean a bit of strength from the chief, but he found only sorrow. It was not just wastelanders who had died that day. Bonded ataçan lay scattered throughout the lifeless throng.

Leaving his father, Alverax stepped into the graveyard. Men. Women. Young and old. United. One in heart and purpose. For the greater good. To defy the gods. Not for the benefit of their own people, but for the world itself. Alverax had once felt shame for being a wastelander. Now, he felt nothing but pride and sorrow.

Pintalla mox.

Surrendered spirit.

He touched them as he walked, a hand placed on stiff shoulders, fingers brushing against crisp hair. Part of him wondered if he had the ability as well. If he knelt beside them, could he surrender his own spirit? Should not the King of the Hive be with his people? Perhaps the only way to kill a Blightwood was if he gave up his own life.

Before he knew it, Alverax was on his knees.

It felt so natural, the grass beneath him, the odd scent of

the wastelanders drifting in the wind beside him. Even the oppressive sun seemed to cool as he knelt. A chill ran along his spine where the scar had once been before the elixir had opened his wastelander heritage once again.

Heritage.

The word swirled in his mind. The physical differences were not his only inheritance. His heritage was one of sacrifice. A heritage of surrender, a spiritual offering.

Alverax closed his eyes, breathed the air, and communed with his birthright. He looked inside himself, searching for the power of *pintalla mox*. His mind swerved in and out of memories, through canals of strength and endowment. Somewhere inside him, he would find his true ancestry. Hidden. Waiting. A snake in the sand.

But the longer he looked, the more he understood the truth. He had not inherited the power of *pintalla mox*. His sacrifice was not to die but to live with the consequences of that day. He would live so the memory of their sacrifice would endure.

As he knelt, he thought he could hear Laurel's words riding on the wind.

People are like trees, remember? The least we can do is stand.

Alverax picked himself up, slowly, legs bearing countless burdens, but still he stood.

Not far away, his father had made his way to the children, whispering comfort and embracing their pain as his own. They were young; perhaps they would forget. But Alverax and Roshaw would not.

Xuçan suddenly grunted and rose, huffing out a blast of warm air through his wide nostrils. A slight tremble in the ground caused Alverax to turn. From the base of the mountain, a troupe of ataçan knuckle-ran through dirt and grass, slamming their massive fists against the ground, skirting around the field of statues until they came to a stop in front of Xuçan.

One by one, they walked forward and fell under the massive arms of their chief. Xuçan squeezed with all his might before looking to Alverax with approval. *Do not doubt the path*, his voice bellowed in Alverax's mind. *No matter how dark the way may seem, there is always light beyond the bend, if you will take the steps to find it.*

Alverax looked up into the midday sky, searching for a star he could not find. Somewhere, hidden behind the blinding light, drifting through an infinite universe, the Moon's Little Sister stared back at him.

He would not soon forget what happened to these people.

Their blackened skin would haunt his dreams.

Hard as the path forward would be, he would not be alone.

And that was enough for him to take the next step.

THE HERALDS ARE DEAD.

Chrys awoke in a padded leather arm chair. A thick fog rolled along the edges of his vision, remnants of the herbs he'd been given to aid in his recovery. He pushed himself to his feet, groaning at the stitches in his side and the bruises decorating every other part of his body.

He was in the Great Lord's study, and though he was alone, he could still feel the ghost of Malachus watching him, judging him, perhaps even letting slip the slightest smile as he often did when he approved of Chrys' choices. But the truth was that Malachus was gone—and even if he were there, his bichromic gaze would have been replaced by achromic brown. Still, Chrys could feel his mentor's presence, and he hoped the Great Lord would be proud of all they'd accomplished.

The Heralds are dead.

Only a single day had passed, but it seemed an eternity had come and gone. Chrys remembered the shrieks of the corespawn being destroyed. He remembered standing over Relek and driving the blade through his chest. He remembered falling to the ground beside Iriel as the two armies backed away from each other. And yet, it still did not feel real. He was certain that at any moment, the Apogee would return, echoing in his skull or claiming the body of another man.

It would take time—he knew that. It would take help—he could not do it alone. But he *would* move on. With his wife and son at his side, they would find peace.

A knock at the door startled him, and he stood, his hand instinctively reaching for a blade that was not there. The door opened to reveal the two women he had been waiting for, surrounded by a host of blue-clad Alchean guards. High General Henna offered a nod as she entered, her white Alirian hair freshly cropped above her ears. Entering behind her, in a long black dress with an intricate swirling pattern of golden brocade, was Eleandra Orion-Endin.

The night before, after the death of Malachus and the Heralds, the war had ceased, and Chrys and Iriel had been carried to Endin Keep. A council of Alchean officials had approached Chrys, despite his weak state, and asked him to take up the mantle of Great Lord, to establish peace with Felia and lead the people to a safe and prosperous future. But a war-time general was not what Alchea needed. The nation needed a healer, someone who would inspire them to rise up, come together, and rebuild. When the council disagreed, Chrys had an idea.

So, he took up the mantle, becoming Malachus' successor, becoming Great Lord Chrys Valerian. As soon as it was made official, as his first order of business, Chrys named a new Great Lord, one who had cared for Alchea for decades, putting the needs of the many above their own. And so, despite the council's previous objections, Eleandra Orion-Endin, the Mother of Alchea, became the new Great Lord.

"Chrystopher," she said with a gleam in her eye.

He gave her a friendly smile, though his pain still

lingered, then crossed the room and offered his hand. "Great Lord."

She shook her head and wrapped him in a warm embrace. "Eleandra," she corrected.

"Only if you call me Chrys."

She laughed and gestured for him to take a seat. As he did, she walked around the desk and took her place on the other end. In the flickering lamplight, she looked older than Chrys remembered. A long night of negotiations and the loss of her husband had taken their toll. Still, she looked strong and graceful, far more ready to take on the Great Lord's responsibilities than Chrys would have been.

"Have you heard the news?" High General Henna asked as she took a seat beside him.

"That's why I'm here," Chrys said. "Did the negotiations with Felia go well?"

Eleandra smiled. "They've agreed to fifty years of peace and open trade. There are, of course, conditions from both sides, but the events of yesterday have brought us all together in unexpected ways. Even the religious institutions of Felia and Alchea have been meeting. They plan to bring together their truths based on the information you've shared, including some of the changes you've requested."

Chrys felt a spark of joy in his chest. "The priests?"

"As Great Lord, I am the head of the Order, and changes have already been instituted, even if there are many traditionalists who are furious with me. The priests will no longer be blinded, and joining will be voluntary. No more conscripting infants or limiting the number of children a family may have."

"That's wonderful." Chrys reached down and touched the waterskin at his side. "And the caves?"

Henna nodded. "We have soldiers headed up the pass as

we speak to ensure that the passage is sealed for good. An exploratory party will be accompanying the ataçan on their return to Kai'Melend. They have been ordered to seal the cave entrance and bring back whatever is left of the waste-lander culture, including sketches of the city and lifestyle."

"Good," Chrys said, recalling the story Alverax had shared the night before. "They deserve to be remembered."

"The southern field will become a monument to the wastelanders," Eleandra said. "And the children have been taken in by the Order of Alchaeus. They will be cared for, as will the statues of their heritage. As for your final request, of course your friends are welcome in Alchea should they return."

Chrys took a deep breath. Everything he'd asked for—changes to the Order of Alchaeus, peace with Felia, destruc-tion of the paths leading to the Provenance and elixir, a pardon for a friend. With Eleandra in charge of Alchea, Chrys could step away with confidence that the nation would be well cared for.

His mind turned to his family. They were already home, resting, Willow helping with Aydin while Iriel recovered from her many wounds. Chrys yearned to go to them, to lie in bed beside Iriel and sleep until the world returned to some semblance of normal.

But he had one last thing he needed to do.

He thanked Eleandra and Henna, left Endin Keep, and jumped in a carriage headed west.

AFTER A LONG, uncomfortable journey, during which his many stitches seemed constantly on the verge of splitting—the carriage did not do well on the army-trampled roads—Chrys finally spotted the farmhouse. It was exactly as it had been described to him: two sprawling barns with fenced-in hogs between them, fields of barley, green pastures with a dozen grazing cows, and a home complex of small, interconnected structures. Enough space for several families.

Chrys stepped down from the carriage and walked toward the center farmhouse. A few paces from the front door, a half-finished bull was carved into the stump of a tree. As he approached, he could hear the sound of children playing inside. Singing, stomping, laughter that was so close to a scream that Chrys wasn't sure which it was. He stepped forward and knocked.

A big man with red hair and a dubious look in his eyes opened the door. "Who are you?" he said with a deep, Laz-like accent.

Chrys raised his hands to show that he was unarmed. "I'm a friend of your cousin. Laz and I worked together. My name is Chrys Valerian."

The man's eyes grew wide. "Is really you? Laz talks about you! Good things, mostly. Come, come. I am Jeshua. You must share drink!"

"Thank you," Chrys said, seeing so much of his old friend in this cousin. "But I can't stay long. I just came to drop off a gift for Luther. I was told he is staying here with his family."

"Yes. Come, come." Jeshua threw open the door and gestured for Chrys to enter. "Is here in back. The kids are so loud, but I love them."

As they entered, Chrys caught sight of Luther's children peeking from around the corner. When they saw him, wide grins spread across their faces and they rushed forward, nearly tackling him with their excited embrace. He was quite certain that one of them tore the stitches in his side.

"Uncle Chrys!"

Despite the pain, he couldn't help but smile. Over the five years that he had worked with Luther—the Emerald to his Sapphire—Chrys had grown very close with his family. Once upon a time, they had hoped that Chrys' child and Luther's third would grow up to be best friends. Two little threadweavers growing up side by side. The Rite of Revelation for Luther's son had changed everything.

While the young girls clung tightly to Chrys' legs, begging him to drag them through the house, Luther and Emory stepped through the hallway. The last time Chrys had seen Luther was days after their son had been taken into the Order, and he'd been a mess. Drinking, threadweaving, and certainly not sleeping, Luther had not dealt well with the outcome. But now, on the outskirts of Alchea, hidden away on a remote farm with nothing but his family and Laz's strange cousin, Luther looked truly happy. Bright-eyed and clean-shaven—head and face—this was the friend who'd stood beside him for so many years.

Next to him, Emory held their infant son, barely older than Aydin but noticeably larger.

"Stones," Luther cursed as he recognized his friend. Emory nudged him for cursing—cut from the same cloth as Iriel. He ignored the comment and walked over, peeling both children off of Chrys' legs and throwing his arms around his friend. "I thought you were dead," he said quietly. "I mean, you don't look far from it, though the beard works, somehow. And, is that blood on your shirt?"

Chrys looked down and noticed that a bit of red had bled through his beige shirt just over the stitches in his abdomen. "Turns out that killing gods isn't as easy as it sounds."

"Is that..." Luther paused and looked at his kids. "News travels slowly out here. All we know is that the Felian army was leaving. Why don't we take a walk? I want to know everything."

"There will be time for that," Chrys said quite seriously. "But there's another reason I came. First, Great Lord Eleandra has pardoned you and your family. If you want to, you are welcome to return to Alchea, no questions asked."

Luther turned to Emory, and they gave each other a knowing look. "Great Lord Eleandra? That's... Thank you, Chrys. I don't know what we'll do, but thank you."

Chrys smiled at them both. "You seem happy."

"A bit of solitude has a way of helping you remember what's important," Luther said. "You know, in the last months, I've spent more time with my children than I had the entire rest of their lives. And it turns out, I even like them. Who would have guessed?" He winked at his oldest. "It's been really nice being able to help out more with the newest member of the family."

"Actually," Chrys said, looking down at the bundle in Emory's arms. "That's the other reason I came. There have been a lot of incredible things that have happened over the past few months, and I'll tell you all about those, I promise. But I picked up a souvenir for you along the way." He reached down and grabbed the waterskin at this side. Even though he had checked it a hundred times already for holes and leaks, he still felt for the slushing weight of what remained.

Luther gave him a confused look. "What is it?"

"I think about your son's Rite of Revelation a lot," Chrys said, untying the drawstrings of the pouch. "Between what happened to you and what happened to Iriel, that day changed both of our lives. But those times are over. The Order of Alchaeus is dissolving, Luther. No more rites, no more revelations, and no more blinding children." He paused and opened the pouch, a soft golden light emanating from within. "No one can take away the pain of what you went through, but I found a way to make it just a little better."

"I don't understand," Luther said.

"Two threads; one bond," Chrys said. "Do you trust me?"

Luther nodded. "Of course, with my life."

"Emory," Chrys said, though he looked to the bundled child in her arms, "do *you* trust me?"

A flicker of hesitation danced in her eyes, but she, too, nodded.

Chrys stepped forward and stood in front of Emory, cupping the waterskin in his hand. "The wastelanders call this *oka'thal*, or life water. Others have called it elixir. But the name doesn't matter. What matters is what it can do."

Chrys held the waterskin over their son's face and let the remaining liquid pour down. The child squirmed, squeezing his eyes shut as the elixir puddled over them, glimmering in the daylight. For a moment, Chrys felt like he was a priest of the Order of Alchaeus. But where they had hurt, he would heal. The child calmed as the magic seeped into him, relaxing into the warmth of his mother's arms.

But then, the child's eyes opened, and the white haze that had clouded them only moments before was gone. For the first time in his short life, he saw his parents.

Luther and Emory wept for their son.

Chrys wept for his friends.

And at last, Chrys Valerian looked forward to what the future held.

~ SIX MONTHS LATER ~

WILLOW HELD up her grandson so he could see out the window of their carriage. It was late morning, and the green hills were filled with dandelions that danced beneath the summer sun. As a sparrow darted past the window, Aydin slapped his palms against the sill, grunting and gasping with excitement. She couldn't help but smile at the boy's enthusiasm for life.

Shortly after, the carriage came to a stop, and Willow stepped outside. She barely jumped out of the way as a horse lumbered past pulling carts filled with kiln-dried, white clay bricks. Dozens of men moved back and forth, hauling lumber and wheelbarrows of sand and lime. Despite all of the nearby activity, the majority of the noise came from farther west. It was there that she spotted Chrys and Iriel.

She wandered over, avoiding the line of traffic between the newly arrived carts and the half-built brick structure. As they approached, Willow pointed out Iriel and Chrys, and Aydin's eyes lit up. When Iriel turned and saw them, she waved them over with a wide smile.

"Thank you so much for watching him this morning," Iriel said, taking the young boy in her arms. She kissed him and let his bottom settle into the crook of her arm. "Chrys is great with ideas, but he needed some help in coordinating all of the moving parts."

"He's always been like that," Willow said. "Thinks he can do everything himself. It's even worse now. No one wants to correct one of the...godslayers."

"Oh, stop it!" Iriel said, blushing. "You know I hate that."

Willow laughed. "Actions have consequences, and sometimes they come with nicknames. Either way, I'm glad Chrys has you beside him. Someone has to tell him when he's being a fool."

"That, I can do." Iriel smirked. "The others are around here somewhere. I think they're helping mix the mortar. Let me grab Chrys, and we'll meet you over there."

Willow nodded and stepped away, walking past a handful of men cautiously guiding an ataçan as it pulled on a thick rope attached to a pulley at the top of the structure. A crate filled with bricks made its way up to a few workers at the top who slathered them and set them in place. With her arms now empty, Willow felt the urge to reach down and lay some bricks herself, to help in whatever way she could. But she also knew that Iriel had clearly laid out assignments to each of the workers, and whatever Willow did to help was more likely to create an imbalance in their plans. And if she was honest, Willow was getting older, and Aydin was getting bigger. Her arms could use a break.

As she walked around the brick-wrought structure, she found men and women dumping loads of sand and lime into buckets, mixing it up, then adding in water until the mortar came out to just the right consistency. The buckets were then taken by others and brought to the bricklayers. In the far station, Willow spotted two handsome men with their shirts off, wrestling with a barrel of freshly separated lime from the kilns back in Alchea. Sweat glistened off their hardened bodies, even if one was a little more hardened than the other.

She stepped through the other mortar makers and stood with her arms crossed until the two men noticed her.

"Willow!" Roshaw said, smiling as wide as the sea. He wiped his forehead with the back of his hand, then slapped that on his pant leg before walking over and throwing his arms around her.

"Roshaw!" Willow said as she pushed him away. "You're disgusting right now."

"Right now?" He smirked as he lifted her up and planted a sweaty kiss on her lips. He set her back down and turned to Alverax. "Sorry. Can't help myself sometimes."

Alverax shook his head with a grin. "You're not sorry."

"No," Roshaw said, looking back to Willow. "No, I'm not."

Just then, Chrys and Iriel—holding Aydin—came walking around the corner. Even though more than half a year had passed, Willow still saw glimpses of the dirty, frightened couple who had taken their child across the world to stop the gods. Now, Chrys' beard was trimmed close, his clothes well-pressed, and he seemed to stand a little bit taller than he once had. Iriel, on the other hand, seemed another woman entirely. She'd hired a night nurse to care for Aydin and had restarted her rigorous training regimen. Despite her hair now being cut above the shoulder, the biggest change was the fire in her eyes.

When they approached, Chrys gave his mother an embrace. "Could use your thoughts on the designs for the new trails. Want to make sure they're safe and that they'll last. Not convinced about the latter yet."

"Classic Chrys," Alverax said, giving them both a wave. "Right to business."

Roshaw let out a clipped laugh. "I thought you were going to say 'Classic Chrys...needs his mum to save his ass.'"

Willow gave him a look. "And what's wrong with that?"

"Oh, it has nothing to do with Chrys," Roshaw said quickly. "Has much more to do with how badass his mother is."

Willow rolled her eyes and turned to Iriel. "He thinks he's quite clever."

"They all do," Iriel said.

Chrys folded his arms. "Every time I get you all together, you turn on me. I'm going to have to start sabotaging these reunions." He paused before letting the slightest smile creep across his lips. "Why don't we all take a break and show Willow the progress."

Roshaw and Alverax cleaned off their hands and followed as Chrys led the others away from the mortar station. Willow noted the sidelong glances from workers across the field as their group passed. After a life of relative anonymity, Willow had still not adjusted to the fact that everyone in Alchea knew who she was, knew all of them. Except Laurel.

But that was going to change.

When they rounded the corner, Willow looked up at the stairway. Even incomplete, it was a marvel. White bricks laid twenty feet wide, as high as a feytree, jutting forth out of the grassy field and reaching up to the top of the Fairenwild. Some had taken to calling it Heaven's Gate, but that wasn't what mattered. What mattered was where it led.

Willow turned to Chrys as they stared up at the enormous structure. "It's brilliant."

Chrys clenched his jaw. "It will be. There is still a lot of work to be done."

"You know," Willow said, "you don't have to wait for the work to be done to revel in the beauty of it. But more importantly, we received word from Felia this morning. They've already broken ground on their own staircase. They've provided supplies to the Zeda people and workers to help. Zedalum is being rebuilt, bigger and more resilient. A year from now, it'll be a thriving trade route between the two nations."

Chrys took a deep breath and nodded. "I wish Laurel could see it."

"We all do," Willow said quietly. "Her brother most of all. Bay is quite the architect, I've heard. Which is great, because it's going to take some real ingenuity to build a proper trade center on the top of the Fairenwild. Ah, speaking of. Felia also agreed to change the name! They loved your suggestion and are already updating their maps. From now on, it will officially be known as the Laurelwood."

He closed his eyes, and Willow thought she saw a quiver in his lower lip. The stairway. The new name. They had both been his idea, a way for the world to remember the heroism of a young woman who had sacrificed everything. Willow thought it a beautiful gesture.

A handsome young woman with white grime covering her hands called out from the far end of the stairway, gesturing toward a cart filled with fresh bricks. Alverax stepped away with Chrys and Iriel to go help, and Willow watched them go. She was surprised when the young woman stepped up to Alverax, blocking his path, and grinned. He looked down at her with the Blightwood smile, leaned in, and planted a soft kiss on her lips.

"Did he just—?"

"He did," Roshaw said. "It's good for him. She's a sweet girl."

"He looks so happy," Willow added.

Alone, Willow and Roshaw clasped hands and stared up at what would surely become one of the great wonders of the world. It was nearly finished, or so it seemed. Though it was difficult to tell when the higher it rose, the more bricks were required. Still, they could stop at that very moment, and it would still stand through the centuries as a testament to peace and sacrifice.

She placed a hand on Roshaw's shoulder and set her head atop it, her other hand wrapped around his forearm. "On the way here, I was thinking."

"Uh oh," Roshaw teased.

She ignored him. "I was thinking about how, when this started, we all thought Chrys and Iriel's child was going to save the world. The Amber-eyed baby, the chosen one, destined to stop the Heralds, to create a coreseal. But that was all wrong."

Roshaw leaned his head against hers. "What do you mean?"

"It wasn't their children that saved the world, Roshaw." She looked up into his dark eyes and squeezed his arm. "It was ours."

ACKNOWLEDGMENTS

It takes an army to win a war, and writing epic fantasy is a series of hard-fought battles. As readers, you step onto the battlefield after the war has been fought, taking in the aftermath, the quiet devastation, and perhaps the victory. But for the author, we see the orchestrated efforts and advice of countless individuals that have come together to do something spectacular, to imagine and create worlds and stories meant to inspire and entertain. Sometimes, I feel like a high general presenting a plan, then listening as my captains say "Don't go that way" or "That doesn't work". Without them, there would still be a war, but there may not be a victory.

So, thank you.

To my first line of defense, Hillary and Brandon. Your influence on the story (particularly in the early days) laid a foundation for everything.

To my beta reader team, Sean, Alma, and the Forge. Thank you all for putting up with the unclean garbage I throw your way and helping me spin it into something worthy.

To my narrator, Adam. You're a god, and I will forever remember the first time I heard you voice the Apogee.

To my editor, Taya. You have taken this manuscript farther (not further) than I ever could.

To everyone else, readers and listeners, reviewers and bloggers, booktubers and bookstagrammers, thank YOU for spreading the word and helping me share this story with the world. I could never do it without your support.

May the winds guide you all.

ABOUT THE AUTHOR

Zack Argyle lives just outside of Seattle, WA, USA, with his wife and two children. He has a degree in Electrical Engineering and works full-time as a software engineer. He is the winner of the Indies Today Best Fantasy Award and a finalist in Mark Lawrence's Self-Published Fantasy Blog-Off. Zack and his wife are the founders of the Indie Fantasy Fund, a non-profit that provides cash grants to help with the cost of self-publishing.

zackargyle.com
twitter.com/SFFAuthor
instagram.com/ZackArgyleAuthor

Join Zack Argyle's newsletter for updates on his next project,
Symphony in the Skies!
http://news.zackargyle.com/